'A book with three-dime
well-researched procedural passages and, mo..
all, dialogue that is consistently convincing.'
Diver Magazine

'A great deal of humour depicting real characters with all
their ambitions, fears, foibles and embarrassments. A real
"whodunnit", technically spot on and an excellent read.'
National Diving Officer, Sub Aqua Association

'The story is scarily believable and difficult to put down.
Whether you have ever been scuba diving or not this is a
great read.'
Diving Diseases Research Centre

'Diving is a technical sport, but Rawle – who is a diver
herself – makes sure complicated terminology is explained
for non-divers while still being accurate and detailed enough
to convince those who do dive'.
Dive Magazine

DEEP TROUBLE

The Perfect Murder... Underwater

Happy Diving at NDAC

Sue Rawle

SUE RAWLE

Sundance Publishing

Sundance Publishing
PO Box 61
Coleford
GL16 9BA

ISBN 978-0-9566372-0-8

British Library Cataloguing in Publication Data.
A catalogue record for this book is available from the British Library.

Typeset in 11pt Bembo by Troubador Publishing Ltd, Leicester, UK

Printed in Great Britain by the MPG Books Group, Bodmin and King's Lynn

To Les, Rob, Rich and George
For their unfailing support, interest and encouragement.

About the author

Sue Rawle is a Forester as she was born in the Forest of Dean. She returned to her roots in order to raise her family in the Forest, on the edge of the Wye Valley Area of Outstanding Natural Beauty. Although this area is land locked, she decided to take up scuba diving, having been inspired by the adventures of Jacques Cousteau in her formative years. She is the secretary of the Forest Pirates dive club and is grateful to them for providing the necessary training to become a diver. She decided to combine her two favourite hobbies (diving and reading crime fiction) in the creation of a novel set within a scuba diving club in the UK. As it is based on the 'perfect murder' concept, but underwater, her dive buddies are now concerned in case she uses them to test out potential murder methods.

Sue lives in the Forest of Dean with her husband, two sons and a bear, as she is something of an arctophile.

ACKNOWLEDGEMENTS

I would like to thank the Forest Pirates club for introducing me to scuba diving. In particular I am indebted to Nick Lane, (for acting as my technical adviser on all diving related matters) and to Kierran Blayney, Nigel Bennett and Nick again for their patience when training me.

The various members of my writing group have been very supportive and encouraging over a long period, so I wish to thank Jane Baker, Fran Nowell, Nicola Langford, Ian Pincott, Kevin Cullinane (and Paul Groves for the first lessons in creative writing).

For their advice on medical matters my thanks go to Dr Lyndsae Wheen, Dr Mike Williams, Dr Phil Bryson and Arwen Nixon. Similarly for advice on police matters, my thanks go to Mark Linnell.

Thanks also to the band of readers who commented on the story as it evolved: Jenny Armstead, Sarah John, Rachel Lowe, Phil Green, Martyn Western, Bob Wood, Naomi Lane, Angie Beard, Trish Bennett, Zoe Elsmore, Jon Hurley, Andrew Blake, Kim Roberts, Mark Bristow and John Winter.

Ian Pincott provided an impressively detailed checking service on the text whilst my thanks go to Darren Stacey for creating the cover design. My mother, Désirée Rawle, was very helpful in identifying grammatical errors whilst my younger son, Rich, was my most constant source of encouragement. Last, but not least, my thanks go to Andrew Taylor for being an inspirational local crime writer.

PRINCIPAL CHARACTERS

Tony Fleming – Forest Divers Club Chairman & Training Officer
Cleo Fleming – Tony's wife & Social Secretary
Rachel Fleming – Cleo's daughter and Tony's stepdaughter

John O' Donnell – Diving Officer

Lynne Beckett – Secretary

Graham Bright – Boating officer
Elaine Bright – Graham's wife
Paula Bright – Graham & Elaine's daughter

Brian Phelps – Treasurer

Martyn Share – Trainee

Ian Jamieson – Detective Inspector
Bill Fry – Detective Sergeant

CHAPTER 1

He could work out how long it would take to die. On his air gauge, the indicator pointed to sixty. In his fifteen litre bottle of compressed air that meant that he had nine hundred litres of air. He was stuck underwater at a depth of twenty metres, so if he used the standard calculation of breathing twenty five litres of air a minute at the surface he might be using up seventy five litres a minute down here. Except that he was an experienced diver and he did not breathe at that rate. Normally he only took shallow breaths so his air consumption was a lot lower than that. But that was when he was perfectly calm. Now he was fighting to suppress a rising panic. He must relax, otherwise he'd be panting his life away. Take it easy, work it out, he thought. He could have twelve minutes left alive, but if he kept still he might be able to stretch it out for longer.

John would have noticed that his diving buddy was missing by now. He would come back looking for him and then he'd be fine. How long had he been here? A few minutes, maybe. But John didn't know he'd gone back, did he? He thought they were both on their way to the diving bell. The routine if you got separated from your buddy was to look around for a minute and then surface, in the expectation that you would find each other again there. It was never a good idea to continue diving on your own. What time was it now? It might take John a while to raise the alarm and then someone would come.

He cursed himself for not following proper diving procedures. If he had tapped John's shoulder and pointed to the dark, inviting hole in the side of the wrecked boat, then they would both have come down to investigate it and he'd have his buddy at his side to help him, but he hadn't done that, had he? He'd thought John was a bit too far away to reach and he'd just pop down, have a quick look and then catch him up. Stupid, really stupid. He went back over their plan earlier. 'Down on this buoy, look around the boat, then head over to the bell and up over there?' They usually dived down head first to make a quick descent and have maximum time on the bottom. The visibility had got worse since their first dive in the morning, so they could barely see two metres ahead. They found the wreck and started to make their way around it. They had dived together for years so they were very comfortable with each other, always knowing where the other one would be, what their preferences were and how they tended to behave. Tony loved to explore dark holes and would head for black spaces within wrecks, whilst John had no wish to investigate every inviting crevice. They had been over and around the boat for some time when John indicated moving off in the direction of the diving bell. Tony had signalled OK, but then caught sight of the enticing gap. The vessel was lying at an angle, with the masts pointing out above his head as he went lower to examine the hole in the side. It was big enough for him to put half his body in, so he unhitched his torch and shone around the inside, identifying parts of the engine. He brushed some trailing ropes out of his way in order to see. Maybe they had been used to tow the boat into position, before sinking it. Having satisfied himself that he had seen everything of interest, he went to back out.

He was stuck. He could twist from left to right, but it felt as if something had caught on the top of his bottle. There wasn't enough room for him to turn around completely, nor was there enough flexibility in whatever held him. He turned the torch around to inspect the edges of the aperture. Of course! Ropes! One of them must have caught around his kit. He automatically bent a knee and reached down to where his knife should be. Not there! He tried to reach behind him to unhook the rope but his arm would not bend backwards in the right direction. He squirmed again. No good. He was held firmly. Perhaps if he undid his jacket he could slide his body out beneath it whilst still retaining his regulator so that he could breathe. Then he might be able to work the rope free from above. He undid his waist strap and then the two shoulder straps. The bottle was held in place above him, but he was free so he eased down and pushed backwards. There was more space on his left than on his right, but there wasn't enough length in the tube connecting his regulator to allow him to move back further. He checked his gauge. Air seemed to have gone down rather a lot. He must just relax. He decided to think back over the morning and wait as calmly as possible.

CHAPTER 2

It was a bright, clear Sunday morning at the converted quarry near Chepstow. The entry to the site provided a view across the sparkling green water which now filled part of the huge cavity gouged out of the landscape. The surrounding cliffs were sheer apart from the sinuous track that led down to the floating pontoons. They were located at the shallower end of the quarry, where the depth started at about ten metres, then sloped gradually to the midpoint. After this, there was a sudden drop off to a much deeper eighty to ninety metres. Scuba divers were drawn to the National Diving and Activity Centre here because of the spectacular setting and the range of depths available. There were also interesting features underwater where they could explore old diving bells, wrecked boats, tanks and even aircraft.

Tony and Cleo had been the first of the Forest Divers to arrive. Cleo! Would she be worried about his absence? No, she wouldn't know yet as she'd still be underwater with the new trainee, Martyn. Would she even be concerned when she did find out? If it were her that was missing, how worried would he be? Not very, in all honesty, he thought. Maybe no one would come. How much air now? Be positive, he told himself. They will come. Think about this morning. They followed the regular routine which was to park along the top edge, near the cafe. There you could admire the full glory of the shimmering water contrasting against the solid rock. He had even smiled with satisfaction at the time, contemplating the beautiful day and the prospect of diving. John was his business partner as well as the diving officer in the club and he had arrived with Martyn, the trainee.

He and Cleo unloaded kit from their boot, placing each item on a mat at the back of their car, to protect them from the gravelly surface. He lifted his bottle onto his shoulder in order to carry it over to be filled with compressed air and grunted with the effort. He was getting older, there was no doubt about it. His suit was getting tighter as his waistline expanded, despite his efforts to keep it in check. He was slightly jealous of John's well-defined muscular body that retained the slim profile of his youth in contrast to many other divers who were on the downward slope to middle-aged spread. He watched John smooth his dark hair back from his temples and knew that he would be wondering if the voluptuous girl was on duty in the office today. He smiled because he knew that John would find a scrawny lad there instead and therefore his charm would be wasted.

Whilst they waited for the bottles to be filled, John explained the plan for the day, starting with, 'Martyn, you'll be with me first. You've been fine with the kit practising in the pool over the last few weeks, but now we'll be able to go deeper to about ten metres. Cleo, you can look after Martyn on the second dive.'

It always took some time for everyone to retrieve bottles, get into suits and organise their kit. The men in the club all wore dry suits so they kept normal clothes on underneath. Cleo remembered she had been impressed when she first heard this because she had imagined a James Bond style tuxedo beneath. Sadly she had yet to meet a man who lived up to this image. Today all the men were pulling thermal under garments on, in order to protect them from the cold water. It was never going to be warm in the quarry, but a few degrees in temperature could make a big difference to the length of time you might want to be down there. She turned to consider Martyn, enjoying the view of such a lithe young man and feeling pleased that she was trusted to instruct him. He was struggling into an old wet suit given to the club by an ex-diver of about the same size. As he glanced in her direction, she looked away quickly, not wanting to be caught staring at him.

Cleo always used a semi-dry suit because she was comfortable in it and had never wanted the additional hassle of adjusting the buoyancy in a suit as well as in her jacket. She had tried a dry suit like the men once, but found it a mortifying experience. It was easy for them. They could just unzip and shrug the suit down in order to relieve themselves off the back of the boat. Once when they were out at sea for hours and she needed to go, she had waited and waited, hoping that the urge would disappear until they were on dry land. In the end, when she felt that her bladder might be about to rupture, she had crumpled the suit around her ankles and wriggled her bare bottom over the side of the boat. The men had all gazed studiously in the other direction, but hadn't been able to resist the 'Are you done yet?' comments. It had taken ages. She couldn't seem to go, knowing that they were all waiting. When she had finished, she looked up to find binoculars trained on her, from a couple of men at the top of the lighthouse nearby. She had vowed never to use a dry suit again. It was much easier to wee in her suit underwater and hope that it rinsed out as she swam along. She had a two part design as one piece covered her whole body and then a shorter version went over the top to provide increased insulation. She needed help to get into the upper part, so Tony heaved the back up over her shoulders and his hands lingered there.

'Come on, you lovebirds,' John called as he carried his kit to the central area where they would wait for the truck to take them down to the water. Cleo couldn't think of a more inappropriate description. She had already moved away from Tony and couldn't understand why he behaved like that. At home he never touched her and barely spoke in civil terms. Yet when they were out he was different. Surely it wasn't just a question of wanting to appear like a happily married couple? Was it some primitive instinct to mark her as his territory? She sighed as she gathered her stuff and followed John.

'What you lost, Tony?' John called as Tony searched in his bag.

'Can't find my knife.'

'It's amazing, isn't it? The number of times we come away and someone always forgets something,' John grumbled. 'You coming or what?' he continued.

'Yeah. I was sure it was there though.'

'Did you look in the boot as well in case it fell out?' asked Cleo.

'Not there either. I'll just go without it, doesn't matter.'

'Right, people. Let's be careful out there,' John said as they set off.

It was quite busy on the pontoons with a few groups of divers sorting their equipment and preparing themselves. John led Martyn towards the far end, closer to the shallowest part of the quarry and started checking his equipment for him, explaining the importance of each process as he went.

'This is a lot more thorough than when I went diving on holiday you know,' said Martyn.

'Well, you're training now. You need to understand how everything works and be able to check your own stuff in due course.'

John held the gauge away from them as he turned the tap on the bottle so that air could travel to Martyn's buoyancy jacket and regulator. 'You always hold the face of the gauge away from you, so that if the glass should blow it doesn't go over you.' He turned it back towards them in order to read, '220 bar. That's a good fill.'

'Right.'

'So in this 15 litre bottle, at 220 bar, we have….?'

Martyn looked lost. His mental arithmetic wasn't up to the task.

'… lots of air.' John continued. 'You just multiply the two together to get the number of litres. Then you can work out how long you've got underwater by how much you're likely to use at particular depths. Of course you're likely to breathe quicker than me, because you'll be gobbling air and I'll be relaxed. You need to remember to check your gauge frequently to see how much you've got, so you don't run out. If you do, you die.'

The others grinned at each other as they heard the familiar refrain on John's lips. There were always key moments in his training spiel when there was the 'If you do this wrong, you'll die,' reminder. It certainly helped to focus the mind.

'But you don't need to worry today, because I'll be

checking it for you first and then Cleo will be with you on the second dive. But if you did run out of air, what's the drill?'

Martyn made the right gesture, moving his hand to and fro in front of his throat. 'Then I'd hand you my octopus rig, I mean this spare here,' he lifted it up on his kit, 'and you'd breathe on that until we got back to the surface.' John continued, 'Now, what is going to be different about today compared to where you've dived before?'

'It'll be colder,' Martyn answered.

'For sure. If you're getting too cold, you need to tell me by doing this.' John mimed hugging himself with his arms.

'What else will be different?'

'No pretty fish?'

'No. There are some fish, but they'll be difficult to see and not pretty really. There's quite a lot of people here today so the sediment will be stirred up and visibility will be bad. If you've got any problem, what are you going to do?' Martyn answered by holding his right hand out flat and waggling it.

'Good. So you're alright clearing your ears to equalise the pressure?'

'Yep.'

'I know I'm going through basic stuff with you,' John said, 'but it's safer if I go through everything, rather than assume that you know what you're doing. I'll help you kit up, then I'll get mine on and I'll go into the water first so I'm there when you get in.'

A few minutes later there was a splash as Cleo entered the water, followed closely by John. Tony was still standing on the pontoon, taking a note of the bottle fill of each person so that their 'air in' and 'air out' would be recorded, along with the names of each pair of divers and the time they started their dive. He put the sheet down in order to help Martyn to the water's edge. Martyn took a giant stride off the pontoon and surfaced close to John. John signalled OK, received the same answer back and they moved off towards a marker buoy.

'Right. Hold onto the rope here a minute,' John instructed as they both floated by the tethered buoy.

'We're going to go straight down following this rope from the buoy to the first platform at six metres. We'll stop there a bit, then we'll go onto the bottom and we'll find a small boat over there somewhere.' He pointed towards the end of the quarry. 'We'll have a look at that and then we'll make our way back up the gradual slope to the beach back there. I'll just put this buddy line on so you don't get lost.' He ducked beneath the surface to attach the line from his jacket to a metal ring on Martyn's. As he resurfaced he made an 'OK' sign and pointed his thumb down to indicate that he was about to dive. Martyn repeated the action and they both emptied some air from their buoyancy jackets so that they could descend.

Martyn could hear the sound of his own breathing loud in his head. The water was cold and murky, with small particles floating about in it. John was looking at him, keeping an eye on his face and behaviour as they made their way slowly downwards. He knew that you could tell a lot from the expression in the eyes as it was a good indicator whether someone was feeling comfortable or scared. He thought Martyn was fine at the moment.

The trainee himself was busy remembering the procedures, keeping a tight hold on the rope and concentrating on John. He did not want to go down too fast or lose hold of the line. The pressure in his ears reminded him to clear them so he held his nose through his mask and blew gently. One ear 'popped', then the other one. That was fine, so he could continue and do it again as necessary. His feet soon hit the platform and John indicated that they should re-align from vertical descent to horizontal swimming position. Martyn felt reluctant to let go of the rope. This wasn't like his diving before and that had been years ago. What if he wasn't weighted correctly? What if he let go and rocketed to the surface? Then his lungs would burst and he'd die. Now that he had a chance to look around him, all he could see was an opaque wall of water. John was comfortingly close but he wanted to hold on to something solid. He eased further down the rope, moving his feet out so that he could still keep his grip whilst becoming parallel with the platform. His breathing sounded faster in his head. Surely it shouldn't be that loud. His mouth was feeling dry so he swallowed. What was the other thing he should remember to do? Mask squeeze. He should breathe out through his nose once or twice so that the mask did not cling too tightly to his face. He didn't want his eyeballs to be stuck to the inside of his mask when he came back up. That was another helpful image from the training lectures.

John was waiting for him and indicating that they should swim off ahead. Martyn looked where he pointed and could see nothing solid. No fixed item to aim for, nothing firm to hold onto. In his previous dives on holiday, visibility had been excellent. In clear blue water you could see for miles (relatively speaking), so you knew there was a seabed beneath you and there were fish, crabs and coral all around. But this was an alien place, with no life forms to be seen, apart from John.

John pointed downwards and moved to swim off. Martyn did not want to release his grip on the rope because he felt safe with it. He tapped John's shoulder and then waggled his right hand to indicate he was not happy. Then he pointed to his eyes and gesticulated ahead. Would he understand what he meant? Apparently he did, as John signalled OK, took his arm and moved them both to the side. Martyn let go now that John was steering him and in a few seconds a rock face appeared in front of them. Martyn immediately felt better seeing something solid and reached out for it gratefully. They followed the path of the cliff around the edge of the quarry until they came across the wreck of the small boat.

Back on dry land for lunch, Cleo quietly checked with John how Martyn had done and if there was anything in particular she should do with him on the second dive.

'He did well. Buoyancy was fine. He just had a bit of a problem coming off the first platform when you can't see anything so we went round by the cliff edge. Not surprising though given where he's dived before.'

'Thanks. I'll see if I can get him over to the other side of the quarry.'

They got up to clear their plates and head back to the truck which would return them to the pontoons. This time it was Cleo examining Martyn's kit and she asked, 'How much air have you got left?'

'One hundred bar.'

'Not enough. You'd be better off with a nice full bottle, just to be on the safe side. You can use that spare one over there and then you can kit up and I'll check you're doing it right.'

'Yes, boss.'

'I'll be the boss next week as well when you start on our new bathroom,' Cleo replied.

'I'll look forward to it,' he answered, thinking that it was truer than he wanted to admit. There was something about Cleo that reminded him of Zara. It was not just her physical appearance, although there was a striking similarity there, but she had some of the same mannerisms and a way of looking at him with a smile in her eyes. He had not noticed any women since the accident and was surprised to find someone attractive again but she was married, he reminded himself as he glanced over at Tony, so nothing would happen. It just meant that he would enjoy his work for the next couple of weeks. He collected the other bottle of air and passed by Tony and John on his way back.

'So what shall we do today?' Tony asked John.

'I fancy taking a look at that new boat. The one that they've only just put in. It's somewhere in the middle I think. We'll check the map.' The layout of the quarry was illustrated in a couple of diagrams, along with the signs about safety procedures that were displayed both at the top by the office and down by the water in a hut.

'Fine by me.'

Tony checked the air contents for each diver again, recording that everyone except Martyn was using the same bottle as their first dive because they still had sufficient quantities left. Tony and John were in the water, finning gently backwards towards the middle buoy as Cleo and Martyn got in. They started to descend and Martyn was trying to think about their dive plan and which way they would be heading when they got to the first platform, but he was distracted by Cleo's eyes. Whilst the hood hid her thick hair, the mask seemed to accentuate her deep blue eyes which were studying him closely. His fins hit the platform again and he manoeuvred to float parallel to her body. She gestured forwards, but it was the same dense, murky nothingness that had bothered him before. He could feel anxiety rising inside him, but he did not want to look cowardly in front of Cleo. He looked about desperately for something solid because then he would feel safer, so he wouldn't just disappear in the fog. Cleo indicated the buddy line linking the two of them together and made the 'OK' symbol. Martyn hesitated. He wasn't feeling OK. There was a slight leak around his mask and some water was coming in. What if it filled up completely? It felt different to the routines he'd practised in the clear, safe water of the swimming pool. Of course! He didn't have to take it off. What was the matter with him? All he had to do was to blow gently through his nose and the water would be pushed out. Cleo took his hand and again gestured down and away from the platform. He released the rope and grasped her hand tighter through their thick gloves. This was good. There was no way he could get lost now, Cleo would look after him. He smiled and then hastily stopped as the movement changed the shape of his face and allowed water to seep into his mask again. They moved off together, finning side by side and hand in hand.

CHAPTER 3

Martyn was packing his belongings into a bag. He had to be back in London the next day to sort out the final details with the house. He was sitting on the bed in his rented flat, thinking that he would be better off buying somewhere as soon as possible. He flicked over the details of some properties but none of them appealed to him so he cast them aside, remembering the agent saying that he was in 'a happy position' as he had already sold their home. He had barely suppressed the desire to hit the man. Admittedly part of him would be relieved to see it go, but the overriding feeling was that of sadness. They had worked on it together, arguing over paint colours, tiles, carpets and the optimum position for electricity sockets. Zara had bowed to his knowledge of plumbing to plan the bathroom but argued about every other thing. Mostly he enjoyed the fray and engaged in the dispute for the fun of it, just so that they could make up afterwards.

As he gazed around the room, he thought that she would not have been impressed with the décor in here as nothing matched. Still, if she had been with him, he would not be here. Some of his friends thought he was making a mistake, moving away from everything and everyone that he knew. He could hardly tell them that was why he needed to go. He thought that taking up diving with the local club was a good idea as it gave him an interest apart from work, with new people to meet. Hopefully it would be sufficiently enthralling to keep his mind away from the recurrent memories.

It was not that long ago that he had contemplated throwing himself into the sea to end it all. At the time the guilt that he felt over the accident had threatened to swamp him. He still blamed himself for suggesting that particular limousine company to Zara for her hen night whilst he was on his stag. A local company would not have taken that route down past Sunny Bank in the ice and snow because it was notoriously dangerous. He could not drive down the road now without imagining the scene that night and every time his mind re-ran the accident it seemed to include some other horrific detail.

* * *

Cleo was on her way home after giving an accountancy seminar at the University of the West of England. When she had seen the timetable she had immediately thought that last thing on a Friday afternoon was not likely to be a well attended event. It made no difference to her preparation time if there were one student or twenty. The cost was in the follow up time required to fill in the gaps for those laggards who did not understand something because they had been absent. How much this irked her depended on her mood at the time and the individual in question. There were those who were habitually lazy, but produced very good work whenever they put in any effort and there were those who struggled just to scrape a pass mark. Her sympathies lay with the latter group, but of course both types tended to skip the Friday sessions. As she crossed the old Severn Bridge she switched to thinking about home rather than work.

She always enjoyed driving back towards the Forest and admired the trees in any season. The beech were currently displaying their fresh green leaves which contrasted well with the conifers amongst them as both fought for space on the steep hillsides of the Wye Valley. At the moment the river was a deep green, which blended in with the surrounding landscape better than the muddy brown colour it produced when in full spate.

Cleo checked the time and thought that Rachel should be back from school when she got in. Tony might be there as well as he seemed to be spending an increasing amount of time at home at the moment. She thought about her daughter, how beautiful she was and the way that she was growing up so fast. Tony had said only recently how much Rachel looked like a younger version of her but it hadn't been complimentary to Cleo. The implication was that she was a wrinkled, tired, fat old body that no-one would ever desire again. As the recurring doubt entered her mind about Tony's need to work at home and Rachel's developing body, she tried to push it away. He was just being a caring stepfather and looking after her. She gripped the wheel and sat up straighter, trying to dismiss the thoughts that regularly invaded her mind and spread through her consciousness like cancer. She told herself that she was just being paranoid, because she was feeling a bit low, that was all.

She couldn't think what the opposite of paranoid was, or even if there were one. Tony had been behaving as if he was some sort of hero, just because he'd survived the incident at the quarry, but it was his own stupid fault for putting himself in that situation. She went over his version of events, wondering if she would have had the presence of mind to act as he did. When he had been stuck in the wreck, there wasn't enough length on his main regulator to be able to breathe from that one and unwind the rope that held him. When he switched to his octopus as his alternative air supply he was fine. He could reach further so he undid the rope and pulled his kit out. Then he put it back on and went up to the surface. Of course by that time John had alerted the rescue boat, so they were coming out to look for him. He'd gone on at Tony about being selfish and negligent and careless (she could have added a few more there) because he shouldn't have gone back to look at a dark hole when John had indicated moving away. Of course the telling-off would not make one jot of difference to Tony's future attitude or behaviour because he would continue to do precisely what he wanted.

As she headed up the track towards the house she saw John's Range Rover parked by the converted barn at the back, alongside Tony's Lexus. The men had met years ago when they had both been employed in the motor industry in the Midlands. Tony had been an automotive designer and John an engineer. After some years working together they had decided to set up their own company manufacturing miniature versions of cars for children. The idea had taken off and over time they had extended the range so that they could now supply small Land Rovers, Rolls Royces, Aston Martins and Cheetahs, their very own sports car. When they had needed to expand, they had taken advantage of a government regeneration grant to re-locate to the Forest of Dean. Property prices had been so much lower back then that their house in Birmingham had translated into a much bigger property when they moved south. Tony liked to work at home and tinker about in the workshop, but the factory premises were only a few miles away, closer to the M50 which was better for deliveries. As the company had grown they had both developed their original roles so Tony was now responsible for marketing and sales whilst John was in charge of finance and production. In the beginning they had valued each other's differences and believed that their skills were complementary. However, Cleo was aware of a growing friction between the men. John complained that he was doing the lion's share of the work, whilst Tony frittered away his time wining and dining potential customers. Although Cleo provided the accounting function within the company, she did not actively participate in management and tried to keep out of any disputes. If anything did happen, she only tended to hear Tony's version of events and lately she had felt less inclined to believe him. She parked the car and walked towards the barn, approaching quietly so that she could listen in, before they knew she was there.

As she peeped in at the open window John's back obscured the view of her husband. In the early days just a glimpse of Tony's bronzed good looks would make her smile. She had thought then that he would always make her happy and they would form a complete family unit with Rachel. His appearance had altered little she noted; still the same fair, floppy hair falling into his blue-grey eyes. However his look was rarely warm when it was cast in her direction. Nowadays she was hesitant when approaching him, unsure of her reception. She felt he no longer cared for her, and, indeed, would rather be without her. This produced a sadness which overlay every other emotion, obscuring her feelings and clouding her thoughts. Where had they gone wrong, she wondered, as she gazed at the two men.

Tony appeared to be doing his best to ignore John as he studied some drawings on the table and did not look up when John continued,

'… but it's not as if you have to do much designing any more. We haven't had a new model for the last year.'

'Yes. That's why I need to be here to develop it.'

'And are you?' John's voice had a note of irritation in it.

'What do you mean?'

'Well, if you've been developing it, where are the drawings? Where's the spec? What's it going to be?'

'It's in progress.'

John sounded exasperated. 'I need you in the factory. I can't run the place on my own. I can't be in control of supply, production, quality control and finance.'

'You're not running the place on your own,' Tony replied sullenly. 'There wouldn't be any point producing cars unless I got the orders. Sales don't come out of nowhere you know. I do the marketing plan. I make visits, do promotions, go to the fairs and exhibitions and I get the business.'

'Well, where is it then?'

'What?'

'The business. The orders.' John threw his hands up in the air. 'We've got to know so we can plan the production schedule. You've got to get your ass in gear otherwise we'll all be out of work soon.'

Cleo wondered if this was going to escalate into a full scale argument and whether she should leave them to it and make for the house.

'Don't worry,' Tony replied. 'There are a couple of orders coming. In the pipeline.'

'It's not good enough, Tony. We need to know what

we're doing months in advance. We can't run hand to mouth like we did when it was just us. There are more guys depending on the work to support their families.'

'I know. I know.'

'I think we need to reassess responsibilities or take on a production manager or promote one of the guys.'

'I like it the way it is,' Tony replied stubbornly.

'God. For a designer you're oddly resistant to change. You've got to get your act together so it feels like a partnership again.' John sighed. 'Is it because of the inheritance? Do you feel like you don't need to work any more?' Cleo stumbled against the side of the barn. 'What inheritance?' she thought. 'First I've heard of it.' The men stopped talking. She walked into the workshop as if she had heard nothing and greeted them cheerily.

★ ★ ★

The regular pool night was on a Thursday. Once the youngsters from the local swimming club left, the divers had it for the last hour of the day. Some club members used the session as an opportunity for exercise, clocking up the lengths. If there were trainees, they would be instructed in particular techniques and then practise routines. The more experienced divers were only likely to bring kit down if they had bought something new or if they were checking things were still working after a winter of inactivity.

'Is that him?' Lynne asked Cleo as she nodded towards the man who had just entered the pool area.

'I can't see from here,' Cleo responded as she turned to look back to the shallow end.

'Yeah, right. It's the fit bloke. You can tell which one he is because he's the only man with a six pack on him. The others have left theirs at home.'

Cleo grinned. 'Well, if he's got dark, curly hair, a tanned body and a sort of scar on his eyebrow, then it's not him, no.'

'My 20-20 vision doesn't allow me to inspect the state of his eyebrows from here. It's Martyn Share though, isn't it? Wouldn't mind a share of that, myself,' she murmured as she studied the body that slid into the water, barely causing a ripple.

'I'd best leave you to it, then,' Cleo said as she set off doing breaststroke. As she passed the lean shape of Martyn cutting powerfully through the water, she couldn't help wishing that she'd worn her other swimming costume. It had a reinforced area that created a flatter stomach out of the stretch-marked mass that lay like dimpled blancmange around her middle.

Lynne pushed her hand through her hair, hoping to achieve a tousled look as she watched Martyn crawl towards her. As he executed a neat tumble turn and sped away, she realised that introductions were not going to happen just yet. Still, it gave her another opportunity to admire his firm flesh as it dipped and turned. Pity she had neither goggles nor mask, she thought, as she would like to see how closely his trunks clung to his body underwater. She set off in pursuit and was rewarded by a call from John, 'Hey, Lynne, come and meet Martyn.'

'Are you going to join the club?' Lynne asked.

'Yes, if you'll have me…' She suppressed a groan. 'I started diving on holiday a few years ago so I did a bit back then.'

'But now he wants to learn how to do it properly,' John completed for him. It was a strongly held belief in the club that a few sessions on holiday could not equip anyone with all the knowledge necessary for safe diving. They preferred the much slower approach of weekly lectures, regular pool sessions and then a gradual build up of experience in open water. This was always tailored to the needs of the individual and their particular abilities so that everyone would learn at their own pace. John maintained that a diver who was pushed into conditions that were beyond their capabilities was a safety risk. Some of the others were chatting and some had swum away, so no-one noticed as John edged towards Cleo. 'He'll do,' he murmured as he nodded in Martyn's direction. Cleo chose to ignore him and disappeared underwater so that no-one could see the dark flush that climbed up her neck onto her cheeks. She could not rid herself of the thought that Tony had still not mentioned any inheritance to her. It was almost a week now. He must be keeping it secret from her deliberately. Why would he do that? Did he know?

CHAPTER 4

The doorbell rang and Cleo walked to the front of the house to answer it. They generally went out at the back because the front door tended to stick. She gazed at the wood and focused on the brass lock. She would look a right idiot if she couldn't open her own front door.

'Coming,' she called to Martyn. He tried to push the door open.

'No. I said I'm coming, not 'Come in'. It's locked. Just a minute.'

She struggled with the door. 'Be there in a sec.' The heat was rising to her face. He would think she was daft. 'Stupid thing.'

'Shall I go round the back?' asked Martyn from outside.

'No. Oh, thank you, thank you,' she beamed as the door opened to reveal Martyn before her.

'I haven't done anything yet.'

'Not you. I was talking to the door.'

'You talk to the door?'

'Only when I want it to open.' Martyn's smile got wider as Cleo looked flustered and said, 'It's got a mind of its own.'

'Have you thought of getting a new one?'

'Tony doesn't see the point. He says there's nothing wrong with it.'

'I've got loads of stuff in the van.'

'Do you want to see where to bring it?' She turned and

led the way upstairs. 'There's a toilet downstairs but only the one bathroom up here. Rachel has to come through our room to get to it, so we thought we'd change the smaller guest bedroom into a bathroom for her.'

'That's nice for Rachel,' Martyn replied as he followed the swaying hips mounting the stairs. She did not tell him the real reason why Rachel needed her own bathroom, or rather, why Cleo had decided that her daughter needed it. She did not like the way that her younger image would wander past their bed, clutching the smallest of towels around her growing form. She liked it even less when Tony called 'Morning, Gorgeous' after her. She didn't want to think about Tony lying in bed, replaying that moment in his mind whilst she went to make breakfast. She shook herself. It was nothing. She had thought that Rachel would have been happier about it though. Lots of girls her age would love to have their own en suite, so they could spend half the day in there if necessary.

'Like a cup of tea?' she asked as they returned downstairs.

'Yes, thanks. I'll take it up with me and I'll get started.'

'No. Stay and have a chat first.'

'But I should be working.'

'Don't worry about that. I'll be paying the bill, because I manage the finances around here and I say you can have a tea break.'

'You're the boss.'

Cleo flicked the switch on the kettle and sat at the pine table as Martyn took the seat opposite.

'So, are you happy about having a woman boss?' she asked him.

'Sure, if she's generous.'

'And you'll obey my every command?'

'Your every command?' Cleo noticed the scar more as he raised an eyebrow. She ignored his question and asked, 'How did you get that scar?' as she got up to make the tea.

'I fell off my bike when I was little.'

'So mundane?'

'No. Actually I was held captive by pirates in the Caribbean and they encouraged me to walk the plank by swiping at me with a sword.'

Cleo grinned. 'Much better. I like it.'

'You'd rather contemplate someone torturing me? How kind.'

'Yes, but better that, than the mental torture of not being able to open your own front door.'

'I know what you mean. I hate those plastic cards that are supposed to work as keys in hotels but never do.'

'Yes, those ones where you have to dip it in, wait for the green light and then open it.'

'But you only have a micro second before it turns red again.'

'By which time you've dropped your bag and coat because you're trying to get it in again.'

They were both laughing as Tony walked into the kitchen. 'Glad to see you're hard at it.' He nodded to Martyn but frowned at Cleo. Martyn decided to take his tea outside and gather the things from the van. Tony gazed after him saying, 'He won't be interested in a tired old bat like you, you know.' Cleo said nothing as she poured the rest of her tea away. 'He'd want someone young and fit, without the creases and the sags.' She grabbed her keys and went out. 'He's just being polite to the customer.'

'You could learn a thing or two from him then,' Cleo

muttered as she wrenched open her car door. She drove off down the lane too fast, creating a minor dust storm behind her. It wouldn't be so bad if she could just convince herself that Tony was lying, but she could see the creases and the sags clearly enough herself. If that wasn't bad enough, she felt that she couldn't retaliate by insulting Tony because he still looked fit. Admittedly he was a few years younger than her, but he did not seem to have changed much over the last twelve years and still looked as fresh-faced and boyish as he had when they met. Although this had been part of his charm, Cleo now felt that it was a severe disadvantage to be with a man who appeared to have an ageless Peter Pan quality whilst she was getting as wrinkled as an old witch.

She had left the house with no clear purpose, but decided to go for a walk in the woods. Old trees were comforting. Age was a good characteristic in a tree, because they matured gracefully into something majestic. Some of the woods nearby contained veteran trees, beeches that were hundreds of years old and would provide shelter beneath their boughs. Cleo had a favourite haunt where she could sit in the midst of the branches, transported back to childhood when she had imagined all sorts of adventures in her tree house. However, on the road to her forest haven she switched direction, seeking her other regular comforter.

★ ★ ★

Graham came home, feeling drained after a difficult meeting at the factory. One of the lines needed new machinery and it had to be installed by contractors who didn't seem to know what they were doing. He just wanted to sit down with a

27

beer and enjoy the football, but he walked in to find a red-eyed Paula sitting at the kitchen table with Elaine and a mound of tissues.

'What's up?'

'Don't go mad,' Elaine said, getting up and standing between him and their daughter. She spoke quickly, as if the information wouldn't be such a shock if delivered at high speed. 'Paula's pregnant. We've done a test and …'

'She's pregnant?'

'Yes.'

'You're having a baby?' He turned to Paula, looking at her in disbelief. She looked very vulnerable in her dressing gown, with her tear-stained face. 'But you're only just sixteen. You're just a child.' Suddenly he saw her as other men might, with her voluptuous figure apparent through the thin cloth. 'Cover yourself up,' he said roughly, looking away from her.

'She's not a child. She's a young woman.'

'Did some bastard force you? Is that it?' Paula shook her head mutely, but more tears coursed down her cheeks. She wiped them away and pushed her hair back behind her ears nervously. 'Did he hurt you? I'll kill him. I'll …'

Elaine pulled him back saying, 'Graham, for God's sake. You're not helping.' He sat down at the other side of the table. Everyone was silent. He studied the grain in the pine planks before him. At the perimeter of his vision he could see Paula's hands nervously shredding tissues. He struggled to control his emotions. He wanted to do something violent, to hit out at someone or something. He could not look at his princess. He took a deep breath and decided to take one step at a time.

'When?'

'When what?' Elaine asked tentatively.

'When did it bloody happen?'

Elaine looked to Paula who kept her head down and said nothing.

'So, there have been so many times you can't remember? So many men using your body?' Graham glared at Paula, who flinched as if he had hit her.

'Graham!'

'Whose is it?' Paula's head bent lower over the table, so that her hair formed a screen in front of her face. Her hands ceased their fretting at the paper.

'She won't say,' Elaine answered.

'You mean she knows, but she won't say, or she doesn't know?'

Paula leapt to her feet, 'One man, Dad. Only one man,' and ran from the kitchen.

★ ★ ★

Cleo lay back on the sofa, brushing her auburn hair out of her eyes.

'So you didn't fancy Portland this weekend then?' she asked her friend.

'Not likely. It's rough down there, isn't it?' Lynne answered. 'Why didn't you go?'

'I've caught Tony's cold. Marvellous, isn't it? He gets better so he can dive and then I get it.'

'You do look a bit peaky.'

'I don't feel too bad, but I've got a really thick head.'

'No change there, then.' Lynne smiled sweetly at her friend. 'Do you think they'll be having a good diving weekend away?' she continued.

'I think they'll be having a good weekend, but not diving,' Cleo replied. 'They knew the weather was going to be bad, but that doesn't stop them going. Maybe they'll do that coasters thing again.'

'You make it sound like a beer mat. It's just jumping off cliffs into the sea.'

'Oh, that sounds a lot better,' Cleo retorted sarcastically. 'You know I'd be clinging to the grass roots, I'd never be able to fling myself off a precipice.'

'So you don't want me to arrange it for your surprise birthday treat?'

'I do not.'

'Yes, but surely you want to do something special for your fortieth?'

'I don't want to think about it. My mirror has developed creases, you know.'

'You need to give it some of that Boots No. 7 anti-ageing cream,' Lynne suggested.

'I have. Worked a treat. Smeared it all over and I couldn't see a thing.' They both giggled as Lynne poured out more wine.

'Anyway,' Lynne said as she replaced the bottle, 'I'm sure Tony loves you just the way you are.'

'Hmmm.'

'What? All not well in chateau Fleming?'

'It's just… I get tired of his jokes, you know? It's the way he makes me feel old and fat all the time. He thinks it's funny to make that noise like a Russian whaling ship when I'm out sunbathing.'

Lynne laughed and stifled it quickly at Cleo's look.

'I'm sorry, but that is … deeply wounding, I can see that.'

'It's alright for you, with your blonde locks, your hourglass figure and your honey coloured skin.'

'I haven't got a man though.'

'D'you want mine?'

'I don't think he would go with my blonde locks, my hourglass figure and my honey coloured skin.' Cleo threw a cushion at her.

Lynne ducked and continued, 'I don't know why you're worried, you still look lovely. Any man would want you.'

'Even with this?' Cleo prodded her spare tyre.

'Certainly. Makes you more cuddly. And anyway they'll want you because you're a nice person, fun to be with....'

The doorbell sounded and Cleo got up to let Elaine in, urging her friend to keep going.

'Intelligent, charming, caring...'

'What's this? Are we describing George Clooney?' Elaine asked.

'We're just doing a spot of morale building.'

A few bottles of wine later and all the women lay in various positions about the living room. The room exuded a feeling of cosy comfort as the warm colours of the walls were complemented by the soft furnishings of the squashy sofas and cushions. Elaine was embedded in a bean bag in a corner whilst Lynne was lying on the deep, fluffy rug in front of the stone fireplace. The fire wove its way through a stack of logs, consuming the wood as it went. The firelight and the candles supplemented the effect of the alcohol so that her face was suffused with a warming glow. The heat was burning one of her legs so she sat up straighter and said,

'Why is it you can't just find one comfortable position and stay in it?'

'Lying in front of a fire isn't as bad as wearing a thong,' Elaine reported. 'It's such a small triangle of material. I once spent a very uncomfortable morning wriggling about, thinking it was the worst thing I'd ever worn. Then when I went to the loo I found I'd got it on the wrong way round, with one leg down the waist bit.' They all laughed as Lynne got up saying, 'Well, I must tear myself away. Early start in the morning.'

'But I've only just got here,' Elaine replied.

'Sorry, but I have to go. See ya!' she called as she closed the front door behind her.

'Early start?' Elaine asked Cleo.

'Maybe. Or perhaps she's got an assignation with some bloke.'

'Oh, right.' The news seemed to have changed Elaine's mood for the worse. Cleo went to the kitchen to find another bottle and replenish supplies.

'You alright?' Cleo asked as she returned.

'Yeah, fine.' She sat still, swirling the last of her wine around the bottom of her glass.

'Tell your Auntie Cleo.'

Elaine sighed deeply and then asked, 'How's Rachel?'

Cleo felt a sudden stab of alarm. Was there something wrong with Rachel that she didn't know about?

'She's well, I think. Upstairs. Why?'

'Daughters. Who'd have 'em?' Cleo waited, hoping that Elaine would explain why they should both be worried about their offspring.

'I was in my twenties when I had Paula,' Elaine continued.

'I know.' Cleo wondered where this was heading. Was Elaine ill or was it Paula? She studied her closely.

'And I'd been with Graham for years by then.'

'Yes.'

'I was just wondering what it would be like to find yourself pregnant when you were very young and you weren't in a stable relationship.'

'Paula's pregnant?' asked Cleo, bending forward to meet Elaine's eyes. 'Is she OK?'

'Yes. I think so. She doesn't seem to be sick or anything.'

'What did Graham say?'

'Not happy about it. His precious princess. You know the sort of thing?'

'I can imagine.' Cleo considered how Graham would behave. Very badly, she thought. Elaine had said something and she had missed it.

'Sorry, what did you say?'

'Thirteen weeks, the doctor said,' Elaine repeated.

'Thirteen weeks.' Cleo was counting backwards. That made it sometime in February. 'Didn't she know before now?'

'She's always had irregular periods. And she probably didn't want to believe it.' Elaine ran her finger around the base of the wine glass.

'Her and her Dad aren't really speaking much.'

'Maybe Graham just needs a while to come to terms with it,' Cleo suggested. She did not know whether she should ask the crucial question about the future of the baby. She did not want to sound as if there was only one course of action.

'He seems more preoccupied by who the father is than the health of his daughter,' Elaine added as she turned the stem of the wine glass round and round.

'And..?'

'She won't say.'

'Well, there could be a number of reasons for that.' Cleo was consumed with curiosity, but tried to find something supportive to say. 'She might think she's protecting the father, or it's someone you wouldn't approve of or…'

'Graham thinks it's an older man.'

'Why?'

'I don't know. I can't think straight. I keep going over it in my head, but it all ends up with me being a bad mother.'

'No. You're not. You mustn't think like that.'

'Teenage pregnancy though. It's not what you want for your daughter is it? You want them to have a better life than you did, with more opportunities.'

'She could still have that. It's early yet….'

'Cleo! You don't mean …abortion?' she hissed.

'Yes, I do. All I'm saying is you need to help Paula through the options.'

'But it's murder.'

'It depends on how you look at it. Some people say it's not an independent being so it hasn't got a life of its own.'

'And others say it's a life from the very first second that it exists. You can't mean it, surely? You wouldn't do that, would you?'

Cleo paused. Would she? In those circumstances, when she was sixteen, with her family still around her and a tiny baby growing inside her? Probably not. But was murder of a foetus the same as murder of an adult? Which was worse? To end a life before it had started or to shut it down once it had enjoyed only half of the estimated 'three score years and ten'.

CHAPTER 5

The pub door swung open as Brian edged into the bar.

'Hey, Brian, how's it hanging?' John called from his seat in the corner. Brian nodded to him, fervently wishing he wouldn't say things like that as other heads turned to focus on the new entrant.

'Where've you been?'

'Some of us have to work for a living.' Brian always had this when he arrived late on a Friday night for a weekend away diving. Everyone seemed to think that he could leave the bank the moment it shut its doors in the afternoon, but it wasn't like that. The bank had procedures and processes with forms that had to be completed at the end of every trading week.

'6X,' Tony stated as he offered Brian an empty glass.

'Who's got the kitty?' Brian asked as he gathered the other glasses.

'Here you go,' Graham said as he gouged out notes and coins from his pocket.

'Thanks,' he replied, uncomfortably aware of the warmth of the coins in his hand.

'I saw an MGBGT on the way down – just like my first car,' Tony told the others.

'And it was still going?' John asked incredulously.

'Certainly was. Didn't look as good as mine though.'

'Triumph Spitfires were much better. There's no

comparison. Beautiful lines, great shape and some power to it,' John said.

'Yours had that overdrive flip switch on the gearstick, didn't it?' Tony remembered.

'That's right. My lovely Mark Four. The only problem was the way the bonnet would come undone as I drove along because the catches on the sides were corroding. Sometimes I could see the lip bouncing up and I thought a good gust of wind might lift it and have me cartwheeling along the motorway. Actually that wasn't the only problem. The slave cylinder on the clutch went a few times. Then there were the leaks…'

'Never had that problem with my Vauxhall Viva,' Graham commented.

'You had a Viva?'

'And you want to admit to it?' asked Tony.

'Nothing wrong with it. It was a good car,' he replied defensively.

'Saw a bit of action in there, did you?' asked John.

Graham ignored his comment and went to join Brian at the bar.

'Maybe he didn't?' John continued, looking after him.

'My first car was a Land Rover,' Martyn stated. 'I thought it was the best thing ever. So much more character although I think my Dad probably nudged me that way because it wasn't going to go as fast as some of the others I looked at.'

'There's something special about Land Rovers though, isn't there?' Tony agreed. 'It's why every kid should want one. And that's good for business.'

'Oh no, he's off. He'll be raving about them now for the next hour or so. Hope you know what you've let yourself in for,' John advised Martyn, who grinned back at him. Tony was mouthing something at him, trying to overcome the noise of the jukebox.

'What?'

'I said, 'Didn't the handbrake get in the way of any action in your Spitfire?'

''Course not. I was over on their side with them. Those were the days.'

Graham and Brian had returned laden with pints.

'How old were you when you – you know?' asked Martyn.

'Fourteen, maybe fifteen.'

'You started early.'

John leant forward to collect his beer from Brian and tried to shift along the cushioned bench to make room for him and Graham.

'It's alright. We'll go over here.' Brian nodded over to the nearby window seat where Graham was heading, immersing his top lip in the froth of his pint to prevent spillage. The noise level in the pub had increased as more people crammed themselves into the small space. The barman slid the volume control for the old jukebox up a couple of notches, thinking that louder music was good for business. He hoped it would act like a beacon drawing the thirsty in from the streets. The divers split into separate groups of conversation because they could barely hear what their neighbour was saying, let alone someone several feet away.

'He makes me sick.' Graham told Brian as he sat down.

'Who?'

'John. Always talking about sex and how much he's done it.'

'Hmm.' Brian did not want to get drawn into this type of conversation.

'But if he was doing it at fourteen or fifteen, what about the girls he was with? What about them? What if they got pregnant?'

Brian wondered if this was a rhetorical question. It was. Graham carried on. 'I mean, I know they're growing up fast and everything, but sixteen's too young. Much too young.' Brian decided to stick with nodding sagely until he had some idea what Graham was going on about, but he found his mind wandering back to his own problem. There were attractive girls in here, laughing in their little groups, all done up for a night out on the town. They might want to get lucky with some bloke, but it wouldn't be him. It would be a disaster. He could feel himself cringing at the memory of previous occasions. The first delight when someone was willing to talk to you, the chat up, the growth of excitement, the anticipation, the gradual build up of intimacy, each little hurdle another step closer, leading up to the moment of conquest and then – ignominious defeat. The unbelievable lie of, 'This has never happened to me before,' and the dreadful, soul destroying inadequacy. When it happened he never wanted to see the woman again and he wanted her to forget his face as rapidly as possible. If they wanted to be supportive and encouraging and tell him that it didn't matter, it only made it worse. He wanted to be a million miles away from the body that he had craved so desperately only seconds ago. His rapid exit did nothing to enhance his reputation of course. It merely reinforced the 'he only wanted one thing' mentality, which was far from the truth in Brian's case. What he desired above all else was a deep, lasting relationship with one woman that he could make love with satisfactorily. He reflected on the phrase. He didn't mean in a mundane fashion. He meant in a way that would be satisfying to both parties. He realised with a start that Graham was looking at him, apparently expecting a response. 'I'll get them in,' he said hurriedly, to buy some time.

'I'll have a whisky chaser with mine,' Graham called after him.

Brian checked on the repeat orders and resumed his seat after delivering the next round of drinks. Graham took a sip and continued with his theme, 'I've barely spoken to her, so I don't know what she wants to do.'

'Elaine?'

'No. Paula. It's Paula that's pregnant. Mind you….'

'Paula's pregnant?'

'For God's sake. What do you think I've been talking about for the last half hour?'

'Oh, right.'

'If you're not even going to listen…'

'I am. I am. Sorry, mate. Just thinking about something.'

Graham studied the pattern that the beer made as it slid back down the side of his glass.

'I want to do the right thing, you know, but I don't know what that is. First I wanted to smash the face of the guy …'

'You're not going to, are you?'

'No. I promised never to hit anyone again and I'll stick with that. Anyway, I don't know who it is,' he admitted ruefully.

Just as well, Brian thought, remembering the incident years ago when Graham had almost killed another boxer in an amateur match. The man had been in hospital for days and although he recovered eventually, Graham had not fought since.

Graham stared over at the other divers and Brian followed his gaze. 'You don't think it's one of them?'

'Might be.'

'Surely it'll be some lad near her own age.'

Graham looked at the scantily clad young girls who had cleared a small space and were dancing around each other, whilst wielding Bacardi Breezers. The line of men supporting the bar were all considerably older and they nodded at the women and muttered to each other lasciviously as they watched the entertainment. Graham's mood shifted from sadness to anger, because he recognised the male behaviour that they reverted to when away from their partners. He wouldn't take advantage of some young slip of a thing, but there were those that did. His eyes shifted to John and then to Tony and Martyn.

'Not them. They're too old, surely?' Brian continued.

'She said something about a man, not a boy.'

'But it could be anyone.'

'Not anyone.'

'No, I didn't mean like that,' Brian added hastily, retreating from the idea that Paula had had lots of men. 'I mean someone that she's known for a while, that she can see easily, that lives nearby...' He tailed off as he realised that he could be describing their friends. 'But they wouldn't, they're your mates.'

'What if they couldn't resist? If one of them had the chance with a young, nubile virgin, with someone who looked up to them and thought they were wonderful ....'

Even though Brian wanted to defend the others and

proclaim their innocence, he couldn't help wondering why he was excluded from the round of suspects. 'Why one of them? Why not me?'

Graham laughed with a mouthful of beer and spluttered some back into his glass. Brian felt insulted. Of course he didn't want to be seen as a potential child molester, but why should he be discounted as a man?

'Sorry. You're one of the good guys, Brian. It wouldn't be you.'

Brian felt slightly mollified, but couldn't help wishing that he had some of the devilish, seductive charm of a famous womaniser, maybe Jack Nicholson. At least making Graham laugh seemed to have lightened his mood temporarily.

'The thing is, we need to decide what to do next.'

'We?' Brian was alarmed at his inclusion in this pronoun.

'I mean me, Elaine and Paula. Don't tell the others, just in case.' He glanced back at the table of divers. 'I don't know how Paula feels about it, whether she'll want to keep it or not and what happens about school, all that sort of stuff. It'll change her whole future.'

'You need to talk to her about it.'

'I know. I know. I should have stayed home really so we could all chat, but at the moment I get so angry when I think about it, I can't talk sensibly. It's not just the baby. I mean the baby can't help being there. It makes me feel like a bad father, for not protecting her, for not stopping it from happening.' He had finished his pint so he took a swig of the whisky. 'If she got rid of it, she might regret it for ever and always wonder what it would have been like. If she keeps it, will it be more like another baby for me and Elaine, rather than hers? We thought we were done with all that and could look forward to babysitter-free time. Now we might have to go back to scratch. And there's the house. Will we need more room? Will we have to make the house bigger or move and get a bigger mortgage? God, what a mess.' He took another long swallow of whisky and Brian wondered how a bout of heavy drinking would improve either his mood or his judgement.

At that moment Tony appeared at their table brandishing glasses.

'Nice view from over here,' he commented, nodding at the girls gyrating close by. 'That one there reminds me of your Paula, Graham.' Both Graham and Brian looked at the body closest to them. Her clothes were tightly stretched over fulsome curves which she moved provocatively.

'Nothing like her,' Graham retorted fiercely.

'She's growing up fast, isn't she?' Tony replied as he gathered the kitty money and went to the bar. When he returned to his own table John asked, 'Graham on the whisky then?'

'Yeah.'

'Looks a bit serious over there. What are they talking about?'

'Dunno. Didn't ask.' Turning back to Martyn, Tony said, 'You should go on that wreck that's got lots of vehicles in it.'

'Yeah?'

'It's great there, isn't it, John?'

'It is, but that's a proper holiday dive trip, that.'

'I didn't mean now. I meant some time in the future. Maybe for now we should go and look at the submarine. You know, the one near Plymouth. It's something a bit different and it's more complete than a lot of wrecks.'

'A submarine?' asked Martyn.

'Yes. It's out and around the headland from Plymouth.' Tony answered. 'Bit of a ride in the boat to get there, but a good dive site. It's actually quite close in to the shore, but there's a bit of a drop-off and a ledge so it's about 25m.'

'So when shall we go?'

'Well, we've got West Wales soon, then the Gower coming up in July, so maybe August,' John replied.

'Alright then, August it is.' Tony raised his glass to make a communal toast with Martyn and John.

A group of boisterous young men were making their way to the bar, but one of them collided with the table of drinks. Some of the beer slopped onto the table and each man quickly steadied his pint in order to retain the precious liquid. 'Shall we have one more or shall we move on?' asked Martyn, about to get the drinks in.

'Looks like Graham's set for a session, so let's stay here,' John replied as he glanced across to see Graham emptying another shot glass of whisky.

'He's going to be wrecked in the morning,' said Tony.

'I think he'll be wrecked tonight.'

★ ★ ★

In the morning, all of the men except for Graham were gathered in the bar again, which was now laid up for breakfast. Each of them was demolishing a full cooked breakfast enthusiastically.

'So where's Graham then?' asked John.

'In bed, groaning,' Brian replied.

'Is he coming down?'

'In a bit.'

'Ah, talk of the devil,' Tony smiled at the grey-faced individual who appeared to be trying to walk forwards whilst keeping his head as still as possible. As he lowered himself gingerly to a seat, John slapped him on the shoulder and said, 'Alright, mate? Want some?' as he lifted his greasy plateful of food up. Graham brought his hand up to his mouth rapidly and left the room with scant regard for keeping his head still. All the men except Brian laughed. 'Think he'll be diving today then?' asked Tony.

'Depends if the Diving Officer thinks he's fit,' Brian replied.

'I'll see how he feels in a bit,' John answered.

A few minutes later, Graham returned, looking slightly pinker.

'Bastards!'

'Breakfast, Graham?'

'Not yet. I'll have some tea, though.'

Brian leant over to pour him some and recoiled. 'God, your breath stinks. Has something died in there?'

'Yeah, it was his sense of modesty,' said John.

'What?' asked Graham.

'Don't you remember what you were doing last night?'

'When?'

'Oh dear, I don't think he remembers,' added Tony.

'So you don't recall dancing on the table singing, 'I'm too sexy for my shirt?' asked John.

Graham groaned slightly.

'That wouldn't have been so bad, but then you went on to the other verses and apparently you were too sexy for your jeans, your socks and your Y-fronts,' John continued.

Graham put his head in his hands.

'You had an admiring crowd with all those young lasses at the front.'

'Oh God.'

'Everyone was cheering but the landlord called an end to it when you started showing everybody your vasectomy scars.'

CHAPTER 6

Cleo leant against the doorpost of the future bathroom with a mug of tea in her hand, having delivered some to Martyn.

'How's it going?'

'Badly. I've just realised I've got a bend that goes the wrong way. See this bit,' he held up a piece of piping, 'it should go to the left to fit in here and it goes to the right. I'm going to have to go out and swap it.'

Cleo looked around at the scene of recent devastation. The bedroom furniture had gone but the walls still showed the marks where the cupboards had fitted and previous phases of painting had ceased. Some of the plaster was missing where Martyn had removed it in order to put pipes through the wall and wires hung limply from old light sockets.

'It's looking a bit Spartan in here you know.'

Martyn sat back on his heels to reach for his drink as he surveyed his handiwork. 'Wasn't that what you wanted? It takes a lot of skill to rip out old wardrobes and put in bare pipe work.' He nodded to the corner, 'The freezing cold plunge pool will be over there and the cool shower on this side here.'

'And the luxurious hot bath?'

'Nobody said anything about hot water. That's a whole different ball game. More pipes. New tank. You should have said.' He grinned at Cleo and dimples appeared in his cheeks, making a threesome with the one in his chin. He was happy in his work.

'That reminds me of Kirk Douglas.'

'Hot baths remind you of Kirk Douglas?'

Cleo looked at him and decided not to mention dimples. 'No, I meant *Spartacus*. Haven't you seen that film? It was great. He led a slave rebellion and when the Romans captured them and asked them to give up their leader, they all stood up saying 'I am Spartacus' in order to save him from crucifixion.'

'I've seen Michael Douglas and the bunny boiler in *Fatal Attraction*.'

Cleo experienced vivid recall of the passionate scenes from the film and was suddenly very aware of being in the house alone with an attractive young man. She moved further away to the window.

'I don't remember that,' she lied. 'What's your favourite film?'

'Well, of course I like *Pirates of the Caribbean* but it brings back horrible memories for me..,' he said as he stroked the scar at his eyebrow. 'Then there's *Charlie and the Chocolate Factory*, but I think I'd have to go with *Star Wars*.'

'Which one?'

'Oh the first, definitely. What about you?'

Cleo had been thinking *Brief Encounter* but decided again that was something not to mention. '*Butch Cassidy and the Sundance Kid*.'

'Really? A western?' Martyn asked.

'Not because it was a western, just that Paul Newman was in it.'

'Don't tell me you just like films if they've got handsome actors in them.'

'Of course. What other criteria are there?' Cleo hitched herself up on the window sill as she considered her own question. 'I like funny films as well. The *Pink Panther* ones or Woody Allen ones.' As she looked down at Martyn she thought about the scene in *Manhattan* where Diane Keaton and Woody Allen were talking to each other but their thoughts appeared as subtitles on the screen, highlighting the different pathways of speech and desire. Martyn shifted position so that he was sitting on the floor, with his legs pointing towards Cleo. He put his mug down and leaned backwards. 'I like that Woody Allen one *Everything You Always Wanted To Know About Sex, But Were Afraid To Ask*.'

Cleo looked away from him and could think of nothing to say. She felt herself getting hotter under his gaze. In her confusion she knocked her mug and spilt tea on her jeans. Afraid that he would suggest she take them off, she blurted out, '*Psycho*.'

Martyn wondered if this was a description of him or a term of affection. 'What?'

'That was a good film.'

'Oh. Of course, but scary.' Cleo rubbed at the tea stain and carried on, 'Then there's musicals. I like those, especially *My Fair Lady*.'

'Don't you like any recent movies?'

'Yes. *What Lies Beneath* with Harrison Ford, but that was creepy and I didn't want to go to bed afterwards, especially as it was cold.'

'You'd just need someone there to keep you warm.' Martyn flexed his legs and leant one arm on his knee, wishing that he hadn't said that. She was a married woman he reminded himself. She might take offence and then he'd lose the job. He had to remember that she was not Zara and he should not behave as if he was flirting. Cleo tried to stay on safer territory.

'I love the songs in *My Fair Lady*. Audrey Hepburn's clothes were beautiful and I liked it when they went to the races.'

'I've never been.'

'You haven't lived. How could you not go?'

'I don't know. Just haven't thought about it, I suppose.'

On an impulse Cleo said, 'Let's go today. Now.'

'But I'm working here on your bathroom.'

'I'm the boss, remember. Anyway, you said you needed to go out to change that pipe. We can do that and go to the races as well.'

'When? Where?'

'Chepstow. They're on this afternoon. Let's go.' Cleo slid off the window sill and walked purposefully out of the room. Martyn got to his feet, looked at his tools strewn on the floor and considered an afternoon engineering the pipes or going out with Cleo. He knew he should concentrate on his work and keep a safe distance away from Cleo to resist temptation. As he put his hands on his torn jeans he decided to decline her invitation to the races. However he found himself calling,

'Do I need something better to wear? Oh, you're ahead of me already.' He smiled as Cleo came back into the room to hand him some of Tony's trousers.

'Try these. See you downstairs.'

'Whatever you say, boss.'

★ ★ ★

'Well, we're the smartest people in here,' Martyn said as he glanced around at the other plumbers and builders waiting in line at the counter. Cleo's red dress had a full flowing skirt which swirled around her legs as she walked. Although admirable, Martyn couldn't help feeling slightly awkward, wishing she had left the hat in the car.

'Going to a wedding, are you?' one of the builders asked.

'Yeah. Need a new bit of piping for the present,' Martyn replied.

They were surrounded by all sorts of taps, mixer units, washers, lengths of pipe and pieces of tubing. Each different product lay in a moulded plastic bucket so that rack upon rack of various sizes could be accommodated economically.

'We could have come here on the way back. We're missing the first race now.' Cleo looked at her watch impatiently.

'You said we could do this as well. Surely you don't want me to neglect my work?'

'No, but I want them to speed up theirs. How can it take so long?'

'It's all part of the game. Haven't you ever wondered why builders start a job and then disappear for two weeks? It's because they're waiting here for parts. Time stands still, unlike yourself,' Martyn observed as Cleo started shifting from foot to foot.

'Your turn.' Cleo nodded towards the assistant approaching the counter. Martyn quickly swapped the piece of piping and Cleo sighed with a mixture of impatience and relief.

★ ★ ★

Her mood altered to excited anticipation as they entered the race ground. She needed this fix of adrenalin. Online betting

50

was good and essential when she couldn't get away, but coming to a meeting and watching things live was so much better. She always came with a feeling of optimism, just entering the turnstiles gave her spirits a lift. It didn't matter how much she already owed (and that was considerable), how many red final demand letters she had (and they were many), or how much she had lost, but she always approached the next race feeling invincible.

However, she would have to be careful today as Martyn was with her. She would have to limit her bets in order to make it seem as if it was all just harmless fun. She would only be able to place serious money if she could get rid of him from time to time. She did not consider the possibility of losing money and that was a dangerous characteristic. She knew full well that the best way to bet was to allocate a fixed amount and to stick to it so that once it was gone, you finished and you went home. Unfortunately she was way past that point. As she controlled the household finances, she had access to both her money and Tony's. He trusted her to deal with everything so only she knew how bad things were. She needed more than a few big wins to pay back the debt. She had had a momentary qualm some time back about forging Tony's signature on the second mortgage documents, but that had quickly gone when she had a big win on an accumulator. She had felt justified at that point, but rather than use it to cover the debts, she had placed ever bigger amounts and squandered it rapidly. Now she was in a perpetual search for new sources of credit and constantly moving the debt from one provider to another. There were brief periods when the debt fluctuated and she thought things were improving, but overall the trend was an inexorable increase and the thousands kept mounting up.

As they walked side by side, Martyn noticed her sparkling eyes and animated behaviour and he hoped that it was because she was enjoying being with him. He did feel slightly strange wearing Tony's clothes, with Tony's wife at his side, but she had chosen to be with him this afternoon and he was enjoying himself. He must just remember he could look, but not touch. She was another man's wife, after all. They studied the form guide for the runners in the next race together and considered the horses as they paraded in the ring before being led out onto the course. Cleo seemed knowledgeable to Martyn, but his only experience of making bets was being in a sweepstake in the Grand National.

Cleo was fired up by Martyn's presence, the crowd and the prospect of winning. She pointed out the horses of interest to Martyn and explained their recent history and the conditions and distances that they preferred. She justified her recommendations for selections, weighing up the fact that the going was good and it was a two mile steeplechase. Having picked her horse and advised Martyn on his, they made their way to place bets. Cleo liked to use the bookies that set up their stalls close to the trackside because she felt the odds were better there than using the tote. She explained the process to Martyn as they cruised the length of the pitches with Cleo monitoring the odds for her preferred horse. Years ago bookies had used blackboards to display their figures, but the majority had now adopted new technology and digital numbers flickered on electronic boards. When Cleo was satisfied that she had selected the best offer for her choice she stopped and put £25 on 'My Game' at 15–1 to win, whilst Martyn placed a more modest £5 on 'Likely Boy' for a place at 10–1. He waited as Cleo paid a quick visit to the ladies. As they moved to the stand she stumbled on a step and he caught her arm in order to prevent her falling. She smiled at him but he admonished himself for breaking his 'look, don't touch' rule. He justified his action to his conscience because it was just a reflex. He tried to suppress the jolt of excitement that he had felt at the physical contact. He hadn't experienced that since meeting Zara. Although it raised the sad memory, the surge of feeling was energising. They watched as the horses milled about near the starting gate. A couple of them looked a little jumpy and had to be pushed into the gates by the handlers. Cleo had brought her binoculars but as the strap was around her neck, Martyn had to lean close in order to use them and he caught a waft of her perfume as he did so.

Cleo grabbed the glasses back unceremoniously as the race started. Her jockey was wearing red and white silks on a chestnut horse and was clearly visible in the group of three horses at the front. Martyn's jockey was in yellow with a blue diagonal and his horse was in the middle of the pack. As they went around the far bend, My Game was falling back a bit and Likely Boy was closing the gap. Cleo's grip on the binoculars tightened as she started muttering 'Come on My Game, come on.' Martyn remained silent but craned forward as did everyone else around them, trying to retain sight of their chosen steed as they headed to the distant side of the course. Attention flicked to the huge screen in front of the stands as the live video link displayed the course of the race. The cheering in the crowd increased significantly as the horses turned the last corner and ran down towards the finish. The atmosphere intensified as the whole body of spectators and gamblers craned forwards, urging their horse on verbally, mentally and physically. Cleo's murmurs had graduated to full scale shouts as she saw My Game accelerating. Her jockey had timed his break perfectly and he just eased the horse to the front two lengths away from the winning post. Cleo shrieked with joy and flung her arms around Martyn.

'I won! I won!'

'I know. I know. I didn't,' although Martyn couldn't help but enjoy her enthusiastic celebration.

'Oh, sorry. Where was your horse?'

'At the back. That was a right old nag you recommended for me.'

'Never mind. I'll buy you a drink with my winnings. Meet you in the bar in a minute.'

Still whooping with pleasure, Cleo ran away and Martyn stood looking after her, still feeling the warmth from her body. He felt as if he had won after all.

Cleo produced two winning tickets and claimed £400 on the first one but a much more impressive £4,000 with the second bet. It had been well worthwhile giving Martyn the slip in order to place the larger amount. She was feeling lucky. As she made her way back to the bar she spotted Martyn on the opposite side and beckoned him over. He struggled through the packed bodies queuing to drown their sorrows or celebrate good fortune.

'What would you like to drink?' he asked.

'Sorry, no time to lose. We need to choose the next horses and place bets. The next race will start soon. Come on.'

Martyn had been looking forward to a quick pint, but Cleo's enthusiasm was infectious and he was pleased that she grabbed his arm to lead him away.

'I hope you're going to make a better recommendation for me this time.'

'Nope. Every man for himself.'

Martyn had been studying the entrants for the next race so he replied, 'Right then. I'll go for 'Babe Magnet' because the jockey's called Share and he's wearing blue.'

'What sort of a reason's that?'

'Perfectly logical. See if you do any better.'

'I will. See these little numbers here,' she indicated the horse's previous form on the programme, 'I'm going for 'Red Sky at Night' because he's gone '421022' so he's obviously due for a win as he was second in his last two races.'

'Obviously. How much obviousness are you willing to bet on?'

'£25. You?'

'I'm sticking with my £5, but don't forget you owe me a drink and if you win this one, the number of drinks should go up by whatever the odds are.'

Cleo quickly checked the board as they waited in line to place bets with the same bookie they had used before.

'You want eight drinks?'

'Uh-huh.'

'Guess who'll be driving home then.'

'Only if you win.'

★ ★ ★

They squeezed back through the crowd to get a good view of the home straight.

'This is where we'll see 'Red Sky' romping home to victory,' Cleo told Martyn.

'Up until the last moment when Babe Magnet kicks his

heels in the air and puts on a final spurt to beat him at the tape.' Cleo looked surprised. 'Or the post, whatever,' Martyn corrected himself.

'They're off.' Cleo turned her attention to the horses.

'I didn't think people really said that.'

Cleo did not answer as she was staring intently at the course and the first corner. Red Sky was in danger of getting boxed in as others moved across from the outside edge.

'Move out, move out,' she murmured as the binoculars became the extension of her eyes. Martyn wasn't watching the race. He thought it was a marvellous opportunity to study her when she was least aware of it. He liked the way her hair curled around her ears, and when the wind lifted her hair there were tiny downy hairs on the invitingly soft skin at the back of her neck. He was a few inches taller than Cleo and he could imagine kissing that neck whilst cuddling the rest of her. Cleo trod on his foot as she stretched to monitor the race.

'Oh, sorry,' she said automatically, still focused on the race. He continued his quiet inspection and noted the freckles highlighting the top of her cheek and he wanted to see if they matched on the other side. He shifted position, found that there were some, but they were not matching and he wondered which side he preferred. Maybe her left, as they formed a small crescent 'c' shape for Cleo and he smiled at the thought.

'Red Sky. Move.' Cleo's utterances were more urgent now but unfortunately for her it was Babe Magnet who responded to the request, putting on a surge that carried him past the winning post.

'Oh no.'

'Oh, yes. Money for me. Don't look so sad. You don't have to buy me eight drinks now.'

Cleo tried to smile but she felt the loss like a blow to the stomach. It was not just the £25 she had placed when Martyn was at her side. She had put all of her previous winnings on and second place was no good to her. Martyn was chatting away happily about his success as they moved out of the stand. He did not seem to notice how quiet Cleo had become. She started to think of the payments that had to be made in the next few days. The unavoidable ones were for the mortgage and gas and electricity. There were bills for car services but the garages could wait for a bit. Tony and Rachel might notice if there was no heating or power in the house. She needed to get some money back quickly from somewhere. Of course. She had the company credit card in her purse. She could use that. She knew how much money was in the current account but no-one else did. She could borrow some money from there, make a profit and put it back before anyone knew. By the time Martyn had claimed his winnings she was feeling a lot better and managed to smile again when they considered their next choices. She decided to play safe and go for the favourite. The odds were lower but that meant she would put on a higher stake in order to win more money back.

CHAPTER 7

Tony sat in the solicitor's office waiting for his appointment. He was early, but that was his usual habit as he couldn't bear being late. He must be the last appointment of the day he thought as he checked his watch and found it was five to five. He felt nervous as he thought that the information he received in the next few minutes would change his life. He wondered about all the other people who had sat there and the different reasons they would have for coming. It might be for a divorce or for a will reading or for house sales and how they would feel when they left. It was not an environment designed to lift the spirits, even if you did obtain good news. The waiting area was lined with stiff, formal chairs and the bookshelves held weighty legal tomes that looked as if they had never moved. The small windows meant that the room itself was dark and further gloom seemed to emanate from the mahogany wood. As the window frames had been painted over there was no possibility of opening the room to the outside world. Consequently the area was filled with a slightly musty smell which may have originated from the books. The overall impression was that the air was tired and wished to be left in peace, without the disturbance of someone inhaling and exhaling.

'Mr Fleming? Mr Wright will see you now.' The receptionist indicated the room just as the man himself came out to greet Tony. They shook hands and the solicitor guided Tony into his room, waved him to a seat and then skirted around the desk to resume his position of power.

'Well, good to see you. I hope your journey went well?'

'Yes, no problem, thanks.'

'When the sun's out on a beautiful June day it helps you appreciate the countryside, doesn't it?'

'Yes.'

'Can I get you a drink? Tea or coffee?'

'Coffee, thanks.'

Edwin Wright pressed a switch on his desk and asked Miss Manners to supply the drinks.

'We live in such a beautiful area, it's a shame to rush through it, without the chance to 'stand and stare', eh?'

Tony smiled politely.

'I always think that the view coming round the hill and down into the town is one of the best in England. The rolling hills, the trees, the church spire, the market hall, all classic elements of Englishness as depicted in Shropshire.' Tony wondered when they were going to get down to business and this message seemed to convey itself to Edwin Wright.

'But enough of that. You want to know what your uncle left you.'

'Please.' Tony felt that he ought to show some sign of mourning. 'Of course, it was very sad to hear of his death, but to be honest we hadn't been in touch for years. I was very surprised to hear that he had so much money.'

'Well, that's the lottery for you. Poor one minute, a millionaire a couple of times over the next.'

Tony produced a more genuine smile. 'It's difficult to believe.'

'Yes, it can be a shock. It takes a bit of getting used to, dealing with all that money. We can put you in touch with

59

people who can help manage the funds, advise on investments, all that sort of thing.' Edwin looked up briefly from the documents before him to check if there was any interest in this offer. It was always worthwhile providing services to the newly rich as they could develop into valuable customers.

'There is just one slight hitch.'

Tony's spirits sank. This was where he found out that he wasn't going to get anything after all. There would be some ridiculous condition that he wouldn't be able to fulfil.

'It's taken a few months to investigate since we first contacted you and I'm afraid we haven't got to the bottom of the problem yet. We believe that you're the only living descendant. However, when we were going through the documents, there was some correspondence years back with a cousin in America. It's proving a bit tricky to track them down, as they've moved a couple of times, so it's taking longer than we thought. It's possible that they have died as well of course, as they had been describing their ailments in the letters and then they just stopped coming. We need to check these things, so it's probably as well not to buy yourself a new Porsche just yet.' Edwin smiled and continued, 'Assuming that there are no living descendants other than yourself, your uncle's estate effectively passes to you after a few elements have been removed for various purposes.' Tony nodded, trying to resist the urge to ask 'How much?'

'We can go through the detailed breakdown of the amounts, but the figure that you will end up with is about £2.8 million.'

'£2.8 million.' Tony repeated, generating his widest smile ever. 'Thanks very much.'

'Well, of course, it's your uncle you should thank, rather

than me. Now, if we look at this document here….' Edwin turned some of the papers around for Tony's benefit, but the detail was lost on him. He was in a strange state when the words '£2.8 million' seemed to keep echoing around in his head.

★ ★ ★

Later that evening, most of the divers had congregated in the swimming pool.

'So where's Tony tonight then? Hasn't forgotten it's Thursday, has he?' Brian asked Cleo as she swam towards the crowd of divers at the shallow end.

'He went up to see a supplier somewhere in Shropshire,' Cleo replied. 'Said he'd be back late. Probably wining and dining or something. What's the plan for the Gower?'

John squatted in the shallow end so that his shoulders were beneath the water to keep warm. He said, 'We'll go down Saturday morning. Aim to get there about ten, in the water for eleven. We could do a drift dive at the point and then go round to Oxwich Bay and do the wreck there. Then see what we feel like on the Sunday.'

'Who's going?'

He looked at the assembled bodies in the pool and replied, 'Martyn, Tony, Brian, Lynne, you and me. Oh and Graham, but he's not here. Working late, I think.'

'Full boat then?' Lynne had been listening in and now joined the conversation.

'Nearly. Seven of us.'

'Where are we meeting?' she asked.

'In the campsite at Port Eynon, where we went before. We can leave all our camping gear there whilst we're on the water. I'll drive down with the boat and bring it on to the site so we can load kit up there.'

'Lynne, you coming down with us?' Cleo asked of her friend.

'Yes please.' The arrangements sorted, Cleo and Lynne set off for a few more lengths swimming.

'So, anyone else travelling down in your car?' Lynne asked, looking slyly at Cleo.

'Like who?' Cleo responded, surprised.

'Like Martyn, of course.'

'I don't see any 'of course' about it.' Cleo replied, feeling slightly irritated. She had not told Lynne (or anyone else) about their excursion to the races and intended to keep it that way.

'You and Tony could be in the front and Martyn and I in the back.'

'So you two could snuggle up together? Honestly!' Cleo gave her friend a despairing look. 'I think you might be barking up the wrong tree.'

'He's gay?' The horrible implications of this thought had stopped Lynne from swimming, so she stood up in the middle of the pool.

'Sshh. No, I didn't mean that. Has he, you know, shown any interest in you?' Cleo glanced furtively around the pool, checking no-one was within earshot.

'Well, he's probably shy. Give him time and a little opportunity. A weekend away might be just the thing.'

'We'll see.'

★ ★ ★

'Oh, you're back.' Cleo said as she walked into her lounge after the pool session. 'Good day?'

'Uh-huh.' Tony did not look up from the television. He wanted to suppress the elation that he had felt in the solicitor's office. He had come out of there bursting to tell someone so he had made a quick call, but explained that it was not absolutely definite and they needed to keep it secret. Most importantly, he did not want Cleo to know about his good fortune. It was his money and his alone. Why should he give her any of it? He wanted to spend it with someone whose company he enjoyed. He needed to turn his feeling of euphoria into something different so that Cleo would not think his behaviour strange. He had already planned his strategy. If he started an argument, there would be no opportunity for Cleo to ask him about his day or for him to give himself away inadvertently. Anger was a good cloak to obscure any other feeling.

'Why is there never any food in this house?' he started, still avoiding eye contact.

'There is. You could have made yourself something.'

'I'm always cooking the food. Why don't you do it?' he added aggressively.

'Because you always criticise anything I make, or you interrupt and tell me I'm doing it wrong.'

'You make such crap food.'

Cleo took a deep breath. 'Actually I got some lamb, because it's your favourite.'

'Sure it's not lamb dressed up as mutton?'

'What do you mean?'

'Look at you.' Tony glanced over disdainfully. 'You're too old to wear a short skirt like that. You need good legs, not flabby, cellulite ones.'

63

'Oh and you're God's gift, are you?'

'I don't try and flaunt myself down at the pool.'

'Flaunt myself? When do I ever do that?'

'And you've put on weight. You need to be young and slim to wear that sort of thing. Rach would look good in it.'

Cleo considered whether to walk out again, but she wanted to fight back somehow. She never did well in verbal conflict with Tony. She could not think fast enough and only came up with a perfect rejoinder hours later when she replayed his insults on a constant loop in her head. She said nothing but moved to sit on the sofa, grabbing the TV remote in order to irritate Tony.

'I was watching that.'

'Well, I want to see this.'

'You choose such garbage. And too much of it. That's why you're a couch potato. And you eat so many of them you're turning into one.'

'Better a couch potato than a....' Cleo wanted to say 'ageing lothario' but stopped short. There might be nothing sinister in his appreciation of Rachel. And besides, he was a few years younger than her.

'What?'

Cleo studied the screen, trying to think of a better insult whilst appearing to focus on the chat show programme.

'You're not really looking at that, are you? I was interested in the golf and I want to see who won.'

'I don't know how you can watch that stuff.'

'That's not the point. You can't just come in here and take the controller away from me.'

'I can. I did. You can use the TV in the kitchen.'

'I don't want to use the TV in the kitchen. I want this one, in here,' Tony insisted.

'I've got this one in here,' Cleo clutched the controller tighter in case he tried to remove it.

'But that's not fair.'

'Diddums.'

'You're so juvenile sometimes. Don't know what I ever saw in you.'

'I thought you liked them young.'

'I like beauty. If I see it somewhere,' Tony retaliated pointedly.

'Well, maybe you should go and find it then.'

'Maybe I will.'

They both fumed quietly in their seats.

'Maybe I will this weekend,' Tony said, breaking the oppressive silence. 'Perhaps I'll take Rach up to London. She'd love to go on a shopping trip and we could take in a show.'

Cleo couldn't believe he could be so mean. It used to be her and Tony that would go up to London to the theatre. He knew how much she enjoyed it.

Tony got up and walked towards the kitchen. 'Perhaps I'll buy her a short skirt. She'll look great in it.' Tony felt pleased with himself. He wanted to celebrate his new found wealth and he had found the perfect way to do it. He and Rach would have a great time and Cleo would miss out.

Cleo sat holding the remote, seeing it as a hollow victory. That was how Tony made her feel sometimes, empty and lonely. She needed something to fill that void.

CHAPTER 8

Cleo and Lynne arrived at the campsite first so they had booked in and chosen their pitch before the others turned up. Lynne ran off to the toilet block as Cleo got out of the car and surveyed the scene. The green of the field was bordered by a ragged dirt track and partial hedge which ran along the edge of the beach. Looking out to sea it seemed calm. There were no white-topped crests, but different shades and shadows of blue which fluctuated as she watched. There was a slight breeze carrying the invigorating feel of the sea and she felt uplifted by it. On the way down she had told Lynne about the row with Tony and the fact that he had gone off with Rachel. Having got that off her chest, she wanted to stop thinking about it for today and enjoy the diving.

Where the sea was withdrawing the sand was wet, slick and smooth. This side of the tideline of seaweed and debris, the sand changed into the light, dry, powdery sort that was no good for sand castles, but lovely for walking through with bare feet. They had chosen to camp on the bottom edge of the field, close to the beach, anticipating a barbecue later. There was sufficient space around them for the others at the moment, although pitches were disappearing fast. Lynne returned so they opened the boot and lifted the tent out in order to stake their territory. It was a modern igloo design with two double compartments off a central lobby area so Lynne would have one and Cleo the other. As they drew the poles out of one long bag, a familiar Range Rover appeared towing the boat and Martyn got out with John.

'Where's Tony? Left you two to do all the work, has he?' asked John.

'Gone to London,' Cleo responded shortly.

Martyn opened his mouth to ask why, but Lynne muttered, 'Don't ask. Where's Graham?' she continued.

'He's coming down with Brian. I spoke to them earlier, so they're not far behind.'

'If Brian's driving, they could be hours yet,' John interrupted. 'He'll be stuck at a junction waiting for written permission to leave.'

Lynne smiled. 'He's just a careful driver.'

Cleo was staring at the coloured poles and looking at the canvas laid out before them on the ground, looking perplexed.

'You need any help there?' Martyn asked.

Before she could answer, John intervened, 'She'll be fine. Don't go offering help. You'll get accused of being sexist. We need to put our own house in order. Come on.' Martyn turned to help John erect their own tent, wondering why it was that John and Cleo didn't seem to get on with each other. Maybe it was something to do with the business.

By the time Brian and Graham arrived both tents were up and everyone was in various stages of preparation for the day's diving. John had fixed the radio and GPS on board whilst Martyn and Cleo had pumped up the inflatable sides of the boat to a comforting rigidity, so that it was safe to take out to sea.

'Couldn't you get up this morning?' John asked, looking at his watch.

'I could,' Brian answered, 'but the passenger was a bit

late,' looking at Graham, who responded with a terse, 'Don't go there.'

'Anyway we're not the last by the look of it. Where's Tony?' he asked Cleo.

She gave the same succinct answer, which did not invite further questions.

'Glad to see we're all playing happy families today,' John commented and drew black looks from both Graham and Cleo.

'What's the plan?' Martyn asked.

'Well, sort your kit out here, put it on the boat, then we'll launch on the beach. We'll go out and do a drift dive first because we need to be in the right place for the tide. Then we'll have lunch and do the second dive in Oxwich Bay later. OK?'

No-one disagreed and Martyn asked, 'Who am I diving with?'

'You'll be with Cleo.' Cleo looked up and smiled at Martyn. 'Right people, let's be careful out there,' John continued.

Martyn was standing near Cleo watching as she struggled into her semi-dry suit.

'Shall I do you up?' he offered, moving behind her. He savoured the view of her back which was exposed in the 'v' shape of the open suit. Her swimsuit covered some of her skin but the bones of her spine were still partially visible, more evident at the top of her back than at the bottom where there was a beautiful smooth curve. Cleo moved her arms, causing her shoulder blades to flex. 'Alright back there?'

'Yeah, just sorting out the zip bit,' Martyn replied as he pulled upwards, gradually hiding the view that he relished. As he fixed the Velcro tab at the collar, he noticed the small downy hairs at the back of her neck again. Suppressing the desire to kiss that patch of soft skin, he pulled her outer suit up and over her shoulders so that she could fasten that one at the front. It was a novel arrangement for him to be the dependent partner with a woman, but diving with Cleo was a very enjoyable experience. He found that finning alongside her gave him ample opportunity to appreciate all the curves of her body, emphasized as they were by the suit itself. It was unfortunate that the bottle obscured her back but he could still view her full, rounded bottom, which he liked to savour on dry land as well as in the water.

★ ★ ★

Later that evening they were all sitting around the fire on the beach, having enjoyed the barbecue. They were making steady progress consuming the sources of alcohol that they had brought with them.

'How come Martyn got to dive the wreck in the bay off the boat?' Brian asked. 'In my day we did it as a shore dive and it took forever to get there. First there was a long way to walk out from the beach then when it was deep enough, it was a miles worth of finning. I was exhausted by the time we got there.'

John grinned happily at the memory, 'Well, it was good practice for us.'

'Good practice! Nearly finished me off.'

Graham suddenly said, 'Oh no, I've missed the Lottery.'

'Oh God! We have this every week when we're away. Surely you can just check the numbers somewhere tomorrow?' John suggested.

'You won't have won, will you?' Lynne added. 'What are the chances? How many million to one?'

'It could be you.' Brian pointed at Graham, mimicking the Lottery phrase.

'No. I need to know today. I could go over to the pub and ask, I suppose.'

'They're not going to know, are they? Not unless there's some sad git like you that needs to check every week. And then they're not going to write them down are they?' John pointed out.

'Elaine does.'

'Why?'

'Just so we can double check. I'll ring her.' He pulled out his mobile. 'Typical. No signal.'

'I'll try. I've got coverage.' John said, flicking his phone open.

'Hi Elaine, it's John… Yeah, we're all fine, no problem… Got your nearest and dearest here and he wants to check his numbers.' He ignored Graham's outstretched hand waiting for the mobile. 'No, I might lose the signal… You tell me and I'll tell him. Right. You ready Graham?…' He nodded. '23.'

'That's one of mine.'

'14.'

'And that. If I get three, I've got £10.'

'6.'

'6. I've got £10.'

'39. That's you Cleo.' Cleo felt it unnecessary to mention that just now.

'Yep. That's four.'

'Sorry, didn't get that? 40? 40.'

'Don't believe it. That's five.'

'42.'

'YES! YES! That's it. That's my numbers. I can't believe it.'

John looked incredulous. 'Not really mate, is it? Don't you want to know about the bonus ball?'

'Give me the 'phone. Let me talk to her.'

'Sorry. Signal's gone.' He folded the phone back together.

'I'm rich! We're rich! I can give up work. We'll have millions. Did she say how many people were sharing it?'

'No.'

'I wonder how much. Can't believe it. All this time. Then the numbers come up. We could buy a new boat.' He looked around at the smiling faces, but Brian wasn't smiling. He looked pained.

'What's up, Bri? Jealous of my riches?'

'He's winding you up. You haven't won the Lottery.'

'What?' Graham looked at John, his face full of doubt.

'Of course you haven't won, you daft sod. I'm fed up with you checking your numbers every Saturday when we're away.'

'Really? But Elaine…?'

'She wasn't on the phone.'

'Bastard!'

'Here! Have a beer and drown your sorrows.' John handed him a can.

'I was happy there for a minute.'

'Well, you were happy for a minute. You should be grateful to me.'

As the evening developed into night, the divers found that one side was uncomfortably warm, whilst the other suffered from the brisk breeze coming in from the sea.

Periodically they got up to stand with their backs to the fire, producing their own gradual rotisserie effect. Lynne had tried desperately hard to stay awake as she wanted to be left alone with Martyn when the others had gone. Unfortunately for her, alcohol and the exertions of day meant that she had slumped into an untidy heap by Cleo and was now unconsciously drooling saliva onto her friend's knee.

'Looks like Lynne's had it, then,' Brian observed.

Cleo glanced down at the head lying on her and gently brushed some of the hair away from her face.

'Not looking her best just now,' he continued.

'Maybe you should get her to bed,' John suggested.

'Hmmm.' Cleo wasn't feeling particularly sleepy herself, but Lynne's head was deadening her leg and she needed to move. 'Come on, Lynne,' she coaxed as she pulled her to her feet. 'Bedtime. Night all.'

'Night.'

Brian got up and helped Cleo steer Lynne back to their tent. Rather than try to insert a flaccid body into a sleeping bag, they decided that it would be easier to unzip the bag, roll her in and then fasten it.

'Think she'll be alright?' he asked.

'Yeah. She's dead to the world. Probably have a bad head tomorrow though. Thanks.'

As Brian withdrew, Cleo went into her own compartment. She sat on her sleeping bag but did not make any move to undress. Despite the late hour, she felt unusually awake. Her thoughts returned to the argument with Tony the night before and she wondered how he and Rachel were enjoying their time in London. She glanced at her watch and the luminous hands told her it was half past twelve. She wondered what they would be doing. Was there really anything in Tony's interest in Rachel or was he just a good step father? She couldn't help thinking that there was some truth in Tony's comments about her age, her body and the things she wore. Rachel would look a lot better than her in a short skirt, but how sad was that to be jealous of her own daughter? Trying to push those thoughts away she decided to go for a walk by the beach. She did not want to go back towards the barbecue so she cut along the bottom of the field, screened by the partial hedge and made for the sand dunes. She found a convenient log which made a bench seat looking out to sea. She drew her fleece up to her nose and buried her hands in her pockets, wishing that she had put another layer on. The sea was looking livelier by night as the waves crashed and withdrew in their rhythmic pattern before her. There was something soothing in the repetitive refrain and Cleo became absorbed in its sound and motion, so she did not hear the man who came up and touched her shoulder.

'Hi.'

'Jesus. You made me jump.'

'Mind if I join you?' Martyn asked as he sat on the log, without waiting for a response.

'How did you know I was here?'

'I was going to bed, but I saw you coming this way.'

'Has everyone left the barbecue now then?'

'John and Brian are still there.'

Cleo nodded and looked down at her feet. She was still wearing sandals and had pushed her feet through the soft sand to immerse them beneath the surface. The sand was cool but heavy on her skin.

'Something wrong?' Martyn continued.

'No. It's nothing.'

'It doesn't look like nothing. You can tell me. I'm a good agony aunt.'

'You're a what?' Cleo turned to him in disbelief.

'Well, maybe more of an uncle or a big brother, or just a friend,' Martyn added hastily as he thought that incest was not really an attractive proposition. As he gazed at Cleo, the clouds moved away from the moon, and the light cast slight shadows on the contours of her face, reminding him strongly of Zara.

'You're beautiful,' he said. 'I'm sorry, I didn't mean to upset you,' he added as tears rolled down her cheeks. Cleo sighed heavily and brushed at her cheeks. He moved to put an arm around her.

'It'll be OK,' he suggested, trying to think of something comforting to say, although as he did not know what the problem was, he felt that this was doubtful. Cleo's tears increased as she leaned on his shoulder and he could feel her body heave as sobs shook her. He waited, partly hoping that the crying would subside and partly enjoying the feel of Cleo's body against him.

'So, is it because Lynne drooled over your nice clean jeans?'

Cleo laughed as she tried to wipe away her tears and shifted into a more upright position.

'Don't look at me when I'm wiping my nose on my sleeve,' she commanded. Martyn obediently averted his gaze, but retained his hold on Cleo's shoulder.

'I don't feel beautiful. I feel old.'

'Really? I thought you were maybe early thirties.'

'With a sixteen year old daughter?'

'You could have had her when you were young. What does your age matter anyway? It's only a number.'

'You can say that because you're only….what? How old are you?'

'I'll be 30 soon. I'm really worried. I think I won't be beautiful any more. The wrinkles will come on me overnight, my clothes won't fit….'

'OK. OK. You think I'm over reacting. But you haven't got a husband telling you you're old and fat, with no fashion sense.'

'Nope. I haven't got a husband at all in fact,' he replied smiling.

'Sometimes I wonder what it would be like without him, but… we've been together a long time. All marriages go through ups and downs, maybe this is just a blip and it'll get better again.' She fiddled with the rings on her left hand.

'Do you really think so?'

'No.' Cleo sighed. 'Before Tony, it was just me and Rachel. Her real Dad didn't want to know and disappeared as soon as he knew I was pregnant. So I had her on my own and it was difficult being a single parent, but at the same time it was me and her against the world. Then I met Tony and he and Rach got on, which was lucky, but now I feel like I'm the outsider and it's those two against the world and that includes me.'

'Are they both at home now?'

'No, they've gone to London. Tony's idea, but Rachel will love it, shopping, staying in a smart hotel, going out to a show.'

'There's nothing wrong with that, is there?' Martyn asked, trying to look on the bright side. Cleo did not know whether to tell him that she felt jealous of Rachel as it was such a mean emotion.

'He's not interested in me any more. The thing, is he's four years younger than me. It didn't seem to matter when we were both in our thirties, but I'm going to be in my forties soon and in decline whilst he's getting more attractive.'

'He doesn't appeal to me at all,' Martyn joked.

Cleo smiled. 'But younger women might like him. Some women like older men, because they're experienced, worldly….'

'They have money…'

'Yes. And what if….what if Tony wants to update with the younger model?'

'You mean Tony with Rachel? But he's her Dad.' Martyn looked at her in astonishment.

'Stepdad. No blood relation.'

'Does she like him? '

'She likes him.'

'But in that way?'

'I don't know. But here I am, losing my looks and she's just blossoming into womanhood.'

'You're not losing your looks. You're lovely, fun to be with, great dive leader….,' he said, turning towards Cleo. As he did so, she kissed him gently on the lips and drew back.

'Thanks.'

Martyn stayed in confused silence. The kiss was electrifying. He wanted to grab her and kiss her passionately, but the voice in his head held him back.

'I can't. We can't. You're married.'

'What if Tony wasn't here?' Cleo asked.

'He isn't.'

'No. I meant what if it was just me and you?' She leant against him but Martyn tried to hold himself away. Feeling his resistance, she withdrew saying, 'Sorry, sorry.'

'But...' Martyn cried after her retreating back as she ran for her tent. He had done that all wrong, he thought. He would have to go after her. Surely she would appreciate his need to do the right thing. The fact that she was still married, however unhappily, meant that she was not available. They shouldn't have kissed, he knew that, but his body and mind were in deep conflict. He knew what his body wanted well enough. His mind told him to go to his own tent and let things cool down between them.

'Cleo,' he whispered outside her tent, 'can I come in?' He waited.

When there was a subdued 'Yes', he stepped inside, stooping to bend his head. 'Sorry. I'm really sorry about just now.' He felt like an awkward teenager again, overcome with desire and trying hard to batten it down.

'Is she asleep?' he nodded towards Lynne, who snored in confirmation. 'Please, let me talk to you a minute.' He glanced up at the canvas that was touching his head. 'Can I sit down?'

'Yes, come in but talk quietly so we don't disturb her.' He crawled in, enjoying the feeling of penetrating Cleo's private sanctuary in spite of himself. There was not much room and Martyn felt his way forward so that he did not break any of her camping gear accidentally. As he felt ridiculous on all fours, he turned when he was only a couple of feet away to talk to her, 'I'm sorry. I do want to be friends. I'm thinking about you and Tony.' He was waiting for his eyes to adjust to the semi-darkness as he spoke to the shape that he knew to be Cleo.

'I do like you but I'm trying not to act on it.'

'Maybe you can resist better than me then,' Cleo replied sadly.

'But you're married.'

'I know but I'm not happily married. There's a big difference.'

Martyn struggled with the thought that he had not known what it was like to be married, happily or not. This woman reminded him so much of Zara that he wanted to grab at a chance of happiness for himself. He wanted her. She'd kissed him and he wanted to repeat the experience. No, he told himself again. He pushed the temptation away, distracted by the smell near him.

'What's that…?' he sniffed, '…awful smell?'

'Oh,' Cleo hurriedly leaned over him to pick up her boots and throw them outside, 'It's just my boots.'

'They don't smell of neoprene.'

She was glad he couldn't see her blushing. 'No, I wee'd in my suit today. I think it must pool in my boots. It seems to take longer for them to lose the smell.'

'Well, that's a lovely thought, you swimming along bathed in your own urine. Thanks for that.'

'You've got a wet suit too.'

'Yes, but we boys go off the boat. I don't need to pollute my suit.' Feeling that they had lost the moment somewhat, he tried to get back to talking about them.

'But Cleo…'

'That's not even my name.'

'What?'

'Cleo's not my name. Tony started calling me that years ago because he was Antony and I was his Cleopatra. I liked it then, and friends started using it so it caught on. Now everyone's probably forgotten my real name.'

'What is it?'

'Starts with an S,' she said, teasingly.

'Sheila? Um. Siobhan? Sue? Ah. Sinead? Stephanie? Sophie? Samantha? Sharon?'

'How many girls do you know?'

'Hardly any. Or is it something more sinister? Shrek? Is that why you went away to hide at night?'

Cleo leant forward and punched him. In the darkness he did not see it coming, but he fumbled for her wrists and fell backwards so that she lay on top of him.

'You smell much better than your boots.' He adjusted his grip to hold her in position. 'You can't run off now.'

'I could. I could wrestle you into submission and you'd be begging for mercy.'

Martyn moved quickly to roll her over and lie on top.

'No, other way round, I think.' He held her arms above her head so that she was defenceless. Cleo could feel his weight pinning her to the floor. She would not be strong enough to throw him off, but did she want to? He bent his head and she tilted her chin up, waiting for his lips.

He hovered with his face millimetres away. He almost gave way to the desire that coursed through him but he rolled off her and walked out of the tent.

CHAPTER 9

Elaine and Paula sat at opposite ends of the sofa in their living room, the emotional distance between them emphasised by their different postures. Elaine sat back fully in the seat in a relaxed manner that she hoped conveyed that she was open to anything being discussed. This subtlety was lost on Paula, however, as she sat hunched over, hugging her knees so that her growing bump was not apparent. It was as if she wanted to suppress the evidence that had prompted Elaine to make time for them to be alone.

'How are you feeling?' Elaine asked as she studied her daughter and worried. She had withdrawn from her and Graham in the last couple of weeks, becoming very quiet and keeping to her bedroom for most of the time that it was possible to do so. Elaine was concerned that this was Paula's strategy to avoid any confrontation with Graham, but it meant that she was effectively isolating herself from the support and love that Elaine wanted to provide.

The prolonged silence from Paula was eventually broken by a 'Dunno'. She had been suffering in her self-inflicted confinement to her room and did want to talk to her mother, but she had been delayed in her response by the sheer range of possible answers that had risen in her mind. Sick? Angry? Tired? Scared? Sad? Surprised? Lonely? The speed with which she could move from one of these feelings to another was confusing in itself. She felt as if they were all simmering in a small cauldron in her stomach and it was only when the molten liquid bubbled that one specific emotion popped into being. In spite of the brevity of its presence, that one burst bubble then dominated the whole of Paula to govern her thoughts, behaviour and posture, as if it had released a vapour that enveloped her in a cloud. Trying to cope with her alternating moods was tiring in itself. The physical changes that her body was undergoing also sapped her energy, but the most draining aspect was the constant undercurrent of the weighty responsibility she held. She knew that she had to decide what to do about 'it'. She did not like to refer to the thing as a baby or an embryo or a foetus because that almost made it into a person, so for now the label was just an 'it'.

Elaine took a chocolate from the box on the table in front of them and nudged it closer to Paula.

'Have a chocolate. I got your favourite.'

'Can't. Gone off chocolate.' Paula continued to stare at the patch of carpet by her feet. The edge of the rug intruded into her field of vision and she started to count the triangles in the pattern.

'Oh. Sorry.' Elaine hastily removed the box and wished she hadn't taken a hard caramel. She chewed furiously in order to swallow it quickly.

'So...' Elaine coughed as she had tried to speak too soon and the food seemed to have stuck in her throat. She coughed again violently. Paula looked at her mother in alarm. As Elaine continued to struggle and her face turned red, Paula jumped to her feet and moved to hit her mother on the back. It had no effect and Elaine gasped 'Bread'. Paula ran to the kitchen and ripped a chunk of bread from the loaf. Returning to the lounge she offered her mother a small piece. Elaine swallowed it and her coughing reduced as the blockage cleared. As her colour faded from the violent puce back to something more normal, Paula said, 'Need some water?' Elaine nodded so she fetched a cup and gave it to her, sitting close by and watching anxiously for any further sign of a coughing fit.

'Thanks. I'm supposed to be looking after you, not the other way round.' They both smiled. 'You could be a good Mummy.' Paula looked away at the floor again and sighed.

'But do you want to be?'

'I don't know.' Elaine sipped her water as she waited for Paula to continue.

'I don't know what to do. If I had it, what about school? If I got rid of it….' Paula stopped as she thought what that would mean.

'I know. It's difficult.'

'It's just there. All the time. I can't turn it off. Sometimes I wish it wasn't there. Sometimes…..' In her head the sentence continued 'I wonder what it would be like.' 'Rach says I should write a big list called 'Have it' and 'Don't have it' and see what comes out top.'

'Well, that's one way of looking at it. Shall we do that?'

As Paula nodded, Elaine searched for some paper and a pen and put them in front of her daughter. She was relieved that they were talking about it and Paula seemed more animated now. The chocolates had worked after all, but not in the way she had planned.

'OK.' Paula drew a line down the centre of the page and put the titles at the top.

'Have it.' They both thought silently.

'It would always be there,' Paula said.

'Is that good or bad?' Elaine asked.

'Oh. It could be either, couldn't it? Do you think we need another split in each column?'

Worried that they might get distracted by the layout of the sheet, Elaine suggested that they just think of as many things as possible, using the two categories for now. They continued with 'Have it'.

'I'd be a Mummy.'

'You'd have to look after it.'

'I'd have a son or a daughter.'

'You'd be getting up a lot in the night to begin with.'

'I could play with them.'

'They'd cry a lot.'

'I could teach them things.'

'You wouldn't be able to go out clubbing.'

Paula considered the list so far.

'Mum, you keep coming up with negative things.'

'Oh. Sorry. There are lots of positives. You'll love them, whatever happens.'

Paula smiled acknowledgement of her mother's message as she wrote. Elaine had been thinking of the practical aspects, but at the back of her mind she was trying to suppress the 'What will the neighbours say?' feeling because she thought that that would destroy the recent rapport that the two of them had just established.

'I'd miss some school,' Paula continued as she wrote.

'You'd go back to school afterwards then?'

'Well, I s'pose. Dunno.' They both considered the unspoken question regarding who would look after the baby if Paula returned to school. Elaine thought about her job at the estate agency in town. She enjoyed the work and she liked her colleagues. She would not want to give it up, but maybe she could reduce her hours if necessary.

'It would be mine.'

Elaine looked surprised at this statement, believing it to be obvious.

'I mean, from me, all mine, not something that other people have given me.'

It was on the tip of her tongue to point out that only half was Paula's and the other portion came from the father, but Elaine bit that tip and did not speak. As if the thought of the father figure had communicated itself to Paula, she said, 'Dad'll go mad,' as she wrote on the next line.

'He won't. I know he was a bit upset...'

'I'll say.'

'... but that was just the first shock when he found out. It's taking time, but he's getting used to the idea.'

'Which one though? The 'Have it' idea or the 'Don't have it'?'

'I meant that you're pregnant. Give him a while before he has to think of the next stage. Right. Let's try 'Don't have it.' Paula wrote down the word 'abortion' without saying it aloud.

Trying to gauge her daughter's feeling, Elaine said, 'That's a bit scary, isn't it?'

'Hmm.'

'It doesn't mean that you can never have children. Just that you don't have this one, right now.'

'I know. But for this ... I mean, it's a bit final for 'it', isn't it?'

'Yes.' They both looked at the paper.

Elaine continued, 'Or you could have it and give it up for adoption.'

Paula looked horrified. 'You mean go through all that time, the pregnancy, the birth, see it arrive and then hand it over to someone else to bring up?'

'I'm just thinking of the options.'

'Well, I don't like that one. Someone else would have it and it wouldn't be mine.'

Elaine continued, 'But it would mean that you could carry on at school...'

'As if nothing has happened?'

'No, I didn't mean that. The thing is, this will always be with you. Whatever you decide now, 'Have it' or 'Don't Have it', you will have to live with that decision, either because you have the baby or because you got rid of it.'

Paula had started slightly at the word 'baby'.

'Don't call it that. It's an 'it', that's all.'

'But it will become a baby.'

'I just don't want to think about 'it' like that.'

'Because it makes it real?' Elaine asked tentatively.

'Do you want me to have it?'

'I'm trying to give you a balanced view. I don't want to influence you one way or the other, because it's your decision and we'll support you whatever.' As she uttered the words, Elaine wondered if they were true. They sounded as if they should be what a good parent would say.

'So you don't want me to have it.'

'No, I'm not saying that.'

'It would be your grandchild we'd be getting rid of.' Paula sounded accusatory as she turned to face her mother.

Elaine stopped, stunned. How stupid she was. She had been thinking about Paula and her welfare and she had not thought about the fact that this would be her grandchild.

Sometimes, when she and Graham had discussed their retirement and what they could do, they had talked about the next generation, but they had expected it to be years away, not now. She did want to have grandchildren one day. Wrestling to bring herself back from the image of playing with a whole new person who would call her 'Grandma' one day, Elaine said,

'But it's you that's important.'

'I'm tired.' Paula fell back on to the sofa. 'It's doing my head in.'

Elaine looked at her child and remembered the wave of love she had felt at her birth.

'You rest there. At least we're talking about it and that's good. Shall we have a cup of tea?'

Paula was irritated at her mother's habit of supplying tea to deal with any family issue, but she accepted. As she listened to the sounds from the kitchen, she flicked the television on. It was force of habit rather than a desire to watch any particular programme as she neither listened nor looked at the screen. When Elaine returned holding a mug in each hand, Paula had resumed her previous position and was apparently studying the carpet again.

Elaine tried to put the mugs on the table without dropping the clutch of leaflets secured under one arm. She was unsuccessful and they cascaded over the wooden surface and onto the carpet.

'Oops. Here we go. A nice cup of tea.'

'What's this?' Paula was stirred into action again as she reached to pick up the brochure at her feet.

'You do want me to get rid of it then?' She threw the Marie Stopes leaflet back at her mother.

'No, no. I just went into the surgery and picked up a few

booklets. I got all sorts, look. This one's about pre-natal classes and this one's about teenage parenting and this one's about nursery places and….' She spread the pile out across the table, 'and I also found this about adoption. I thought it would be helpful because I don't know all the answers. You might want to go and talk to some of these people yourself and that might help.'

'Mum, I use the internet.'

'Oh, of course.' Elaine realised that her method of looking for information was old fashioned. A modern teenager sourced everything on the net. 'Yes, yes, I hadn't thought.'

'That's why we're talking.'

'Is it?'

'Uh-huh. I found this chat room specially for girls same as me. I got talking to this one called Spike and her family had thrown her out. She said I was really lucky that I didn't have to live on the streets and I should appreciate that and talk to my Mum.'

'I like Spike already.'

'Yeah, well, she's having a tough time.'

'I can't believe some families. Throwing someone out just when they need you most.'

'Something to do with religion, I think.'

'Oh.' Elaine leaned forward to sort through the paperwork. 'So do you already know some of this then?'

'Not the details, no. I tried to look up some things and then I just got scared and thought I couldn't do it on my own.'

'You're not on your own, love.' Elaine moved to put an arm around Paula. 'We're here together and we're all going to support you.'

'Thanks, Mum.'

'Now, where had we got to? Not far down the 'Don't Have it' column.'

'I found this web page where people had written their stories. There was one there that was so sad. She'd had an abortion and something had gone wrong, so she couldn't ever have children in the future. She'd spent years wondering what her kid would have looked like and how it would have grown up and what it would have done.'

'Well, that must be an extreme example. For some people, it's just the timing that's wrong and they do go on to have a happy family later.'

'And then I started reading about adoption and the way that children can turn up out of the blue years later, blaming you for having given them away in the first place.'

'Yes, well, none of the options is easy. If...'

They both jumped as the back door opened. Graham entered the kitchen and called to them through the doorway, 'Hi, back earlier than I thought. Any food left?'

'Lasagne's on the side,' Elaine replied automatically. She moved away from Paula to gather up the various leaflets as Graham walked on into the room.

'What's all that then?'

Paula had curled herself into a tight ball in the corner of the sofa, trying to reduce the amount of space that she took up.

'Paula and I were just having a chat about... things.'

Graham reached down and snatched one of the brochures from Elaine's grasp.

'What did you get that one for? 'Contraception explained'. Bit late for that. Shutting the door after the horse has bolted.'

'Graham!' Elaine tried to silence her husband, afraid that

he would undo all the good work that she and Paula had covered by talking to each other. She glanced anxiously at Paula, who wanted to disappear into the sofa. There was no way she'd discuss contraception with her parents. That first time she had thought that she couldn't get pregnant standing up. After that she had believed him when he said that it would be alright. She had never liked to question him about how he was going to make sure, she had just trusted him.

Graham had also grabbed the 'Have it / Don't Have it' list and was scanning it rapidly.

'I see there are more things on the 'Have it' side, but I can't see any mention of the cost, or making the house bigger, or getting a different car.' Elaine thought Graham must have had another bad meeting at work. She tried to point out that they were still developing the list on the other side, but Graham's eyes hit on another item.

'All mine. Hah! Well, that's not right, is it? What about the father? Where's his half?' Elaine mentally lamented the fact that Graham lacked any instinct to bite his tongue. Paula cringed under her father's tirade.

'You can't make this decision…' he brandished the list, 'without consulting the father, can you?'

Paula shook her head and remained dumb.

'Why don't we all meet up – you, me, your mother and HIM, whoever he is? We can all sit down on a nice, cosy sofa and have a nice little chat about whether to bring his bastard into the world or kill it off…'

'Dad!'

'Graham!'

Paula ran from them, hurtled up the stairs and slammed into her bedroom.

CHAPTER 10

Tony took a deep breath of the crisp morning air as he stood gazing out of the bedroom window. It looked like it was going to be a beautiful August day, one of those that gave you the 'it's great to be alive' feeling. The sun was glinting on the mirror smooth water and the creamy buildings on the far side of the harbour were reflected on its surface. The faint noise of engines came over the water as some small boats were making their way out to sea. The tranquillity of the scene disappeared as Tony re-focused onto the activity immediately below him. On his side of the harbour, he could see various groups of divers carrying kit to boats or climbing onto RIBs, making ready for their day's diving. He knew that it could be hours yet before all the divers in his club would be up and ready to go. The sleeping bodies would be lying in various positions on their beds, some breathing quietly whilst others snored. He would usually be one of them, but this morning he had woken early, feeling strangely alert and impatient to be up. Their last trip in July had been a non-event in diving terms because of the bad weather, so he was really looking forward to getting back in the water today. He heard the sound of coughing and retching coming from the adjacent room. Graham or Brian? he wondered. Graham definitely. He recognised the groaning. He'd been hammered again last night. He was certainly drinking vigorously at the moment.

★ ★ ★

In the girls' room, Cleo lay awake, listening to the sound of Lynne's breathing. It was quiet and regular and signified sleep. She glanced at her watch – only five minutes since she had last done so. Time was crawling. It was ridiculously early to be awake – eight o'clock on a diving weekend was not usually experienced by any of them. They didn't normally get in the water until midday, by which time they would encounter other clubs returning from their first dive, ready for lunch. She felt restless, but did not want to disturb Lynne by tossing and turning too much. The bunk beds seemed to magnify any slight movement for Lynne lying above. Her self-enforced stillness made Cleo's mind race. She was anxious about the day ahead and fretted whether things would go to plan. John always went through their dive schedule, where they were going and what they would do, but he wasn't here today and Cleo felt part dread and part excitement. She knew that they were going to dive on the submarine. She had never done that before, but the others in the club who had done so reported an eerie feel to it.

She wondered if Tony was awake yet. They had hardly spoken to each other on the way down. Relations had been distinctly cool since their separate weekends away and that had been weeks ago now. It seemed neither of them wanted to discuss their situation. Tony had said little about his trip with Rachel and Cleo did not particularly want to describe her encounter with Martyn at the Gower. Of course, she had heard about London indirectly, but that was only because she had listened in on Rachel's enthusiastic conversation with Paula on the phone. She had been willing the other girl to ask the questions that she wanted answered. How had Tony been with her? Had he been a caring step-parent or an attentive lover? Had he moved on to the younger model? Was that the way it was going to end? She twisted the rings on her left hand as she considered her future. She took her engagement ring off and placed it on the duvet over her stomach. Her wedding ring remained in isolation. 'For better, for worse. For richer, for poorer.' Was it over? Was her future with Martyn, not with Tony? She took the second ring off and sighed deeply.

★ ★ ★

A diver stood alone in a cave. It was a remote spot and he was pleased that he had not met anyone as he left the hire car in the lay-by and carried the kit down to the beach. He surveyed the rebreather equipment. He had bought it last week from a dive shop in Wales. It had cost a small fortune of course, but it would be worth it for the larger amount of money that he would gain. It had been useful to go on that refresher course just to remind himself how everything worked. He checked his watch. He had plenty of time but he wanted to be in position well in advance. He was glad that he had decided to go in this morning to locate the wreck. This time he could just follow the rope that he had left and it would be a lot quicker, not having to stop and check his bearings in order to navigate.

★ ★ ★

Hours later the first dive to the Invincible had been completed and everyone had had lunch. They had switched to their second cylinders, so that they would all have plenty of air.

Tony called, 'Right, so it's time for the sub.'

'Pity John's not here because he would have liked it.' Brian pointed out.

'He said he had to work, didn't he, Tone?' asked Lynne.

'Yeah. Got to sort out some production problem.'

'Sometimes it doesn't seem like you two work in the same company.' Cleo glanced at Tony to see if he was going to take this as a criticism, but he was fiddling with his dry suit seal and was not paying attention.

'Graham had been looking forward to it as well, hadn't he?' Brian commented.

'Yeah,' Tony chuckled, 'but there was no way he could dive today. He was positively green. Did you see him?'

'I saw him staggering back to his room when we were coming out. He doesn't learn, does he?'

'What's up with him at the moment?' asked Martyn 'He seems to be hitting the drink hard.'

No one answered, so Tony continued, 'Well, we'll dive with the same buddies this time so I'll go with Martyn, and Brian you can have a threesome with Cleo and Lynne.'

'Was that the order as well?' Cleo asked.

'What?'

'Well, I'm still feeling a bit sick after the first dive. Can we go down first?'

'Are you alright? I thought you didn't eat much lunch,' Lynne asked her friend.

'Yes. No. Well, don't know really. Maybe it was something I had for breakfast.'

'You still want to dive though?'

'I'll be fine in the water. It's just sitting on the boat, when it's going up and down. I'd rather get in first, before I feel worse.'

'Right then,' Tony resumed. 'We've got a bit of a ride to get there, because it's out beyond the headland and round, so it's probably 45 minutes away. The wreck's at about 25–30m, depending on the tide, but we have to dive at the right time in slack water. There'll be a window of opportunity for us for about an hour. You three go first then Martyn and I will go straight after. The sub is in an unusual situation because it's quite close in to shore, so there's an interesting ridge of rock to look at and it's nestled at the bottom of it. It's up to you where you go but maximum time down is 30 minutes, otherwise you'll be caught in the tide.'

Tony pulled his head through the top of his dry suit and asked Martyn to zip him up, pulling the tag tight afterwards to check that it was completely closed. He performed the same service for Brian and everyone took up their favoured positions on the RIB as they set off, cruising slowly through the harbour area and then picking up speed in the open water. The breeze had increased since the morning, so there were now noticeable waves as the boat skimmed the surface of them. When they skirted the headland the waves grew in size and every so often Tony shouted a warning as a larger one loomed before them. Cold spray hit everyone on the boat, but the people at the front partially screened those at the back. As they neared the wreck site, Tony asked Brian for specific directions.

'You need to line up between the cave in the rock over there and that small island on the other side of the bay.'

Tony manoeuvred the boat and they both studied the fish finder, looking for something solid that would denote the wreck.

'How deep are we?' Martyn asked.

'35metres here. Bit further in, I think.' Tony answered.

'There.' He had spotted a shape on the screen. 'Throw the shot in someone.' Brian grabbed the shot and threw it overboard, rapidly moving his feet out of the way as the rope uncoiled from the bottom of the boat. He also threw the buoy in, connected to the other end of the rope so that the divers could be dropped by the buoy and follow the line down to the wreck.

Tony cut the engine and said 'First lot kit up then.' They moved to the back of the boat where there was more space but as they did so, Lynne said 'Something's leaking. Hear that?'

Everyone stopped and listened to the quiet hiss of air escaping. They leaned over the kit secured in the centre of the boat.

'Think it's mine.' Tony said, grabbing his demand valve and holding it up. 'Yeah.' He hit it against his other hand, and it stopped.

'How much air have you got now?' asked Martyn.

Tony checked his gauge. '180. I'll still be OK with that. Plenty of time for us to have a good look round.'

'You could use the spare bottle here.' Lynne suggested. 'It's full.'

'No, I'll be fine. Martyn'll probably need more air than me.'

Martyn moved to help Cleo with her kit whilst Tony assisted Lynne. Brian grappled with his own equipment and then completed the dive marshal sheet, recording buddy pairs and time of entry into the water.

'All set?' Tony asked, receiving nods in confirmation. He

drove the boat into position near the buoy and yelled 'Go!' so all three divers rolled backwards off the RIB into the water. Lynne and Brian surfaced indicating 'OK', but Cleo rose and swam to the side of the boat.

'Forgot fins,' she said guiltily.

'Who did the buddy check?' Tony asked as Martyn quickly found them and leaned over the side to guide Cleo's feet into them. 'Sorry' he said as he did so.

'Thanks.' Cleo replied, moving around the boat to meet up with Lynne who was already holding onto the rope under the buoy alongside Brian. They all signalled 'OK' and 'Down' and disappeared below the surface.

Martyn and Tony remained in the boat organising their equipment in order to take their turn when the others surfaced.

Tony asked, 'So you're alright about going down to maybe 25metres to look at the sub on the bottom?'

'Yeah, sure.'

Tony considered for a minute. 'The thing is, I really want to take a look inside.'

'Inside the sub? I didn't know you could get in.'

'Well, you're not supposed to. War grave and all that, but the thing is one of my mates said they'd attacked the hatch and you can squeeze in now. I always want to go and look inside any dark holes. You want to come?'

Martyn's instincts screamed 'No.' He did not really like the idea of going into wrecks even when they were quite spacious. Caves at sea level made him feel anxious, but the thought of deliberately going inside a very small space metres under the water was completely out.

'No, not really.'

'Oh. Thing is, I really want to go. What if I just left you at the top of the conning tower while I popped in for a few minutes?'

Martyn looked doubtful. He was a novice and this was his instructor telling him he'd be left on his own for some time. Tony carried on regardless.

'Of course it'd be our secret. We can't tell Brian, he'd disapprove, but it'll be an adventure. I won't be gone long. You'll be able to see me inside the tower and you can hang onto the hatch at the top. It'll be fine.'

In spite of his feeling that it would be far from fine, Martyn agreed as he did not wish to seem cowardly and he felt he should trust the judgement of his more experienced buddy.

After their allotted time, Cleo and Lynne broke the surface first, closely followed by Brian and as soon as they were aboard, Martyn and Tony entered the water and headed for the shotline. Tony gestured 'OK?', received the same signal back and then they both descended. Martyn slid his fingers down the rope looking below to see Tony disappearing beneath him. He squeezed his nose and blew gently to clear his ears. He was surrounded by bubbles and felt disorientated, not knowing if he was going down or they were coming up. He looked down. Tony had gone. Where was he? Why wasn't he waiting? He could hear his breathing, which sounded loud in his ears. It seemed to be hard work. It hadn't been like this before. His feet weren't vertically below him, they were out at an angle as he pulled himself down the rope. The water was opaque and there was nothing solid to focus on. He moved a few more metres down the line and found Tony waiting for him, looking up and checking that he was OK. They continued downwards and the huge dark shape of the sub loomed before them. It looked like a gigantic cigar, but the last one in the box as it appeared to be hiding by the ridge of rock that was closest to the shore. The shot was sitting on the surface of the sub, at the bow end so they made their way there. Martyn checked his depth gauge, which showed 22metres, and his air contents which was at 150bar. He seemed to have used up quite a lot of air on the way down. He showed it to Tony who nodded before indicating that they should swim off towards the bow.

They spent some time examining the length of the sub on the top surface but then they moved over the edge and descended slightly further. Tony drew Martyn's attention to the fact that his depth gauge indicated 24metres and waved his hand flat out from side to side. Martyn looked at him blankly, not knowing what he meant. He looked at his own gauge which read 24.2metres so he indicated 'OK' to Tony and they continued, making their way up the conning tower and rising to its hatchway at the top. There were iron bars at either side of the entrance so Martyn held onto one as Tony peered inside. He undid his torch and shone it into the darkness, where the bright ray of light illuminated the ladder that disappeared beneath. Martyn could not believe that Tony wanted to go down there as his attention was taken by the many metal projections that lined the aperture. Tony indicated that Martyn was to hold on and he would only be away four minutes. Martyn leaned backwards to ensure that Tony's fins did not connect with his mask as he manoeuvred himself into the hole. It looked like a tight fit but he appeared to descend easily enough. Martyn peered down, expecting to see him directly beneath. However, the hatchway must have been designed in two stages as he saw Tony's Kowalski torchlight pick up a further dark hatchway offset from the first. As Martyn silently thought, 'No, don't go down there,' he saw the light vanish. He checked the dive computer that he had borrowed from Graham. They had been down 17 minutes. Tony had just gone in, maybe at 16 minutes, so he would be back in 3. He felt angry with Tony. He said that he would be able to see him and he couldn't. He did not like being down here alone. The sub was a war grave and that meant that it should not be disturbed. What about the men who had died on it? Would they object to a live intrusion into their midst? Martyn shook himself. Superstitious nonsense. What time was it? 18 minutes. He had 100 bar left. What had Tony meant by waving his hand at 24metres? What was it about 24metres? They had been at 25metres on their first dive. Then he realised. Tony was telling him that they shouldn't go any deeper than their first dive, so they couldn't go all the way to the bottom of the sub where it rested on the seafloor because that could be 30metres. That had been fine by him, but he should have explained that when they were still in the boat. Cleo would be in the boat now. God, she was gorgeous. But he shouldn't want her, she had a husband. Here he was, waiting for the husband. 19 minutes. Did Tony do this sort of thing to her he wondered? Just went off and did whatever he wanted with scant regard for anyone else. He didn't deserve Cleo or – he still hadn't found out what the 'S' stood for. Sally? Had he said Sally? 90 bar left. There wasn't much fish life about. Maybe they steered clear of the dead. There wasn't much to see at all in fact. Where was the shotline? When Tony came back which way did they need to go?

A light flickered below him. Thank goodness, he was

coming back up. As Tony rose up the shaft to meet him, he gestured 'OK?' and Martyn moved to respond when Tony suddenly stopped. He tried to move again but seemed to be stuck. He looked up to Martyn for help, but his body and kit filled the gap and Martyn could not see past him. He tried to twist to the left and right but he seemed to be held fast. He reached his hands up and Martyn grasped them. He pulled but their fingers slipped apart. Martyn changed his grip to Tony's wrists and tried again. He didn't have anything to pull against so he tried to hold onto the iron bar with one hand and pull with the other. It was no good. Tony squirmed, trying to twist around to see what held him, but it was impossible in the narrow space. He looked again to Martyn, who gestured to his eyes and pointed behind Tony. Too dark, he couldn't see. Tony's torch was still attached to him on a line so he unhooked it and passed it up. Just as Martyn grasped the handle, it slipped and, finding the only gap between the trapped body and the unyielding metal, fell away into the darkness.

Shit! Why did he want to go down there anyway? Stupid bastard. How was he going to get him out? Seemed easy enough when he went in. But there were all those metal things sticking out. Must be stuck on one of those. Martyn leant into the hatchway to see if he could feel around Tony's head in order to release him. Tony tried to wrench himself free but he accidentally knocked into Martyn, causing his mask to slip and the demand valve to fall out of his mouth.

Water in his mouth. Water in his nose. Get out! Get out! He scrambled frantically to find his demand valve. Water in his eyes. He couldn't see. Mouth closed. Air! Where was it? Get out! Get out! As he reversed rapidly out of the hatchway, his demand valve came up towards him in a blur. He grabbed it and breathed in. Water filled his lungs and he coughed. Air! He needed air! Get to the surface. He breathed again and found air. Continuing to cough and splutter he put air into his jacket and started to go up. There was a beeping noise. What was it? Too fast. Shit! He couldn't see the dive computer properly. Too fast and he'd kill himself. Let air out. He pulled on his dump valve. He was going down. Ears. Hurt. Blow. Hurt. Blow again. His fins hit the bottom of the sea floor. Too deep. All the way down. Get back up. Air. Surface. He pressed the button to inflate his jacket again. He was going up, breathing hard. He could hear his breath and his heartbeat pounding in his head. How much air did he have? Beeping again. Shit. Slower. No. Get up. Get out. Surface.

CHAPTER 11

Tony watched helplessly as Martyn panicked trying to retrieve his regulator. He waved as he saw that Martyn was going to leave him there, but to no avail. Martyn was no longer concerned for him; it was a case of his own survival taking priority. When he disappeared, Tony considered his position. His air gauge was stuck somewhere below him and consequently he did not know how much air was left. He had 180 bar when they came down. They'd been swimming around for about twenty minutes, but it was hard work on the descent. When did he last check his air? Maybe five or six minutes ago before he came in here. It was about 110 bar then. If Martyn got to the surface OK he'd alert the others and they'd come looking for him, but what if Martyn did not get to the surface? Tony had felt his panic. He would be ascending without an instructor, with no shotline to hold onto, having had a frightening experience, possibly contending with a rising current. Tony cursed himself for bringing a novice on this dive. Why did he do it? He had put someone else at risk. John would give him a bollocking for diving in the sub. Did he have enough time to sit and wait to be rescued? Probably. He had his pony for extra air as well as his main cylinder and the octopus for the pony was easily reachable on his chest. He also had the emergency cylinder containing additional air in his Buddy jacket. However, he did not want to wait passively. It was not in his nature. He remembered what happened in the quarry. This was just the same situation. His kit had got stuck on something. He would take the same actions and be able to free himself.

He undid the buckle at his waist and released his shoulder straps. He still seemed to be jammed into position. He needed more room in order to be able to squirm around and release himself. He decided to let some air out of his jacket because that would make it thinner. Maybe that was what was making the difference. He pulled on his dump valve and immediately felt the jacket and kit sinking away from him. Happy that his solution was working and he could escape, he turned to grip the handle on the inside of his jacket in order to pull it free.

Who..?

Tony's regulator was forcibly removed from his mouth and he breathed water accidentally. He coughed instinctively and then tried to suppress it. He needed to keep his mouth closed. He tried to grab his kit but it fell away beneath him. He made the 'out of air' signal. The diver watched. He did nothing. Tony did it again, furiously. He couldn't mistake it. Nothing. Air! Need air! Tony's hands flew towards the diver's regulator but he was ready and he caught them at the wrists. They struggled as Tony felt the need for air rising within him. Octopus. He switched direction, going for the spare air supply. Fear gave him extra strength but the man's grip on his wrists was tight. Shit! What was he doing? Was it a man or was it something inhuman? He was held away from the life-giving source. Air! He tried to gesture to his throat again. Why didn't he help? Tony wrestled from side to side in a frenzy of need. His elbow hit the diver's octopus but he couldn't grab it. Air! He tried to bring his knees up to kick but there was no space. He was pinned against the metal wall. The mask was tight on his face. He had breathed through his nose to get his last intake. His eyes bulged with the effort of keeping his lips closed against the water that would soon enter his body. Air! His lungs were starting to burn. His brain was screaming. He tried to headbutt the regulator out of the other man's mouth. Then in a last desperate lunge he opened his own mouth to try to bite it off him. Water rushed in and his body convulsed.

Make it stop, the diver wished as he hung on, waiting for Tony to die. His teeth were tightly clenched around his regulator and Tony's eyes were millimetres from his, full of fear and panic. Would he recognise him? Would he know who was killing him and why? He looked away, fighting to control the body as it bucked against him. Please stop it. The body went slack. He eased his grip slightly. Tony hung before him, his eyes now dead and vacant. He wanted to get away. He released Tony's wrists, but they fell on his shoulders as if in a last embrace. He tried to thrust him back but there was no room. He felt vomit rising through his throat but swallowed hard to fight it down. It wasn't supposed to be like this.

In the plan Tony would get stuck because the diver would hold him in place in the conning tower. He would turn his air off and let Tony die quickly, without all this panic and struggle. His knowledge of the design of the tower had been wrong. There were so many impediments on the sides of the walls that he barely caught up with Tony before he got to the top. He was lucky to have a clip, attaching him to a metal ring in the tower in order to hold him fast as he squirmed. Then he could not reach up high enough to turn the air off. He worried when things did not go according to plan. There was so much more risk, having to make things up as you went along. But then, Tony suddenly made things a lot easier for him and played straight into his hands. They planned that he would turn Tony's air back on, to await later discovery of an accidental death, but now it would be even better, as Tony died due to his own stupidity.

Now Tony remained before him, his neoprene suit caught on one of the metal projections, blocking his exit. He couldn't wait in here any longer. His nerve had almost failed him having to sit quietly in here all the time waiting for Tony to arrive. He felt that the ghosts of the dead men all around him were oppressive, resentful that their grave was going to have to accept a new individual. He had turned his head torch on periodically, telling himself that it was easier to read the luminous hands on his watch that way and cursing himself for a fool, being afraid of the dark. He hoped that Tony's light would be sufficient for him to see and follow him up, but the momentary delay when he turned his own head torch on had almost given Tony the chance of escape. They knew that he would find the sub irresistible and they knew that he would come in alone. That much was correct. He did not know where Martyn was but it would not be long before someone came looking for Tony. He must get out now, even if there was a risk of finding Martyn there. He decided to send Tony up first. If Martyn was still at the hatchway, the sight of Tony's body whistling past him would send him to the surface for sure. The diver released Tony's suit and guided him up through the hatchway. Without the weights in his jacket to keep him down, the body continued upwards without interception. He followed cautiously. Raising his head above the hatchway he could see no-one. He moved upwards and out and then took a line diagonally downwards, searching for the rope that would lead him back to the cave. The reel was secured amongst some rocks a short distance away from the sub, so he collected it gratefully and wound it up as he made his way back to his safe haven.

★ ★ ★

Above him the others were sitting in the boat, calmly awaiting the return of Martyn and Tony. Cleo looked pale and was leaning over the side.

'You gonna throw up, Cleo?' Lynne asked.

She groaned in response.

'Best wait 'til they come up, then you could catch them with it.'

'Do you remember doing that Brian?' she continued. 'John had just put his arm up and got a handful of vomit. Then he surfaced in the middle of all that gunge. He wasn't a happy bunny.'

'They should be up soon, actually, shouldn't they?' Brian said as he checked his watch. They all automatically searched the water around them for any telltale bubbles. The swell had increased, much to Cleo's discomfort, and it meant that there were now substantial peaks and troughs to scan.

'Diver up, there.' Lynne pointed to the black head amongst the waves.

'Only one?' Brian asked as he started the engine and turned the boat.

'Is it Tony?' Cleo asked as she raised herself to look towards the diver.

'Think it's Martyn.' Lynne answered.

'Something's wrong.' Brian was concentrating on the black shape. 'He's just lying in the water.'

'Where's Tony?' Nobody answered Cleo's question as they were all intent on the narrowing gap between the boat and Martyn. Brian slowed the engine to bring it alongside.

'Got him,' called Lynne, holding on to the floating body.

'Martyn, you OK?' Cleo asked, as she grabbed hold of his jacket.

There was no response. Martyn lay in the water on his back, parallel with the boat. 'He's unconscious. We'll have to pull him in.'

'But where's Tony? They should be together,' Cleo said.

Brian was already undoing Martyn's weight belt and he groaned at his touch.

'He said something.' Lynne leaned over, 'Where's Tony?'

'Sub.'

'What did he say?'

'Sub, I think.'

'What? Get him in here so we can hear.'

'He's hurt. Be careful.'

'Stuck.'

'What? Where?' Brian asked looking for any obvious injury.

Martyn ignored him. 'Tony's stuck.'

'Tony's stuck? What happened?' Cleo was leaning over the side, looking anxiously at Martyn.

'Stuck in the sub? What's he doing in there?' demanded Brian.

'Someone'll have to go down. I'll get my kit,' Cleo said, moving away.

'No-one's going anywhere until we've got Martyn on board,' Brian stated. 'Where does it hurt?'

'Back.' Martyn grimaced. Brian was undoing his waist

strap and shoulder straps carefully as Cleo held onto the cylinder. He then eased the jacket away as she held on to Martyn.

'Legs OK?'

Martyn shook his head.

'Can you move your legs?'

Martyn's fins moved feebly in the water as a wave lifted him against the side of the boat.

'Lynne. Get his fins off. I think he's got a bend. We'll have to lift him in. Did you come up fast?' Brian continued to talk to Martyn as hands reached over the side to haul him in.

'Too fast.'

'Did you stop at 3metres?'

'No. Tony.'

'Cleo, get the oxygen. Lynne, call the coastguard. Let's put him here,' Brian commanded as they laid Martyn in the bottom of the boat with his legs up on one side. Cleo had not moved.

'Cleo, oxygen.' Cleo was transfixed looking at Martyn.

'But Tony?'

'Lynne. Bilge pump on. We're underwater back here. There's not enough room to lie flat.'

Brian clambered past Cleo to the front of the boat. He threw goody bags around in order to retrieve the green oxygen container that was buried at the bottom of the pile. He moved back along the boat and undid it, took out the cylinder, connected the mask and placed it over Martyn's nose and mouth.

'Lynne, hold that there,' he instructed. 'Water. He needs water.' He felt for a pulse and found it was beating rapidly.

Lynne fixed the oxygen mask around Martyn's head so that she could grab a water bottle.

Brian was thinking fast. He should have pressed the 'man overboard' button in order to freeze their position on the navigation screen. He flicked the radio to Channel 16, trying to remember what to do. Tony or John would know the drill but neither of them were there. MIPDANIO sprang into his head, but what did each letter mean? He struggled to focus his thoughts. He needed to make a Mayday call, give the Identity of the boat and their Position, explain the nature of their Distress, detail their Actions, Number of people on board, provide any other Information and finish with Over.

'Mayday. Mayday. Mayday. This is Forester. Forester. Forester. I have a diving related incident. We are at…' he squinted at the figures on the screen and read them out. 'Require immediate medical evacuation. Over.'

'Mayday. Mayday. Mayday. This is Brixham Coastguard. Brixham Coastguard. We have received your distress. Is your boat in any danger of sinking?'

'No.'

'Please repeat position.'

Brian complied.

'Helicopter has been scrambled. Please describe state of casualty.'

Cleo was struggling to put her kit back on.

'Cleo, stop that. You're not going down.'

'I am. Didn't you hear him, Brian? Tony's stuck.'

'You're in no fit state.'

Lynne took over on the radio, 'Casualty reporting pains. Think it's a bend….Yes, he's getting oxygen… Yes, we'll give him water.' Turning to Brian, she said, 'I'll go.'

'You won't have enough air left. You've done two dives today. We don't want any more casualties.'

'We can't just leave him there!' Cleo shouted. 'He'll be running out of air. What time is it? When did they go down? We've got to go.'

'You've only just come up. You haven't had a proper surface interval.'

'BRIAN! That's Tony down there,' Cleo cried.

Brian hesitated. 'Lynne, you and I will go. Let's switch the bottles over to the spare ones.'

'Cleo, you stay here. Help Martyn. Give him some water.'

Lynne started to unfasten her first bottle as Brian moved back to the radio. 'They'll be coming out from Culdrose,' he reported. 'Takes about 15 minutes to get here.' He continued speaking into the radio, 'About 25metres....Yes, casualty conscious.... Five of us on board.... One missing.'

Brian put the radio down again in order to get to the spare cylinders. He heaved one upright and lifted it across to Lynne on the other side of the boat. As he bent for the other spare, his eye caught sight of another black shape in the water.

'Diver up!' he yelled, immediately going back to the controls and putting the boat in gear.

'Is it Tony?' Cleo asked, searching the surface of the sea all around.

'Where?' Lynne asked as she looked up.

Brian pointed to the black mound bobbing amongst the waves on the port side. Martyn rolled to one side, and the oxygen mask fell away from his pale face. He was clammy to the touch as Lynne tried to rouse him.

'Martyn? Martyn?' His eyes flickered open again. 'Stay with us. Feeling OK?'

'Worse.'

'Can you move your legs around a bit? Need some space for Tony.'

Martyn grimaced but his legs did not move.

Lynne checked the gauge on the cylinder to see how much oxygen they had and whether they could use the other mask for Tony.

The boat drew alongside.

'Tony! Tony!' Cleo cried in alarm. He was lying face down in the water. His suit was distended, giving him a strange inflated appearance all over. The blackness of his suit contrasted with the red, slushy material that bobbed around his head. 'Oh God. What's all that stuff?'

'Tony? Mate? Where's his kit gone?' Brian asked in surprise as they pulled him closer.

'He's unconscious. Pull him in.' They all reached over the side and seized parts of Tony's suit but he was difficult to hold. A wave lifted him up part way into the boat, but he slipped back into the sea, splashing some of the red foam onto the boat. Cleo wiped her face automatically, 'Blood! It's blood!'

'For God's sake! Get a firm hold. Lynne, get his legs.'

'Is he alright?' Cleo cried as they heaved him over the side. 'Is he breathing?'

Tony's face was grey, apart from the scarlet gunge that still oozed from his mouth. A frothy, bloody mess trailed onto his chest. In spite of the evidence, they did not want to accept that he was dead. Brian slit the neck seal and they pulled his head out of the drysuit. He checked for a pulse in his neck but found none. He shook his head.

'NO! You've got to do something. Help him!' screamed Cleo.

'Cleo, we can't. It's too late.'

'No! No!' Cleo collapsed onto Tony and slid down to the floor by him, sobbing. The others stood looking down, momentarily stilled, not believing that they could have lost a friend.

Brian was the first to move, realising that he still had a patient to attend to. He stepped over Tony and squatted beside Martyn, who was unconscious.

'Shit. Come on, Martyn. Come back to us.'

'Is he OK?' The others looked over as Martyn opened his eyes.

'Yes, he's going to be fine. Aren't you? Have some water.' Brian removed the oxygen mask temporarily.

'Tony? You've got Tony?'

'We've got him, yes.'

As Martyn drank, the only other sound was the seawater lapping gently against the boat. It had exercised its power of death over life and now returned to a quiet calm. Cleo's burst of sobbing stopped. Now she sat, staring dully at the body. Brian went back to his station by the radio to talk to the rescue team.

'Two casualties. We've got the other diver, but he's dead.' He called back, 'I'm going to have to move the boat to get into the right position for the helicopter.' No-one answered. Cleo and Lynne still looked dazed.

'Where's his kit gone?' Brian asked of no-one in particular.

CHAPTER 12

Brian lit a flare to produce the orange smoke that would indicate wind direction and help locate them speedily. There was silence on the boat as they waited. He gazed at the others: Lynne crouched by Martyn, Cleo tear-stained as she sat with a hand on Tony's chest. Brian's eyes fixed on Tony, on the frothy, bloody mess that clung around his mouth and slid over his chin. They should clean him up or cover him at least so he looked around for something. Apart from their kit, they only had goody bags on board, which seemed strangely inappropriate. Then he remembered that both Cleo and Lynne would have put coats on board to keep them warm after diving. He pulled one of them out. He didn't know whose it was but didn't think it mattered as he laid it gently over Tony's head and chest.

The sound of the helicopter made everyone look up. The red Sea King appeared to be getting larger as it approached them. Brian put a hand over his ear so that he could hear the instructions coming over the radio. They were in the right position. As the helicopter got closer, they would see a trailing rope but they must not touch that as it carried static electricity. Brian shouted this instruction, but doubted if the women heard him. A Sea and Air Rescue diver would jump into the sea and swim to them. He leant back towards the others to tell him what would happen, but the noise from the engines above made speech futile. The downdraft from the rotors was whipping the sea around them and had effectively dispersed the coloured smoke. Brian realised that there was very little space for a man to climb on board. The helicopter seemed to be far too close as Lynne looked up and wondered why it had an ace of clubs painted on it. Was that lucky? What if it was unlucky and crashed on top of them? Was it supposed to make that noise or was there something wrong with the engines? She looked at Cleo's pinched white face and tried to put an arm around her but the thundering noise made them both put their hands over their ears. Lynne thought her heart was beating fast before but now her whole chest seemed to reverberate. They were all getting dowsed with spray and the boat lurched again, so they each grabbed one of the handles on the sides. None of them wanted to be thrown into the churning sea which had suddenly become an enemy since it claimed Tony's life.

Lynne held the oxygen mask over Martyn's grey face. She leant over him to try and shield him from the wind created by the helicopter. Martyn's eyes were closed now and she hoped that they were not going to lose him as well. She looked up to see the rescue diver leap from the open doorway and splash into the water near them. He swam over and pulled himself aboard, gesticulating as he did so to his mate above, leaning out of the bay of the helicopter. The noise reduced temporarily as the helicopter veered away and hovered nearby.

'Hi. Name's Sam. Two casualties?' the navy man asked.

'Yes, two, but he's dead.' Brian nodded towards Tony.

Sam spoke into his radio, telling them they would have to winch two casualties aboard. He checked Tony's body briefly but then focused on Martyn.

'Is he conscious?' he asked, glancing at Martyn as he unfurled the harness that he would use to lift him.

'Keeps coming in and out,' Brian replied, but at that moment Martyn opened his eyes.

'What's his name?'

'Martyn.'

'Right, Martyn, we're going to get you out of here and you'll be fine.'

As there was no answer, he continued, 'He's been on oxygen, yeah?'

'Yes. He was on a dive to about 25 metres but he came up too fast we think.'

'He's still got his dive computer on?'

'Here.' Lynne raised Martyn's wrist.

The man knelt closer to Martyn. 'Martyn, my name's Sam. I'm going to put this over your head and shoulders so we can get you up, OK?'

'He can't move his legs.'

'Oh. Martyn, can you feel this?' He tapped his legs as he asked the question. Martyn did not respond.

'Was he like this when he came up or has it developed?'

'When he came up.'

'Right.' He spoke into his radio and asked for a stretcher to be lowered. If there was a danger of paralysis, it would be better to keep the casualty as immobile as possible on a stretcher, rather than have him swinging around on the harness.

'Have you got the details of time in and out and air contents?'

'Here. They were last down, Martyn and Tony.' Brian handed over the sheet with all the diving information recorded.

The helicopter manoeuvred back into position and

lowered the stretcher. Brian held it steady whilst Sam released the cable. He explained how they were going to ease a board under Martyn to keep his neck and back straight and then they would slide him onto the stretcher. Brian and Lynne helped move him into position as gently as possible, but they could not control the waves and Brian worried that they might have added to Martyn's injuries inadvertently. With the operation complete and the straps tightened to hold him onto the stretcher, they locked his head in position using supports on either side. Sam clipped himself on so that he was alongside Martyn and summoned his crew back.

As they were lifted off the boat, fear suddenly made Martyn much more alert. He was completely immobile, strapped to the stretcher. If the cable snapped or the clip broke, he would plummet into the sea and descend rapidly to the seafloor. Sam would be alright as he could move his arms and legs. His were pinned down. He would not even be able to flail helplessly at the water as he drowned.

The noise of the engines thundered overhead as they rose, spinning slightly underneath the helicopter. Hot air enveloped them as they got closer. In spite of the oxygen mask, Martyn could detect the burnt kerosene polluting the atmosphere. He felt sick. A side wind made the helicopter lurch just as they neared the door. Martyn wished he could lapse into unconsciousness wilfully so that he could remove himself from this experience. Sam caught hold of a bar by the open doorway whilst the winch man grabbed Martyn and guided him inside. Sam followed and waved to the boat below to indicate that all was well. He quickly unfastened himself from Martyn, reattached to a new stretcher and was being lowered back down for Tony's body, all within a few seconds.

The air was better inside and Martyn breathed deeply, feeling the stretcher being manhandled. The pain in his back was excruciating. There had been a temporary relief when the fear of falling had blocked it out but now there was no such distraction. He hoped that the transfer to the stretcher had not created any further damage. Perhaps if it got unbearable he would black out. As his head was held firmly in position he could only look straight up at the pipes running overhead. One of these was leaking fluid of some sort that dripped onto him steadily. No one paid it any attention so he hoped that it was not important. The grey interior was painted in five different shades, chipped and scuffed in places to show bright glints of bare metal beneath. Near his head there was some worn material that kept flapping and he wondered how old the helicopter was and how often it was called out on rescue missions. He hoped they would make it back to dry land safely.

It seemed that by the time he had thought this, Sam was back in the hatchway, with the second stretcher, waiting to be manoeuvred inside. The crew accepted it and lined Tony's body up close to Martyn's. The last thing he heard was them discussing the need to fly low on the way back, in order to minimise any decompression effects that he was suffering. He hoped that he was secured onto something solid as the floor tilted in an alarming fashion and the helicopter made a climbing, banking turn. He had a clear view of the gaping doorway and the choppy green water awaiting his re-entry. He looked away and tried to think of something else.

* * *

'Well, they certainly know what they're doing. Hope he'll be alright,' Brian said as they watched the helicopter disappear into the distance. 'We'd best get back.'

Lynne looked at the bloody pools where Tony had lain and moved to block Cleo's view of them. She could not think of anything to say but Cleo showed no inclination to speak or move. They were all silent on the way back to Plymouth, each enveloped in their own thoughts. As they progressed through the harbour, they could see a police car near the floating pontoon they had left that morning. Two policemen stood watching their progress, along with other groups of divers looking sombre, so they must have heard the news. Graham was also obvious, pacing up and down along the length of the wooden platform. Brian brought the boat alongside the pontoon and Graham immediately greeted them with, 'What happened? Someone said there'd been an accident. Then there was a horrible rumour that someone had died. I thought it couldn't be our boat and then they mentioned the Forester.'

Brian stepped off and put a hand on his shoulder, 'It's Tony. He's dead. Martyn's injured.'

'Dead? But how could he be dead? He was fine this morning.' Brian moved him away a little, out of earshot of Cleo, but closer to the waiting policemen. One of these introduced himself with, 'I'm Sergeant Fry and this is Constable Dixon.'

Brian replied, 'I'm Brian, one of the Forest Divers.' He pointed to the others as he continued, 'That's Lynne and this is Cleo, um, Tony's wife. Tony's the casualty,' he finished awkwardly. 'But Martyn's the casualty that's still alive,' he added, then cursed himself for his clumsiness.

'Thank you, sir,' Sergeant Fry answered. 'We will need statements from everyone in due course.'

Graham asked 'How's Martyn?'

'We don't know,' Lynne said. 'The helicopter took him off to the hospital.'

'We'll see you there later,' Sergeant Fry added. Brian put an arm around Cleo as he helped her on to the pontoon. He said, 'It'll be alright,' and then wanted to kick himself for saying something so thoughtless. Fortunately Cleo did not seem to register that he had said anything.

'But what happened?' Graham asked Lynne.

'Dunno,' Lynne shook her head. 'Martyn and Tony were last down so the rest of us were on the boat waiting. It was probably about time for them to come up and then we spotted Martyn on the surface. When we got to him he said Tony was stuck in the sub and someone would have to go down.'

'In the sub? What was he doing in the sub?'

'He shouldn't have been there but Tony always wants to go into dark holes, doesn't he? Martyn was having pains and we'd just called the coastguard then Tony popped up. Funny thing was, he had no kit.'

'Where was his stuff?'

'Must be on the bottom of the sea somewhere – or in the sub I suppose.'

'God. It's terrible.'

'We'll need to impound all your dive kit, sir,' Sergeant Fry interrupted.

'What? Why?' Graham asked.

'It's standard procedure with these sorts of incidents. We'll need to check the equipment, look for any faults, try to identify the cause of the problem, that sort of thing.'

'Do you need all our stuff then or just Tony's?'

'Everyone's, just to be on the safe side.'

'We don't know where Tony's gear is though. He came up without it.'

'Right. Might need to call the dive unit in then,' he said to Constable Dixon. 'Can you organise that?' Turning back to Brian he said, 'Can you tell us precisely where you were diving so that we can send them to the right spot? Another thing, sir. As it was an unnatural death, there'll have to be an inquest so we'll inform the coroner. He'll probably convene the court first thing on Monday morning.'

'Oh. Do we have to be there? It's just that we'd all be going home tomorrow, back to work on Monday.'

'Not necessarily. It's just a formality at this stage. The coroner has to start proceedings, but then he'll adjourn, pending further enquiries.' Sergeant Fry glanced up to check where Cleo was and saw her standing next to Lynne. 'He will have to request a post-mortem though, and that will happen as soon as possible, maybe Monday afternoon.'

'A post-mortem?'

'We have to determine how he died you see, sir.'

Brian was thinking about Cleo, wondering if he had to tell her this news but Sergeant Fry appeared to have understood his concern as he said,

'I'll explain the process to Mrs...?'

'Fleming.'

'...Mrs Fleming when we see you up at the hospital. We'll need to get statements from everyone about today,' he repeated.

★ ★ ★

Cleo stayed in the shower for a long time, feeling the hot water wash over her. She had sunk down onto the floor and now sat hugging her knees contemplating the plughole as the water swirled around and spiralled down. Every so often she heard Lynne come back into the bathroom and then leave again after asking if she was alright.

Was she? She didn't know. The water running down her face mingled with the tears and washed them away. Her head ached and her limbs were heavy. She struggled to her feet knowing that the others would be waiting for her and they would all have to go to the hospital. She wrapped a towel around herself and went back into her bedroom. Tony was dead. Alive this morning, dead this afternoon. She was now a widow. Suddenly aware of her single status, she wondered how Martyn was. Where would they take him? Would he be at the hospital as well or would he go straight to the Diving Diseases Research Centre? The worst thing was thinking about Rachel. How was she going to tell her? What was she going to tell her? Her thoughts switched again. What about him? Was he OK?

They were expecting her to go to the hospital. She pulled on a jumper and reached for her coat. As she pushed an arm through the sleeve she noticed the dark stain on the back. What was that? She took her arm back out and studied the patch. She drew her fingers over it. Something red and slimy came away in her hand.

'Oh God!' She ran to the sink and was violently sick as she realised that Tony's blood was on her. Lynne came back in to find her still retching.

'Cleo. Oh.' She saw the coat lying on the floor and threw it outside the door.

★ ★ ★

'Mrs Fleming?'

Cleo turned to face the doctor who was addressing her.

'We've taken your husband into the x-ray department.'

'Why?'

'It's standard procedure with all diving accidents. We need to x-ray him so we have a record of where any gases are in the body before they dissipate.'

Cleo nodded dumbly.

'We have some forms to complete and of course we'll have to keep the body here until the police are satisfied with their investigation.'

'Investigation?' Cleo asked in alarm. 'But it was an accident.'

'The police are always involved in these cases. Nothing to worry about really, but Sergeant Fry is waiting to ask you some questions. I'll leave you in his hands.' The doctor nodded to the policeman standing nearby and Sergeant Fry took his cue.

'Hello, again. Sorry about this but we have to treat every diving casualty as if it is a suspicious incident until we are satisfied otherwise. Therefore we need to ask each of you for a statement.' He looked from person to person. 'The sooner we do it, the better. We can do it now or you can come down to the station later.'

'Can we just check how Martyn is?' Lynne asked.

'Martyn? That would be Mr Share? Yes, he was taken directly to the Diving Diseases Research Centre – the DDRC and I believe he's undergoing treatment there. You'll be able to go over and see him but as he'll be in a hyperbaric chamber for some time, there's no immediate need to rush.' He smiled, 'Mrs Fleming, shall we start with you? If you'd like to follow me.' He led the way into an empty office that they were using as a temporary base for taking statements.

★ ★ ★

'This one's blown up a bit by the look of him,' Jason said as he wheeled Tony's body into the x-ray preparation room. Tom looked up, 'He is, isn't he? Divers often have a bit of a belly on them though, don't they? I wonder if it helps with buoyancy?'

'We'll soon see how much is him and how much is gas.'

'I've got the evidence bags ready for his suit. Oh and he's still got his dive computer on.' Tom made a note. 'That's good. The police'll need that. Have you got the docket from the Path. lab?'

'Here. They said Francis will probably do the post-mortem on him on Monday so after we've finished with him, he'll go in the fridge over there.'

'So, Mr Antony Fleming,' Tom said as he wrote the name on the bags, 'let's have a look at you.'

He passed a scissors to Jason so they could both start cutting the suit off Tony.

'Helpful the way someone's started our job for us,' Jason commented as he examined the cut neck seal where the others on the boat had made the desperate attempt to revive him.

'He must have looked dead when they got to him, though. Look at all this blood on him.'

'People just panic, don't they?' Jason commented. 'It'd be horrific if it was your mate.'

'Wouldn't mind if it was you,' Tom answered.

'Thanks, mate.'

The men concentrated on their task until Tony lay naked before them. 'Well, that's not going to impress Francis much, is it?' Jason nodded at the exposed genitalia.

'Come on, let's get the pictures of him.' Tom was sure that Jason was straight but he sometimes found his banter unnerving.

'Smile please,' Jason said, as he pressed the button to take the first x-ray of the chest. 'Does it say do him all or just head and chest?'

Tom checked the form, 'Just the top half but let's do the pelvic area as well, for Francis.'

'OK.' Jason pressed the buttons to take further pictures of the body. 'And now for the side shot.' They manoeuvred the equipment so that the x-ray of the head would take a side view as well as face on.

'Great. That's him done then. The boss can have a look at the pics on Monday and send the report over before Francis starts hacking him about.'

Tom smiled at the description. The pathologist was meticulous and had called them to task previously if anything was less than perfect. He would not like to be described as a 'hacker.'

★ ★ ★

John was greeted by the caretaker as he left the factory buildings.

'Right Mr O'Donnell? Another long day at the office?'

'That's right, Jim. It's a hard life.'

'Mr Fleming not with you?'

'No. Diving trip for him this weekend. They'll all have been down there, sunning themselves on the boat, enjoying the sea, while some of us have been slaving over a hot desk. Still, it'll be nice and warm for you.'

'Oh, right you are.' Jim chuckled at the idea that he would be sitting at a director's desk. 'Goodnight then.'

'Goodnight.'

As he did his rounds later, Jim looked in at John's office. He knew he was joking about having left it nice and warm as it was August, but there was no harm just checking that the fire was turned off. The large table across from the desk was littered with all sorts of papers. The same sort of maelstrom seemed to have attacked Tony's office as well. It must have taken him some hours to go through that lot. As he closed the door, he reflected on his good luck that his job didn't involve much paperwork.

CHAPTER 13

When Cleo came out of the room that the police had commandeered temporarily for taking statements, Sergeant Fry called Brian in. The others gathered around her.

'How did it go?' Lynne asked.

'Fine. They just need to know what we've been doing today and what happened when Tony and Martyn went down and came back up and... afterwards.' Cleo made her way to a line of orange plastic chairs in the corridor and sat down.

'We've been thinking about calling home,' Graham started.

'What have you told them?' Cleo asked, alarmed.

'Nothing yet,' Lynne replied calmly, placing a hand on her friend's arm. 'Graham said that Rachel will be round at their house with Paula anyway. So that's good, isn't it? At least she'll be with someone.'

'Yes. Yes. That's good.' Cleo was desperately trying to plan what she would say to her daughter.

'Shall I ring Elaine first so she knows?' Graham suggested.

'No. Yes. I don't know.' Cleo's head was still reeling from the session with the police. All those questions. It was an accident. Why did they need to ask so many things? 'No. I should tell Rach first, and then you can talk to Elaine after.' She reached for her bag to find her mobile and moved a little way apart as she pressed the buttons to call Rachel. The others watched anxiously.

'Rach? … Hi. Are you OK? … You're round at Paula's?… No. Well, Yes, I'm alright. It's your Dad… No, he's had an accident… He's in hospital, yes, but it's worse than that… Yes, it's serious… I'm afraid… He's… He had an accident diving and he's dead… Yes, he is… Oh, Rach, I'm sorry… There was nothing we could do… Yes, I tried! … Rach?….I wish I was there… Rachel?… Rachel?' Cleo turned back to the waiting group. 'She's dropped the phone. Just crying.' Graham stepped forward to take the mobile.

'Elaine?… Elaine? … Pick the phone up!… Come on!… Where were you?..Yes, that's right, Tony's dead… We don't know how … Of course we're sure… Yes, he's really dead… Well, you'll have to believe it… I don't know, some sort of accident when they were diving today… No, I didn't go… Too sick… Look after Paula. I mean – both of them… Stop saying you can't believe it. I'm telling you, he's dead… The police will investigate it, they're taking statements now… They always do apparently… No, we'll phone the others. I'll talk to you later, bye.' As he came off the phone he said, 'God, that woman's stupid sometimes.'

'Graham,' Lynne said, leaping to Elaine's defence, 'she'll be in shock. You could have been a bit gentler.' He shrugged.

'We need to tell John. Do you want to call him?' Lynne asked Cleo. As Cleo turned to her with tears starting a slow descent down her cheeks, Lynne decided for herself, 'No. I'll ring him.'

'John? It's Lynne… Yes, hello… No, diving was not good… No. There's been an accident. Martyn's in the DDRC and he's getting treated but Tony… Tony's dead… John?… Yes, that's right, he's dead… No, we're all a bit shocked. We were on the boat and when they came up… it was terrible.' She stifled a sob, trying to suppress the image of Tony's body that came to mind. 'We don't know. They must have been on the sub because we all were... Brian's talking to the police now... They want statements from everyone... He says should he come down?' She turned to Cleo, who did not answer. As Lynne put the mobile back to her ear, she continued, 'Yes, we're all staying here tonight. Yes, see you in the morning then...'Bye. He's coming down.'

Cleo nodded. 'How was he?'

'How was he? I don't know. I didn't ask him.'

Brian came out, 'They want you next, Graham.'

'Me? But I wasn't even on the boat.'

'They just want to talk to all of us.'

'Oh.' He disappeared into the room as Lynne walked over to Brian.

'We've been calling home. Cleo rang Rachel and she's round with Paula and Elaine.' Brian glanced across the corridor at Cleo who sat staring at the floor.

'Anyone told John?'

'Yes, he says he's coming down tomorrow.'

'What for? What's he going to do?'

'I don't know. Suppose he just wants to be here.'

'But it's Sunday. We'll be going back tomorrow anyway. We all need to be at work on Monday.'

'Not all of us,' Lynne reminded him. 'I don't know what Cleo will want to do and Martyn's in the DDRC. I feel I should stick with Cleo wherever she needs to be. I'm sure work will give me time off in the circumstances.'

'The police said their diving team will go down looking for Tony's kit tomorrow.'

'Why do they need that?'

'It's just what they do. They need to check his equipment for malfunctions. Identify cause of death and so on.'

Lynne looked surprised as she remembered the state of Tony's body on the boat. Brian answered her unspoken question, recalling the gruesome image in his own mind. 'Yes, I know, but they still need to do a post–mortem. They'll do that on Monday when the pathologist is in. They don't work weekends. No urgency, I guess.'

Graham came over to them saying, 'Your turn, Lynne.'

'Oh, right.'

He sat down on the line of chairs and Brian moved next to him.

'I don't know what they needed to talk to me for. I don't know anything, only what you told me when you got back. God, I could do with a drink.'

Brian looked shocked. 'Well, couldn't you?' Graham asked.

'I don't think it's the time, right now.' Brian nodded towards Cleo, sitting further away on his left. She appeared to be immersed in her thoughts as she studied her feet. The toes were pointing to a red line painted on the floor, leading patients to a distant department like a yellow brick road. Cleo was making infinitesimal adjustments so that her toes just kissed, but did not cross, the line.

'Life goes on.'

'Graham. For God's sake,' Brian hissed as he took him by the elbow and forced him away down the corridor.

'Cleo's just lost her husband. Have a bit of feeling.'

'Do you think she's bothered? Not exactly the hysterical grieving widow, is she?'

'She'll be in shock. People react differently. Why are you being like this?'

'I'm just saying, I don't think everything was lovey-dovey in their marriage, that's all.'

'Now is not the time,' Brian said firmly, taking him further away. 'Why don't you go back to your room? We'll all be coming soon enough, once the police have finished with us.'

As Graham turned to leave he mumbled something about teenage girls. Brian did not hear him properly.

'What?'

'People shouldn't mess with teenage girls.'

Brian stared after him in bewilderment. What was he talking about?

Behind him Cleo had shifted her attention from her toes to her fingers. She was using her right hand to rub each finger of the left in turn. She stopped when she got to her ring finger and considered the gold and diamonds before her. 'Til death us do part.' He was gone. Would that make everything better? She rubbed at her nail. The finger was discoloured around the edge of the nail as if she had been picking blackberries and the last vestiges of the fruit had clung on in the crevices. Reddish brown more than purple... Blood! Tony's blood. He was still with her! She leapt to her feet, raced for the ladies and ran to the first basin, turning the taps on full. In the torrent of water she scrubbed at her nails frantically. She had been interviewed by the police with blood on her hands! It meant nothing. She hadn't killed him. She hadn't been anywhere near him. They probably hadn't even noticed. She continued washing, repeatedly soaping and rinsing in a compulsive ritual.

★ ★ ★

Elaine put the phone down and turned to the girls. Rachel had sunk to the floor sobbing and Paula sat with an arm around her shoulders, asking what was wrong.

'What is it Mum? She just started crying.'

'It's Tony. There's been an accident. A bad accident. He's dead.' Rachel's sobs deepened at Elaine's words and she seemed unable to catch her breath.

Paula froze. 'Tony?'

'Yes.' Elaine did not know what she should do to look after Rachel. Was it like an asthma attack and should she get her to breathe in and out of a paper bag?

'He's dead?' Paula asked.

'Yes.' Elaine answered impatiently but then realised she should be looking after her own daughter. Paula made no sound as the tears rolled down her face, but the noise from Rachel was appalling. Elaine felt completely inadequate. She had always felt that the crying of babies was designed so that their needs could not be ignored, but Rachel was shredding her nerves fast. She wanted to cry too, but her role as the responsible adult in the house was to comfort the other two. She didn't know what to say to Rachel or Paula. The thought that Tony was only a step father, not a real father, did not seem an appropriate thing to mention to the distraught girl at her feet. Practicalities, maybe that was the best thing.

'Come, on, girls, let's move to the sofa.'

Paula now had both arms wrapped around Rachel as they cried together, lying prone on the floor. Elaine knelt down with them and put her arms around both.

'I know. I know.' She wished that it was true. She actually thought that she knew nothing and was feeling deeply uncomfortable. The childhood platitudes about having a good cry and then feeling better were not going to help here. In spite of her forty-odd years, Elaine had not had any close contact with death. She searched desperately for something to say or do. The girls' sobbing seemed to come in bursts. Rachel would ease up as she got her breath back and then Paula would resume and they'd both be off again. When Rachel raised her head briefly, Elaine could see her red eyes and the mucus running from her nose. The sight made her own eyes fill up in sympathy, but she tried to stifle the welling emotion. She turned around to reach the box of tissues on the coffee table and plucked at the flimsy paper, handing some to Rachel and some to Paula. Some sort of accident Graham had said. Why were the police involved? Did he say the others were alright? She couldn't remember. Why hadn't he gone with them? Sick, he'd said. Did he mean drunk? He had been drinking a lot lately, but she thought that was his way of dealing (badly) with Paula's pregnancy.

'Shall I make us all a cup of tea?' The girls ignored her. If anything, Paula increased in volume. Rachel stopped crying suddenly and pulled away.

'Why are you crying?' she asked Paula.

Paula struggled to answer, 'Why ...?'

'He's not your Dad. Why are you so upset?'

Paula held the tissue to her face.

Rachel was staring at Paula's bump. 'You've never said who the father is.'

'What?'

The doorbell rang loudly in the ensuing silence. No-one moved. Elaine and Rachel were both intent on what Paula would say next.

'He's not your Dad either. Why are you crying?' Elaine

looked from one to the other, uncertain about the rapid change from sympathy to accusation.

'Who's the Daddy?' Rachel insisted.

'None of your business.' Paula got to her feet with surprising agility and ran upstairs to her room.

Elaine wondered if she should go after her, but the distant slam of the bedroom door made answering the front doorbell a more attractive option.

'Oh, hello John. Come in.'

Elaine was instantly relieved that she wouldn't have to cope with the girls on her own.

'Elaine. How are you?'

'Well, it's terrible isn't it? What a dreadful accident. I've only had the briefest of calls from Graham and he said the police are involved and they're taking statements. Martyn's in the DDRC...'

'And the girls. How are they?' John cut in, entering the house as he could not wait for Elaine's report to finish.

'Well, you can see. Rachel's here,' she waved vaguely behind her, 'and Paula's upstairs. I was just making some tea. Would you like some?'

'Please.' She left the lounge for the sanctuary of the kitchen and as she retreated to her domain, John sat beside Rachel and enveloped her in a hug. Elaine could hear a dull murmur of conversation and was relieved that John could find something to say. She would make the tea very, very slowly. As she lifted the caddy out of the cupboard she noticed a black ring on the shelf, outlining its position. She took a cloth from the sink to wipe it clean and wondered if it was black treacle or balsamic vinegar. It was particularly stubborn. As she nudged other bottles and spice jars in the cupboard she noticed similar rings and marks. Before long she was completely absorbed in emptying the whole cupboard and cleaning it thoroughly. Next she decided to re-sort some of the jars in the cupboard as they needed to be in descending order of height. As she shifted items around, she wondered about the course of the conversation. Tony dead. Crying. Who was the father? Running off. She sighed. Probably hormones. All sorts of strange things happened when you were pregnant. She leant back to assess the array of products before her. It was not right. She needed to do it again, perhaps by ascending order of height.

John and Rachel had moved closer to the kitchen door and Elaine could hear John saying that he would go down to join the others in the morning. Elaine wondered what he could achieve by going down there, but decided that it was not the time to cross-question him.

'You'll see Mum?' Rachel asked him.

'Yes. I'll look after your Mum.'

'She didn't look after Dad.'

'What do you mean? It was an accident,' John continued. 'Nothing anyone could have done. Cleo was on the boat anyway. It was Martyn who was down there.'

Rachel sank back onto the sofa, pulling a cushion close to her chest to hug it fiercely.

'How's Martyn?' Elaine asked as she eventually brought the tea out of the kitchen.

'I don't really know,' John replied. 'At least he's in the best place. They'll look after him there.'

'What is the DD... whatever it was?'

'It's where they take injured divers so they can put them in a pressurised container if they've got some sort of decompression illness.'

There was the sound of doors opening and closing above them, prompting Rachel to ask, 'Should I go up to see Paula?'

John turned to the stairs, 'I'll go.'

As Elaine watched him mount the steps she couldn't help wondering if Paula would want to see him.

CHAPTER 14

As the stretcher was taken out of the ambulance and rolled inside a building, Martyn came to, wondering where he was now. Apart from the ambulance men wheeling him along, there was another man, dressed in what looked like hospital scrubs. This person smiled at him and said,

'Hello Martyn. You're in the Diving Diseases Research Centre. My name's Mick and we'll be looking after you here. You're going to be examined by Dr Helston and then you'll probably need a few treatments in a hyperbaric chamber.'

'What?' Martyn wondered what that meant but he did not really care, so long as someone was going to look after him.

'Don't worry. It's what you need for now. You're in good hands.' Mick patted his shoulder as if to demonstrate the point. They wheeled him into an examination area and he was lifted onto a bed by a member of staff who came to assist Mick. He was in a very clean, bright white environment he noted. A bag of intravenous fluids was transferred to an adjacent stand and he wondered when they had inserted the needle into him. Had they cut off some of his suit in the helicopter? A new oxygen mask was placed gently over his head by a young red–haired nurse.

'Hi Martyn. I'm Gill. I'm just going to get the rest of your suit off so we can examine you properly.'

As Martyn wondered if he needed to agree to this, Gill took a large pair of scissors that were curved on the lower side and started to cut away the side of his suit. Obviously no assent was required. He could feel the scissors as they moved down from his chest towards his hip. He raised himself up to see why she had stopped but then realised that the scissors were continuing down his leg although he had no sensation of it. He lay back gingerly, considering the strange disconnection between his senses. Sight and touch used to mean the same thing. What if he never got the feeling back in his legs? What if he couldn't move them ever again? He didn't want to spend the rest of his life in a wheelchair. How would he work? Who would want him? What would Cleo say? He wished he'd taken more dynamic action in the tent that night. She had wanted him, he was sure of it. Then at least he'd have the memory. Tony! What had happened to Tony?

'Tony. Is he here?' he asked.

'Sorry?'

'My buddy?'

'No, I'll get…' At that moment Dr Helston appeared. She was a small but curvaceous woman who greeted Martyn with a welcoming smile.

'Martyn was just asking about Tony,' Gill continued.

Dr Helston immediately became serious.

'I'm afraid he died. He's been taken to the hospital but he was dead when he got to the surface.'

'Oh.'

'That's all we know. Now we need to concentrate on you.' Her manner became brisk as she put some papers down and started to check Martyn's blood pressure and heart rate.

'Are you on any medication?'

Dead. Tony, dead. Was it his fault?

'Martyn? Are you on any medication?'

'Um. No.'

He'd left him down there. He must have run out of air.

'Any history of heart or lung problems?'

Never leave your buddy.

'No.'

'Did you have a medical exam before you started diving?'

'What? Yes.'

'And you were passed fit?'

Cleo was a widow – available. Shouldn't think like that.

'Yes.'

'How is the pain now?'

'Bad.'

'We can give you something for that. Where is it?'

'In my back.'

'And your legs?'

'Can't feel them.'

'Right. We need to do a few tests then.' The doctor moved away as Martyn thought of Tony. Was this paralysis of his legs punishment for letting him die?

'I'm going to touch you at various points and I want you to tell me if you can feel anything.'

'Yes.'

'Yes?'

'I meant OK. Can't feel anything.'

'I'll try again. Here? And here?' As the doctor repeated her queries and Martyn continued his negative responses, his spirits sank further. He was not going to be able to walk again. How was he going to cope?

'Can you try to move your legs?'

'They moving?' Martyn asked hopefully as he raised his head to look down his body.

'No.'

'Will I be paralysed?'

'Too early to say. What we can say is that you had very good first aid care as you had oxygen and water on the boat and more fluids and oxygen on the helicopter, which got you here very quickly. That treatment was all excellent and many people do recover well so…'

'I'll walk again?' Martyn interrupted.

'You'll need to have a few sessions in the hyperbaric chamber and we'll keep doing these tests on your legs. We would expect to see some improvement over time. At the moment you're scoring one out of five, which means that you can't move your legs.' Martyn lay back as he considered her words. 'What's wrong?'

'Looking at your dive profile and your symptoms, you've probably got an arterial gas embolism.'

Martyn raised his left arm looking for his dive computer.

'We took the computer off in order to check your dive records. It seems that you were at about 24metres, then went down to 30, which was deeper than your first dive and then you had a fast ascent. That sound right?'

'Uh-huh.'

'That means that the microbubbles that were in your blood stream from the first dive will have been compressed by going deeper. As they are smaller, the bubbles are forced into solution and they can pass around your body but then come out of solution later, making bubbles again. If one of those bubbles expanded during your ascent and got lodged in your spine, that would account for your problem.'

'But I'll get better?'

'We'll get you into the chamber now and there's every hope for improvement.'

139

Martyn noticed that the doctor did not give him a straight answer but he kept repeating her last words to himself as a mantra to keep the fear of paralysis at bay. At least they knew what it was. They seemed to know what they were doing. He was glad that they'd been diving close to Plymouth, not somewhere remote where it would have taken hours to rescue him. The doctor had said he'd had good first aid care.

He was moving again as they wheeled him out of the examination area, across a corridor and into a larger room. Martyn had a brief impression of a boiler room, but a very clean version of one, as there was a huge cylinder filling most of the space, connected to all sorts of pipes and instruments on the outside. Mick was back by his side, 'We're just putting the ramp in so that we can wheel you straight into the chamber.' There was a metallic clank as the step inside was effectively smoothed out. 'Let's get you in then.' Martyn had a brief glimpse of other staff around the corner, checking gauges and monitors as he was manoeuvred through the doorway. It seemed like quite a tight fit, but once they were through the entry compartment the chamber itself was surprisingly spacious. A tardis, he thought. They just needed some of Dr Who's magical instruments to make him well again.

Mick had closed the door and was saying, 'I'm just connecting you up to a few things, so they can monitor how you're doing on the outside. I'll be with you all the time in here. We've got an intercom so we can talk to them and they can see us on a video link. We'll be in here for seven and a half hours for this first session, so you'll probably fall asleep. You'll be more comfortable in one of these.' Mick was opening a hood and helping Martyn into it. 'This fits over your head completely and it gives you the gas that you need so you don't have to have a mask over your face.' Martyn had stopped listening. The moment Mick had said that he might fall asleep, he realised how tired he was feeling. Now that he was safely cocooned within the chamber, in the hands of experts, he could sink into their care.

★ ★ ★

Later, the other divers clustered at the control panel outside the chamber, listening intently to Dave, the chamber operator. He described the treatment that Martyn was undergoing and what would probably happen to him over the next few days.

'We think he's got an arterial gas embolism that's causing paralysis in his legs. We're giving him Co-mix thirty for seven and a half hours, so that's a mixture of helium and oxygen. The helium should replace the nitrogen that's in his body and it's a lighter gas so it dissolves in and out faster.'

'What's that on his head?' Cleo asked, gazing through the porthole to study Martyn as he lay inside the chamber.

'It's a Scott aviator bib – a built in breathing system, so he can breathe easily without bothering about a mask and tubes. We can check how he's doing from here, but Mick is in there to keep a close eye on him. Sometimes we have more than one diver or we might have some non-divers – patients from the hospital who need treatment in the chamber for one reason or another.'

'Is he going to get better?' Brian asked.

'He's got a good chance. He looks quite fit and healthy and he got to us quickly. It will be quite critical how he reacts in the next couple of days.'

'Will he need several treatments then?'

'Yes. If he's going to recover well, there should be a drastic improvement on maybe the second day. He'll be here until midnight tonight, then he'll transfer over to the hospital. In the morning he'll come back for a second session, but then he'll be on US Navy Table six. That treatment will be a bit shorter, but he might need a few of those on successive days.'

'Is that still helium & oxygen?'

'No, that's 100% oxygen, but with air breaks, otherwise continuous pure oxygen all the time would give him fits.'

'It looks a bit like an operating theatre in there,' Lynne commented as she edged closer to Cleo to gain a better view of Martyn inside.

'Do you think so? Of course we don't do anything like that. We have doctors here to check how casualties are doing but we don't do invasive procedures. Everyone has to wear that uniform though so that we know that no-one is wearing anything that might produce a fire risk.'

'Is that what that long list of things is by the door to the chamber?' Brian nodded in the direction of the entrance.

'That's right. We have a regular check list to ensure that no-one goes in there with anything dangerous on them. That can include glasses, wigs, hair gel, all sorts of things.'

'They don't sound dangerous.'

'Well, we're just making sure that people don't introduce a fire hazard into an oxygen-rich environment. Of course your mate will be fine because he didn't come in with anything.'

'There's an awful lot of dials and gauges to monitor.' Lynne was looking at the bewildering array of switches, lights and screens in front of them.

'Yes, but you get used to them once you've been trained up and you're never on your own. We need to keep a close check on how they're doing on the inside and the pressure that they're at, of course.'

'Is he asleep?' Lynne asked, continuing to watch Martyn's inert body.

'Yes, he's been asleep for a couple of hours and he'll be in there for another five or so.'

'But he's going to be OK?' Cleo said as she stared intently at the small window.

'Difficult to say at the moment. We'll probably know better tomorrow or Monday.'

Brian was standing back to look at the other bits of equipment.

'It's a good set up you've got here.'

'Yes, we think so. We can take up to twelve divers altogether in all the different chambers.' Everyone hoped fervently that they would not need their services, impressive as they were.

'Have you ever been full?' Lynne asked as she looked at the smaller two storey chamber adjacent to the one containing Martyn.

'No, but sometimes we get busy weekends. There can be times where the weather's been bad for a few weeks then everyone goes diving and someone does something silly.'

Brian thought that diving in a sub would come under that heading, but he didn't say so.

'Like what?' he asked.

'Well, recently we had a few divers who were so intent on taking pictures they forgot to check their air, so they came up too quickly when they thought they were going to run out.'

'Martyn should be OK though?' Cleo repeated.

'He's got a good chance.'

'He had a problem with his legs. Will he be paralysed?' she asked anxiously.

'We'll have to wait and see.'

'Oh.' Cleo and Lynne answered simultaneously, both saddened by Dave's answer.

'Come on. There's nothing we can do here. Let's get back and get some rest,' Brian said as he ushered the others out of the room.

★ ★ ★

Martyn was fighting for breath. Water in his eyes and mouth. Something against his head trapping him, so he couldn't get up. His legs and arms weren't working properly, but he needed to escape. Water in his mouth, coughing, how could he get out? Falling, falling, deeper. He woke with a start, gripping the bed. Where was he? Metal. Portholes. Sub? No, safe. He was safe. As his initial shock on waking subsided, he came back to reality. He looked down and tried to move his feet but no answering movement came. The pain had diminished but now he felt pressure on his bladder. He looked around for Mick.

'Need a leak.' Mick didn't hear him. Maybe this hood was soundproof. He raised an arm just as Mick turned to him.

'Need a leak,' he repeated.

'Right. I can help you with that.' Mick moved to find the right equipment. As he returned he said, 'Of course you might not be able to go in the normal way but don't worry, we can fix that for you.'

As Martyn struggled to no effect, he was horrified at the failure. To lose the use of his legs was bad enough but he hadn't thought he wouldn't be able to use a toilet (or a bottle as it was now). It was such a basic thing that you took for granted.

Mick was continuing cheerily, 'No problem. Someone'll come in and fit a catheter for you and then you'll be fine.' He relayed the request to the external supervisor and almost immediately there was the sound of the outer door opening. 'That'll be Dr Helston coming in to the air lock. She'll be put at the right pressure so that she can join us in here.'

In a very short time, Dr Helston entered the inner compartment.

'Hello Martyn. Don't worry. It's quite usual to have to do this early on. It doesn't mean that you've got worse and things can still go back to normal in time.'

Martyn nodded as he lay back. She seemed to know just the right thing to say to allay his worries before he'd uttered them. He tried to absent himself from the procedure. He didn't know whether he would prefer a male or female doctor manipulating his bits in normal circumstances, but at the moment he didn't care. He flinched as a drop of the cold lubricating jelly fell onto his stomach.

'Sorry. Won't be a minute and then you can go back to sleep.' Dr Helston smiled encouragingly and Mick wondered how often she said that with a man's penis in her hands.

CHAPTER 15

Brian woke up early on Sunday morning. He glanced across at Graham who was still snoring and decided that he was not going to get any more sleep. He might as well go for a walk down by the harbour. Although they had all been on the boat and at the hospital, he still found it difficult to accept that Tony was dead and they would never see him again. As he sat on the edge of the bed reaching for his shoes, he considered Graham and thought that his reaction in the hospital had been strange. Surely they should be pulling together, to be supportive of each other at a time like this?

He made his way downstairs and outside to look at the water. It was a calm day and would have been good for diving, but none of them would be taking the opportunity today. He sighed and ambled around the corner of the building, nearly bumping into Cleo and John as he did so.

'Oh, sorry, Cleo. Hi, John.'

'Morning, Brian. You're up and about early,' John said.

'You must have been even earlier. What time did you leave to get down here so soon?'

'It doesn't take long.' John moved further away from Cleo and Brian felt as if he had interrupted something.

'I couldn't sleep,' Cleo said, turning away from the men.

'No. Nor me, but then I had the Snoring Supremo in with me.'

★ ★ ★

'No, I'm sorry, you can't interview him now.' Dr Helston was speaking to Sergeant Fry as they stood by the hyperbaric chamber. 'He's gone in for his second treatment and it'll take nearly five hours so you'd best come back later.'

'And we'll be able to talk to him then?'

'Yes. We'll be moving him back to the hospital of course, but you'll be able to catch him either here or there. He'll be with us for a few days yet.'

'Did you take his dive computer off him?' Sergeant Fry asked.

'Yes,' Dr Helston replied. 'We needed to check the records of his dives to help us determine what might be wrong with him.'

'Of course. Can we have a copy of that and the computer itself?'

'By all means. We'll have kept it safe somewhere. I'll track it down for you. Do you want to follow me?' Sergeant Fry ignored the eager nod from PC Dixon and stepped in line behind the doctor.

Martyn was observing this exchange through a porthole. 'Who are those guys?'

Mick turned to follow his gaze. 'Oh, that's Sergeant Fry and Constable Dixon. They're always on dive-related incidents. Think they must like the water – or the overtime, one or the other.'

'The police. Why are they here?'

'It's par for the course. They investigate any sudden death. Are you feeling a bit better today?'

'Yes. The pain's not so bad now.'

'Good. Dr Helston will want to run the same series of checks on your legs when you've finished in here today. Hopefully there'll be some improvement. Do you want me to put a film on? It helps pass the time.'

'A film?'

'Yes. The Friends of the DDRC put these screens in so that you can watch something if you want. We've got *The Abyss*, *Deep Water*, *Open Water*, *Titanic* – all good classics.'

'Great choices. Anything on dry land?'

'Oh, yes. Got those too.' Mick grinned at him as Martyn suggested, 'Something with a happy ending?'

'I'll see what I can do.'

The police, Martyn thought. They would come back and interview him later. What should he say? He'd left his buddy down there, knowing he was stuck and would run out of air in due course. He'd just panicked and abandoned him. What sort of a man did that make him? What sort of a man was he going to be in future? Would Cleo want him?

★ ★ ★

Sergeant Fry checked his watch as he walked back to the car with Constable Dixon.

'Well, as we can't interview him now, we might as well see if we can meet the new Marine Liaison Officer a bit early. Then the dive boys can go and retrieve the kit, wherever it is.'

'If they find it today, that'll be handy. Then we'll know whether there was an equipment malfunction before the pathologist starts slicing the body up tomorrow,' Sean Dixon said as he unlocked the car and got into the driver's seat.

'Well, we already know from Tony's computer what his last dive profile was like. Now we've got a copy of Martyn's we can check where the two differ and when they parted company.'

'It's a bit odd for him to come up without most of his kit on, don't you think? Never heard of that before.'

'That guy – one of the divers…'

'Brian?'

'Yes, him. He said that Tony had been stuck in a wreck before and undone his jacket to slip out of it, free himself and then put it on again.'

'Do you think he'd have done that down there in the sub?'

'Stranger things happen at sea. Let's go.' Bill Fry slammed his door as Sean started the engine. 'That's another thing,' he continued. 'He should never have gone in the sub anyway. It's a war grave. The Diving Officer should have expressly forbidden any of them from going inside.'

'But the Diving Officer wasn't with them, was he?'

'No. Anyway it'll be useful to talk to his buddy, when we can get to him. I wouldn't have thought it's the sort of thing you do on the spur of the moment. You'd know it's going to be tight and dark and dangerous.'

'Wouldn't catch me down there.'

'No, but they said he liked going into dark holes. That's alright as an experienced diver if you stay with your partner, but he should never have left whatshisname on his own.'

'Martyn.' The younger policeman smiled at Bill's apparent inability to remember names. How did he cope when he was interviewing suspects? Bill continued, 'They were all pretty consistent about their description of events on the day, weren't they?'

'Yeah. Tragic accident and all that.'

'What did you reckon about the grieving widow?'

'Tasty.'

Bill Fry sighed. 'Do you have to see every woman as potential fodder for your salacious appetite?'

Sean shifted uncomfortably in his seat. 'Don't know what you mean, Sarge.'

'Never mind. I didn't like that other guy – the one who was sick and didn't go diving.'

'Can't do him for being drunk in charge of a bed though, can we?'

'Maybe it's just as well he wasn't there. Then we might have had two corpses to deal with, not one.'

'Twice as much paperwork.' Sean did not like the amount of form filling he did in his job. He preferred to be out and about or, if he had to be inside, he would rather be using a computer.

'There is that. We'll have to call by the station to check we've got budgetary approval before the dive boys go out.'

'Lucky they were on for a training session then. Maybe it won't cost as much.'

★ ★ ★

Everyone took the same places at the breakfast table as on the previous day. That meant that Tony's place was empty but they were all doing their best to ignore the vacant seat. As requests for milk, coffee and tea passed up and down the table, John appeared and made his way towards the group.

Lynne greeted him with, 'John. You must have got up early. Joining us for breakfast?'

'Don't mind if I do.' He slipped into Tony's place and there was a communal glance around the gathering, noting the fact.

'What?' he asked.

'Tony sat there yesterday,' Cleo answered.

'Oh.' John looked uncomfortable, wondering if he should get up and leave it as a mark of respect but he stayed put. 'Pass me some coffee, please,' he asked.

Brian did so as Graham finished munching on a piece of toast and raised what most people around the table were thinking,

'What have you come down here for?'

'I thought I should. It's a terrible tragedy.'

'But we're going home, soon as we're done here,' Graham said.

'If the police don't need us,' Brian added.

'Why should they want to talk to us again? We've given statements.'

'I can't believe he's gone,' Lynne said as tears sprang to her eyes again. 'It was only yesterday and we were all here. The way he looked when he came up...'

'Lynne,' Brian interrupted her, looking at Cleo.

'Oh, sorry, Cleo.'

Cleo put her hands up to her head and stared down at the table, saying nothing. There was an awkward silence as all those who had been on the boat tried not to remember Tony's appearance. Brian cleared his throat and said, 'They'll be doing a post mortem on Monday.'

'What have the police said?' asked John.

'They were a bit unhappy about Tony diving in a war grave,' Lynne answered reluctantly.

'That's right. He shouldn't have been down there,' John pointed out.

'It was his own fault for going in there,' Graham said. 'He never did have sufficient regard for safety, always going off into dark holes. This club has a good safety record and we provide excellent training. There is no way any of the rest of us would take a trainee down there and leave him on his own. We'll be lucky if Martyn doesn't sue us for negligence and it'll be down to Tony doing something stupid, just like he did in the quarry.'

'Don't call him stupid.' Cleo felt she should defend his name.

'I think he was stupid. And bad. And a dirty old man,' Graham said.

'Why did you say a 'dirty old man'?' Brian asked. 'He was only thirty-six.'

'Because of the way he looked at my Paula. Always gawping and drooling after her.'

'No, he didn't,' Lynne said. 'You're making it up. And you shouldn't speak ill of the dead. He was a good bloke, Tony. I'm sorry he's gone,' she added, stifling a sob.

'Has Paula said who the father is?' John asked.

'You don't think…?' Cleo turned from John to Graham.

'He always liked them young. Never knew why he married you. You're older; rather, you were older than him, weren't you? Did he say you were past it?'

'Graham! Stop it!' Brian tried to defend Cleo.

'Wasn't he getting any at home? Was that it?'

'I don't think this will help anyone.' Brian tried again to calm things down.

'I'm not going to cry any crocodile tears for him. Not

like her!' Graham pointed at Cleo. 'Can you honestly say you're sad he's gone?'

'I...'

'You can't, can you?' Graham accused. 'You'll be glad to be rid of him. Now you can move on to the next available male.' Cleo looked alarmed as he continued, 'I've seen the way you look at Martyn. You've got the hots for him, haven't you?'

Lynne whirled around in her seat to look at her friend. 'Have you?'

John also turned to her, repeating the question.

'Of course not. He's making it up.' Cleo took up her serviette in an attempt to hide the blush that was rising from her chest up her throat.

Lynne was still looking thunderstruck. 'Martyn? Do you like Martyn?'

Cleo was feeling attacked from all angles. She bowed her head and started rubbing her left hand with her right. 'Not like that. He's just nice, that's all.'

'More than you can say for your husband,' Graham said. 'I'm not going to be some sort of hypocrite. I'm not sorry he's dead and that's what I'll say to anyone who asks.' He got up from the table abruptly and left the room.

'I'm going to pack,' Lynne said as she got up.

Two waitresses entered, laden with plates full of cooked breakfast for everyone.

'I'll have two,' John claimed. 'One for now and one for lunch.'

'How can you?' Cleo asked.

'Easy. I've been up for hours and I'm hungry.'

'Sorry.' Cleo addressed the waitresses. 'Some of the others have gone to pack.'

'Just put them down and we'll see what we can eat.' Brian seemed keen to follow John's example.

Cleo nudged her own plate aside as she contemplated the men around her, both quietly intent on their food. Wasn't it Oscar Wilde who said that the fastest way to fall out of love with someone was to watch them eat? Bacon and beans and dribbly egg all squashed onto a large forkful. The open mouth, the bulging cheeks, the chewing, munching and swallowing. How could they? Her own throat was feeling tight and dry and not in the least desirous of food. She had struggled to keep the tears back for fear that Graham would label them false. Maybe he had a point. They were not for Tony. Were they for her, or for Rachel's loss, or for Martyn? She did not want to go up to the room and face an inquisition from Lynne about her feelings for Martyn, so she stayed put. Black pudding. She looked at it with disgust. How could they eat that? Wasn't it made with blood? Her hands were still massaging each other beneath the table and she glanced down at her ring finger. Clean. Definitely. Should she still be wearing her rings now? People did, didn't they? Even if they'd lost their husbands decades ago, the widows still wore their bands of gold. A widow. She'd have to get used to that description. Graham must be wrong about Tony and Paula though. Surely it was Tony and Rachel? He must be barking up the wrong tree there. She wished she'd said something cutting in riposte. Why didn't she ever think of an appropriate retort at the time? It was no good when the moment passed. She would constantly replay his wounding remarks, probably long after he had forgotten them himself. It was the same with Tony. Tony and Rachel. Was she wrong about that? She should ring Rachel to find out how she was this morning. What sort of a mother was she? She ought to be at home looking after her daughter, but she needed to be here for now.

Brian and John both switched plates for their second helpings. Brian thought he should make an effort to break the silence.

'So what'll happen to the business without Tony?'

Cleo jumped and Brian wished he had made some innocuous comment about the weather.

'I don't know. John?'

John finished chewing his mouthful of food before replying.

'I need to chat it through with Cleo. The immediate concern is the new equipment that was installed last week. It was needed for an order that Tony had and I've been looking for it everywhere, but can't find the paperwork. We need to know to plan production. Oh and I need to pay the contractors. Couldn't find a chequebook either,' he continued in an aside to Cleo.

Fear coursed through Cleo. Would there be enough in the account to pay the contractors? She'd had a couple of wins lately but that had not made up the deficit from earlier in the year. A string of bad choices had depleted her own funds so she'd raided the company finances again. At the time, she told herself that there was nothing wrong, she would soon recoup the losses and no one would be any the wiser.

'How much is it for?'

'Twenty-eight thousand.'

'Right.' She thought it was far from right. It was so far left it was out of sight. When would Tony's money come through? She wasn't supposed to know about it, so how could she check? There must be some papers about it at home. She'd have to get back to look, but Martyn would still be here, stuck in the chamber. She hoped he would recover fully. She wanted to cuddle him and make him better. Perhaps she should have taken more dynamic action in the tent that night.

John's knee brushed against hers beneath the table. She got up to leave. 'See you both later.'

★ ★ ★

Bill Fry and Sean Dixon were on their way to the DDRC to interview Martyn on Sunday afternoon when they got a call from the dive team. Bill put his mobile down.

'They've found the kit in the sub. Let's go to the harbour and meet them when they get back.'

'What about interviewing Martyn?'

'He'll keep. I want to see what they think about the equipment.' Sean turned the car around and headed back over the dual carriageway into the centre of Plymouth.

They did not have long to wait by the waterside before the police boat came into view. As the divers lifted Tony's equipment onto the pontoon, Sergeant Fry asked, 'Where was it?'

'At the bottom of the conning tower.'

'It must have dropped straight down then?'

'Pretty much. There's so many bits of metal sticking out, it's surprising it didn't get hooked up on something.'

'Maybe it did. That might have been the problem.'

'Guy must have been crazy to go in there at all. I'm not a big bloke, but it's unbelievably tight. Sampson here would never have got out again.'

His buddy grinned. 'I was doing cover. No need for both of us to risk getting trapped.'

'Is there anything wrong with his stuff?'

'Doesn't look like it, but we'll check it over thoroughly anyway.'

Constable Dixon said, 'All the other kit from the rest of the group is at Deep Divers over there.'

'Best keep it all together then at least we know it's been checked in the same way. That OK with you?' Sergeant Fry asked.

'Sure. Lead on.'

As they walked, Bill Fry continued, 'Some of his friends on the boat said that his kit had been leaking air on the way there, but it stopped when he knocked the regulator.'

'But he didn't change anything or switch to a different bottle?'

'No, he thought he had enough apparently.'

'Well, we'll check everything and see if whatever happened on the boat occurred again at depth. Of course there's often no way of telling what happened down there. It's not like a scene of crime up here with everything cordoned off.'

'Don't I know it,' Sergeant Fry muttered.

CHAPTER 16

Sergeant Fry gazed around the court as they waited for the coroner to appear. There were the normal officials and a bored reporter, who looked as if he'd rather be spending his Monday morning elsewhere. Bill's interest was aroused at the sight of Cleo entering the court, escorted by a man that he did not recognise. He was not one of the divers who had been down on the weekend trip, so perhaps he was the business partner. He had a confident air about him even though he must be in unfamiliar surroundings. He would check later, but he noted the way that the man put an arm around Cleo to guide her to a seat, but he did not think that she welcomed the touch. Of course she was now a widow and he was probably attractive to women. They would be impressed by that sort of rugged face, the close cropped hair, and a body untouched by middle-aged spread. Bill rested his hands on his knees as he contemplated his own growing paunch and lamented the lack of a woman in his life.

Everyone stood when the coroner entered the room. As Bill Fry had anticipated, it was all over very quickly as there was nothing much to say at the moment. The coroner officially recorded the death of one Antony Richard Fleming, explained the role of the coroner, adjourned the court pending further investigations and ordered the post-mortem. Bill moved to intercept Cleo as they made to leave.

'Oh, Sergeant Fry,' Cleo said in surprise, 'I thought the coroner's court was separate to the police.'

'It is indeed, Mrs Fleming, but we attend because our functions are related. Where they stop is often where we start, but there is some overlap.'

'Yes, it was quite interesting that they only focus on the cause of death and the four key questions: who he was, where he died, when and how,' the man commented.

'And you are...?' Bill Fry asked.

'Oh, sorry. John O'Donnell, partner to Tony in the business, friend of the family and diving officer in the club.' He smiled confidently.

'Thank you sir. Of course we're more interested in the why – why did he die?'

'But it was an accident,' Cleo answered. 'There is no why with an accident, is there?'

'That's what we need to find out. See you again, no doubt.' Bill Fry turned to leave but as he glanced back he noted that they remained looking after him, both wearing a similar frown.

★ ★ ★

It was a beautiful sunny day outside, but Francis could not see any evidence of it as he sat in his office in the Pathology department, buried deep in the bowels of the hospital. As he perused the documents before him, he had a sense of excitement that a new body would soon be ready for him in the mortuary. It was an emotion that he thought politic to keep secret, but he could not deny that he enjoyed his work. A 'fresh' corpse was like settling down in a comfortable armchair, away from phones, with what you hoped would be a completely absorbing book. He likened the investigative process of determining the cause of death to a plot, which gradually revealed itself as you went deeper into the body. He smiled as he thought that the mass of his favourite author's books on the shelves at home could be described as a 'body' of work.

He refocused his attention on the police report before him. There was a brief summary of the examination of the deceased's kit, reporting no equipment malfunction that could have precipitated the accident. There had still been air in his bottles, so it wasn't as if he'd run out, apparently. All of the statements taken from his friends confirmed the notion that it was another tragic diving incident. There was a wife too, he noted, poor woman.

Dead divers always held a particular fascination for him, because although he could identify and explain the condition of the body on the table, no one could know what the sequence of cause and effect had been in order to determine the precise reason for death. Had the person just panicked for some reason? Then there would be no obvious sign of it now, just the visible consequences of coming to the surface with uncontrolled rapidity. On the other hand, if there were evidence of a heart attack, that could have rendered the casualty unconscious at depth, subsequently causing a fast ascent with all its concurrent injuries. But it would be impossible to ascertain the actual moment that the fatality occurred – whether on the sea floor or on the way up. They could have died from coronary failure, from drowning or from the rise to the surface. His 'dry' corpses were less intriguing; sudden deaths on land were more straightforward in that it was possible to conclude that a heart attack had been fatal, given that no other extraneous factors could have intervened.

As he looked at the printout of the dive profile from Tony's computer, it confirmed the rapid ascent from 25metres. Francis noted the distance from the submarine to the surface. There was no way anyone would survive rocketing up at that rate. He turned back to the statements from Tony's friends who mentioned that he had been found without his kit. Now that was odd, although the man must have been mad to go in there in the first place. He could sometimes appreciate why divers went underwater to see tropical fish in clear, warm conditions, but why they would want to go into a cold sea, in poor visibility, to put their lives at risk entering small spaces in wrecks was incomprehensible to him. Surely he must have known it was dangerous? Still, his was not to reason why; that was up to the police.

He took a sip of tea as he turned from the written documents to his computer. He could see that there was a report from the consultant radiologist waiting in his 'in' box, but he wanted to look at the images first. He clicked on folders until he found the x-rays of Antony Fleming. He still marvelled at the efficiency of the Picture Archiving and Communication System which meant that x-rays were stored digitally and therefore easily accessible. Both the quality of the picture and the speed with which they could be referenced had radically improved over the old method where the flimsy films had to be affixed to light boards. It was so much better to be able to manipulate the image nowadays. You could zoom in on particular features or re-orientate the body. The detail was remarkable as not only bones were visible, but also the outline of flesh and the major arteries and veins.

Deciding to examine the chest first, he clicked on the file and considered it. Of course, one of the interesting facets of his work was that he did not have x-rays of the individual when alive in order to compare what differences there were when deceased. However, the evidence before him showed all the signs associated with a 'classic' diver death. Gas trapped in the body showed up as dark grey sections, compared to the white of the bone and the intermediate shades of the flesh. The heart appeared to be darker than it would have been in a healthy individual, indicating the presence of gas in both the right and left ventricles. Other organs had similar visible traces and Francis thought that the man had probably been quite distended when he was found. Sometimes they looked pregnant when they came in, which was bizarre. He moved on to inspect the head. The first image was taken from above looking down onto the face, but he moved to the second which showed a side view. Here he could easily spot the areas which had been full of liquid. The sinuses showed flat lines with meniscus, indicating fluid, rather than tissue, lying in what should have been empty spaces. He checked in the folder to see if that was the lot and discovered that there was a third area as the guys had included the pelvic region for him. Opening the image, he was rewarded with excellent examples of dark grey femoral arteries, indicating the presence of gas where there should have been only blood. This was likely to be nitrogen that had evolved in the vessels because there had been no time for it to diffuse out of the tissues and be breathed out normally.

Glancing at his watch, he scanned through the radiologist's report, noting the items that he had just identified. There did not seem to be anything remarkable about this man and his injuries. He checked the time in the bottom corner of his computer screen and then compared it to the clock overhead. Why did his three reference points for time never coincide? He was scrupulous about punctuality and needed to give himself enough margin to change into 'scrubs' for the mortuary and be ready to start at two o'clock this afternoon. He expected Sergeant Fry would make an appearance as it was normally his duty to attend such events. If the observers were interested in his work he was happy to explain things to them, but he could not abide those who averted their eyes or who were likely to vomit on his pristine floor. Inspector Jamieson had suffered that ignominy once before when Francis had been eviscerating a body that had been washing about in the sea for weeks. Admittedly it had not been a pretty sight or smell, but usually the air conditioning was quite efficient in removing unpleasant odours. Ever since then it had been Bill Fry who had been delegated to attend.

With a few more mouthfuls he finished the tea, gathered the papers together and made his way to the mortuary. He knew that his staff would be checking all the equipment he, and they, would need. He expected that Rob would be nervous as he was going to perform his first incision into the chest cavity today. Of course, he had watched the procedure many times before and Francis would be supervising closely, but it was still different having to do it oneself, under the critical eyes of colleagues and police personnel. He would do well though; he had the right attitude and worked hard to learn their trade. Francis went through the staff entrance to the mortuary where there were changing facilities and showers. The police would enter from the other side and would wear gowns over their normal clothes and covers on their shoes in order to prevent any cross-contamination with the deceased. It was also a form of self protection as no one wanted to be infected with any blood-borne diseases. Francis changed quickly, removing his trademark bow tie and waistcoat, before folding everything neatly into his locker. He checked the time again to ensure that he was early, and then entered his arena.

He greeted Bill Fry and the police photographer who were standing just outside the official 'viewing area'. Although you could see the table and the waiting body from there, it was no practical use for a close examination. If Francis wanted to draw attention to some particular feature, he needed them both to be by his side. With first-time observers he knew instantly how well they were going to survive the experience according to how near they got to the corpse. Those who were concerned about losing their lunch tended to hang well back in case they had to make a rapid exit. Both Bill and the photographer were inured to the process now.

'All set, Rob? Cath?' Francis asked. Rob was the 'wet' assistant so once he had touched the body he would stay by it, so that he would not spread any matter around the mortuary. Cath had the 'dry' role today; she would hand any equipment required to either Rob or Francis. The bodies for examination were stored adjacent to the operating area, so it was easy for Rob and Cath to remove Tony from his cool storage and place him on the shining silver surface. To Francis the array of drawers was reminiscent of a bank of safety deposit boxes. Each one held a secret known only to its owner, until it was opened up to reveal the mysteries inside. Their currency was disease and abnormality and Francis relished the prospect of exchanging the unknown for the known. He did not have to rely on the patient's version of events and he did not need to cultivate a bedside manner in order to comfort them and extract the relevant information regarding symptoms. It was so much better for him to have the intellectual challenge of piecing together the factual evidence in order to arrive at the cause of death.

The blackboard affixed to the end of each container proclaimed the identity of the body within; the name chalked on the board presaging the gravestone to come. They were almost full at the moment, as most of the slates were labelled. Some 'customers' had been examined and were being stored; others were awaiting the attentions of Francis or his colleague.

He glanced around at the gleaming surfaces. All was set. The corpse lay supine on the table in the middle of the room. He did not cover the whole area so the drainage shelves beneath him were visible. Holes in the surface allowed any body fluids to drain through, but any small fragments would be caught and sent for analysis, if required. Francis picked up his dictaphone and approached Tony, detailing his name, the date and a brief resume of how he had been found. His eye was immediately drawn to the bruising around one wrist, but he wanted to savour the excitement that stirred within him as this had the prospect of being the 'treat' on Tony's body. He scanned the rest of the remains, noting the slight distension of the stomach. This had probably subsided from the condition when he was found on the surface, when the gas inside would have given him a bloated appearance. There was dried blood on his chin and neck which had hardened into miniature peaks and crags. Francis assumed that this was a consequence of a rapid ascent to the surface and anticipated finding major disruption to the lungs when the chest was opened up. As he made his way methodically around the table, he was gratified to see bruising also on the other wrist, but he did not voice his thoughts aloud just yet. He checked the head closely and discovered that the eyes looked a little bloodshot. The man may have had some experience of mask squeeze if there was insufficient air in his mask, and this would have had a detrimental effect on his eyes. He beckoned Bill Fry as he raised Tony's right arm for a closer inspection.

'Look at this. Bruising. That's interesting.'

'Why?' Bill asked, bored. He had been through many of these examinations before and just wanted Francis to get to the point so that he could return to the office and wrap this one up.

'It's unusual to see marks like this on a diver. Normally their suit acts like a cushion to protect them from bumps. An impact that would create a bruise on dry land would not have the same effect underwater.'

'So?'

'The only place on a suit where the insulation is less and the fabric thinner is around the wrists. That's why there is discolouration here and here.' Francis had walked around to the far side to pick up the other arm.

'Yes, but his mates hauled him over the side of the boat in order to get him on board. He should have marks all over him.'

'Ah, no. This bruising means that it happened before death, when the blood was still being pumped around the body.'

'Right.' Sergeant Fry was annoyed with himself. He had attended enough of these to know about the differences between bruises before death and afterwards. He really should concentrate.

'But maybe his buddy tried to pull him free. The others said in their statements that this guy was stuck down there.'

'OK.' Francis put his dictaphone down on a nearby table. 'Imagine I'm stuck in a narrow aperture in a submarine. I'm putting my arms up to you for help. What do you do?'

Bill hated these sorts of role-play re-enactments. He sometimes thought that Francis must have had some frustrated ambition to be on the stage. With his hands firmly buried in his pockets, he replied, 'I'd get hold of you and pull you out, obviously.'

'Not good enough, Sergeant. Show me.'

Reluctantly, Bill removed his meaty paws from the warmth of his trousers and clasped the fine-boned wrists of the pathologist.

'Excellent. Ryan, take a photo.'

Bill let go rapidly, as if the skin were corrosive. He could imagine the comments going round the station if pictures of him holding hands with Francis were circulated.

'Don't be childish,' Francis chided. 'I'm just trying to illustrate the bruising pattern that would result.' Bill resumed the position and Ryan duly clicked his camera, but could not conceal a faint smirk as he registered the sergeant's discomfort.

'Now, your hands are on top of mine, with the thumb and fingers closing beneath my wrist, so the pressure points are on the underside.' He detached one hand in order to indicate his point on the other, which was still firmly grasped by Bill. 'That is where the bruising should be, if it had occurred in that way. Now, pin me against the wall.'

Bill looked truly aghast. It was going from bad to worse.

'I mean, hold my wrists as if you were pushing me against something, to prevent me from moving.'

Ryan was now displaying a wide grin as he waited for Bill to assume the position. Bill hesitated, not knowing if Francis wanted to be held with his back to the hypothetical wall or his face to it. Neither prospect filled him with enthusiasm.

'Come on, man. Like this.'

Francis picked up Bill's wrists which had been dangling loosely at his sides and held them up near his shoulders. He released one again in order to explain.

'You see. Now I'm holding your hand from the underside with my thumb and fingers clasped on top of your wrist, so the pressure points and the damage would be there.'

'Now,' he turned back to Tony and Bill hoped that his duties as a mannequin were over. 'You see these marks here are on the top side, as if he had been restrained.'

Bill was trying to focus his attention on the bruises as he rubbed his arms, attempting to erase the memory of Francis' touch unobtrusively.

'He was held?' he queried.

'I believe so.'

Bill's mind was turning this information over slowly. 'But what would that mean?'

'Well, we know that this diver came up without most of his kit. If he was somehow separated from his equipment and kept away from it so he couldn't breathe, he would die.'

Bill thought that Francis was letting his imagination run away with him.

'But why? And who else is going to be mad enough to go down into the sub with him?'

'I have no idea.'

Bill considered the scenario that Francis had outlined.

'It would be terribly difficult to separate a man from his kit without his co-operation and who's going to agree to that?'

'It's just a hypothesis.'

'You don't think it was an accident?'

'I can't tell you that. All I can report on is the evidence before my eyes.'

'But if it was murder, I need to get the boss.'

'Yes. I'm sure Inspector Jamieson will be delighted to attend.'

Bill wondered if Ian Jamieson would be delighted to participate in the same demonstration that he had just endured. He thought not.

'I'll have to call him. I expect he'll want to come and see for himself.'

'By all means. I'll carry on though, so we can go over the highlights when he gets here.' Francis was pulling on surgical gloves as he prepared to investigate the body. He always used two pairs for extra protection.

Bill went to the office in the designated viewing area in order to call the station. He returned quickly. 'He'll be here in the next hour or so.'

CHAPTER 17

As Rob inspected the equipment in preparation for cutting into the body, Cath handed the face visors around to everyone else.

'Remember, this is a diving casualty,' Francis told him, 'so you're going to have to go especially carefully once you're through the ribs. There's likely to be bits of lung everywhere.'

Rob took a deep breath and made the first cut through the skin which produced a dark red line widening into a gash as the edges were pulled apart. He used what looked like long handled pruning shears to penetrate the sternum and, as he withdrew the tool, a fragment of tissue splattered onto Bill Fry's visor. He recoiled as if struck by a spitting cobra, but tried to camouflage the movement by reaching for a handkerchief. He only succeeded in transforming the moist lump into a brownish smear, so he persevered with blurred vision until the chest cavity was fully exposed.

Francis leant inside and commented on the extent of the damage to the lungs as the camera flashed to record the evidence from several angles.

'Well, let's see how much we can salvage.' Francis reached into the body again to remove the lungs. Some blood clots slid down from the oesophagus once the trachea had been cut. Rather than coming away intact as in most previous cases, it was necessary to make a number of forays to retrieve particles of tissue that had apparently been blasted onto other organs. Happy in his work, Francis drew attention to the portion of lung he had just extracted, as it retained an impression of the ribs which it had pressed against. He explained that the volume of gas would have expanded on ascent due to the decrease in pressure as the body got closer to the surface. This would have caused the tissue to rupture as the gas could not be released through exhaling.

He likened it to a balloon full of air at the surface, being squeezed to a smaller volume by the pressure at depth. At 20metres down the balloon would be a third of its size and at 30metres a quarter of its size. If the balloon were then returned to the surface, it would regain the original volume. However, if the capacity of gas expanded beyond the size of the balloon, then it would burst. This was in effect what had happened to Tony, causing 'burst lung'. Although the analogy of the balloon was a useful explanatory tool for Francis, he knew that in reality the lungs were more like a whole series of very tiny balloons all strapped into one big bag, so there were lots of small 'bursts' within the complete organ. In normal circumstances, divers did not experience this problem, because their regulators maintained the right pressure for the air that they breathed at depth, preventing the lungs from being compressed. As long as divers continued breathing in and out normally on ascent they would not have any trouble, but it was why it was an essential rule that they never hold their breath on the way up. Although this was not new information to his listeners, Francis had a habit of providing a running commentary, which was useful on those occasions when he had less experienced ears paying attention. He liked to display his knowledge to those less well informed than himself.

Once Francis felt that the entire organ had been collected, he nodded to Cath who took it away to be weighed. She then recorded the result on a white board at the side of the mortuary. Francis checked the figures.

'Yes, definitely heavier than it would have been on dry land, because it's waterlogged.' They continued to remove each major organ in turn, with Rob assisting and Cath weighing and recording. Bill Fry was glad of the efficient air conditioning which took away any noxious smells from the mortuary. Although he prided himself on having a strong stomach and the gory sight did not affect him, sometimes the stench of decaying flesh at a murder scene could make him swallow hard and wish desperately for fresher air.

As they moved on to the stomach, Francis commented that it too contained water, which would be consistent with drowning. The heart was gently extracted, weighed and stored, awaiting further more detailed examination later. Cath had placed the shears and the visors in one of the sinks for subsequent cleaning. It was part of her work to clear up after the post-mortem, ensuring that each tool was returned to its appropriate place, pristine once again. There was something satisfying about being able to clean the trays, hose the table down and mop the floor so that the mortuary was absolutely clear of all traces of one corpse before the next customer arrived. Dealing with the dead bodies was not an issue for her, but she dreaded coming into contact with the bereaved relatives. Although one of her tasks included the preparation of the corpse for the relatives' room, she was glad that she did not have to be present when distraught family members viewed their parent, son or daughter.

'Right. We need to address the head next and then examine the brain. We might find some haemorrhaging or perhaps some air in the cerebral arteries. We should also check for damage to the middle and inner ear.'

Although Francis had delegated the chest cavity to Rob, he wanted to keep the honour of the head for himself. He examined the neck carefully for any injuries and then slit the skin, peeling it backwards to reveal the facial bones. Cath handed him a small saw to cut a circular hole in the top of the skull and as he prised the top half off it gave the customary 'pop' when the seal was broken. Bill Fry could not help but flinch at the sound every time he heard it.

The atmosphere of quiet concentration was suddenly broken by the arrival of Inspector Jamieson, who entered the mortuary hurriedly.

'Ah, good afternoon, Inspector. Glad you could join us.'

'Francis. What have you got?' Ian Jamieson replied, nodding to his colleagues. He approached the group gathered around the table, intent on the brightly-lit body and its constituent elements.

'We've got some very interesting bruising on both wrists. Here.' Francis indicated to entice the Inspector closer to the corpse.

'What have you done to him?' Inspector Jamieson asked angrily as soon as he saw the state of the body. Francis did not answer as he thought it was obvious.

'You shouldn't have carried on with the post-mortem. As soon as you thought there was a possibility of murder you should have stopped and waited for the Home Office pathologist to take over. You should never have gone on like this. Have you taken leave of your senses?'

Francis was severely embarrassed at being told off in front of his junior staff. 'No, I…'

'And what were you thinking of?' The Inspector turned on Sergeant Fry. 'You've seen enough of these to know the procedure. What the hell's the matter with you? What were you thinking? Or were you not thinking at all?'

Bill Fry could not answer so no one broke the uncomfortable silence. 'This is disastrous,' Ian Jamieson continued, blaming himself for not spelling it out to Bill, but he had thought it was so obvious there was no need to do so. 'If there's a chance it's murder, then we have to get the forensic pathologist to come and do another examination.' He realised that the expense of bringing the second medical expert in would make a substantial hole in his budget, but it had to be done. He sighed heavily, thinking that he would get it in the neck from the Assistant Chief Constable for this lapse in protocol. 'But as we're here and you've got this far, you'd better tell me what you've found out.'

Francis shrugged his shoulders as if to dislodge the criticism and re-assert his authority.

'The bruising on the wrists, here and here.' As the Inspector attempted to circumnavigate the table whilst averting his eyes from the dismantled person before him, Bill Fry noted the discomfort of his senior officer. He hoped that Francis would re-enact his explanation of the possible causes of the marks, whilst using Ian as the dummy this time.

'How did he die?' the Inspector asked. He concentrated on Francis' face so that his eyes would not be drawn to the bloody scene on his right. It was an occupational hazard to come across gruesome remains, and he had tried to steel himself to withstand them better over time, but he still preferred to read a post-mortem report than to see it first-hand. It was different with a crime scene. Then he had to attend in order to understand the context, but here he could rely on Francis' expertise.

'It's most likely he drowned,' the pathologist replied.

'You don't know for sure?'

'He has some of the signs of drowning, but we won't know if that was the cause of death until we examine all the other possibilities.'

'Such as?' Ian Jamieson queried.

'The heart, for example. We need to check for any indication of coronary disease that might have precipitated a heart attack.' Francis pointed towards the orphaned organs lying on a counter nearby, which he would explore at a later stage of his investigation.

'So what's the importance of the wrists?'

'That's for you to find out. I am merely drawing them to your attention.'

The Inspector sighed heavily, awaiting further explanation, so Francis decided to continue, 'As I explained to Sergeant Fry, the pattern of bruising suggests that his hands were held like this.' He grasped one of his own arms with the other in order to illustrate the point. 'With the fingers clasped on the top.' Bill Fry watched this with a sense of disappointment, which quickly transformed into alarm. Why hadn't Francis gone through the same pantomime, manipulating the arms of the Inspector? If he could demonstrate the idea just as well using his own body, why had he used Bill? The notion that Francis had just wanted to touch him made him distinctly uncomfortable and he shifted from foot to foot.

'But his buddy had tried to pull him out, hadn't he?'

'Indeed. Then it's more likely the marks would have been on the underside like this.' Ian Jamieson studied the demonstration whilst considering the possibilities.

'Or his mates on the boat could have made marks when they hauled him in.'

'Yes, but as I explained to the Sergeant here, these injuries happened before death, not afterwards.'

'And he would have been dead when he was on the surface?'

'Oh yes. Of course it's impossible to tell precisely when he died. However, we have got the dive profile from his computer, so I would think he was probably dead before rocketing upwards. If he'd been alive and conscious he would have made every effort to avoid doing that, so you just need to check the record of his depth against the time.'

'The dive profile,' Ian repeated. 'We'll need an expert to interpret that data for us. Bill?'

'Sir. PC Dixon can do that for us. He's familiar with the technology.'

'Good.' Ian returned to Francis. 'So, we've possibly got something odd happening in the sub resulting in a suspicious death. You think it's murder?'

It was more of a statement than a question, but Francis chose to answer it evasively.

'I am merely reporting on the evidence and alerting you to the possibilities.' Francis decided to stay on the side of caution, given the Inspector's criticism of his actions earlier.

'Right. I've seen enough. Bill?' As he walked towards the doorway, Bill Fry followed and the others closed ranks over the body.

'Do you think he's got something there?' Ian asked as he removed his gown, folded it up neatly and placed it in the waiting bucket. Bill threw his bundle of cloth in the same direction as he answered. 'Maybe. I don't know.' He leant on the wall so that his weight did not cause him to overbalance as he stood on one leg to remove a shoe cover. Ian wondered if Bill was ever concerned about his own mortality after such close contact with a corpse. Personally, he made a resolution to live more healthily whenever confronted by sudden death, but Bill's increasing waistline suggested that he was untroubled by such concerns.

Dismissing these thoughts, Ian continued, 'Well, we'll have to act on the belief that it's murder. You call up the other pathologist and then we'll have a second opinion. I'll have to tell the Chief so we can get the budget and resources in place. You gather us a team and make sure that we've got PC Dixon, and a WPC and whoever else we need to manage the HOLMES database.'

'Yes sir.' Bill had already mentally assigned Sean Dixon to the role of managing HOLMES. He knew that he had an aversion to paperwork but a positive love of computers. The Home Office Large Major Enquiry System had revolutionised the way police forces managed intelligence. It enabled them to assimilate a database of evidence, statements, technical reports, and forensic data which, supplemented with its analytical software, greatly improved the organisation of information gathered during a serious crime investigation. The advantage with Sean was also that his experience with other diving incidents would mean that he would be able to interpret the data from the dive computers. There was bound to be appropriate software that Sean would either have access to or be able to obtain in order to do this.

Ian was continuing, 'We'll hold the briefing at,' he glanced at his wristwatch, 'six pm. We need to find out more about this guy, his family and friends. What do you know of them?' They left the Pathology department and mounted the stairs, leading them back to the province of the living.

'Seemed like a regular chap. Nothing odd about the grieving wife, she was distressed, as expected. He's got a number of mates that he was diving with, they're all a bit shocked.'

'We have to dig deeper. If it is murder, there will be a reason. Money or sex, it always comes down to those two.'

Bill privately wished he had more of both.

Ian continued, 'If something fishy did happen underwater,' Bill glanced at him to see if the pun was intentional and noted the hint of a smile, 'then we need to start with the buddy. What's his name?'

'Martyn Share, sir. He'll either be at the DDRC or in here somewhere in a ward upstairs.'

'Find out where so we'll be able to track him down later.'

* * *

The diver woke suddenly in his bed. It was only afternoon and he wished he had stayed awake, rather than let his eyes close and drop him back into torment. It was the same nightmare he had experienced on the previous two nights. He was fighting for breath, frightened of doing the wrong thing and terrified of being killed. He shook himself and rubbed his chest which was wet with sweat. He tried to remove the image from his mind and focus on the room before him, but he felt he could still see the eyes, imploring him for help.

* * *

Bill gathered the team for the briefing and checked that everyone was in attendance. He had PC Sean Dixon for the HOLMES database, PC Enson to assist him, WPC Wright if they needed to interview women and PC Close was floating on general duties. He felt that he had done well to summon all these personnel at short notice. Of course there was no guarantee that they could keep everyone on the investigation. It would depend on other claims on their time, but it was important that they started together. Inspector Jamieson entered the room and greeted them with, 'Right then, listen up. Sergeant Fry is going to take us through the known facts about the murder victim, Anthony Richard Fleming, his family and associates.'

Bill Fry turned to point to a photo of Tony on the board behind him.

'This is the guy. Up until Saturday morning he was alive and well, enjoying a diving expedition with his mates. They had come down from the Forest of Dean for the weekend. During his last dive something went wrong, possibly at the hands of his murderer and he was dead when he got to the surface.'

'Only possibly, Sarge?'

'Yes. He had some curious bruise marks on his wrists and, although he could have been held, we don't know when that took place or if it contributed to his death. If he were prevented from using his breathing apparatus, then we'll have a murder on our hands. We'll be getting another report from the Home Office Pathologist in due course.'

Bill continued, 'He leaves a wife, Cleo, and step-daughter,' he referred to his notes, 'Rachel. He also had a business partner, John O'Donnell and although he is a diver he wasn't on this particular trip. Those who were on this weekend away were all members of the diving club, so we have Brian Phelps, the treasurer; Graham Bright, the boating officer; Lynne Beckett, the secretary; Martyn Share, who's the guy that was injured. On Saturday night we were working on the belief that the death was accidental, so all of the people who had been on the boat were interviewed and provided brief statements.'

'And Graham Bright, who wasn't on the boat.' Constable Dixon added.

'Oh yes. He was too drunk to go out due to over indulging on the Friday night. However, he was only too happy to tell us what he thought of the deceased – which is not much, as he had him down as a dirty old man, likely to defile his daughter.' He turned to address the comment muttered at the side of the room. 'Thank you, Close, for putting that a little more graphically.'

Inspector Jamieson got to his feet to address the gathering. 'The consensus from those statements was that it was a tragic accident. What we want to do now is check for motives. Who might want to get rid of Tony Fleming? Who would gain by his death? Who might be lying? The lines of enquiry will therefore be based around his relationships and contacts, family, friends and business. The prime suspects will be the members of the dive club who were present at the scene. Sergeant Fry and I will need to go back over each statement and interview that person again, once we have any queries or discrepancies that we want to clarify. PC Dixon will be managing the HOLMES database and I believe he has already started entering those preliminary statements into the system?' Sean Dixon confirmed this with a brief nod. 'PC Enson will be assisting him so make sure whatever data you gather in the course of your enquiries gets fed back to one of them and they will enter it in the appropriate way. Sergeant Fry here has the allocated tasks detailing who should do what. Any questions?'

PC Enson spoke up. 'Guv, are they all still here or have they gone back to wherever?'

'Good question.' Ian turned to Bill to answer it.

'Some of them are here and some have left. The wife, the business partner and the injured guy are around but everyone else has gone home.'

'Who's going on a jolly then?' PC Enson enquired hopefully.

'It will certainly not be a jolly,' Inspector Jamieson asserted his authority, 'but it is possible that some enquiries will take us up to Gloucestershire. However, there's plenty of checking that we can do from here first. We need to find out about the man's finances, his business and his family. Right, that's all for now. Let's get to it.'

★ ★ ★

Mick greeted Martyn cheerfully as he came into the ward,

'Hey, look at you. I have one day off and you're transformed.'

Martyn smiled in response. 'Yes, this is so much better. Now I'm standing I can look down at you, rather than up.'

'Careful, careful. I can always kick your stick away, you know.'

Martyn sat down on the bed as he asked, 'What are you doing here?'

'I'm on my way into work, so I thought I'd just call by and bring you some reading matter.' He put *Jaws* down on the chest of drawers next to the bed. 'You said you'd be bored.'

'Thanks.' Martyn glanced at the cover. 'Great choice,' he added sarcastically. 'Dr Helston said I might be able to do without the stick in another couple of days.'

'She's happy with your recovery then? Did she give you an 'A' grade for improvement?'

'Better than that. She did all the testing with various objects, blunt ones, sharp ones; she stroked me gently, tapped me with a tuning fork and tested my reflexes. I got four out of five so I graduated from the walking frame to this.' He waved the stick about. 'It's amazing to get my legs back again.'

'I can tell.'

'It's great knowing that I'm not going to be confined to a wheelchair and that everything works, you know.' He nodded downwards.

'Catheter gone?' Mick asked, following the direction of his glance.

'Yep. Can do it all by myself again now. Tomorrow I've got physiotherapy and another session in the chamber.'

'Back in my tender care. You've probably made a rapid recovery because of the excellent attendant you had.'

'Dr Helston says it's because I had very good early treatment, so I should get back to one hundred percent. The only thing I haven't done yet is to pass that test where you have to stand with both feet together, with your hands out and your eyes closed.'

'The Rhomberg position?'

'Think so. That's another thing I have to do before she'll be satisfied that I'm better.'

'Maybe you'll be able to do it tomorrow.'

'Hmmm.'

'So you should be dancing around these beds then – now you've got your legs back and all?'

Martyn hesitated. 'Yes, but I can't help thinking that Tony's not able to leap around the ward.'

Mick leaned against the bed as Martyn gazed down, studying his feet.

'You can't blame yourself for his death. It wasn't your fault. Just a terrible accident, that's all.'

'It was me down there with him. Me that left him.'

Mick knew how important it was to keep a positive view on things.

'But you tried to help him. You told me you did. You couldn't do any more.' Receiving no answer, Mick prompted, 'Could you?'

'I don't know. Maybe if I was a better diver, I could have done something. I shouldn't have panicked like that.'

'But you're a novice. You're not an expert. You couldn't be expected to know everything. Sounds to me like he was doing the wrong thing, being there in the first place and taking you with him. No-one else could have done anything differently, could they?'

'The others blame me.'

'How do you make that out?'

'No-one's come to see me. They must think it's my fault.'

'You're wrong there. They all came to see you Saturday night, but you were out of it.'

183

'It's still my fault.'

'No, it's not. It's…' Mick was interrupted by the arrival of the two policemen.

'Evening, Mr Share. I'm Sergeant Fry and this is Detective Inspector Jamieson.' He looked pointedly at Mick.

'Right, I'd best be off. See you tomorrow then, Martyn.'

'Yeah.'

Both men focused their attention on Martyn and Ian Jamieson began, 'We have reason to believe that Tony Fleming was murdered.'

Martyn nodded slowly. 'It was me. I killed him.'

CHAPTER 18

'Mum, when are you coming home?'

'I don't know yet, Rachel. Soon I hope.'

'But the place is empty and it's creeping me out.'

'You're back at our house then?' Cleo asked.

'I couldn't stay round at Paula's any longer. She's acting weird and when Graham arrived I really didn't want to be there. Why can't you come?'

'There are things I've got to sort out with... with the funeral.' Cleo was stalling for time. Her maternal instincts were screaming at her to go home and look after her daughter, but she did not want to abandon Martyn. She knew that as a recent widow she should not visit him in hospital but if she had to return to the Forest for Rachel she could not go without seeing him. She wanted to know how well he was, but more importantly she needed to know how he felt about her, given everything that had happened. She knew that it would be some time before they could arrange the funeral, but she needed to give Rachel a reason for the delay. Sergeant Fry had told her a bit about the inquest process and the investigations and reports that would have to be completed with a diving accident. She hadn't been able to think how to describe it to Rachel, without using the word 'body' and she did not want to send her daughter off into another bout of crying. Cleo thought that she sounded reasonably alright at the moment.

There was a sob at the end of the line. 'Please come home, Mum.'

'OK, Rach. I'll be there in a few hours. Go and have a hot chocolate and that'll make you feel better.'

★ ★ ★

John sat in the interview room, wondering how long they would keep him waiting. He had asked the silent PC Dixon but gained no answer and the man now stood like a waxwork, stolidly staring into the middle distance. John was leaning back in his chair, hands in his pockets with his long legs stretched out before him, crossed at the ankles. This relaxed posture belied the fact that his mind was racing, wondering why they had called him in, what they would ask and how he could best engineer his answers to meet his objectives rather than theirs.

The door opened and three men entered. The first spoke, introducing each of them.

'I'm Inspector Jamieson and I believe you already know Sergeant Fry here.' John nodded to the other man. 'This is Mr Hewlett, the duty solicitor, so we'll leave the two of you to get acquainted for a while and then we'll be back.'

John had rapidly uncrossed his legs and sat forward.

'What? Wait a minute. Why do I need a solicitor?'

'We have reason to believe that Tony Fleming was murdered and therefore…'

'Murder? How could it be? I thought he died on a dive. It was an accident, surely?' John looked very surprised.

'You should talk to Mr Hewlett here. We'll be back.'

'But… no offence to Mr Hewlett, but don't I need my own solicitor?'

'Have you got one trained in criminal law?' Inspector Jamieson asked.

'I don't know, he does wills and stuff. But I haven't committed a crime.'

'There's no need to worry then, is there?' the inspector countered. 'Mr Hewlett is here to advise you and he has to be present before we can interview you. All solicitors would follow the same procedure at this point.'

Whilst John was wondering what 'at this point' might mean, all of the policemen left, leaving James Hewlett to sit down opposite John.

By the time they returned, the solicitor was sitting alongside his new client. John had been convinced by the reasoning that it was better to have a professional who knew the police and the coroner in the area and understood the procedures of investigating a diving death. It had also occurred to him that hauling old Murmur down from Gloucestershire would cost a lot at his hourly rate and provide no tangible advantage. Besides, it had been an accident. He had nothing to worry about.

Inspector Jamieson and Sergeant Fry took their places across the table and PC Dixon resumed his position by the door. Sergeant Fry conducted the formalities of detailing who was present, cautioning John on what he was about to say after pressing the 'record' button on the tape recorder.

'As I said, we have reason to believe that Tony Fleming was murdered.'

'But he died on a dive,' John protested.

'He did, yes, but there are some unusual circumstances.'

'What unusual circumstances?' John asked.

'I'm not at liberty to divulge that information.'

John looked blank. 'But if you can't tell me, how can I help?'

'We need information about the events leading up to the incident.'

'But I wasn't here at the weekend. I was working, not diving.'

'And what work do you do?'

John relaxed again. 'I'm Tony's... I was Tony's partner in business. We run a factory designing and manufacturing miniature cars that we sell all over the world.'

'How is it going?' the Inspector pursued.

'The business? It's fine.'

'And your relationship with Tony?'

'That's fine, too. I didn't have a motive to kill him, if that's what you're thinking.' Inspector Jamieson did not respond. He waited. 'Well, in any business partnership there are arguments. Just minor things.'

'What were those about, sir?' prompted Bill Fry.

'I thought he was spending too much time away from the factory. He said he was tinkering around in the workshop coming up with a new design.'

'And was he?' the Inspector resumed.

'Not that I saw. I don't know what he was doing. He could have been anywhere for all I know.'

'So you had concerns about him pulling his weight. Were there any money issues?'

'Not really. We had the normal sort of waves of orders and some fluctuations in cash flow, but nothing to worry about. Cleo does the accounting for the company, so you'd better ask her if you want to know any details.'

'Cleo. That's the wife?' John nodded. 'A happy marriage, would you say?'

John looked uncomfortable. The clock ticked steadily on the wall. 'It's not for me to say.' He looked to his solicitor for guidance but he said nothing.

'This is a murder enquiry, sir. Please answer the question.' Inspector Jamieson did not feel inclined to tiptoe around social niceties.

'They sometimes seemed happy when they were out.'

'But?' John had started picking at the cotton on his jacket. There was a fine thread dangling from a seam and he helped it unravel a little more.

'You should talk to Graham,' he suggested.

'Graham?' The inspector looked to Bill Fry with a raised eyebrow.

'The one that was sick, guv. He didn't go on the boat.'

'So why should we talk to him?'

John sighed and appeared reluctant to continue. 'Go on,' the inspector urged.

'I don't know if there's any truth in it, but he thinks that Tony got his teenage daughter up the duff.'

'So there's no love lost there then?'

John shook his head so the inspector continued, 'And would Graham want to do some damage to Tony?'

'He did do some serious damage to a guy years ago, but that was about Elaine.' John shifted in his chair. 'This thing now, it's just talk… probably.'

'Probably he got into a fight or probably it's just rumour?'

'Either. Both. I'm not sure.'

'Do you think it's true about Tony and the daughter?'

'I don't know. Tony always fancied young girls – but

who wouldn't?' John raised his hands disarmingly.

'If he were playing away from home, how would the wife feel about that?'

'Cleo? Hurt, I think. Up until...' John stopped and looked as if he was struggling with something.

'You were saying 'up until...' Up until what?' the inspector asked.

'It's nothing. I shouldn't have said anything.'

'But now that you have…?' the policeman prompted.

'The new guy, Martyn. He's been sniffing around her, that's all.'

'Anything serious, do you think?'

'Not on her part. I expect she's flattered. A young blood like that.'

'What do you know about him?' As Ian Jamieson asked the question, Bill Fry wondered if he was going to divulge the fact that Martyn had just confessed to the murder or whether he would keep it up his sleeve for now. Personally he had been delighted by the result. It solved things in record time, they could put this one to bed and he could retire to his own after a couple of well-earned pints in The George. Sadly, Ian had not accepted Martyn's story at face value and wanted to investigate further. What was the matter with the man? Maybe he hadn't had enough years on the force to know that he should accept a gift horse gracefully, without checking its teeth.

'I don't know much about him really. He's a plumber, moved into our area. We happened to meet him one weekend and he was interested in learning more about diving, so he came along to the club. He seems like a nice enough guy, but you never know, do you?'

'Capable of murder, do you think?'

'We're probably all capable of murder, given the right incentive, don't you think?' John replied, smiling.

'That would send the crime statistics rocketing,' Bill commented.

The Inspector cast him a look which made him wish he hadn't spoken.

'Do you think Martyn did it?' John asked.

'We're pursuing a number of enquiries. Do you know anything about any altercation that Tony might have had last Saturday morning?'

'No, like I said, I was working at the factory. I wasn't down here.'

'Is there anyone who could corroborate that?'

'Sure. Jim, the caretaker, he saw me there.'

'Thank you for your help. Mr O'Donnell.'

'Does that mean I can go?'

'You can, yes. We have your details if we want to contact you again.' The inspector looked to his sergeant for confirmation of that fact and received a nod in response. 'Will you be staying in Plymouth or returning home?'

'Probably going back soon.'

'We may need to come up there and interview some of the others in the club, so we might see you again.'

'I'll look forward to it,' John replied. He got up and shook hands with James Hewlett, thanking him for all his help with a tinge of sarcasm in his voice.

As the policemen walked back to their office, Ian asked Bill what he thought of their interviewee.

'Wouldn't want to buy a used car off him.'

'Hmmm. I thought he was a bit rattled at the start when we mentioned murder.'

'Yeah. He recovered well though. He's probably charming to women, but I wonder if he's a bit dodgy underneath.'

'Yes. I had the feeling he was just feeding us bits of information,' Ian agreed. 'I don't like that. I want to know everything he knows, not only the things he sees fit to tell us.' He turned to the constable following behind them. 'Sean, bring Mrs Fleming in to see us would you? Then we can get her view of things,' he continued as he turned back to Bill.

★ ★ ★

'Hi. How was your day?' Elaine asked Graham as he came through the back door into the kitchen.

'Quite exciting really. Everyone wanted to know what had happened to Tony.' Elaine was stirring a large pot of bolognaise on the cooker, but she stopped abruptly.

'How did they know anything had happened to him?'

'I told them, of course. It might have been on the news, but I think it's more likely to be in the South West region rather than Points West, so maybe not.'

'What do you mean, "You told them"? You weren't even there. You mean you gave them your version of events?'

'I may not have been on the boat itself, but the others told me the details. And I left them in no doubt what sort of man he was.'

'You didn't... Did you...?' Elaine hesitated because she could not ask how indiscreet Graham had been whilst Paula was in earshot.

'Dad?' Paula walked into the kitchen, having heard part of the conversation from the lounge.

'Hey, princess. You're looking more beautiful every day.'

'What did you say, Dad?' Paula asked. 'You didn't mention me?'

'No, I didn't mention you.' Graham was hastily re-running his various conversations in his head. He had made general accusations about Tony's depravity and inappropriate behaviour and stated that young girls were not safe around him, but he had not referred to his own family.

'Nothing specific. Just said he wasn't pure as the driven snow, that's all.'

'Well, that'll set the rumour mill working like nothing else will,' Elaine commented.

In an attempt to divert the conversation away from what he had actually said, Graham proposed his plan to build an extension. He drew out a chair for Paula and placed a cushion carefully behind her back.

'I thought it would be a good idea to plan ahead a bit. We're going to need some more space. Obviously the baby will be in with his (or her) Mummy to begin with,' he smiled across at Paula, 'but they'll be needing a room of their own as time goes by.'

'What do you think about that, love?' Elaine folded her arms over her own (non-pregnant) bump and looked fondly at her daughter.

Privately, Paula was thinking that it would be a great idea to get away from her parents and visiting the council housing department had been recommended by one of the nurses at the surgery. Of course it depended what 'he' thought and how soon they could get together. Maybe this would do for now.

'Awesome. Won't it be expensive?'

'I've been thinking if we built out from your bedroom over the garage then that would give the baby a new space and maybe we'd put another bathroom round the back. Then you could bath him and put him to bed all close by.'

Without disturbing us in the middle of the night, Elaine thought. She wondered if her husband had been thinking of his own self-interest at all.

'That's lovely, Dad. Can we really do that?'

'Yes. Can we really do that?' mimicked Elaine. 'How are we going to pay for it?'

'We'll get a loan. I'll go in and have a word with Brian tomorrow.'

'I know he's in the bank, but surely it's not just up to him to lend you money?'

'No, but he can advise me on the different packages, then I'll make an appointment to fill out the forms with whoever.'

The phone rang and Elaine went to answer it as Paula started to imagine what the baby's room might be like.

'Do you think yellow would be nice, Dad?'

'What's wrong with blue?'

'Murder! They think it's murder?' Elaine's question silenced the others in the kitchen. 'But why? How could it be?... Who would do such a thing?... Martyn? Surely there must be some mistake... The police will come here?... Right, yes, thanks for calling.' She turned back to face the others. 'That was Lynne. John's just phoned her. The police have been questioning him about who might want to murder Tony.'

'Simple. I would,' replied Graham.

'Don't say that.'

'Dad! You ruin everything.' Paula struggled to manoeuvre her bulk around the kitchen table. Once free, she plodded up the stairs to her own room.

'I can't believe it. Surely it's not murder. Things like that just don't happen around here.' Elaine looked towards the stairs and remembered what had caused Paula's most recent exit. 'You can't go round talking like that now.'

'Oh, come off it. I didn't kill him.'

'Innocent people get wrongly convicted all the time. Be careful what you say, that's all I'm saying.'

'Bit late now,' Graham muttered as he thought back over his day at work.

'You don't even know that he is the father. You've got no evidence.'

Choosing to ignore this comment, Graham asked, 'What did Lynne say about Martyn? You mentioned him on the phone.'

'The police have been questioning him.'

'Do you think he did it?'

'Oh, don't be ridiculous. It was an accident. They have to ask questions, but nothing will come of it. I don't know why you lot want to go diving, ever. It's dangerous and you could get killed. Now one of you has.'

* * *

Cleo stopped at the nurses' station and asked where she would find Martyn. A friendly nurse explained where he was and Cleo walked down the corridor, turning into the bay of beds to find Martyn. She gazed at him while he slept. The hospital corners were intact at the bottom of the bed, but as her eyes followed the contours of his body upwards the regimented lines gave way to softer tumbles of cloth. He was lying on his side so one arm was beneath the covers and the other lay bent towards his head. She noticed the scar near his eye and smiled at the thought that he had received it from a pirate's sabre. He had not shaved so he had a good growth of stubble on his chin. She loved the sound of a man rubbing a stubbly jaw and she wanted to stroke his cheek to feel the bristles under her fingertips. The beginnings of a beard made him even more attractive to her and she wondered briefly about kissing him awake. Deciding that this would be a bad idea, she tried to dismiss the thought by considering what it was about a man's forearm that she found so captivating. His was muscular and bronzed, with golden hairs that continued on the top of his hand. The hand itself showed raised channels and mounds where the warm blood flowed through his veins. As she imagined those fingers moving over her skin, his eyes opened. She jumped a little, fearing her thoughts had disturbed him. 'Oh, hello.'

'Uh, hi. How long have you been there?' He pushed himself up into a sitting position and ran his hand through his hair. 'Why didn't you say something?' He left a tuft sticking up wildly, but Cleo suppressed a desire to smooth it into place for him.

'You looked so peaceful. I didn't want to disturb you.'

'You look gorgeous. I mean, it's great to see you, thanks for coming.' Martyn smiled broadly and watched Cleo's grin answer him. They both looked at each other quietly. Cleo's hands rested on his bed and Martyn collected one of them in his. At his touch, Cleo felt as if an electric current shot through her body, but she did not want to remove her hand. Breathing in deeply to try and regain control of herself, she realised that she should say something to break the silence, but she could not focus on anything beyond the sensation of his skin on hers. After what seemed like a long interval she asked, 'So, how are you feeling?'

'Oh, I'm loads better, thanks. I've moved from a horizontal position to vertical.' Cleo glanced at his bed with a silent query which he answered, 'And back to horizontal again. But I've been walking today a bit, with my trusty stick.'

'You've been walking? That's fantastic. Your legs are alright then?'

'Yes. I will get back to complete normality...'

'I didn't know they did personality transplants in here as well,' Cleo cut in.

'Ha, ha. You're not supposed to kick a man when he's down.'

'Wouldn't dream of it. But you are going to make a full recovery?'

'I am. I promise.' Was it his imagination or was Cleo asking him about his future abilities as a lover? 'I won't disappoint.'

'What?' Cleo appeared flustered all of a sudden. She dropped his hand as a blush crept up her neck and flooded her cheeks. 'I just came in to see you because I've got to leave now. I need to go home and look after Rachel.'

'You're going? But you only just arrived.'

'She's upset. I have to get back.'

'Of course.' Martyn's guilt about Tony's death had been pushed into the background by Cleo's presence, but it came back strongly at the mention of Rachel. 'I'm so sorry. It's all my fault.'

'Don't be silly. It was an accident.'

'No, really. It's my fault. I've told the police I killed him.'

'You told the police you killed him?' Cleo repeated dully. 'But you didn't. I mean, you couldn't have, surely? You tried to help him and he was stuck and you came up without him.'

'Precisely. I left him there to die. He would have run out of air. I killed him as surely as if I'd turned his air off.'

'But this is all wrong. You didn't do it. I know... I know it was an accident. It was his own stupid fault for going in the sub. You couldn't have known he'd get stuck.'

Martyn threw his blankets back and put his feet on the floor.

'Well, if you've got to go, the least a gentleman can do is walk a lady to the door.' The stick was on the other side of the bed so he had no support once he stood.

'No.' As Cleo was trying to steer Martyn back into the bed, he toppled and she caught him so that they appeared to be in a passionate embrace just as PC Dixon entered the ward.

CHAPTER 19

Cleo was sitting in the interview room, in the seat previously occupied by John. She studied the impassive features of PC Dixon as there was little else to focus on. Unlike John, she could not manifest a relaxed posture as she found it difficult to stop her mind flitting from Martyn to Rachel to Tony. Why had they called her here, what should she say and, more importantly, what shouldn't she say? She fidgeted, crossing and uncrossing her legs. Why would the police think it was murder?

The door opened and three people entered. The first spoke, introducing each of them.

'I'm Inspector Jamieson and I believe you already know Sergeant Fry here. This is James Hewlett, the duty solicitor, so we'll leave the two of you to have a chat for a while and then we'll be back.'

Bill Fry had a sense of déjà vu as he watched Cleo uncross her legs and sit forward.

'Inspector? Sorry, why do I need a solicitor?'

'We have reason to believe that your husband was murdered and therefore...'

'Murdered? But why? Who would do such a thing?' Cleo looked very surprised, but her expression changed to sadness as she looked down at her hands on the table. 'It's terrible.'

'Yes, Mrs Fleming. That's why we have to investigate. You should talk to Mr Hewlett here.'

'Oh. Thank you.' As the policemen left and the solicitor

took a seat, they heard Cleo asking him why she required a solicitor and what it was that they should talk about.

Cleo looked tired when the policemen re-entered the room later.

As before, Bill Fry dealt with the formalities and then Ian Jamieson started with, 'As I said previously, we need to talk to you about the death of your husband, Mrs Fleming. We have reason to believe it was murder.'

'What do you mean? Who would want to hurt him? What makes you think it's murder?'

'The circumstances of his death are suspicious and we need to investigate further.'

'But he was on a dive. It was an accident.'

'Well, he was on a dive. It may not have been an accident,' the Inspector replied.

'What do you mean?' Cleo repeated. She looked from one to the other, wondering what a loving wife would say in this situation. 'How did he die?'

'It's most likely he drowned.'

'Most likely? You don't know for sure?'

'There are more tests yet to be done and we have to await confirmation.' The Inspector hesitated, 'You do know about the post-mortem?'

'Oh. Yes. The coroner explained a bit about the process with an... an unnatural death.' Cleo had started to rub the fingers of her left hand with her right. 'But surely if he drowned, it was an accident? He got stuck in the sub and... and he died.' She reached into her bag for a tissue.

'Yes, but the thing is, he still had air in his cylinder. There was no equipment malfunction. Why did he die then and why did he come up without his kit?'

'I don't know. It was awful, seeing his body like that.' Cleo put her head in her hands. She did not want them to see the fear in her eyes. She should cry, but the tears would not come. She ought to think of something terrible and then reminded herself that the death of her husband was terrible and she should look more grief-stricken.

'Was he a safe diver usually?' the Inspector asked.

'He always wanted to go into deep, dark holes and I never went there with him.'

'You didn't dive together?'

'No, we thought it was best for Rachel's sake that we kept separate in case there was ever an accident.'

'So you think it was an accident?'

'Of course. It had happened before. A few months back in the quarry, when he was stuck in a wreck, he'd undone his jacket and wriggled free and everything was fine.'

'Yes. We know about that.'

She wondered if she sounded convincing. Perhaps they needed more explanation, so she added, 'So he probably thought he could do the same again.'

Inspector Jamieson decided to change tack. 'Are you having an affair with Martyn Share?'

'What?' Cleo was genuinely surprised at the switch in direction.

'It seems you were in a passionate encounter at the hospital.' Cleo glanced at PC Dixon but he kept his eyes focused somewhere above her head.

'No. He fell, I caught him. He's still weak from the accident.'

'So you're not having an affair?' Bill Fry repeated the question.

'Of course not. I'm a married woman. I mean, I was a married woman.' Cleo tried to quell the emotions that stirred at the thought of having a torrid affair with Martyn. She needed to concentrate.

'That's an interesting description. Most people would say 'I'm a happily married woman', Bill Fry continued. 'Were you happy with your husband?'

'Yes.' Cleo thought rapidly. Who had they spoken to? What would they know already? What would other people say? 'Well, not all the time. Sometimes we didn't get on that well and then it would get better again, you know.' Both men looked sceptical.

'So, you like Martyn?'

Cleo was rubbing her fingers again, holding them between her knees as she sat forwards.

'Yes, I like him, but that doesn't mean...'

'And he likes you.' Bill Fry leaned forwards, watching her intently. She flushed under his stare, cursing herself for blushing so easily.

'He's just a nice man in the club, that's all.'

'So you wouldn't want to get rid of the husband you no longer love in order to be with the new man in your life?'

'Of course not.' The colour had drained from Cleo's face as rapidly as it had appeared. She hoped that this would be interpreted as outrage at the suggestion, but it was in fact alarm that they knew about her desire.

'But you went to visit him in hospital.' Why had she done that? She should have stayed away. She should have gone straight home.

'Rachel. My daughter. I need to go to her.' She half raised herself out of her seat, but Ian Jamieson put a hand on her arm and exerted a slight pressure. She sat down again.

'Just a few more questions, Mrs Fleming,' the Inspector said.

'Did your husband have anyone who wished him ill?'

Cleo hesitated. 'No....Well, he's not been Graham's favourite person lately.'

'Why is that?'

'Graham's got this crazy notion that Tony fathered Paula's child.'

'Do you find that a crazy notion?' Ian Jamieson repeated her words back to her.

'Well, yes. He wasn't interested in Paula.' Wrong thing to say, she thought, swearing silently. She needed to think faster. She should have encouraged the story about Tony and Paula. It gave Graham a motive. After all, she had no idea who the father was.

'Although...' She appeared to be considering and the policemen waited. 'He spent a lot of time away from the factory recently. I don't really know where he's been or who he's been with.'

'We have a statement suggesting that he liked young girls.'

'He's just a normal bloke who liked pretty women. Don't you?' Cleo stopped. She should not antagonise the officers, but she needed to get off this topic. She did not want her own suspicions about Tony's interest in Rachel to surface. That would give her a motive for murder.

'How are Tony's finances?'

'Alright, I think.' She was cautious, wondering what they knew. She was not supposed to know about his inheritance. Hopefully they were not aware of it either, in which case there was no need to mention it. Besides, that was another reason to want him dead.

'So he didn't have any money problems?'

'Not that I'm aware of.' Had she covered her tracks adequately? What if they examined the company accounts? Would the irregularities necessary to cover her gambling debts be obvious to a trained eye?'

'And if there were any, you would be aware of them?'

'Yes. I do the accounts for the firm and I manage the household finances as well.'

'Unusual isn't it, for the wife to hold the purse strings?'

'Not if the wife is an accountant. Tony wasn't interested in that sort of thing. He loved designing cars and he loved diving and he loved our daughter.' Thinking about Rachel back in the house, without either parent, feeling more alone in the world than she ever had before, tears sprang to Cleo's eyes. 'It'll be terrible for Rachel, without him now.' She concentrated on an image of Rachel crying as her own tears started to flow. 'Can I go to her?'

'You mean to travel back to the Forest of Dean tonight?' Bill Fry checked.

'Yes. Sorry.' Cleo brushed at her cheeks with the tissue.

'You are free to leave, but we may wish to talk to you again.' The Inspector rose, drawing the interview to a close. Bill Fry also stood so they both watched Cleo stumble slightly in her desire to get away from them rapidly. Mr Hewlett also left the room with PC Dixon. Ian sat down again and Bill followed his lead.

'What do you think of that performance then, Bill?'

'I don't think she's particularly cut up about his death, do you?'

'No. I thought it was interesting that she didn't pick up on the 'the husband you no longer love' phrase. She was anxious enough to deny an affair, but if she did still love her husband, you'd have thought she'd want to proclaim the fact and be prostrate with grief.'

'She's definitely not that, although she did well to squeeze a few tears out at the end,' Bill said.

'You're a cold-hearted sod.'

'Not me. I've just seen a lot of genuine grief, that's all. People take it differently of course, but there was something,' he paused, 'calculating about her, I think.'

'Hmm. If she has set her eyes on Martyn, I hope he knows what he's letting himself in for,' Ian commented.

'You don't think they're in it together?' Bill asked.

'It's odd the way he's claiming to have killed him. I believe he's sincere about that belief and the guilt he feels. If he is, then he can't have planned to murder him. Not unless it's a case of double bluff and he's a very good actor, but I don't think he's that clever.'

'But she couldn't have had a hand in Tony's death anyway, because she was on the boat with the others, when he was still underwater. Seems like a great alibi to me.'

'That's true.' Ian nodded. 'So then we're left with the father wanting to avenge his daughter's honour. Do you think that would motivate someone in this day and age?'

'Doubt it. But I didn't like the guy.'

'That's no reason to consider him a suspect. Even if it was a motive I think it'd be more likely to be a spontaneous rage thing when he found out, rather than a premeditated attack.'

'Not if he still wants to talk to the daughter. If Tony were the father of the baby and Paula's dad was responsible for killing him, it wouldn't do a lot for his role as Grandad if she knew, would it? Anyway, he wasn't even on the boat so he was nowhere near.'

'We don't know where he was during that time though, do we?'

'No. He was too sick to go out, according to him. Maybe he could've got on with another group and dived down to do the dirty deed?' Bill suggested.

'Without any of his mates on their boat seeing him? Sounds a bit far-fetched to me. Anyway, we don't even know for sure that it is murder. We've just got those curious marks on his wrists.'

'Well, that brings us back to Martyn. He was definitely with him and trying to help him out, so he says. What if his efforts were to keep him down there instead?'

'And almost kill himself in the process?'

'Well, he panicked,' Bill added defensively. 'Something went wrong.'

'Surely the timing's out? Martyn came up first. They'd got him on the boat, called for assistance and then Tony came up. We need to go back upstairs and check all the times. We'll have the dive profiles for Martyn and Tony and the dive marshal time for when they went down.'

'I doubt anyone recorded what time they came up.'

'No, probably not. But the coastguard would have logged the call, so we'll be able to work it out. Come on, let's go.'

Bill wearily heaved himself up, mentally mourning the fact that the possibility of a couple of pints in his local was diminishing fast.

He placed a cup of coffee on Ian's desk and held onto his own as he watched the Inspector log on to the computer.

Everything on the Inspector's desk was in regimented neatness, unlike his own which was chaotic. Of course Ian had more space because he had his office and filing cabinets and bookshelves, but Bill knew that his systematic filing and ordering bordered on the compulsive. Overall, he preferred his own way but he appreciated that his boss could generally find what he was looking for quickly. Ian was looking through the folders on the HOLMES database but could not find what he wanted in this instance. Bill wondered whether he should suggest that Sean Dixon would be able to search for documents much more efficiently when the same thought apparently occurred to the Inspector.

'Could you get Sean to come in for a minute, Bill?'

'Sir.' Bill returned with the constable who slid into the seat recently vacated by the Inspector. As both senior officers stood behind him, peering over his shoulders, Sean had an uncomfortable feeling reminiscent of his parents supervision of his homework.

'Sean, we need to look at the dive marshal's sheet first, then the dive profiles for Tony Fleming and Martyn Share,' Ian instructed.

'Yes, sir. The sheet was scanned in and stored here. What do you need to know?' He clicked the mouse and a document appeared on the screen.

'What time did Tony and Martyn go into the water?'

'2.55 pm,' Sean answered. Bill put his coffee on a beer mat at the corner of the desk and reached for his notebook. Computers were all very well, but he still preferred pen and paper, particularly if he had to work something out.

'Right. Now can you find the dive profiles?'

'And can you explain what we're going to be looking at?'

Bill added as Sean clicked on folders and documents.

'Yes, sir. The profile is the output from the data stored in the diver's computer on their wrist. It's a great piece of safety equipment as it monitors depth over time so a diver always knows what depth they are at and how long they've been down. They should be referring to it regularly, along with their air gauge, in order to check how they're doing against their dive plan, which is essentially how deep they were going and for how long. They will also use the computer to monitor their ascent rate on the way up. It will beep to warn them if they are coming up too fast (so they will then slow down) or if they need to stop for a while to avoid any decompression illness. The more sophisticated models can also check air consumption, but that's not what we're dealing with here.'

A graph appeared on the screen before them.

'Isn't technology amazing?' Bill asked. Neither man answered and Sean continued, 'So what we've got here is the record of Martyn's dive. It's like a cross section through the sea because it shows depth on the vertical axis against time on the horizontal axis.' Sean pointed to the top left corner of the screen. 'This is where he entered the water and you can see he went down at a steady rate to about 20metres.' His finger tracked the diagonal line on the screen. 'Then he spent quite a few minutes at about that level.' His finger followed the horizontal line.

'OK, thanks. Got the idea,' the Inspector cut in. 'Is it possible to superimpose Tony's dive profile on this graph of Martyn's? We want to know what time it was when they separated. If there was a big gap between the times when the two of them surfaced, we can assume that he was still alive when Martyn left him, because he would only rocket up like that if he was already dead or unconscious.'

Sean frowned at the screen as he opened Tony's profile and copied the data into the programme plotting Martyn's dive. As the screen changed to show two lines, Sean said 'So, this red line is Martyn's dive that we were just looking at and this green line is Tony's dive.'

'Great. So what does that tell us?' asked Ian.

'Well, they're close together most of the time (as they should be) up until here and...'

'What depth is that?'

Sean checked the data point. '22metres. They separate there and Tony goes a bit deeper.'

Bill said, 'That must be when he was in the sub.'

Sean continued, 'Then he's back and they're together again.' His finger followed a sharp dip in the graph and a steep diagonal line to the surface. 'Martyn goes down and then up quickly...'

'That'll be when he's panicking and making for the surface,' Ian interrupted.

'... which he reaches after 23 minutes,' Sean concluded.

Bill calculated quickly, 'So it's 3.18 pm.'

'Right, let's see if that checks against the time that the coastguard logged the call for assistance from their boat. Have you got that in there somewhere, Sean?'

'Yes, sir.' Sean minimised the graph and opened a different folder and another document filled the screen. He scanned through the page. 'That's 3.21 pm.'

'Could be right. He comes up, the boat goes over, they pull him in, call up on the radio. It could take them three minutes to do that,' Bill said as he considered his notebook.

Ian nodded. 'So we left Tony on the sub at about 22metres. Let's go back to the graph, Sean. Right, he's there for what? Five minutes altogether?'

'That's right, sir.'

'First he'll be stuck when Martyn's trying to pull him out, that might take a minute. Then he'll be on his own when Martyn's gone, wondering whether to stay put and wait for some help to arrive, maybe another minute. He gets fed up and undoes his jacket and loses his mouthpiece, another one gone. How long can you hold your breath for?'

Bill thought, '60 seconds, max. Maybe less if I'm exerting myself. Perhaps more if I think it's my last.'

'Well, we'll give him a minute, then he dies. How long will it take him to drown? '

'Don't know.'

'Well, if each action I said was a bit longer so overall it adds up to five minutes. Then his body ascends rapidly at the end of his dive, which is at 27 minutes.'

'That would make it 3.22 pm,' Bill said, writing down his figures. 'What time did he hit the surface?'

Ian sighed. 'We don't know. Nobody recorded that.'

'Huh. Well, that's a lot of use, then.' Bill said irritably.

'No, wait. Assuming that he's only going to zoom to the surface when dead or unconscious and, say, that would take a minute at most. That means that he only died at 3.21 pm or after.'

'And Martyn's already been on the surface for three minutes by that time.'

'Exactly. So he couldn't have killed him. We'll be able to remove that weight of guilt. It's not his fault he died.'

'But whose fault is it?' Bill had the feeling that he had just said something else that his superior officer found unnecessary.

CHAPTER 20

On Tuesday morning Graham approached the doors of the
bank and put his hand out towards them. Before he made
contact they opened automatically so he quickly replaced the
hand in his pocket, hoping no one had seen him. He noted
the long queue of people leading up to the cashier's windows
and felt irritated immediately. The small offices on the left
used for private consultations were empty, so why didn't they
have more staff at the counter? He couldn't spend all day in
here waiting to be told that he was in the wrong queue and
that personal meetings were 'over there'. The woman at the
front seemed to be unearthing various repositories of money
from about her person. The bank clerk was going to have to
count every penny of the woman's life savings. Behind her
there was a young mother with a toddler. She should stop
that child from swinging on the rope alongside the line of
adults. Too late! The post for the rope toppled over, taking its
neighbour with it. The child howled as it was pinned
underneath the metal rod. The mother was covered in
confusion as she tried to quieten her offspring and re-erect
the barrier. She was impeded by the elderly gentleman behind
her who gallantly strove to help, but his walking stick got
tangled in the loose rope and for a moment he tottered
dangerously, until the woman next in line put out a supportive
hand. As Graham observed this domino effect, he caught a
glimpse of Brian in the corridor. Cutting through the queue

whose path snaked across the floor, Graham called loudly, 'Brian. Morning.'

Brian looked up and said, 'Oh. Hi, Graham,' before turning back to his colleague with, 'Excuse me a moment. I'll get back to you.' Brian ushered Graham into one of the cells equipped with a table, a computer, a couple of chairs and a plethora of leaflets and brochures about the bank's services.

'What's the matter?' he asked as he took a seat.

'Nothing. I wanted to ask your advice about a loan,' said Graham.

'I'm busy. Why didn't you make an appointment with one of the girls?'

'Well, I'm here now aren't I? Might as well talk to me as we're in the "personal meeting" space.' He made quote signs in the air with his fingers and glanced back through the glass wall. 'Customer service isn't very good today, is it? All those people waiting.'

'We've got a couple of staff off sick and it's just a bit hectic.' Brian did not want to say that part of the cause of the delay at the counter was due to the 'back stage' activity prompted by a request from Plymouth police for information about Tony's finances. There was also the fact that two point eight million pounds had just been credited to the new account that Tony had recently opened and this was an unprecedented transaction. Trying to concentrate on Graham in order to be rid of him as fast as possible, he asked, 'What do you want, Graham?'

'It's the baby. It'll be coming in November and we need to get ready for it.' Brian looked blank. He thought: Towels? Hot water? It was only August. Graham added, 'I'm thinking it'll need a room, so we could build onto the back of the house and make another bathroom as well.'

'You want a loan for an extension on your house?' Brian checked.

'Precisely.' Brian flicked over the leaflets in the display stand. 'There should be some loan stuff in here that'll give you all the options.' He continued to search. 'No, there aren't any. Someone should have re-stocked these. Wait a minute, I'll get you one.'

'Can't you just tell me?'

'I haven't got time. Anyway, you'd have to come back and talk to someone who can go through the details with you. I don't do that.' Brian emphasised his last sentence as he left the room, leaving the door open in his haste. Getting up to examine the leaflet rack himself, Graham was aware of a conversation on the other side of the wall. His attention was caught by the mention of a familiar name. A female voice was saying, 'Tony Fleming. Yes, it must be him. We've only got one Anthony Richard Fleming. Just think, all that money coming too late.'

'It's terrible, isn't it? He was only in here last week, looking the picture of health,' another voice replied.

'Two point eight million. What would you do with that?'

'New car? New house? New husband?' They giggled together.

'And the police enquiry. I wonder what that's about?'

'Ssshhhh.'

Graham was still standing with his head close to the wall when Brian returned briskly, passing Nicky and Rose in the corridor.

'Alright?' he asked as he shut the door and resumed his seat.

Graham could not contain his new knowledge.

'Is that right? Tony's come into a small fortune?'

'What? What makes you say that?' Brian wondered if he should deny it.

'I just heard some of your staff talking.' He gestured to the wall. Brian cursed them for gossiping in the corridor. He'd give them a severe lecture about customer confidentiality. 'You can't keep something like that a secret. It'll be all over town by lunchtime,' Graham continued.

Brian sighed heavily. 'Yes, it's true that a lot of money has come into Tony's account, but we need to check things.' He assumed that Tony had discussed it with the branch manager, but he wasn't in today and had not seen fit to brief his deputy about it. Brian was annoyed. He begrudged him the position anyway; he should have been manager by now and the other man's poor communication skills were only one of his failings, in Brian's eyes.

'Two point eight million.' Graham whistled. 'Do you think Cleo will buy the club a new boat?'

'What? How can you mention that at a time like this?'

'Easily. You mean you haven't thought about all that money? And the wealthy widow and how she might spend it? Maybe that's why she killed him.'

Brian looked shocked. 'Killed him? What do you mean?'

'Haven't you heard? The police think it's murder.'

'It can't be.' Brian thought back. 'We all saw his injuries. She was on the boat with us.'

'Well, they're investigating. Apparently they've already questioned John.'

'How do you know?'

'Had a phone call last night. They might come up here and talk to us again.'

'Why? There's nothing more to say, surely?'

'Ah.' Graham tapped his nose in what he hoped was a knowing gesture. 'Motive!'

'Motive?' Brian echoed dully, trying to get to grips with this new perspective on events.

'Don't you think Cleo getting a huge wad of money would provide her with the motivation to get rid of her husband?'

'Cleo might not know...' Brian cursed himself. In his anxiety to protect her he had inadvertently let slip further information. There he was condemning junior clerks for breaching confidentiality and then he shoots his own mouth off.

'Cleo might not know?' Graham repeated, quick to pick up on it. 'She might be a millionairess and not be aware of it? How could she not?'

Brian remained silent.

Graham considered. 'It's in a different account, isn't it? Maybe he didn't want her to have it?'

'Stop it, Graham. Don't invent stuff. And please don't repeat anything you've heard in here.' In spite of this instruction, Brian knew that Graham would not be able to keep such a great story to himself. That's if Nicky and Rose hadn't already blabbed to the rest of the community.

He handed the paperwork on loans over, 'Here, take these and arrange an appointment next time.'

'Sure. Thanks, Brian. It's been a piece of heaven.' Graham grinned at him as Brian rose to return to his office and checked his watch. He'd take an early lunch to go and tell Cleo the news before someone else did – unless she knew already, of course.

★ ★ ★

Rachel sipped her tea as she sat with Cleo at the table on the terrace, gazing down from the house. The land sloped away from them so they could see across to the wooded hillside on the far bank, which displayed multiple shades of green from the patchwork of deciduous trees. Although they knew that the river Wye meandered through the tree-lined valley, there was no sight of it from this vantage point. There were still some crumbs on the table from their late breakfast and she brushed them aside as she set her mug down. A calendar lay before them and Cleo held the current August page up.

'What date is it when you get your results?' she asked.

'The twenty third, I think.'

'And you're happy about staying on into the sixth form?'

'Why wouldn't I be?' Rachel asked in surprise.

'I'm just checking, that's all.'

'It's not as if I'm like Paula. She'll be half way through term when her baby arrives.'

'Yes, of course. It's November, isn't it?' Cleo looked at her own daughter and could not imagine her being on the brink of motherhood. She wondered how Elaine and Graham were coping with the prospect.

'I know she's not going back in September, but I don't know what she's going to do afterwards,' Rachel continued.

'No.' They both gazed at the picture of Harry Potter wielding a wand which pointed to the beginning of the month.

'But you'll be starting A levels.'

'Unless I do a BTEC.'

'A what?'

'It's the thing that Dad suggested, more of a practical

217

hands-on qualification in automotive engineering.'

Cleo felt that she should tread carefully. Her first instinct was to say, 'Well, he's not here now,' but she bit that back.

'Do you want to do that?' she asked incredulously.

'I don't know. It'd be different without Dad here to help me.'

'But didn't you have to confirm your choices last term?' Cleo asked, trying to skip over the fact that the possibility of Tony's future involvement had been removed.

'I had a chat with Mr Jones and he said I could take it if I wanted to and just to think about it and get back to him after the results.'

'But what would you be dropping?' Cleo was wondering about the other A level choices and how it would affect Rachel's future.

'I'd keep Biology and Drama. Maybe get rid of Chemistry or Geography.'

'I suppose you should think about what you're going to do after A levels and then work back to what you need in order to do that,' Cleo suggested, trying to take a practical approach.

'Well, I had thought I'd be helping Dad in the business. I won't now.' Rachel started to cry silently. She wiped the tears from her cheeks as she fought for control.

Cleo was stunned. How could they have been planning this without her knowledge? They must have discussed it. Why would Tony have excluded her from talking about their daughter's future? She struggled to pull herself together.

'Oh. Sorry. I didn't know.'

'It wasn't definite.' Rachel looked uncomfortable, just the way she had when she tried to conceal a guilty secret as a child.

Cleo tried to suppress her feelings. It was a betrayal of sorts, but nothing like as bad as the one she had envisaged, unless that had been going on as well? She should focus on what was best for her daughter.

'Surely you should follow what you really want to do? I know you'll miss your Dad, but don't take on something just because he might have wanted you to do it.'

'Maybe I should talk to John about it.'

'John?' Cleo was taken aback. Did he know about their plan as well?

'So we could discuss what I might be able to do in the business in the future.'

'Yes. Yes, of course.' Cleo felt like she'd missed out on some vital information somewhere. She was reeling from the thought that Tony and Rachel had been discussing plans for the company together.

'Anyway, we need something fun to think about.' Rachel sounded determined to be cheerful and pointed to a square highlighted in red. 'What about your party on the eighteenth?'

'What?' Cleo could not keep up.

'Your fortieth. We have to celebrate it.'

'Oh, I don't know. After what's happened, surely we can't have a party?'

'I think we should. It's a big event in your life. Dad would have wanted you to have a good time.'

'He would?' Cleo asked faintly, wondering if Rachel's perception was actually the correct one. Surely not? Maybe it was just a teenager's preoccupation with her own destiny. She would assume that her parents were happy unless faced with incontrovertible evidence to the contrary. A car came up the driveway. As Cleo rose to see who it was, Rachel said, 'I'll start planning it then.' She went back into the house and paid no attention to Cleo's call of 'No, wait.' Cleo stood by the low wall that edged the terrace, watching as Brian got out of the car and walked over to join her.

'Oh. Hi, Brian. You're looking very smart.'

'Hi. Yes. I've come straight from the bank. Lunchtime.'

'Want a cup of tea or something?'

'No, thanks.'

Brian looked worried, prompting Cleo to ask, 'Is something wrong?' as she gestured to the table and he sat down. He hesitated so Cleo took the place opposite him as she asked, 'What is it?' anxiously.

'Well, it's good news – and bad.'

'What's the good news?'

'Tony's come into a significant amount of money.'

'What do you mean?' Cleo asked, trying to keep her voice steady.

'He's inherited two point eight million from an uncle who died recently and the money's just come through.'

'Wow! That's a lot of money.' Cleo thought for a moment as the prospect of unimagined wealth washed over her. She could not help but smile and tried to disguise it quickly with a frown of concentration. 'Why didn't he tell me?' Brian shrugged as he could find no appropriate answer. He wanted to believe that she did not know about it, to bolster his conviction that she had nothing to do with his death. 'But surely that's good news?' Cleo continued. 'What could be bad about it?'

'I had a call from the police in Plymouth. They need to know the details of Tony's finances.'

'Oh. Right. And have you told them?'

'I've given them the normal stuff about Tony's joint account with you and the company information. But this huge amount has come into a new account that Tony had set up using his second name, rather than his first. Such a big transfer caused quite a stir, I can tell you.'

'And why wouldn't you tell the police about it?'

Brian looked pained. 'I didn't want to have to say this, but Graham was in this morning asking about something, and he said the police think Tony was murdered.'

'Yes. They told me that yesterday,' Cleo said calmly, looking down at her hands on the table.

Brian wondered if Cleo had missed his point.

'But, you see...,' he shifted in his seat awkwardly, 'from the police point of view, Tony getting two point eight million gives you a motive to kill him.'

'It can't do. Not if I didn't know about it. Besides,' she added quickly, 'he was my husband. I wouldn't hurt him, would I?'

'No. No, of course not,' Brian tried to sound reassuring. 'But you see how it could look.'

'What are you going to do?'

'Well, it's not up to me. The bank will have to respond with all his known records. I don't think the slight delay between the first instalment of data and the second will matter, given that he used a different version of his name. I just thought you should know, that's all.'

'Yes. Thanks, Brian.'

As she watched his car disappear down the driveway, Cleo could not suppress the smile that reappeared. All that money. Hers. Soon. She needed to ring the solicitors and make an appointment to see George Murmur.

CHAPTER 21

On Wednesday morning Bill Fry walked into Ian Jamieson's office waving a piece of paper. 'Know what you said about money and sex being motivators for crime? Well, we've just got the money.'

Ian looked up from his desk and held his hand out. 'What is it?'

'This is the info from Tony Fleming's bank. He's just inherited two point eight million.'

'That's a lot of motivation. Does it go to the wife?'

'I presume so, but we don't know that yet. We need to track the will down.'

'Well, that's very interesting. Now we have a wife who is not mourning her husband much, who stands to gain a lot from his death. I wonder if she engineered it somehow? Do you think she's having a torrid affair with Martyn Share and they cooked it up together?'

'But you didn't think he did it, in spite of his confession.' Bill pointed out ruefully.

'No. I still don't, but maybe it's a double bluff. I think we need to see Mr Share again, don't you?'

'Sir.'

'Then we should prepare to spend a couple of days up in the Forest of Dean. Can you organise that with the local force there? If they've got some rooms we could use that would be great. Otherwise sort something out, can you?'

Dr Helston examined Martyn again and proclaimed him fit and well enough to leave. He no longer needed a stick to walk and had regained his physical abilities remarkably well. Even though he was keen to get home, Martyn went to find Mick and the rest of the staff to thank them for looking after him. He found them in the day room. Mick greeted him with, 'Martyn. Have you got the all clear then?'

'I have, yes. Just come to say thanks and goodbye.' He smiled at Gill, the red-haired nurse who had admitted him.

She said, 'I'm glad you're better. Will you be going diving again soon?'

'Maybe in a bit. Not straight away.'

Mick said, 'You should hear the story Dave's been telling us. Go on, tell him.'

At Mick's encouragement, Dave related the tale again: 'I was out with a mate and we found thousands of pounds worth of kit just lying on the sea floor.'

'Does that count as treasure?' Martyn asked. 'Do you have to report it like lost property?'

'Not likely,' Dave answered. 'Finders keepers. Looks like someone must have accidentally dropped it off the side of a boat. Everything's there, all connected up and ready to go.'

'Had it been down there a long time?'

'No, looks brand new. That rebreather equipment's not cheap so someone'll be sore as hell at losing it.'

'Wouldn't they have gone looking for it?'

'You would have thought so, wouldn't you? But the seabed there is full of little gullies and thick kelp. You could search for ages and not find it. I only spotted it because we were looking for congers in dark places.'

'Are you going to use it then?' Martyn asked.

'Not yet. I don't know how to at the moment, but I've booked on a course.'

Mick shook his head. 'I'd never want to dive with a rebreather, myself. I've seen too many casualties who have had problems with it and it's been the end of them.'

'Is it particularly dangerous?' Martyn asked, thinking that he wanted to minimise any risk to himself on future diving trips.

'No, not if you know what you're doing,' Dave answered. 'Sometimes people forget to turn the right valves on, so they gradually breathe more and more carbon dioxide and it kills them.'

'Why would anyone risk that?'

'The benefit is that you can stay down for longer and there aren't any telltale bubbles of air when you breathe out. Photographers might want to use it for that reason,' Mick explained. 'Anyway,' he rose to his feet, 'you're off home, then.'

Martyn shook his hand. 'Yes. Thanks for everything.'

'Hope we don't see you again.'

'It's mutual. Bye then,' he called to the others.

Mick walked with Martyn to the reception area where they encountered PC Dixon at the entrance.

'Mr Share?' he asked.

'Yes.'

'Could you come down to the station please, sir? Inspector Jamieson wants to talk to you.'

★ ★ ★

'Morning, Mr Share,' Inspector Jamieson started. 'I see you've met Mr Hewlett.' He took the seat opposite Martyn as Bill Fry slid tapes into the machine to record the interview.

'Yes, but I don't really see why I need a solicitor.' Martyn knew he had done nothing wrong but the bald nature of the room and the pervading atmosphere of the station was intimidating.

'This is a murder enquiry, Mr Share. We need to interview you in the presence of a solicitor and follow the appropriate procedure so that evidence will be admissible in court.'

'In court?'

'Yes. Once we've finished our investigations and we understand what happened and how Tony died.'

'I already told you. I killed Tony.'

'Yes. In your version it was effectively death by neglect though, wasn't it? You felt you'd abandoned him and it was your fault?'

'Yes.'

'So let's just think about how you tried to help him out. Show me what you did.' Ian offered his hands to Martyn.

'You want me to pull you?' he asked. Receiving a nod, Martyn took hold of the Inspector across the chipped table and heaved. Ian and Bill exchanged a glance. That grip would not have produced the marks that they had seen on the body. 'But our hands slipped, so then I took his wrists.' Martyn moved his fingers down to a new position. 'That was a better hold so I tried that for a long time, but it still had no effect. Then I tried to get some purchase by holding an iron bar with one hand and pulling with the other, but that was useless as well.'

Both Inspector and Sergeant nodded, in apparent agreement.

'But rather than try to get him out, you could have held him away from his breathing apparatus,' the Inspector suggested.

'Why would I do that?'

'To kill him, obviously. So you could benefit from his death.'

Martyn instantly thought of Cleo as the glamorous widow, but he dismissed the idea.

'I don't benefit from his death. I didn't intend to kill him. It was an accident.'

'Of course. An accident. But you and Cleo are having an affair. Surely you wanted to get rid of the husband?' Ian asked.

'We're not having an affair,' Martyn exclaimed. If only, he thought.

'She's an attractive woman. You were wrapped around her in the hospital recently…'

'I fell and she supported me. Obviously she's a good-looking woman and…

'And you like her,' Bill Fry added bluntly.

'Yes, I like her. But we're not lovers. Even if we were, she'd just separate or get divorced. There's no need to do away with her husband.'

'Ah, but there would be if you hoped to get your hands on his money,' Ian pointed out, leaning forward intently.

'What money?' Martyn looked surprised.

'So you don't know about the two point eight million that Tony's just inherited?' Ian added.

'No. I've only known everyone in the club a few months. I didn't think he was that rich.'

'He wasn't, up until recently. The point is that all that

money is enough motivation for someone to want him dead,' the Inspector explained.

'Not me.'

'So now you're saying you didn't kill him?' Sergeant Fry asked.

'I never said that.'

'You did.' Bill Fry casually flicked over the pages of his notebook and read out, 'It was me. I killed him.'

Martyn was rattled. 'I didn't murder him. What I meant was, he died accidentally, when I was the last person with him. I felt responsible, that's all.'

Ian Jamieson inclined his head to acknowledge the point. 'So, someone else who stood to gain from his death then?'

'Not Cleo.'

'So you automatically assumed that it would be Cleo who might murder him?' Sergeant Fry pursued.

'No, I didn't. You're twisting what I said.'

'Would Cleo be able to plot his death, do you think?' the Inspector resumed.

'No. Absolutely not.' He looked from one to the other of them. 'It must be someone else.' Cleo was good and kind and beautiful, he thought.

'Who else?' Inspector Jamieson persisted.

Reluctant to put another name forward, Martyn did not answer, but mentally he checked through the members of the club, wondering who would fall under suspicion.

'Or maybe it's no one,' Martyn concluded after a pause. 'How could anyone have done it? I was there and it was only Tony and me. It was an accident,' he repeated.

'What was the visibility like?' Bill asked.

'Not that good. A few metres, maybe.'

'So someone else could have been lurking nearby and moved in when you'd gone?'

'But who? The others were on the boat,' Martyn replied.

'They could be lying. How do we know they were up there all the time?' Bill continued.

Martyn was stunned. He had not thought of that. Surely they could not all be in a conspiracy?

'Do you remember who was on the boat when you got there?'

Martyn tried to remember. 'Brian... Cleo... Lynne, I think. I don't know. It's all a bit hazy. I was ill.'

'Never mind about who for now,' the sergeant continued. 'It's possible there could have been another diver?'

'It's possible, but there wasn't anyone else down there...'

'As far as you know.'

'Yes.'

'You didn't see any signs of other divers?'

'No.'

'No bubbles of air from someone else's kit?'

'No.' The phrase triggered the memory of Mick's description of the rebreather equipment. "No telltale bubbles" – that's what he'd said. Should he mention that? Maybe not until he'd spoken to Cleo. There was no way she could be mixed up in this. She wouldn't do that. But if she wasn't involved, he should mention it. Something still held him back.

'If no one else was there, that brings us back to you being the most likely murder suspect. I could arrest you for the murder of Tony Fleming,' Inspector Jamieson intoned the formal words. 'I think we might need to hold you for further questioning.'

'What? Can they do that?' Martyn asked his solicitor.

'They can hold you for forty-eight hours whilst they make enquiries, yes.'

'Wait. Wait. I didn't see anyone else down there,' Martyn said cautiously.

'But…?' the Inspector prompted.

'I wouldn't have to see bubbles to prove that another diver was there. If they used a rebreather they don't release any gas into the water.'

'That right?' Ian asked Bill.

'I'll check.'

'I don't know much about it myself. I only just heard about rebreathers,' Martyn added.

'So you've invented this to deflect our attention away from you?' Bill Fry asked aggressively. 'It could be a cock and bull story about another diver on the scene and there's no evidence of it whatsoever.'

'Oh, no. There is evidence.'

Both policemen looked incredulous.

'There's a guy who found some new rebreather kit abandoned in the sea. You should ask Dave at the DDRC about it.'

'We will.'

'Can I go now?'

'Yes, you can go,' Inspector Jamieson confirmed.

The two policemen climbed the stairs back to their offices and Ian said, 'Get onto that guy about the rebreather kit. We need to know if that ties in or not. Why didn't anyone mention the possibility of an undetected diver in there?'

'No reason to, I suppose.' Bill Fry hesitated over his next question, knowing it would sound critical of his boss, 'You think it's alright to have released him?'

'Yes, don't you? We know he didn't do it. This way he might put the wind up whoever did and then we'll be there to see what happens.'

'I guess so.' Bill sounded doubtful. 'I've booked us into a local hotel in the Forest for the next couple of nights.'

Ian checked his watch. 'Well we could be there this evening, but it depends on the guy who found that kit. I'd like to talk to him before we go so we might need to delay until tomorrow.'

'Yes, sir. I'll track him down.'

CHAPTER 22

Martyn sat on the train listening to his mobile ringing Cleo's number. It switched to her answer phone so he turned it off. He would try again later. However, after repeated attempts over the next couple of hours and still no response, he decided to ask Brian for a lift instead.

He was the only person to get off at the station, although that was rather a grand term for it, he thought. There was only a raised concrete platform on either side of the rails. No ticket office, no café, not even a dilapidated shelter. The only building was the signal box on the other side of the road. There were no staff to deal with enquiries about trains, taxis or buses. The best you could hope for was that the timetables stuck to the decaying boards were up to date. As he walked into the car park, Brian greeted him cheerfully with, 'Taxi for Share.'

'Hi, Brian.'

'Do you get loads of people coming to join you whenever anyone says that?'

'Not often, no,' Martyn replied wearily as he got in the passenger seat.

'How are you?' Brian asked as he drove over the level crossing, taking the road back towards the town. The station was some way from the shopping centre and new arrivals often looked about them as if they had disembarked at the wrong point, wondering how to get to some semblance of civilisation. Brian threaded his way around the outskirts of the town and headed towards Martyn's rented flat in the next village.

'I'm fine, thanks,' Martyn said. He thought the reflex polite response was completely inadequate to express the confusion of emotions that he felt. He was more than usually tired from the journey; maybe he still hadn't recovered fully from the accident. Mentally he was reeling from the fact that the police could have accused him of murder and held him for questioning. Above all that, he wanted to see Cleo desperately. Naturally he did not like the police suggestion that he would profit from someone else's death, but the fact remained that he was still alive and so was Cleo. He had not actively contributed to Tony's death but he did have a desire to 'seize the day'. If he and Cleo could be happy together, why shouldn't he go for it, as long as she wanted the same thing?

The road twisted through trees overhanging the tarmac, forming a green tunnel. Every so often there were patches of dappled sunlight ahead, where the leaf cover was sparse. As the car accelerated out of the bends, the light flickered as if the sun had a faulty bulb. Realising how grateful he was for the lift, Martyn said, 'Thanks very much for coming to pick me up.'

'No problem. You'd have been there hours if you were hoping for a bus. I normally leave work about now anyway and today of course we've got the committee meeting later, so I need to go home and eat something. Shall I come back and pick you up for that?'

'No, it's alright, thanks. I've got a few errands to do, since I've not been home for a while.' Brian nodded, whilst

Martyn thought that his most urgent errand was not for food or to do washing, but to dump his stuff and go round to see Cleo.

★ ★ ★

Cleo and Rachel were chatting as they cleared up after their meal, so they had not heard the van come up the driveway. Cleo jumped at the knock on the back door and Rachel laughed at her reaction, saying, 'It's not likely to be a mad axe man, is it?'

'Martyn,' Cleo said in surprise when she opened the door. Trying to suppress her large grin, she turned back to say, 'Not the mad axe man this time.' Rachel disappeared upstairs.

'Sorry to disappoint you,' Martyn replied as he stepped into the kitchen and stood before Cleo, savouring the proximity.

'I'm not disappointed. Far from it,' Cleo murmured as she pushed the door shut.

'How far?' he asked as his arms snaked around her waist and pulled her towards him. She had no time to answer as his lips gently brushed hers. Speech was unnecessary as they kissed with increasing passion but as their limbs entwined, Cleo suddenly thought about Rachel. She could come back in at any moment. The realisation acted like a bucket of cold water and she stopped kissing the gorgeous man in her arms. He took her glance over his shoulder to indicate the kitchen table and turned her around to make for it.

'No. No. We can't.'

'You want to.' Martyn stated this as a fact whilst he nuzzled her neck. As he moved up to kiss an earlobe, she placed her hands on his shoulders and pushed him away.

'Rachel's here. We just can't,' she repeated.

He looked so crestfallen she almost laughed. Taking his hands in hers, she said, 'I can make you some tea.'

'Tea? You mean you're going to put bromide in it?'

'No. Just water, milk and Tetleys.' As she moved to the kettle he said, 'Well, I'll help you then, just to make sure,' and stood close behind her, with one of his hands on each of her wrists. Together they moved from the counter to the sink where Cleo filled the kettle. Then they stepped in synchronised motion to the fridge for the milk.

'I don't think we can keep this up, you know,' Cleo giggled as they tracked back with the bottle.

'I can,' he replied confidently, lifting her hand up to the cupboard to collect the mugs.

'How are we going to sit down?'

'Easy. You sit on my lap. See?' he said reversing onto a chair and drawing her down onto him. When he started to kiss the back of her neck they both heard footsteps on the stairs and Cleo leapt away so that she appeared to be leaning on the far side of the pine table by the time her daughter came in.

'Hi Martyn. You going to do any more plumbing for us?' Rachel asked.

'Hi. No, not at the moment.' He thought quickly, 'I just called round to see if your Mum wanted a lift to the dive meeting.'

'You're a bit early,' Rachel replied, checking her watch. 'It's only quarter past six. It's not 'til eight, is it, Mum?'

'No,' Cleo answered, wondering how to explain such an early arrival. Fortunately no such explanation was needed as Rachel continued, 'Great, you can help us plan Mum's party.'

She settled herself opposite Martyn as Cleo placed a full mug of tea by him and stood sipping her own. She gazed at the pictures on the wall above the counter. They had been there for years as Rachel had made them in primary school and, although the paper was going brown, Cleo still kept them. Her favourite was Rachel's depiction of herself cuddling Cleo, with the badly formed letters underneath proclaiming 'I love my Mummy'.

'You're having a party?' Martyn asked, looking from the daughter to the mother.

'I didn't want one, but…'

'But she has no choice. She's getting one because you can't be forty and not celebrate it. And she was working hard all day today so she needs a treat.'

'You were?' Martyn enquired.

'Yes. I start teaching a new module next term so I thought I'd better get my head stuck in some books.'

'It's hopeless when she does that. She goes into this work zone and doesn't hear the phone or anything.'

'You're exaggerating. I'm not that bad.'

'You are. I rang you today and you didn't answer,' Rachel said accusingly.

'When?' Cleo asked, frowning.

'Afternoon. Just after lunch and again later.'

'I was here all day.'

'Did you have your phone on?'

'I don't know. I think so.'

'She's hopeless,' Rachel confided to Martyn. 'Sometimes forgets her mobile altogether, then when she does have it, it's switched off.' Resuming her party organiser mode, she continued, 'Some of my friends are in a band. They're really good and they could come and play.' He began to see that her plan was more for a teenager's party than for Cleo. He would have to get a present though.

'When is it?'

'Saturday.'

'This Saturday?'

'Yes.'

Cleo registered the surprise on his face and said, 'I think it's too soon, Rach.' She took a seat at the table. 'Surely this isn't the time to celebrate?'

'It is. You can't move your birthday.' She ticked things off on her fingers: 'The band is booked, they've got a sound system, the bowling club's available, I've sorted out the food. All we need now is some beer and decorations and stuff.' As she felt the adult's opposition, she played her final card, 'Dad liked a good party. He'd want us to do it. I want us to do it.'

There was a silence while Cleo considered. 'Please, Mum.'

'OK, then.'

'Great. You won't regret it,' Rachel said, hugging Cleo. 'I'll tell the guys they're on,' she called as she ran back upstairs.

'Well, she seems pleased about that,' Martyn observed.

'I don't know if I've done the right thing,' Cleo replied. 'At the moment she's up one day and down the next. It's better than her crying. This will distract her for a while.'

'Yeah. I'm a bit worried though.'

'What about?' Cleo said, suddenly anxious herself.

'I didn't know you were that old.' She tried to kick him under the table but connected with the wooden support instead.

'Ow.'

'See? Your co-ordination's going now you're getting older.' She scowled at him, rubbing her injured foot.

'Let me,' Martyn said, moving his chair around and taking her foot into his lap where he massaged it gently. 'Better?'

'Hmmm.' Cleo leant back and lifted her other leg to double the pleasure.

He continued the motion on both feet as he asked, 'Shall I give you a lift to Brian's?' but then he felt her body tense.

'No. I don't think we should arrive together.' She withdrew her legs.

'But I want to be with you.' He was afraid he sounded petulant.

'What about tomorrow?'

'I'm due to start demolishing a bathroom. In fact I'm overdue. Should have been doing it on Monday. The guy's already complaining.'

It was Cleo's turn to look disappointed.

'Maybe I'll tell him I can't start until Friday,' Martyn suggested.

'Yes. Let's have tomorrow just for us.'

'I'll call you in the morning. On your mobile or home?'

'Either.'

'Your mobile doesn't always get a signal though, does it?'

'It works fine here.'

He wondered about her phone and her whereabouts earlier, but he quickly dismissed it. He was happy that he was going to have a whole day with her and nothing else mattered.

★ ★ ★

All the members of the diving club committee were gathered around the dining table in Brian's house. The kitchen gleamed with aluminium and polished granite surfaces. The stone tiles added to the clinical feel of the place and contrasted strongly with the cosiness of Cleo's home. Waiting for the meeting to begin, she felt that the warm peachy tones in her own house contributed to a sense of welcome. This was absent from the cool blues and greys here. Although they complemented the materials in the kitchen admirably, it was utilitarian rather than comforting. Brian passed a can of beer to Graham and said, 'Right then, I suppose before we get to the first agenda item we ought to elect a new chairman.'

Nobody said anything for a moment as they contemplated the fact that Tony's death had created a vacancy on the committee.

'I still can't believe it,' Lynne said, looking as if she might start crying at any moment.

'I know,' Cleo replied, wondering if she should say that she missed him or something, but she couldn't bring herself to do it.

'This time last week he was fine,' Brian said, as if this was news to everyone. 'It'll be odd to go on dive trips without him now.'

'At least we won't have him going off doing something stupid that puts other people in danger,' Graham said.

'That's a bit harsh, isn't it?' Lynne replied.

'Well, I'm sorry,' John said, 'but the fact remains that Tony put both himself and Martyn at risk. This club had an excellent safety record and the only two incidents we've had have revolved around him ignoring basic rules.'

'So he broke the rules a bit. Doesn't mean he should die,' Lynne responded angrily.

'Of course I didn't mean he should die,' John said defensively.

'Come on, everyone,' Brian said, 'It's no good us all getting at each other.' He looked around at the assembled faces, to Cleo, John, Graham, Lynne and his gaze stopped at Martyn. 'It seems obvious to me that we second Martyn on to the committee and then we can elect him to be chairman.'

'Can we do that?' asked Lynne. 'Don't we have to vote everyone on to the committee at the AGM?'

'We're not going to wait until then to have a chairman, are we?' Brian retorted. 'Martyn's in the club, but not on the committee and he hasn't got a job, whilst everyone else has.'

'Shouldn't you ask if anyone else fancies the job of chairman?' asked Graham.

'OK. Does anyone want to do it?'

'Yes. I do,' Graham stated immediately, putting his can down as if staking his claim to the position.

'Fine. Does anyone object to Graham being chairman?' Brian asked.

Everyone either muttered 'No' or shook their heads.

'And can we second Martyn on to the committee?' This suggestion was greeted with more enthusiastic nods and vocal assents.

Graham picked up his agenda and sat up straighter in his seat, 'Well, I'd like to welcome you all to the meeting. Has everybody read the minutes from last time?' Almost everyone agreed and those who had not done so rapidly scanned the papers before them. 'And can we pass them as a true record?' All confirmed that it was. 'Right, passed. Lynne, you might want to make a note of the spelling mistakes at the bottom of page two and the top of page three.' He pointed out the relevant words to Lynne on his left. She felt like stabbing his podgy, freckled hand with her pen. He'd only been the chairman two minutes and he was already finding fault with her. Tony had never done that.

'Right, then. Dive officer's report?' Graham looked to John who answered with, 'I don't think there's much to say about last weekend, except of course that it was a terrible accident and safety issues should always be of paramount importance.'

'He shouldn't have gone in the sub anyway,' Graham pointed out.

'And he definitely shouldn't have left Martyn at the top,' Brian added.

Graham continued, 'We obviously haven't got a training officer now, so I'd like to volunteer for that position if that's alright.' As no-one objected he continued, 'We had an enquiry from someone who wants to do a try dive in the pool, so they'll be coming down next week. Next item, treasurer's report.'

Brian spoke up, 'The club account stands at £5,065, which is a long way off our target for a new boat. We really do need a fund-raising campaign.'

'Or a generous donor,' Graham said, looking pointedly at Cleo. He glanced at his agenda. 'As we're on Cleo, Social Secretary next.'

'I feel a bit awkward about this,' Cleo began. 'Rachel wants to hold a party on Saturday. You know it's my birthday?'

'Of course,' Lynne replied.

'Well, I don't know whether it's a good idea, with everything that's happened. What do you think?'

'It's only a party, isn't it?' John said. 'Where's the harm?'

'I'll tell you where the harm is,' Graham responded rapidly, 'It'll be like dancing on Tony's grave, won't it?'

Cleo flinched as if struck.

'Graham…,' Brian said, about to remonstrate.

'That's what I'm worried about, that some people might feel that,' Cleo said uncertainly.

'It's not really my place,' Martyn felt he should say something supportive, 'but Cleo was thinking of Rachel. She thought it might distract her a bit and she's got friends who play in a band. It would be good for them and for Paula, wouldn't it?' he asked Graham.

Graham had the wind taken out of his sails somewhat. He knew that Paula loved to party and that with her impending motherhood, opportunities to do so in future might be more problematic, particularly if he and Elaine had to babysit. It might be better to let her enjoy herself now.

'Well, maybe,' he admitted grudgingly.

'So, will everyone spread the word and come to the party on Saturday night?' Cleo asked.

'We will,' Brian answered for everyone. 'Sorry, I forgot to mention the next dive trip earlier, but we're due to go to West Bay in a couple of weeks. Who's going? Because I need to book accommodation.'

'I'm away that weekend,' Lynne said.

'I don't want to go just yet,' Martyn added.

'I don't think I can make it either,' Cleo replied.

'Listen to you all,' Graham said with quiet venom. 'Everyone's too scared to say what they really think. It's trust, isn't it? You have to trust your buddy, otherwise you're up shit creek. Tony was murdered and one of us in this room could be the murderer. Who wants to go diving when they might be next?'

As if on cue, a police car drew up outside Brian's house and all eyes watched as Inspector Jamieson and Sergeant Fry got out and walked up the path.

'They're coming to arrest you, Cleo,' Graham continued, spitefully. 'They're coming to take you away for murdering your husband.'

Cleo had gone very pale. Martyn wanted to reach across Lynne and hold her hand. They sat in frozen silence as Brian opened the door to the policemen and escorted them in.

Ian Jamieson said, 'Graham Bright, we'd like you to come down to the station with us, please.'

CHAPTER 23

Ian and Bill sat across the table from Graham in their customary positions when interviewing suspects. The local police force had been remarkably accommodating, so they effectively had the run of the station now as PC Field was the only other officer on duty that night. Graham had refused the offer of a solicitor to sit in on the interview when he found out that it would take forty-five minutes for one to get there. He had been stunned that they had come for him at Brian's house, and had acquiesced quietly at the time, but now he was feeling bullish. He had done nothing wrong, so he shouldn't be in a police station at this time of night when he wanted to be at home, savouring the fact that he was now club chairman with another beer.

After Bill had started the tapes, Ian began, 'How long have you been diving, Graham?'

'Ten years or so, why?'

'And have you always used the same type of kit?'

'Pretty much, yes. I've had two different sorts of regulator but surely you haven't brought me down here now to ask me about my shopping habits?'

'No. Have you ever used rebreather equipment?'

'Wouldn't touch it with a barge pole.' Graham sat back in his chair with his arms folded, displaying the attitude of a man who wanted to get things over and done with quickly.

'But do you know how to use it?' Ian persisted.

'No. There's no need. Why are you asking me this?'

'You see, someone found some rebreather kit abandoned in the sea, not far from the diving location where Tony died.'

'Very interesting. What's that got to do with me?' Graham asked impatiently.

Sergeant Fry took up the questioning. 'You didn't like Tony much, did you?'

'He was alright,' Graham replied carefully, wondering where this was leading.

'Rumour has it that you thought he'd got your daughter pregnant and you weren't too chuffed about it. That right?'

'You can't believe rumours.'

'Do you have any proof that he was the father?'

'No,' Graham replied sullenly.

'No? But that didn't stop you mouthing off to your work colleagues, did it? Apparently,' Bill referred to his notes, 'you said he was little short of a paedophile and if he hadn't died you'd have "cut his balls off and made him eat them". That doesn't sound very friendly, does it?'

'Ha!' Graham laughed nervously. 'Just a joke, that's all.'

'Did anyone find it funny?'

Graham shifted uncomfortably in his seat, remembering the shocked silence that had greeted that particular outburst.

'I didn't kill him. You can't pin it on me.'

Ian resumed control of the interview, taking a reasonable tone of explanation. 'You see, Graham, we have to follow certain methods in police investigations. You've probably heard of the key factors to consider – motive, means and opportunity. You've got a motive to kill Tony, the means would be to hold him away from his breathing apparatus and you had the opportunity on the Saturday. That makes you a prime suspect.'

Graham leant forward, frowning, trying to follow what the inspector was saying. 'Wait a minute, wait a minute. I was ill on the Saturday. I didn't go diving with the others.'

'Precisely,' Ian agreed. 'You weren't with them. You could have gone diving on your own. You could have used the rebreather kit and killed Tony underwater, when there were no witnesses.'

'No, I couldn't. I didn't. I don't know how to use the bloody rebreather kit,' he blustered. He looked from one to the other, trying to find some way to prove his innocence. 'That stuff that was found. It's expensive right? And you have to go on a special training course to use it?'

'Yes,' the inspector agreed, based on their new-found knowledge after having spoken to Dave at the DDRC.

'So I'd have thought that anyone buying that sort of equipment was on a register somewhere.'

'Also true. You sound well informed,' Ian commented. He stretched his long legs out before him as he studied Graham and weighed up the likelihood of him being the murderer.

'No. I'm just trying to point out it's not me,' Graham stated. 'If you've got hold of it, can't you track the owner from a serial number or something?'

'We could and we did. It led us to a false address.' Graham looked as disappointed as they had been at the outcome. He looked down at the table wondering how he could prove that it wasn't him. He wished that he had never said those things at work. Elaine had been right about the danger that put him in. The thought irked him. He did not like it when he was in the wrong and she was proven right.

'Have you got anyone who can vouch for your whereabouts that day?' Bill asked.

'I was sick. I was in my room,' Graham protested. 'No one else was there, because they were out on the boat.'

'That's unfortunate,' Bill replied, although his tone lacked sincerity.

'But I was incapable. I was drunk. I was in no fit state to go diving.'

'You could have been pretending to be unwell.'

'Brian,' Graham said desperately. 'Ask Brian. He'll remember. I threw up in the basin and I pissed in the wardrobe.'

A flicker of distaste passed across the inspector's face.

'I thought it was the bathroom,' Graham added unnecessarily.

'When did you do this?' Ian asked.

'In the night sometime. I don't know.'

'So it doesn't prove where you were during the day?'

'I went out for a walk late morning, just to get some air.' Ian thought that the atmosphere in Graham's room must have been somewhat unpleasant.

'Did anyone see you? Who can corroborate that?' Bill interjected.

'Lots of people saw me. I went for a hair of the dog down by the harbour side. The pub there, what's it called... The Anchor.'

'Will anyone remember you there?'

'I don't know,' Graham replied. Realising that the situation was not looking good for him, he tried to re-direct their attention. 'I didn't do it. You shouldn't be questioning me. You're on the wrong track here.'

'And what would the right track be?' Bill queried, adjusting his ample frame on the uncomfortable plastic chair.

'Cleo. His wife. You should be interrogating her.'

'We've spoken to the lady in question,' the inspector replied, 'but she was on the boat and therefore has a cast-iron alibi, unless the whole club is lying.'

'She's no lady,' Graham scoffed. 'She'll be in league with a lover, won't she? They probably planned to bump him off together.'

'And who would that be?'

'I don't know, do I? Martyn, maybe? She's been making up to him.'

'Mr Share is not a suspect.'

'Well, someone else, then. She'll have conned another gullible fool to do her dirty work for her so she can get his millions.'

'You obviously know about the inheritance,' Ian commented, 'but are you certain that Cleo will get it?'

'What? Well, won't she?'

The inspector decided to ignore the question as it was something that he wanted answered himself. 'Right, we need to keep you here until we can check out your story.'

'What do you mean?' Graham said, alarmed.

'We need to find someone who remembers seeing you on Saturday, in order to prove that you weren't out at sea, killing Tony.'

'But I wasn't,' Graham protested. 'How are you going to find anyone now?' He checked his watch. 'It's after ten o'clock.'

'Quite. I'm sure PC Field will make you comfortable in a cell overnight and then we'll see what we can find out tomorrow.' Ian rose as Bill turned off the tape recorder.

'Wait. You can't keep me here. I haven't done anything.'

Graham got up and moved towards the men aggressively.

'I wouldn't advise assaulting a police officer,' Ian stated. Graham stopped immediately.

'I haven't done anything,' he repeated as the policemen left. 'Wait. Elaine'll wonder why I haven't come back.'

'You can call her on the way to your cell,' Bill suggested, nodding to PC Field to organise this for him. Turning back to Ian he added in an undertone, 'But she might be happy to be rid of him for a while.'

As they walked up the corridor to the office they had requisitioned for the duration of their stay, Ian replied, 'It won't hurt him to stew in there for a night until we can check his story. I hope you've booked us into somewhere a little more luxurious?'

'Yes. It's supposed to be a good quality hotel nestling in the valley with picturesque views of the river.'

'We're not tourists, you know.'

'No. Although I must admit my choice was influenced by the fact that they stock beer from both the Wye Valley and Kingstone breweries, so I thought we could sample the local delicacies.' Bill stroked his protruding belly in anticipation.

★ ★ ★

The following morning Cleo was in a state of nervous excitement as she drove to Martyn's flat. She felt it was better to meet there as she would be more likely to relax, knowing that Rachel would not walk in on them. However, she was far from relaxed currently. Her stomach was turning over, but in a bizarrely pleasant way. Her hands were sweating on the steering wheel and she wiped them on her jeans. She did not want to meet him with slimy hands. She had not been to the house before so she slowed, following his directions. There was a crossroads in the village, then up the hill, past the church on the right, through some woods, around a corner by a school, then the house was on the left. She turned into the driveway and looked up, noting the turret room on the side that was part of Martyn's flat. He said that the house belonged to an old lady who was somewhat hard of hearing. Remembering the phrase, a delicious surge of desire flowed through her. Did he mean that if they had a noisy lovemaking session she would be none the wiser? Or did he mean they could put Radio 4 on loudly and she would not complain? She smiled to herself, hoping it was the former. Surely she couldn't just arrive and leap into bed with him though? Should they go for a walk first? As she turned away from the car she saw the travelling rug on the back seat. It had been an anniversary present years ago to her and Tony. She brushed the unwelcome thought aside and walked to the porch eagerly.

Upstairs in the flat, Martyn was checking that it looked tidy. He pulled the duvet straight and wondered if he would be back under it soon. It would be ungentlemanly to jump on her the moment she came through the door, but he didn't know how much longer he could wait. When he heard the bell, he ran downstairs and opened the door, greeting Cleo with, 'Well, fancy seeing you here.' She grinned, replied 'Morning,' and stepped inside. They kissed briefly and then Martyn stood back to let her lead the way up the stairs. It was too awkward to do this holding hands, so they let them fall and he admired her closely fitting jeans as he followed.

'Here we are,' Martyn said as they walked into the sitting

249

room. 'I'll give you the guided tour.' He remained standing still as he continued, 'This is the kitchen/living area, bathroom to the right and bedroom to the left.' Cleo's eyes lingered on the doorway to the last room mentioned, but then she took in the cosiness of their current location. There was a sofa, a thick rug in front of the brick fireplace, colourful curtains and a mahogany table and chairs which matched the cabinet beside it. 'It's lovely,' she said. 'Compact, but lovely.'

'Yes. It'll do for now and then I'll look around to buy somewhere later, when the business is established.'

'Was that guy alright about you starting his bathroom on Friday?'

'Yes. You'll know him actually. I forgot, but it's Jim that works at your factory as a security guard.'

'Jim Common?'

'That's right.' Martyn moved to face her and his arms encircled her body. 'So, what would you like to do? Don't say you want a cup of tea.'

'Coffee?' Cleo asked as she allowed her body to melt into his.

'Sorry. Coffee's off.'

'We could go for a walk in the woods?'

'Got a bad leg, I'm afraid. I can barely limp anywhere.'

'Do you need to rest it?'

'I really need to lie down somewhere.'

Cleo pulled away from him. 'Perhaps I should drive you to the hospital and see if they have a bed available?'

'No need, really. I have one here.'

'I can't see it.'

'Come this way,' Martyn urged, taking her hand and leading her into his bedroom.

'Wow, I've always wanted a turret room.' Cleo went ahead of him to admire the forest. There was a series of windows around the room so that almost every aspect of the view was covered. Martyn came up behind her and slid his hands around to the front of her jeans. Cleo tried to pull her stomach in, realising with horror that the timing was all wrong. Why had they engineered this so that their first passionate encounter was going to be in broad daylight? He would be turned off by the hideous patchwork of stretch marks on her dimpled blancmange stomach. Either they could delay until nightfall – unlikely, she thought as Martyn started kissing her neck, or she would have to get him out of the room while she undressed. Her gaze fell on the car in the drive below.

'Oh no!'

'What?' he asked, murmuring in her ear.

'I forgot to lock the car.'

'It'll be fine. There's no one about.'

His fingers were undoing the button of her jeans and now one hand was unzipping whilst the other slipped beneath the fabric.

She stopped his hands. 'No, really. I'll be worried about it.' She pulled her keys out of her pocket. 'Could you go down and lock it for me?'

'What? Now?' Suppressing the urge to say 'Forget the car!' or to rephrase it more forcefully, Martyn grabbed the keys and took the stairs two at a time.

Cleo undressed at lightning speed, ripping off her jumper and shirt together whilst kicking off her shoes. As she tried to remove both pants and jeans at the same time she crashed into a bookcase. Regaining her balance and discarding her clothes in a chaotic pile, she undid her bra. She could hear Martyn's feet pounding up the stairs as her best underwear, carefully selected that morning, was thrown onto the heap. When Martyn came back into the room, Cleo was safely hidden under the duvet.

He grinned appreciatively. 'You want to go for a walk in the woods then?'

'Maybe later.'

As he pulled his t-shirt over his head, Cleo admired his well-muscled torso. She squirmed in the bed, trying to remove her socks unobtrusively but still managed to notice the golden hairs on his tanned forearms as he tossed the shirt aside.

'Are you going to draw the curtains?' she asked.

'Lock the car! Draw the curtains! Is there no end to your demands, woman?' he answered as he removed his jeans.

'I do have others,' she replied, studying the impressive bulge in his boxers. She felt the weight of him draw the bed down as he sat on the edge to pull his socks off.

'I don't want to be in darkness,' he replied, turning to face her. 'I want to look at you and I want you to see me.'

He stood to take his boxers off but had his back to her. God, what a hunk, she thought, noting the way that the soft jersey cotton clung to his pert buttocks. The shape of the muscles created slight dents leading down to meaty thighs. And he's getting into bed with me. He turned, lifting the duvet at the same time and climbed in beside her. She felt his warm body pressing against hers. He moved up to give her a peck on the cheek, said 'Night then' and turned over.

Cleo lay in complete confusion.

Was this what he wanted? To sleep together? Literally? Had he felt the stretch marks earlier when he undid her jeans and been repulsed? Should she slide out of bed and scuttle off home, hoping they could both forget the whole sorry incident? As she contemplated the distance from the bed to the pile of her clothes and on to the door, Martyn moved beside her.

'Come here, gorgeous,' he said, turning back as his arms enveloped her and one of his strong legs pushed across her stomach, claiming the rest of her body.

'Swine!' Cleo uttered, before his mouth closed over hers at the start of a passionate kiss.

CHAPTER 24

Cleo was on her way to the solicitors later on Thursday afternoon. She smiled as she thought back over the hours with Martyn, still feeling an inner glow of satisfaction. Rachel was in town with friends so she was going to meet her at the office, along with John. Cleo wondered why George Murmur had asked him to attend, but presumed it was something to do with the company. John had told her about his plans for some re-structuring. Some of the existing team would have to take on Tony's work, but they would need to advertise for a marketing manager. Alarm bells had started to ring for Cleo if the new responsibilities meant that eyes other than hers would be examining the finances. Using the company account to subsidise her gambling would not be possible in future. At the moment she was almost back on an even keel, having had a great result yesterday. Online betting was both a boon and a temptation. It was so easy, but it lacked the excitement and atmosphere of going to the races. Then again, Martyn was currently providing all the excitement that she needed and when the will was read out later, that would take care of all her financial worries. Brian had already told her about the inheritance so there would be no need for her to appear shocked and surprised at the amount of money that Tony left her.

★ ★ ★

John, Rachel and Cleo were ushered into George Murmur's office and took their places on the seats ranged before his desk. The chairs and the desk were beautifully crafted combinations of oak and leather which looked as if they had seen a couple of generations of solicitors and clients through multitudes of meetings. The computer was an alien presence in this office which paid tribute to years of tradition. The grandfather clock ticked stolidly and Cleo wondered if its audible movement encouraged solicitors to charge every accountable second to one client or another. John thought the pictures of George's forebears on the walls pretentious, as if the place purported to be a minor stately home. It added to his feeling of discomfort. The sooner the business was done and he could get back to work, the better.

The solicitor entered the room and took his place at the desk. He shuffled the papers before him and began with, 'Thank you all for coming. As you know, you are here for the reading of the last will and testament of Antony Richard Fleming.' Cleo noticed that Rachel was searching in her pockets as a tear leaked from her eye. She handed a tissue to her daughter, hoping that it was not going to be too much of an ordeal for her. The action was noted by George who was sympathetic to young people losing their parents. He had anticipated that this would be a difficult meeting so he was anxious to proceed quickly. He continued, 'I won't burden you with all the legalese, because you won't want to be here any longer than absolutely necessary. Shortly before his death Antony inherited a substantial sum from an uncle.' Rachel looked up, surprised and then glanced at her Mum, whose expression remained impassive. 'The money has only recently come into Anthony's account. There is now an additional two point eight million added to his estate.'

'Mum!' Rachel exclaimed, 'Two point eight million. Did you know?'

'Well,' Cleo admitted, 'Brian did tell me that there had been a huge transfer of funds at the bank.' Rachel looked incredulous. 'But I didn't want to mention it until I knew it was true.'

'How could you not mention it?'

'I thought...'

'Can we get on?' John interrupted impatiently, thinking that his time was going to be wasted with a mother and daughter dispute.

'Yes, certainly,' George replied. 'If I can summarise the main items of interest for you: Cleo will get the house...' She smiled in acknowledgement. 'But the rest of Antony's estate, the two point eight million and his share in the company, is to be divided equally between Rachel Anne Fleming, his step daughter and John Ryan O'Donnell, his business partner.' Cleo had stopped smiling. John and Rachel looked shocked. Cleo was the first to speak.

'Sorry, I'm not sure I understood you correctly. I get the house, but Rachel and John get the fortune and the business. Is that right?'

'Perfectly, yes.'

'Oh.' She glanced at John who shrugged as if it was nothing to do with him, but it was Rachel who said, 'Why would he do that, Mum? Why wouldn't he leave everything to you?'

Cleo was desperately asking herself the same question. What had he known that had caused him to change his will? In the last one she knew about she had been the sole beneficiary.

'Um. I don't know. We hadn't been getting on that well recently…'

'Hadn't you?' Rachel said. The child must be blind and deaf, Cleo thought bitterly.

'When did he make that will?' Cleo asked.

'June twenty third.'

'And it is legally binding?'

'Oh, absolutely. He came in and we drew it up and when he was happy, he signed it.'

'Who were the witnesses?' Cleo wondered who else was privy to this time bomb of information.

'Jeff Saunders and his son, Gary, from the undertakers next door. They quite often pop in to witness wills for us. We need to work together sometimes, obviously, and we can rely on their discretion.'

'So it is all above board?' John queried.

'I can assure you that it is, yes.' George replied and continued quietly, 'Of course Rachel is only sixteen at the moment, so her money will be held in trust until her eighteenth birthday.'

★ ★ ★

That evening Martyn was first in the pool, relishing the feel of slicing through the still water as if it was for his sole use. He knew that Cleo would not be there tonight, because they had planned to meet up later, when their assignation could be kept secret from the rest of the club. As he turned back for his fourth length he saw Graham and John enter from the changing room and could hear Graham ranting about his treatment at the hands of the police. He stopped as they got into the water, making the customary complaints about the temperature. Greeting Martyn briefly, Graham continued with his diatribe about unfair imprisonment at the hands of the 'Laurel and Hardy' of the constabulary. As more of the dive club regulars arrived and Graham's audience swelled, so his description of his maltreatment expanded. As far as Martyn could make out, the police had not acted at all improperly, or abused his civil rights in any way. Recalling his own experience with Inspector Jamieson and Sergeant Fry he said,

'Surely they're allowed to hold anyone they like for questioning when it's a murder enquiry?'

Graham scowled at this unwelcome interruption which challenged his credibility as the injured party. 'What were they like with you?' he asked Martyn. 'Why didn't they hold you overnight?'

'I don't know. Maybe I told them what they needed to know and they didn't require me any longer.'

'What did they want to know?' Brian asked.

'They seemed particularly interested in how I'd held on to Tony when I was trying to pull him out of the sub. Wanted me to re-enact it holding onto the inspector's hands, which was a bit weird really,' Martyn remembered.

'How do you mean?' John sidled over to the group to join in the conversation.

'Well, I had to explain how I tried different grips and various positions when I was trying to get him out.'

'They ask the strangest questions, don't they?' Graham commented. 'Went on at me about whether I'd ever used rebreather kit. Couldn't see the point of that at all unless they're just trying to have free diving lessons.' Martyn decided to keep quiet about why they might be questioning divers on their use of rebreather equipment and he watched Graham turn to John. 'Maybe they'll come to you for a training session next.'

John smiled and launched himself into a rapid front crawl which excluded him from further comment temporarily. When he took a rest in the shallow end, only Graham remained and he leaned against the back wall, spreading his arms along the tiles,

'So, I guess they saw sense and released you this morning then?'

'They did, but with the caution that they might need to speak to me again about my whereabouts on the Saturday, once they've made "further enquiries"'.

'Why?' John asked, apparently relaxed and now making swirling patterns in the water with his hands.

'Well, I can't prove where I was that day, can I? You know I was too sick to go on the boat, so first I was in my room and then I went to The Anchor, but I doubt anyone will remember me. The police have got some crazy notion that I could have used a rebreather kit and gone out to murder Tony.'

'Really?' John replied, looking incredulous. 'What if someone could vouch for you at that pub?' he continued, thoughtfully.

'Well, that would be great, but there isn't anybody,' Graham replied morosely.

John stopped his movements but the undercurrents continued. 'There could be if you want there to be.' Speaking softly, he leaned closer to Graham, 'A mate of mine. He could have seen you in there and remembered you because you kicked up a rumpus when the fruit machine didn't pay out.'

'That could be right. That might have happened and I've

259

only just remembered it,' Graham considered. 'But why would this mate of yours want to say that?'

'He'll do it because friends do each other a favour now and again. He owes me, that's all. It would help you, wouldn't it?'

'Oh, yes. I'd really appreciate it.'

'Right then. It's done,' John said, shaking Graham's hand.

John resumed his swimming as he reviewed recent developments. He would soon be able to have a pool of his own in the new house which he could buy with Tony's money. He smiled to himself. Really, it had been quite funny to see the look on Cleo's face when she found that all she had was the house and that the inheritance was divided between himself and Rachel. She had been so confident that all the money would be hers. She should have thought that Tony might have made other arrangements, given the state of their relationship in the weeks and months before he died. Good old Tony. A last insulting act from beyond the grave to demonstrate how little he cared for his wife. Of course everyone would get to know sooner or later, but for now he wanted to keep the knowledge to himself, to savour the beauty of it.

★ ★ ★

When Martyn returned home from the pool, Cleo was waiting for him outside his flat.

'Hi, you must be desperate to see me,' he said, grinning at her. Cleo did not smile back. 'I've had some bad news.'

'What?' he asked, concerned.

'I don't get any of the money. It's gone to John and

Rachel, one point four million each. I can't believe he'd do that to me.'

'It's only money. I thought someone had died from the look on your face,' Martyn joked. Cleo looked as if she hated him. He didn't understand, but how could he? He didn't know about the strain her gambling put on her financial situation and she didn't want to tell him. The easy solution where Tony's inheritance would make up any shortfall was not going to happen. She would have to find funds somewhere else and fast. Luckily there was racing on tomorrow. She would bet wisely and everything would be alright.

'Why didn't he leave it to you?' Martyn continued, trying to be sympathetic, but in a way he was glad that she had not become fabulously rich, because then she might not want him any more.

'We hadn't been getting on that well before he died,' Cleo admitted reluctantly.

Martyn thought this must be something of an understatement, but he had walked ahead of her to unlock the door and now turned back saying, 'Come inside and I'll make you forget all about it for a while.'

Cleo smiled in spite of her mood. That was what she needed; a passionate encounter that would drive all other thoughts from her head. She took his outstretched hand, thinking that she was lucky to have this man who could make her feel like this. If she could get the finances back on an even keel, could she be happy with him? Could they move on from Tony's death and put everything behind them?

CHAPTER 25

On Friday morning Martyn drove his van to Jim Common's house and was welcomed warmly by the owner who ushered him into the bathroom. Mrs Common brought Martyn a cup of tea with a couple of digestive biscuits as Jim explained again what their plans were. Martyn was more used to a mug of tea that could be deposited anywhere in the workplace and he felt uncomfortable holding a proper china cup and saucer. It was obvious that the bathroom needed a complete refurbishment as the fixtures and fittings must have been untouched for decades, he thought. The rest of the house was immaculate; they had been on a gradual programme of renovation, with Jim doing the harder work with carpentry and wiring whilst Phyllis did most of the decorating. Jim explained that they had the time to do things properly now that he'd retired and they enjoyed working on the house together, although plumbing was beyond him.

'I thought you worked at Kidcars,' Martyn said, curious at his description of being retired.

'Oh, I do, yes, but only as a night watchman. In fact that's a bit of a grand term. I'm only there for a couple of hours in the evening, doing the rounds, checking the premises and locking up.'

'I'll just bring some of my stuff in,' Martyn said as he walked back along the plastic sheeting that Phyllis had put down to protect the carpet. He noted that he would have to be careful to skirt the flower arrangement that dominated the hall and clashed with the floral print wallpaper. Jim continued to talk as Martyn strode backwards and forwards carrying equipment. It did not seem to matter to Jim if Martyn was within earshot or not and he hoped that the continuous conversation was not going to dog his every movement, otherwise the job would seem to take a lot longer. As he knelt on the bathroom floor to sort out tools, Phyllis joined Jim in the doorway and they both talked at Martyn; his required participation was minimal. He decided that he would start with some heavy demolition in the hope that severe hammer blows to the bathroom furniture might make them think it was not a spectator sport.

'It was terrible about that nice Mr Tony wasn't it?' Phyllis said to Jim as they watched Martyn at their feet. 'Did you know him, dear?' Martyn had not registered at first that this question was addressed to him as he was trying to reduce their talk to an inconsequential murmur in his head. The ensuing silence attracted his attention and Phyllis repeated her question.

'Oh, yes, I did.'

'Such a dreadful accident.' Jim shook his head as he inspected some of the piping leaning against the doorframe.

'Well, we all thought it was an accident, didn't we dear? And then the police rang up and said it was murder.' Martyn thought that Phyllis and Jim were remarkably well suited in terms of their capacity for chatting. Jim took up the tale.

'Yes, a lovely young gentleman. Sergeant Fry his name was and I said 'as in bacon' and he laughed and wished he'd had some for breakfast. He asked if I could confirm that Mr John was at work that Saturday and I said that I could of course. I told him what lovely people they all were and such good employers and how we were all so upset for Mrs Cleo and Rachel.'

'Poor girl,' Phyllis added, 'losing her dad like that. The good Lord didn't see fit to bless us with children, but I really feel for her.'

Poor Martyn, he was thinking, if he had to endure this level of communication for days.

'It might get a bit dirty and dusty,' he said. 'Perhaps we ought to shut the door to keep all the mess inside?' For a horrible moment he thought they were both going to come in with him to supervise his every move, but fortunately Jim closed the door with them on the other side. He could hear them retreating to the kitchen, still chatting. 'Odd,' he thought, 'don't they realise that people who've been married for years and years are supposed to run out of things to say to each other.'

★ ★ ★

Ian Jamieson and Bill Fry sat in their adopted office in the police station reviewing the case. The room was not habitually used and had the neglected air of a spare room, filled with mismatched pieces of furniture and boxes of files. Bill was slightly hung over due to the amount of beer he had consumed the previous evening, but he had felt compelled to try out the various local brands which were on offer. It was one of the perks of staying away in the back of the beyond, as he viewed it, but of course it did not sit well with having to work on a Saturday morning. In contrast, Ian seemed alert and enthusiastic as he placed his coffee cup precisely in the centre of the coaster and straightened the papers before him.

'Right, let's be systematic about this. The questions we need to answer are: What happened? How did Tony die? Why did he have to die? And who could possibly have killed him?'

'Surely we know what happened and how he died,' Bill replied. 'He didn't use his breathing apparatus when underwater, so he drowned.'

'My point is that we don't know whether he couldn't get to his air because of some unforeseen accident or because he was held away from it.'

'But we've got those bruises,' Bill complained.

'Yes, but those marks do not provide us with cause and effect, unfortunately. There's always the chance they could be completely unrelated to his death,' Ian cautioned.

'I thought we'd decided that it wasn't an accident?'

'Yes, but it's just a thought, lurking at the back of my mind, that pretty well everyone involved says it was a tragic accident.'

'Well they would do, wouldn't they?' Bill responded tetchily, rubbing his forehead and wishing he had drunk more water. Ian noted the irritability of his sergeant and decided to move on.

'Let's consider the 'why'? Why would anyone want to get rid of Tony? Who had a motive?'

'Graham,' Bill answered promptly, 'because he thinks Tony was the father of the baby. Cleo, because she wants to be with her lover, Martyn.'

'They say they're not lovers, remember,' Ian pointed out. Bill shrugged as if this was neither here nor there and continued with his mental checklist.

'Martyn, because he wants to be with Cleo. John, because he'll inherit half of Tony's money.'

'Yes, John,' Ian said slowly. 'That was very useful our visit to Mr Murmur yesterday. Very helpful indeed to know who benefits from Tony's death.'

'I'll bet Cleo was cut up about that.'

'I would have thought so, yes,' Ian agreed. 'So then, is that our shortlist? No-one else in the club or out of it who might want him dead?'

'Not as far as we know,' Bill confirmed.

'OK. Let's take each one in turn. Graham,' Ian said. 'Bit strange the way he suddenly remembered having that argument in the bar, don't you think?'

'Stranger still that he can produce a witness to back it up,' Bill agreed. 'I don't know that I believe that story. I do believe he could be off his face enough to forget periods of time, but that would apply to the night when he was drinking, not the morning after when he was sobering up.'

'Well, if we don't believe his newly-made alibi, that means that he could have got to the dive site, used the rebreather kit and lain in wait for Tony.'

'Do you really think he'd do that?' asked Bill.

'Not really, no. I can see him committing a crime of passion when he was enraged about something and just went mad on the spur of the moment. I don't think he's got the temperament or the intellectual capacity to carry out such a premeditated murder. Next, Cleo.'

'I reckon she's a cold-hearted manipulator, so she could kill a man for sure,' Bill stated categorically.

'But why? She doesn't get the money, remember? And she was on the boat when Tony was underwater dying.'

'Well, she could be in collaboration with someone else. Martyn maybe.'

'But we'd eliminated him on the grounds that the times didn't fit, hadn't we?' Ian reminded Bill.

'So that leaves us with John. What do you think of him?' Bill asked his superior officer, hoping that he would come up with something inspired that would answer all their queries.

'I think he has both the personality and the intelligence to plan a crime, to stay cool under pressure and to maintain his innocence. However,' Ian said regretfully, 'he can't be a prime suspect because he's also got an alibi that you checked. He was here that weekend wasn't he, not diving with the others?'

'That's right. Jim, the night watchman, said he was at the factory.'

'The night watchman? You didn't say that before. You just said his alibi checked out.'

'Well, it does. He said he was there.'

'For God's sake, man, think. "The night watchman"' he stressed the words, 'would only be there in the evening at best. He can't have known whether John was at the factory all day and if he wasn't at the factory all day....'

'He could have been in the sea killing Tony in order to get his money,' Bill finished for him. 'Sorry,' he added, looking shamefaced.

'That's the sort of shoddy police work that I might expect from a green PC not an experienced detective like you.' Ian was clearly annoyed and Bill felt suitably reprimanded. He wondered how he could have made such an elementary mistake and cast his mind back. He thought he had made the call shortly after Martyn had confessed, so in his mind the file was closed and the culprit identified. Consequently there was little need to question the veracity of a statement about someone who was hundreds of miles away from the scene of the crime. He had to admit it was a bad error and he wanted to redress the balance by producing some intelligent analysis of the situation. Unfortunately his mind was blank apart from the oppressive ache that permeated his whole head.

★ ★ ★

Rachel was at the bowling club sorting out decorations for the party that night. Paula was helping, along with some of their friends. The building was long and low, all on one level with a bar at one end and a raised platform at the other for the band. In between there were clusters of tables and chairs, with most of these being at the sides so that the tiny dance floor was accessible in the middle. Two of the girls were standing on chairs to fix balloons above the bar. They had forbidden Paula from this task in case she fell off and hurt the baby. As Paula patted her large bump, she thought that it would be impossible for her to climb onto the chair anyway, given her size, but she was determined to have a good time dancing tonight.

'How long have you got to go now, Paula?' one of the girls asked.

'About ten weeks or so. I was looking in my book today and the baby looks like everything's there, now it just gets bigger and bigger.'

'Do you have to go for lots of checks?'

'Not really. I had one today at the doctors and she said everything's fine. At the moment the baby's head is up here,' she pointed to the top of her bump, 'but it could still turn round. Oh. It kicked just then.'

'Can I feel it?' Rachel asked. The others climbed down so they could all put their hands on Paula. 'Oh, yes.'

'Yes, there.'

Rachel spotted Cleo coming into the room and went to meet her as the others clamoured around the mum-to-be. Cleo was glad that she had insisted on no birthday banners. This way it could be any average party and the criticism of her partying the night away so soon after her husband's death might not spring so readily to people's minds. At least that was what she hoped.

As the day had progressed, she had felt increasingly uncomfortable about the whole idea of the party but Rachel seemed to be enjoying herself. Perhaps Lynne's suggestion that they should view it as a wake for Tony was a good one, because then people could have a good time celebrating a life rather than mourning a death. Of course Rachel did have something to celebrate, in the form of the one point four million that she would receive from Tony. How could he have changed the will like that without telling her, or the beneficiaries themselves? Could John and Rachel really have known nothing about it?

★ ★ ★

After another hour, the party at the bowling club was in full swing. The young band formed by Rachel's friends had proved surprisingly competent and they had played a set which got people up dancing. They had now switched to the disco while they had a break and would play again later. Elaine and Graham sat at a table at the side of the room, watching their daughter whirling around wildly on the dance floor with one of the boys from school.

'Isn't she going to damage the baby dancing like that?' Graham asked.

'What?' Elaine wondered why the music had to be so loud and if she was too old for this partying lark now. Graham repeated the question, leaning closer and shouting near her ear. She had been thinking much the same thing but did not want Graham to storm onto the floor and drag her off it.

'She'll be fine,' she said, glad that he was concentrating on Paula rather than suspecting any man she danced with as the possible father of the baby.

'Do you think it's him?' Graham asked loudly, apparently in tune with her thoughts.

'No,' she replied, with more confidence than she felt. Paula had already danced with lots of her friends from school, both girls and boys mingling together in a group. It would be very difficult to identify any individual she had been with as the probable father. As the current song finished and the next tune started up, Paula accosted John on his way back from the bar, asking him to dance. He had two pints of beer in his hands so it looked as if he refused. Paula looked crestfallen, but then threw herself into the rhythm of the music more energetically than ever. Elaine thought that her daughter ought to take a rest and got up to get her some water. It was very hot and Paula was looking flushed and sweaty rather than merely glowing. It had been a warm summer day and although the windows and doors were open the heat from so many bodies was oppressive in the confined space. Elaine stood at the edge of the gyrating crowd and managed to attract Paula's attention long enough to raise a glass of water.

'Thanks, Mum,' Paula said as she gulped the drink down gratefully.

'Are you alright? Do you need to rest for a bit?'

'Don't worry, Mum. I'm fine. I'm having a great time.'

'What about the baby?'

'It likes the music,' she yelled, returning to the throng.

CHAPTER 26

Cleo saw John walking out of the door and followed him. She wanted to ask if he had known about the will. She looked to the right where the tennis courts used to be, then to the left and saw John by the edge of the bowling green. She had a fleeting impression that someone else had just moved away from him, but decided it must have been her imagination as there was no-one else about as she got closer.

'We need to talk,' she said.

'Do we want to be seen together, here? Now?' John asked.

'Let's go into the playground then,' Cleo suggested. They walked up the driveway and turned right, cutting down through a gap in the hedge to the top corner of the field. There was a seesaw by them, next to a series of swings across the top edge of the sloping field, with a slide, roundabout and climbing frame further down. There was also a small shelter on one side of the play area and that was where Cleo and John headed.

'Did you know that you and Rachel were going to get all Tony's money?' Cleo asked in an accusatory tone.

'No. I thought you'd get it, and then we would share it, like we'd planned,' John replied.

'So are we going to share it, now that you've got it instead of me?'

'I've only got half, haven't I? I've got what would have

come to me as his business partner. You should be asking Rachel about hers.'

'Don't be ridiculous. How can I say to Rachel that I should have a part of the money because we planned the death of her father to achieve just that result?'

'That's your problem, not mine,' John snapped.

'But we were going to share the money,' Cleo repeated, cursing herself for the pleading tone that had crept into her voice.

'You've got a different Share on your mind now though, haven't you?'

'What do you mean?' Cleo asked defensively.

'I mean Martyn. You want him, don't you? It's not me and you any more, is it? Or is it?' He stepped closer and moved to put his arms around her but she retreated.

'We're in this together,' he stated.

'It was you that killed him,' Cleo pointed out as she backed up against the wall. John laughed softly.

'I really wouldn't recommend you going down that route.' He followed her and placed a hand on either side of her shoulders. 'You might find that a dangerous path to pursue, not good for your health.' Cleo felt trapped. There was no chance of escaping from John's powerful arms and returning to the safety of the clubhouse. She had admired his physical strength in the past, but now he was a murderer, not a lover, and he was extremely threatening.

'Cleo?' Martyn appeared at the entrance to the shelter. John moved away and Cleo stepped towards Martyn and took his hand thankfully. 'You OK?' he asked, solicitously.

'Ah, how touching, the young lover,' John sneered.

'How did you know I was here?' Cleo asked.

'I came looking for you and I heard voices.'

'What did you hear?' Cleo sounded alarmed.

'Are you worried, Cleo? Do you think he won't love you if he knows what you're really like?' John taunted. He stood with his arms crossed now, feet planted apart as he surveyed the other two.

'What does he mean?' Martyn said, turning to look at Cleo.

'Nothing. Let's go back to the party.'

She made to leave but Martyn pulled her back. 'No. I do love you. Why wouldn't I?'

Cleo was confused. He had just said that he loved her. If she told the truth he would never want to see her again. She could not answer him.

'What does he know that I don't? Tell me,' Martyn insisted.

'If we're going to talk about this, we should move out of here, so we can see anyone before they get within earshot,' John said, leaving the shelter and moving down the field towards the roundabout. Cleo hesitated but Martyn pulled her after him as he followed John. The sky was darkening rapidly into night and the chestnut trees at the top of the field cast deep shadows. 'Right then, a seat for the lady,' John said as he took Cleo's other hand and led her to sit on one section of the roundabout, causing Martyn to let go of her. As soon as she was sitting, John gave one of the hand rails a tremendous push and it started rotating.

'It's a game of chance. Who will win Lady Luck? Him or me?' John gave the roundabout another hefty shove and Cleo had to cling on in order to maintain her balance. 'Where she stops no-one knows.'

'Don't play stupid games,' Martyn said as he moved to stop Cleo's sickening spin. John's strong arms held him back.

'Afraid not, my young friend. The lady has to choose for herself.'

'She has chosen. She's with me,' Martyn replied angrily, wrenching himself free of John's grip.

'Ah, but is she really? Or is she playing what you so aptly describe as a stupid game?'

'I am not,' Cleo shouted as she swung past, putting out a foot to drag along the ground, trying to slow the motion of the roundabout.

'Is she just using you for some purpose that you're unaware of?'

Martyn looked doubtful, uncertain what John could mean. Cleo jumped off, but was unsteady on her feet and fell against Martyn, who instinctively put an arm out to steady her.

'Shut up, John,' Cleo hissed urgently.

'But why? He says he loves you. Surely he should know the real you, otherwise how can he love you deeply, wholly, completely? And you, you trust him, don't you? Shouldn't you need to share your deepest, darkest secret with him to achieve true loving communion?'

'No. Shut up,' Cleo repeated.

'Ah, she doesn't trust you enough, Martyn. Maybe you are just a young stud and she wants you for your body, nothing more.'

Martyn looked at Cleo, asking the question.

'No, that's not true,' she cried. 'I love you. It's just …'

'It's just she can't bring herself to tell you that wasn't in the plan,' John completed for her. 'Sit yourself down, young stud, and I'll tell you a story.' Martyn found himself propelled

275

into the seat recently vacated by Cleo, but this time John held the roundabout still as he spoke quietly, close to Martyn's face. 'Once upon a time there was a husband, a wife and the husband's business partner. The wife was dissatisfied with her husband and started an affair with the business partner.' Martyn looked at Cleo, hoping for a vehement denial, but she turned away. John continued, 'To begin with, it was just sex for convenience but they became close over time. When the husband came into a large inheritance, they planned to kill him in order to be together and enjoy the money.'

'No,' Martyn interrupted. 'I don't believe it. You wouldn't,' he said, looking at Cleo.

'I didn't want to. He made me do it,' Cleo pleaded.

'Don't listen to her. She lies,' John stated casually. 'Anyway, I haven't finished my story. The wife and the partner obviously didn't want to be found guilty of the husband's death, so they needed a fall guy. This is where you come in,' he smiled cruelly. 'We wanted a diver who we could put in the right place at the right time, so he would be the prime suspect for the murder. He would have a motive because Cleo here, the femme fatale, would lead him on and he would believe that she cared for him. More importantly, the police would accept that he had a reason to do away with the husband. Does this sound familiar?' Martyn was shocked. Surely all those times with Cleo could not be based on lies and deception? His head was spinning just as if John had set the roundabout in motion again.

'Cleo. It's not true, is it?' he asked, stricken.

'It's not true that I was just leading you on. I care about you. I love you, honestly.' She came to stand before him, looking deep into his eyes. 'I love you and I want to be with you.'

'But the plan with Tony? You decided to murder him?' he asked incredulously.

'He made me do it. I didn't want to,' Cleo repeated.

'But you said you didn't get any money in his will,' Martyn pointed out.

'Yes, that's right,' Cleo said eagerly. 'So I don't gain anything from his death.'

'But she didn't know that at the time,' John cut in, stepping between them. 'The question is, what are we going to do next? The police are still investigating. If they come asking questions we all need to have consistent answers that tie in together. They haven't got any concrete evidence so they can't prosecute us if we all say the same thing. If either of you say anything to incriminate me, I'll say it was you two who cooked the whole thing up. Martyn, you'll be a murderer. I imagine you'll go down for a long time. Think about it.' John pushed Martyn onto the seat, seized the bar and took a few steps with it to get the roundabout moving again. He released it with a further push and Martyn spun past them. He saw trees, the slide, a house, swings, Cleo, John, trees, the slide, a house, swings, Cleo, John. How had this happened to him? He thought he had found the love of his life and now he was embroiled in a murder.

John stood alongside Cleo. 'He's thinking about it, Cleo. If he gets off and walks away that's you and him over.' Cleo had the same thought and was trying to quell her mounting anxiety that he would do just that. Martyn was remembering the time at the submarine when he was struggling to get Tony out. Then he thought about the police questions. He stopped the roundabout and addressed John.

'You were already in the sub, weren't you? You weren't at work in the factory all day. But you could have got back in time for the evening, so Jim would say he'd seen you there.'

'He's not just a pretty face then, Cleo?' John observed wryly. 'The point is Martyn, unless you play ball, I will tell the police how you and Cleo plotted to kill Tony and how you did the deed in the sub. I can provide convincing details that I overheard the two of you discussing it, so don't even think about going to the police, because you will be signing your life away.'

'But you said they can't prosecute without evidence.'

'Indeed I did. What I should have said, more accurately, is that they can't prosecute me without evidence. Of course there is something severely incriminating about Cleo.'

'What?' Cleo said, alarmed.

'There are those text messages which you sent me. I think the police would be interested in them.'

'But you said we should destroy those mobiles we used to call each other.'

'Yes, I did. I know you got rid of yours. How obedient you were. But I kept mine.' He smiled and his teeth seemed unnaturally white in the first hint of moonlight which strayed over the threesome. 'Just a little insurance, you see.' He turned to Martyn, 'There's really no alternative. You have to play along. Follow my rules and all will be well.'

'But surely the police will keep asking questions?' Martyn replied uncertainly.

'And we'll keep giving them the same answers. They'll stop eventually, because there'll be pressure to move on to other cases. Now, shall we all go back to the party?' John put an arm around Cleo and Martyn and guided them back up the field.

'Wait a minute,' Martyn pulled away. 'I need to talk to Cleo.'

'As you wish,' John inclined his head in a mock bow and walked towards the bowling club.

'Is it true? I'm just the fall guy?' he asked accusingly. 'You don't really care for me at all?'

'No, I do. I love you. The only falling was mine. I fell for you. God, that sounds corny. You must know that. Surely you can feel it when we're making love?'

'I thought so, but…'

'There isn't a but. I know we're in a bad place at the moment, but John's right, there is no choice. All three of us have to stick together for now, with the same story.'

'We could go to the police and say it was John,' Martyn suggested.

'No. You're forgetting the texts. That would incriminate me. I don't want to go to prison.'

'But it's wrong. It's all wrong,' Martyn cried, shaking his head.

'I know. I wish I could turn the clock back, but we're stuck with it. We have to do what John says, otherwise he'll engineer it so we go to prison and he gets off scot free.'

'I can't believe all this,' Martyn said hopelessly. 'Do you really think he'd have kept the phone with your messages on it? Surely it would be bad for him too?'

'I don't know. The threat of it is enough. We should do as he says, don't you think? Unless… maybe we could get some evidence of our own on John,' Cleo said thoughtfully, 'and then we'd be in a stronger position.'

'What?'

'I'll think about it. I do love you, you know,' she said, kissing him.

'Yes. I love you too,' Martyn said, but this time with a sadness in his heart. He knew he was inextricably linked to something that was deeply wrong.

Cleo led Martyn back into the bowling club, through a crowd of youngsters loitering outside smoking. His head was still reeling from the encounter in the playground and all its implications. As he watched John cavorting on the dance floor with Rachel and Paula, looking as if he didn't have a care in the world, he found it hard to believe what he had just heard. Apart from John, the guests seemed to have separated into their respective age groups, with the younger members occupying the end of the room closest to the band. Most of the older diving contingent congregated at the bar, although some of those who had imbibed more liberally were throwing themselves about on the polished wooden flooring. Graham was thrashing the air around him, causing more conservative dancers to duck out of his way every so often. Brian leant against the end of the bar, studying a group of girls who were following a particularly energetic sequence as the band yelled and played and stamped. A group of women were conducting a ritual dance around their bags on the floor, whilst many of the remaining men concentrated on the co-ordination required to lift a pint glass to their lips. Cleo pulled Martyn through the crowd, saying, 'You need a drink.'

He nodded agreement as there was little point in trying to speak above the noise level. As he glanced back across the room, he was surprised to see Sergeant Fry making his way through the crowd, closely followed by Inspector Jamieson. They closed in on John just as the band came to the end of their set. Martyn was close enough to see him cast a disparaging glance at the balloons stirring above his head as he said, 'We need to talk to you again, Mr O'Donnell. If you would, please, sir,' he said, gesturing towards the door. Bill Fry had quietly appeared on the other side of John so that the two of them could escort him from the building. Someone had cut the power to the disco so John's 'Only too happy to oblige,' sounded unnaturally loud and the attention of the crowd was suddenly focused on him. For a moment no one noticed the body that had collapsed to the floor. Then one of Paula's school friends cried out as she tripped over Paula, lying prone behind her. Elaine rushed towards her daughter, but it was the policemen who got to her first. Bill automatically checked for signs of life as Ian Jamieson looked for injuries. Graham stumbled over and almost fell on top of her as he peered down, trying to focus his attention on the emergency before him.

'She's OK,' Bill reported shortly. 'Just fainted. Give the girl some air.' Many of the dancers who had clustered around, immediately drew back, following his instructions. 'How pregnant is she?' Inspector Jamieson asked Elaine, noting the obvious bump. 'Thirty weeks. Is she alright?' Elaine asked anxiously.

Paula was stirring, 'Mum?'

'Are you alright, love?' Elaine was on her knees beside her daughter.

'Ow!' Paula curled over on her side, wincing with pain as she held on to her stomach. Ian Jamieson took his mobile out and called for an ambulance. Lynne bundled up her coat to make a pillow for Paula's head and Cleo brought her picnic rug out of the car to drape over her. Most of the party audience had removed themselves to the far end of the room. Subdued conversation resumed as they discussed the possible emergence of a new life. An occasional shout of laughter punctuated the relative quiet as party spirits did their best to reassert themselves. The atmosphere emphasised the impropriety of such sounds and the individuals responsible cursed themselves and took another drink. Paula suddenly cried out again as a rapidly expanding pool of liquid spread beneath her body and beyond the rug. It soon enveloped the feet of those adults closest to her, whilst those at the bar watched in horror as the pool grew. The outer reaches of the circle were clear but immediately beneath the girl's body there were red globules that coalesced into dark patches. One of the barmaids brought towels from the toilets to try and mop up. Ian checked his watch as he lifted his feet out of the way, thinking that the ambulance should get there soon. This was no way for a new life to enter the world, he thought. As all attention focused on the mum–to–be, John caught Cleo's eye and held a finger to his silent lips.

CHAPTER 27

It was a long ambulance ride for Paula to the maternity unit in Gloucester. She knew that contractions were supposed to come in waves of pain, building in intensity and then dying off, but this agony was continuous, there was no relief. In spite of the mask over her face providing anaesthetic, it only dimmed but did not completely remove the sensations in her body. The paramedic had checked her blood pressure and the cuff remained on one arm, whilst the other held a clip on her finger to check oxygen saturation and her pulse. She was frightened, both for herself and for the baby and what would happen to them in future. Although she had read about the development of the baby in her book, she had not got onto the birth process because it had looked scary. She had planned to wait until the antenatal classes started because the midwives at the health centre were friendly and encouraging. She felt that they would explain things to her in their normal matter-of-fact way. Maybe the baby would be fine staying where it was. They probably just needed to check them both over and then she'd be able to go home again. She glanced at her Mum sitting next her. She looked worried. It was the wrong person for Paula, it should be him. At the clinic she envied those other pregnant Mums-to-be if they arrived with their Dads-to-be, particularly when they looked happy together. Sometimes there was a couple where the man looked like he wanted to be somewhere else and then of course there were others where the woman was alone because the man in question was somewhere else. The man in question, she thought. She knew her parents were still consumed with curiosity about his identity, as was everyone, but he said it was better for no-one to know, not until after the baby was born.

Elaine fretted next to Paula, frequently getting in the way as the paramedic tended his patient. He seemed to speak in a different technical language from the driver, but was reassuring when he spoke to Paula and her Mum. The driver had radioed ahead to the hospital, so a midwife would be waiting for them at Accident and Emergency. The fact that they were in professional hands eased Elaine's anxiety, but she feared for her unborn grandchild. Graham was worse than useless, she thought angrily. Why must he always drink so much? There had been some debate back at the club as to how he was going to get to the hospital, but Elaine wondered if he needed to be there at all. Most people had either drunk too much or had no car at the club and no-one was going to suggest that 'they'd be alright to drive' in front of the policemen. However, Martyn had only had one pint and Cleo offered her car, so it was the two of them, with Graham, who followed the ambulance on its urgent journey.

Elaine could not help but think about her own horrendous experience of childbirth as she looked at her daughter now. It had taken almost two days with the labour apparently starting up, stopping and then starting again. When the contractions came in earnest, it went on for hours and she was exhausted long before Paula appeared. At one point they had thought she might need to go into theatre, but then Paula made a bid for freedom and at last she was out and they had a beautiful baby girl. Elaine did not want that same baby girl to have to go through a similar experience now to produce her own tiny offspring. She was too young and it was too soon. It was her fault of course, Elaine told herself. She should have stopped her from dancing like that. It was wild and violent. She should have told her to stop, or rest or dance in a quieter way. The baby was bound to object to being shaken up like that. And then the faint. Had she fallen on her front? Elaine couldn't remember. She was on her side when Sergeant Fry had checked her pulse and asked people to clear some space. Elaine looked at Paula's position and noted that the bump seemed smaller when she lay on her back. Elaine hoped that if the baby did come now, it would be fine. Thirty weeks was obviously premature, but babies could survive very well at that age these days. She heard the driver speaking into his radio again and realised that they were slowing down. 'Nearly there, love,' she said to Paula and patted her shoulder in what she hoped was a reassuring way.

Almost as soon as they stopped, the back doors opened and Paula was wheeled out into the Accident and Emergency entrance. All attention focused on her so Elaine felt superfluous as she climbed down from the ambulance, wondering where to go next. She followed cautiously as Paula and her team disappeared through the swinging plastic doors. The disjointed procession continued through the hospital corridors until they reached the delivery suite of the maternity unit. By the time Elaine arrived, the patient had been transferred to a hospital bed and was being connected to a set of monitors. A brisk midwife was asking her about her pregnancy, dates, her general health and what had happened today. Elaine was quietly impressed at how this woman managed to elicit such a large amount of information in such a short space of time, from a teenager who could be severely uncommunicative at times. It must be an indication of just how frightened Paula was, she thought.

'Are you Mum?' the midwife asked, smiling at Elaine.

'Um, Yes.'

'My name's Sam and I'm a midwife. Have a seat here,' she suggested, indicating the chair by the bed. 'I'm just going to call a doctor who will come and examine Paula. Won't be long.'

The existing mother and daughter remained in silence. Elaine contemplated the curtains around the bay, wondering if mauve was supposed to be therapeutic. If so, it wasn't working as they could both hear a patient in the adjacent bay strenuously denying the need for medication and condemning the proficiency of the medical staff.

'How are you feeling?' Elaine asked as she sat by Paula.

'Sick.'

'You hadn't been drinking anything had you?' Elaine asked anxiously.

'Mum. I haven't had hardly anything since I've been pregnant.'

Elaine wanted to ask what she meant by 'hardly anything', but the midwife had returned with the doctor, who smiled and introduced herself saying, 'Hi, I'm Dr Nichols. You've probably had an exciting trip in to see us, haven't you?' Paula nodded. 'We've wired you up to these machines so that we can monitor the baby's heartbeat and yours. You're both fine, so that's all good. This other thing on your finger measures the amount of oxygen in your blood and that's working well.' She turned to check that the curtains were closed. 'I need to examine you to see how things are going down there.'

Elaine felt uncomfortable. 'Do you want me to go?' she asked Paula.

'No.'

'You'll have to take your trousers and pants off,' Sam said, as she started to fill in a form, confirming Paula's date of birth, address, doctor and due date. 'You're a bit ahead of schedule aren't you? We shouldn't be expecting you for some time yet.'

Paula smiled awkwardly, unused to conducting a conversation with a stranger when she was half naked.

'Have you had any contractions?' Dr Nichols asked.

'Dunno. It was hurting all the time and then it got better as we got closer in the ambulance.'

'Have your waters broken?'

'Uh-huh, back then.'

'There was some blood too,' Elaine added.

'Right. It's possible that you've had a partial placental abruption,' the doctor began. Both Paula and Elaine looked alarmed, never having heard the term before, but the explanation followed rapidly, 'which means that part of the placenta has come away from the uterus. There are lots of blood vessels in the placenta that allow the transfer of food and oxygen from the mother to the baby. If it has separated a bit, that would account for the blood loss and the continuous pain. Does it hurt much now, Paula?'

'Not so much now, no.'

'Well, that's good. We might be able to give you a drug that will stop any further contractions and delay labour so the baby will have time to get a bit bigger.' Elaine wanted to check that babies born at thirty weeks could be perfectly healthy but she did not want to say it out loud in front of

Paula. The doctor was continuing, 'We'll take you along for an ultrasound scan in a little while to check what's actually happened with the placenta, but for now I'll have a quick look at you.' She pulled on a pair of thin gloves and pressed all around Paula's abdomen. 'The baby's head is still up here,' she said, indicating a point just under Paula's right breast. 'It would be better really if he or she,' she looked up at Paula for confirmation, but Paula did not realise so remained silent. Elaine intervened with, 'We don't know if it's a boy or a girl.'

'Right, well, it would be better if the baby were head down now, in the right position for the birth, which could start anytime soon. But you've felt the baby kicking today have you, Paula?'

Paula thought back. She had been unaware of any movement at the party, but that was because she'd just been thinking that her vast bulk was impeding her dancing.

'This afternoon, yes.' She remembered that all the girls had clustered around her to feel the kicks when they were putting the balloons up. The doctor eased a jelly-like substance onto her gloves and Paula flinched at the cold touch. After a brief interval, Dr Nichols said, 'Well you've dilated to about two cm so there's some way to go yet, but it certainly looks like things are happening tonight.'

Paula had just settled beneath the covers when Graham's voice called, 'Elaine? Paula?' Elaine stepped out of the cubicle, leaving Paula with the medical staff.

'How is she?' he asked. He looked remarkably sober, she thought, given how much he had drunk.

'She's fine for now. The doctor is checking her over. They think she might have had a problem with some of the placenta coming away.' Graham turned pale at the description and Elaine decided to spare him any more details. 'Do you want to go for a coffee or something and I'll come and find you in a bit? I think there's a café in the main hospital foyer.'

'But she's alright?'

'Yes.' Graham smiled in relief and turned towards Cleo and Martyn who stood a little distance away.

'Thanks for bringing him in,' Elaine said, spotting them. She returned to their daughter as Sam came out, smiled and said, 'Are you Dad?' but it was not clear to them who she was addressing. Graham answered, 'I'm Paula's Dad, but I'm not The Dad.' As her gaze switched to Martyn and he realised what she thought, he said, 'No, it's not mine,' hurriedly. 'I mean, I'm not the Dad,' he continued, looking deeply uncomfortable and wondering why he was there. Cleo suddenly felt very old standing next to him. Sam smiled again.

'My fault, I'm always leaping to the wrong conclusions.' She turned to Graham, 'Your daughter's fine.'

'Thanks,' Graham answered. 'Right then, café,' he said, turning to the others. 'Do you think it'll be open at this hour?'

'I don't know,' Cleo said, 'maybe. Something's always open somewhere in a hospital.'

It did not take them long to find the café and establish themselves around a small table. When Cleo left for the Ladies, Graham looked after her, saying, 'You and Cleo an item now then, Martyn?'

'I wouldn't say that.'

'But would she?'

'We just gave you a lift in, that's all,' Martyn answered irritably, not wanting his relationship with Cleo to be under scrutiny.

'Be careful, that's all I'm saying.' Graham took a sip of his latte which left a moustache of creamy froth on his top lip, highlighting the red of his nose above. As he raised his eyebrows in an attempt to give his words significant import, Martyn was reminded of a clown, but it was a sinister sort of clown.

'Careful of what?'

'She's got rid of one husband. Make sure you're not the next.'

'Don't be ridiculous. She's not…' He stopped speaking as Cleo reappeared, but his thoughts continued. What had he been about to say? She's not a murderer? If she plotted and planned and conspired to kill her husband, didn't that make her a murderer? He was still trying to come to terms with what he had learned in the playground. Could he really live with that knowledge and be with Cleo, knowing what she and John had done? He looked at her, stirring the cream into her coffee. His gaze moved up from the hands that had caressed his body, to the breasts that he had squashed against his chest, to the neck that he nuzzled, the earlobes he nibbled and those sensual lips. Desire stirred within him in spite of his thoughts. How could he want this woman and want her so badly? It was all wrong.

★ ★ ★

John sat next to his new solicitor after having waited some hours in a police cell whilst he travelled up from Plymouth. It was a wise move to get rid of that first man who had been an ineffectual spectator rather than an active participant. This guy was going to fight his corner. He would be expensive of

290

course, but it would be worth it so long as he kept out of prison.

'Mr O'Donnell,' Inspector Jamieson started formally, 'where were you on the Saturday of Tony's death, between midday and 6pm?'

'I was working at the factory. Jim Common saw me there. I've told you this already.'

'You have, but the thing is, Jim is a night watchman, isn't he? He wouldn't be there until late evening. If you'd been down in Plymouth killing Tony in the afternoon, you could have made it back in time to be seen by Jim on his rounds.'

'I couldn't get back that quickly, surely?'

'Your friend here has just made it in, what, two hours?' Ian pointed out, checking his watch.

'OK. OK. I admit it.' John held his hands up and shook his head at Ian and Bill.

'Don't say anything,' Richard Waters cut in quickly, looking shocked. There was a weighty pause as everyone else in the room wondered what was coming next.

'Maybe I shouldn't have done it, but I couldn't help myself,' he sighed theatrically.

'My client and I need to confer for a moment,' Richard stated, looking at John in disbelief.

'What can I say? She was young and willing and I took advantage.' The three other men looked confused.

'What are you talking about?' Ian asked.

'I wasn't at the factory all afternoon last Saturday. I was with Paula.'

'Paula?' Ian repeated. 'In what sense, with Paula?' he asked incredulously.

'In the sense of a man and a woman being in bed

291

together. I think Paula will remember, as it was a particularly good performance, even if I say so myself.'

'You're old enough to be her Dad,' Bill blurted out.

'But not too old to be a new Dad,' John answered smoothly. 'Has there been any news from the hospital?'

★ ★ ★

Graham sat tapping his fingers impatiently on the plastic surface of the coffee table. Cleo and Martyn were long gone and he had been expecting Elaine to join him ages ago. He had seen a sign for a relatives room and thought he could kip down there for a bit if it was going to take hours. Tiredness swept over him and the thought of sleep anywhere was very enticing. Not surprising, he thought, as it was now the early hours of the morning. Elaine was suddenly running towards him down the corridor. He got up, alarmed.

'What is it?'

'They've taken Paula in for an emergency caesarean. The contractions came back, stronger. She was in pain and the anaesthetic didn't seem to be doing any good.'

'Why didn't you come and get me?'

'It all happened so fast. Paula wanted to hold onto my hand when the contractions came. They got harder and closer together. Dr Nichols was marvellous, telling us what was happening and keeping a check on the baby's heartbeat as well as Paula's blood pressure. Paula was biting her lips with the pain and there was blood all over her face. I asked Sam to wipe it off. Then she started bleeding again and the baby went into distress with the heartbeat dipping. They couldn't afford the time to let Paula try and have it naturally so they thought they'd better get it out quickly. Paula was very brave the whole time. She's doing really well.'

Graham found it difficult to say anything. His princess was in theatre, about to produce a grandchild. He wanted the baby to be well of course, but his overwhelming concern was to have his daughter back safe and sound.

'We can wait closer to the maternity unit. They'll tell us when we can see her,' Elaine added, walking with Graham out of the deserted café.

CHAPTER 28

Martyn reversed out of the hospital car park and headed back towards the Forest. He glanced at Cleo sitting alongside him, wondering how much he really knew about this woman whose life was now closely intertwined with his. He had imagined their lives together in future, but the assumption that the midwife had made about him being the father of the baby threw another factor into the mix. What if he wanted a family? Cleo was now forty. Her birthday was today, or rather yesterday, he realised.

'Happy Birthday, by the way, for Saturday. Sorry I hadn't said it earlier, been a hectic day.'

'Thanks.'

'If you reach into my jacket on the back seat, there are a couple of presents for you.'

'Great. I love presents,' Cleo answered, as she stretched backwards. 'Is this it?' she asked, producing a package from one of the pockets.

'There are two, one in the other side as well,' Martyn said as he negotiated through the traffic on their way out of the city. The street lights illuminated the brown paper bag which Cleo was ripping through.

'Nicely wrapped,' she commented. But when she penetrated the next layer of tissue she added, 'Oh, it's lovely.' She drew out a gold bracelet and immediately put it on her right wrist, closing the clasp to make the ring complete.

There was an intricate pattern of carving on the outer surface that Cleo could feel as she ran her fingers over it. 'It's beautiful, thanks very much. I would kiss you, but I don't want us to crash,' she said, sliding her hand across on to his lap. Martyn wondered about pulling in to a lay-by on the way home but Graham's warning came back to haunt him. The idea of Cleo as a murderer effectively doused his desire.

'I don't want to crash either, so you'd best open the other one,' he said.

'Of course, the other one.' Cleo turned her attention back to the second parcel which was squashy. As she unwrapped it she could feel something soft and cuddly, but could not make out what it was until they passed a few streetlights. 'Oh, he's lovely too.'

'A Forest sheep for you,' Martyn explained. 'I tried everywhere to get a black one but I could only find white.'

Cleo smiled. 'Thanks for him.'

They continued for some miles in silence.

'He's wrong, you know.'

'Who?' Martyn asked.

'John.' Cleo was mentally re-running the scene with John in the playground, dissecting his argument.

'Any texts that I sent him aren't traceable back to me because I didn't use my name and I destroyed the phone so there's nothing to connect me to them.'

'Oh. I suppose not, when you put it like that. It sounded different when he said it.'

'I know. That's the trouble with John. He's got the gift of the gab. He can make white things seem black.'

'You'll have to show him your sheep then,' Martyn joked.

'Hmm,' Cleo replied absently, still thinking about John's reasoning. 'He had a point about evidence, though. We should try and get something on him so that if the police turn on us, we can say it was all down to him.'

Martyn's heart sank at her words. He did not want to be embroiled any further in this plot, but he could not deny that he and Cleo felt like 'we' and they should be acting together. Cleo was continuing on her line of thought.

'We need something that would prove he was in the submarine.' She thought for a moment and then turned to Martyn in excitement. 'His dive computer. If we found that, it could show that he was on a dive at the right depth for the necessary amount of time, couldn't it?'

'I guess,' he answered reluctantly. 'What do you mean, if we found that?'

'Let's go to his house now and look for it. He'll still be at the police station. There won't be anyone there. Come on. You need to take a right here.'

Martyn obeyed automatically, in spite of his reservations. They parked in the lane behind John's house. There was a footpath leading down to the woods which ran close by the side of the building. The fence alongside it was broken in places and Cleo had followed the route to his back door many times in the past. She knew that the spare key would be hidden in the woodshed, which was always unlocked.

'This is burglary,' Martyn hissed, as they approached the back of John's house.

'Ssshhh.'

A leylandii hedge screened them from the neighbours, but seemed to increase the level of darkness as Cleo fumbled to fit the key in the lock.

'How do we know he's not asleep upstairs?' Martyn whispered once they were inside.

'He'll still be with the police, won't he? But we'll check if his car is at the front.' Cleo led the way, tiptoeing past the utility area where John's diving equipment lay in a corner.

'It's there, look,' Martyn pointed out.

'Not his computer. He keeps that in his study with his logbook.' Cleo turned into the kitchen and bumped into a chair, which made a noisy scraping sound on the tiled floor. They froze, listening for any sound of movement above.

'We shouldn't be here,' Martyn said quietly at Cleo's ear. 'It's breaking and entering, trespassing and we're planning to steal something.'

'We haven't broken anything and John won't report his computer as stolen, will he?' Looking out of the window at the vacant parking space, she continued in a more normal tone. 'And he's not here. We'll be fine. Come on.' Martyn doubted whether anything would be fine ever again, but he followed Cleo into the hallway. A motion sensor located high above the front door flickered red as a rapid beeping came from the alarm unit.

'Shit. The alarm.' Cleo raced to the cupboard under the stairs, frantic to key in the right numbers to stop it within thirty seconds. 'God, what's the code? Think!'

'I don't know. Do you?' Martyn watched helpless, realising belatedly that Cleo was talking to herself and conscious only that the beeping had been going on a long time already.

'His birthday and the number of the house. Is it 0734 or 3407? 07 to start I think.' She keyed in the numbers and a welcome silence greeted them. 'Thank goodness. Let's go,' Martyn said, making for the back door.

'What is the matter with you?' Cleo demanded irritably. 'We're sorted now, so we can go on to the study.'

'What's the matter with me?' Martyn responded angrily. 'You seduce me into a murder plot, make me the fall guy, entrap me into conniving against the police, and now bring me on a burglary and you ask what's the matter with me? You only know his number because you used to come here when he was your lover. Isn't that right?' He was suddenly seized with jealousy. 'Does he keep his dive computer by his bed? Did you see it there when you were lying in his arms?'

'No, I didn't. It's you I want, not him.' The danger of invading John's house was giving Cleo the same kick of excitement that she got from gambling. It turned her on. She leant against Martyn. 'Do you want me to prove it to you, right here, right now?' She looked down at the carpeted floor. 'You could take me in the hall here, or on the stairs.' She turned and led him forwards. 'Or you could really mark your territory by rogering me senseless in his bed.' She pushed her hips into his, slowly, rhythmically, excited by the response that she evoked from his body. 'Where do you want me? How do you want me?' she whispered in his ear.

Martyn struggled to keep his desire in check. 'You're wicked.'

'I could be wicked if you wish, or wanton. I need someone to teach me a good lesson.'

'And I will, just not here,' he said, disengaging himself from her entreating arms. 'The sooner we find the computer, the sooner we can get away. He might come home soon.'

Cleo hung back reluctantly as he tried to move them away from the stairs. 'Not even a quickie?' she asked, disappointed that she was not going to get any immediate gratification.

'No. Be patient and I promise I'll make your body throb with pleasure later.'

'Promises, promises,' Cleo said sullenly, moving into the study.

'How are we going to find anything in the dark?' he asked, trying to concentrate on the job in hand.

'I know where he keeps it. Won't take long,' Cleo replied. 'Oh, it's not there.'

'What?'

'It's always sitting on the shelf by his desk, but it's not there now. He must have put it somewhere else. Look round.'

'It's dark. We'll never find it.' Martyn looked hopelessly at the murky shapes in the room, cursing the size of the search area.

'We'll have to turn a light on. Shut the curtains,' Cleo commanded.

'Ow.' Martyn walked into a small filing cabinet which impeded his route to the window. He hobbled on, rubbing his knee and drew the curtains across the bay window. Cleo turned the desk light on and surveyed the scene. 'I'll check the desk and these drawers. You look over there.'

As they searched rapidly, trying not to disturb anything, Martyn thought that they were on a fool's errand. If John had moved it from the normal place, then it could be anywhere in the house. He might have thought it was a dangerous piece of incriminating evidence and got rid of it altogether. He was just about to point this out to Cleo when they heard a car turn into the driveway. Cleo leapt to turn the desk light off and then cannoned into Martyn in the sudden darkness, causing him to knock a stack of CDs on to the floor. They raced back down the corridor wordlessly, swerved through the kitchen avoiding the chairs and made it to the utility room and outside. Cleo dropped the key in her haste to get it out of her pocket, but Martyn grabbed it and locked the back door, just as they heard the front entrance opening. He handed Cleo the key to replace in the woodshed and then they ran for the gap in the fence. As they got back in the car and Martyn drove them away, he said, 'Remind me never to offer Graham a lift to the hospital again.'

John stood on the threshold wondering why the alarm was not beeping. He strolled along to the cupboard under the stairs and checked the control unit. The green light was on, as if it were daytime and the alarm was off. Normally when he came in and it was set, a red light would be flashing until he keyed in the right entry code. He was sure he'd put it on before going out. He always did. He glanced into the study and saw a CD on the floor. As he got closer he noticed that there were a number of discs scattered across the carpet. They had been neatly stacked on the top of the small filing cabinet so there was no way they could have propelled themselves on to the floor. He looked around quickly to see what had been stolen. Nothing apparently, although some things had been disturbed. He walked into the lounge and then the kitchen, checking that the back door was locked as he went. As he returned to the hall, he looked again at the alarm unit and smiled. Only Cleo and Paula knew the code. It couldn't be Paula because she was in hospital, so it must have been Cleo. Well, she was proving cleverer and more resourceful than he had thought. He liked that in a woman. Maybe that had been some of the attraction in the first place. She would have known both the significance of the dive computer and where it was normally kept. He wondered if she had persuaded Martyn to be her partner in crime. Probably, he thought, but then he grinned at their timing. 'Too late, my friends, just too late.'

★ ★ ★

'We only need two minutes with her.' Inspector Jamieson was pleading with the sister on the maternity ward, hoping to be allowed to talk to Paula on the Sunday morning.

'She's had a very rough night and she's in no fit state to be questioned by the police.' The nurse busied herself with the paperwork at her desk, but the inspector was not going to give up.

'I'm sorry, but this is a murder enquiry and it's vitally important that we speak to her.'

'You do know she's only sixteen? Don't you need her parent's permission?'

Bill Fry nudged Ian's arm and nodded down the corridor where Elaine was approaching. 'You're right, thanks,' the inspector said, moving to intercept Elaine.

'Good morning Mrs Bright, how are you?' he said.

'Oh, Inspector. Sergeant. What are you doing here?' Elaine sounded surprised to see them.

'I'm afraid we need to talk to Paula. How is she?'

'She's exhausted. We all are. Graham's getting forty winks in the relatives' room while Jo's being checked over by the paediatrician. It's very worrying. She obviously has to be in an incubator for a while yet, just being fed on a drip, the poor little mite. As she's so premature, she's got some breathing difficulties because her lungs are under developed. They're not happy about her condition and her Apgar scores are low. Not that I'm sure what that means,' she added sadly.

301

'I'm sorry to hear that. How's Paula coping?' he asked.

'I think she's shocked that it all happened so soon. She wasn't ready for it. She's only a child herself really. When I think back to when she was…'

'Can we talk to her?' he interrupted, concerned that Elaine was going to ramble off on a lengthy reminiscence.

'Yes. I'll just check that she's decent.' Elaine walked into Paula's bay and disappeared behind the curtains briefly, before pushing them back and beckoning the policemen over.

'Hello Paula. Sorry to have to ask you questions at a time like this,' Ian began.

'What do you want?' Paula did indeed look and sound exhausted. She seemed very young curled up in the bed and it was difficult for him to see her as an adult, caring for a child of her own.

'Paula, you know we're investigating Tony Fleming's death?' She nodded, looking down at the edge of the blanket where she was picking at the stitching.

'Well, we've been talking to John O'Donnell about where he was on the Saturday that Tony died.' Paula looked up quickly at the mention of John's name, glancing furtively at her mother. 'The thing is, John says that he was with you that Saturday afternoon. Is that true?'

'Why would he say he was with Paula?' Elaine interrupted. 'Why bring her into this?'

'Why would who say he was with Paula?' Graham asked as he joined the group at his daughter's bedside, taking up a position next to Elaine and opposite Bill Fry.

'Isn't this harassment of a minor?' he asked the inspector aggressively. 'What are you doing here, questioning my

302

daughter at a time like this, with my granddaughter fighting for her life in an incubator?'

'I'm sorry Mr Bright, but our enquiries brought us here and we needed to speak to Paula urgently.'

'What's so urgent that couldn't have waited?'

'John O'Donnell claims to have spent the Saturday afternoon when Tony died, with Paula. We need to know if that's true,' he repeated, looking down at the girl in the bed between them.

'He was with me that afternoon,' she confirmed, keeping her head down and not looking at anyone. She started crying quietly as the adults continued to talk across her.

'John?' Graham repeated incredulously. 'He was with you? Do you mean he's the father? I'll …'

'Graham,' Elaine said sharply, noting her husband's rising colour and clenched fists and hoping he wasn't going to say something stupid. Fortunately her warning penetrated his growing anger and he appreciated the necessity of curbing it in front of the police.

'I want him here. He should be here with our baby.' Paula sobbed as Elaine put an arm around her.

'Please leave us alone,' Elaine said to the policemen.

As they left the ward, Bill Fry muttered, 'I think Paula's in for a bit of a hard time, poor kid.'

'She's already had a tough time, hasn't she? I don't suppose it's going to get better any time soon.' Ian glanced back as the door closed on the ward. He could not hear the small family group but he could see Graham making violent gesticulations in the air.

'What's more important for our purposes is that Paula's statement effectively rules John out as a viable suspect.'

303

CHAPTER 29

Graham was on his way home in a taxi, having been sent by Elaine to get a number of things for Paula's stay in hospital and clean clothes for herself. He was relieved to be out of the building because he felt useless looking at both his daughter and granddaughter in their respective beds. He wanted to do something to help them. Although he loved his daughter, it did not always come out right and the scene at the bedside was just another one where he had let his emotions get the better of him. He appreciated it when Elaine gave him a reason to escape.

His initial rage towards John seemed to have illuminated things for him and this new insight made him see the economic opportunity it presented. He knew that he had to control his fury into a more manageable anger in order to get what he wanted and he needed to plan what he would say. If he went through it carefully in his mind step-by-step, he should be able to make things go his way. It would be important not to blow his top, he thought, as he breathed deeply, trying to calm the seething feelings that threatened to overwhelm him.

There was a momentary spike in Graham's blood pressure when the taxi driver asked for payment. The cost of the ride back from Gloucester was exorbitant in Graham's view. He could have hired a helicopter for that amount of money, he commented angrily, which would have been faster and more comfortable. Begrudging every penny, Graham extracted some notes from his wallet and waited sour-faced for the change.

* * *

John opened his front door to find Graham on his step, shading his eyes in the bright sunshine of a glorious Sunday afternoon.

'Hi, Graham. Coming in?' He opened the door wide, stepping back into the hall. 'How's Paula?'

'How's Paula?' Graham started indignantly. 'How can you stand there so calmly and ask me how my daughter is when you've left her to suffer agonies in hospital giving birth to your child?' Graham had got so far into the house that he was pinning John against the door to the study, prodding his chest with an accusatory finger.

'She's had the baby?' John asked. 'Isn't it too soon?'

'A lot you care. Where were you?'

'At the police station. You know I was.'

Graham had to concede the point, nodding and realising that giving vent to his feelings was not why he had come. Now that he was face-to-face with John the hatred that he felt simmered closer to the surface, threatening to erupt into violence. How could he have done it? To his daughter. And kept it secret all that time. And behaved as if he was a friend. Was it some kind of calculated insult to him? He struggled to focus on his objective.

'The police were at the hospital this morning, asking Paula to vouch for your whereabouts the Saturday that Tony died.'

'Really?' John replied nonchalantly. 'Want a coffee or something?' Released from his position by the study, he moved into the kitchen. Following him, Graham registered the opulence of John's house and saw it as something achievable for himself, hopefully in the near future.

'No, I don't want a coffee. I want you to listen to me.'

John took a seat at the head of his solid kitchen table, spreading his hands flat to savour the cool granite surface. He appeared to be the picture of serenity, his distinguished head holding every hair in place. This contrasted strongly with Graham who fidgeted at his side as he launched into his rehearsed speech. 'I know you weren't with Paula that afternoon and I know that you've bullied her into lying for you. You were in the sub waiting for Tony, weren't you? Like you'd planned with Cleo, waiting to murder him to get your hands on his money.'

'How can you possibly think that?' John asked, sounding shocked and thinking rapidly. Graham was obviously overwrought, wound up about his precious daughter. Provided that he could remain cool and calm himself, he would be able to exploit Graham's hotheadedness and manipulate him in a way that would further his plan. 'I was with Paula, enjoying... how shall I say... savouring her youthful enthusiasm for my body.'

Graham flushed angrily. 'Don't talk about her like that.'

'Oh, but she's good, Graham. Knows how to treat a man, now that I've taught her a thing or two.'

'Shut up.' Graham's face reddened so that his skin clashed horribly with the ginger hair that edged it.

'I think she loves me.' John inspected his nails, casually. 'I think she'll do whatever I ask. I wouldn't be putting it too strongly to say she worships the ground I walk on. I've made

306

her feel things and do things that she's never done before.' He paused, apparently thinking about something. 'Although I wouldn't say she was a virgin. I think she's been around a bit.'

'You bastard,' Graham yelled, flinging himself at John and knocking him sideways off his chair. John fell onto the tiled floor, hitting his head on the cold stone. Graham was on top of him, grappling for his throat in a desperate attempt to throttle him to stop the foul words coming out. His fingers were already pressing into John's flesh before the larger man had a chance to wrench one arm away. Graham shifted the other hand to close over John's neck as their free arms fought for dominance. John rolled over so that the two men collided with the legs of the table and set the chairs scraping across the floor. He was heavier and stronger but he did not have the mad passion that made Graham flail wildly at his head. One of Graham's punches caught John in the eye before he managed to grab his arms and pin them by his sides. John now lay on Graham, using his weight to squash the smaller man into submission.

'Don't do that, Graham,' he said, breathing heavily. 'You'll make me angry and you wouldn't like me when I'm angry.'

'Get off me,' Graham spat. He lay panting and immobile, furious that his outburst was not part of his carefully laid plan. He should try to get things back on track. 'You need me,' he said, through gritted teeth.

'Ha!' John laughed derisively, 'How could I possibly need a poisonous little oik like you?'

'You need Paula to stick to her story.'

John was uncomfortable on the floor. 'Are you going to behave yourself now?' he asked, releasing the pressure on Graham's arms. He gave a curt nod so John climbed off him and righted the fallen chairs, taking one for himself and offering Graham the other with mock courtesy. Graham sat with his elbows on the table, flexing his hand and examining the damaged knuckles. 'The point is, she's lying for you and you should say thank you by giving her some of the money that you've got off the back of Tony's murder.'

'So you're suggesting a "thank you"? You're not using the old fashioned term of "blackmail"? How quaint. As it happens, I will be providing for Paula financially, but only as support for the child.'

'You're not planning on marrying her then?'

John laughed gaily. 'Oh good lord, no, Graham. What are you thinking? She's a good lay, or rather she was, but I'm not going to link my life with hers.'

Graham tried not to rise to the bait. 'But your life is linked with hers, isn't it?' He leant forward, thinking that perhaps he had a slight advantage for once. 'Your prick did that for you. Paula is expecting you to be with her and the baby. When you tell her that's never going to happen, she might change her story to the police. Your freedom is dependent on her word. That's why you should pay, for her silence, not just for the baby.'

John became serious suddenly. 'She wouldn't do that. She loves me.'

'How much power do you think you'll have over her when you refuse to live with her and you shatter her dream of playing happy families?'

'Let's just say, hypothetically, that you might have a point,' John replied, leaning back in his chair. 'How much were you thinking?'

'A million.'

John fell forwards as his chair crashed back on to the stone tiles. 'A million? You must be mad.'

'Not mad at all. Surely it's worth it? Twenty years or more in jail or your liberty. I'm not greedy. You can have the other four hundred thousand.'

Graham saw that his argument had hit home as John was clearly thinking things over. Perhaps he had realised how Paula would feel when he refused to marry her or live with her.

'Half a million's more than enough for Paula and the kid.'

'Ah yes. I should have explained. Half a million for Paula's silence and half a million for mine.'

'So you're not just looking out for your daughter and the kid?'

'My granddaughter. Glad to see you're interested enough to enquire about the sex of the child.'

John dismissed this comment as if it were an irrelevance. 'If I'm going to pay all this money out I want to know that I'm not going to be left under suspicion and the police are going to close the case. They've got a particular hang-up about the bruises on Tony's wrists. If you say that you had an argument with Tony in the pub that Saturday lunchtime and you pinned him against the wall, like this,' he grabbed Graham's wrists to illustrate the point, 'then we've got a deal and you can have the million.'

'Done.' As the men shook hands in apparent agreement, Graham thought that he was going to be a rich man, able to provide for his growing family. 'I'll pop down to the police station before I go back to the hospital,' he said. 'Will you be going in to see Paula and Jo later?'

'She's called it Jo?' John asked. 'Nice.' He smiled as he escorted Graham back down the hallway. After he left, John leant against the inside of the door, thinking about his strategy. He did not rate Graham as an intellectual adversary, so he thought it would work. Greed would blind him, he was sure.

★ ★ ★

'We weren't expecting to see you again so soon, Mr Bright,' Inspector Jamieson said as he and Sergeant Fry took up their respective positions in the interview room across the table from Graham. 'You're not going to grumble at us for interviewing your daughter this morning, I hope? We did have your wife's permission.'

'Oh, no, nothing like that. I just thought I'd come in and clear up a little misunderstanding there might have been about the Saturday when Tony died.' Graham smiled at the two men, who looked at him nonplussed. Sergeant Fry put a tape into the machine, uttering his habitual introductory phrases and checking the time as Ian Jamieson said,

'Do you want to have a solicitor present for this interview, Mr Bright?'

'No. No need. It won't take a moment.'

'Perhaps you'd like to tell us what you mean by a little misunderstanding on the Saturday when Tony Fleming died?'

'Well, it's just that on that day, at lunchtime, when I was in The Anchor having a 'hair of the dog', I bumped into Tony in the passageway at the side of the pub. I confronted him about fathering Paula's baby and he denied it. I thought he was lying and there was a bit of a tussle. I pinned him against the wall, telling him there was no point denying it. He continued to say it wasn't his and we argued until he kneed me in the balls and I doubled up. He went off to join the others back on the boat for the afternoon dive. OK?' Graham got up to leave but Bill Fry ushered him back to his seat.

'No, Mr Bright. Things are far from OK,' Ian replied. 'Could you demonstrate, using Sergeant Fry here, precisely how you pinned Tony against the wall.'

'Sure.'

Bill Fry was not happy about being used as a human dummy again, but nodded his confirmation to Ian, as they both realised that Graham was using the correct grip to produce the bruising seen on Tony's wrists. 'Well, Mr Bright, we have a problem here. The first time we interviewed you about your whereabouts on that Saturday, you told us you'd gone to The Anchor, but no-one would remember you there and you seemed to have difficulty remembering your actions yourself. Then, the next time we talked about it, you managed to produce a witness who recalled you on the premises, arguing about the payout from a fruit machine.'

'Yes, but…'

'And now all of a sudden you remember that you wrestled with Tony in a back alley and therefore that would account for the bruising we found on his body. To be honest, witnesses do sometimes change their statements as they recall details some time after the event, but no one, no innocent person that is, provides three different versions of events for a crucial period of time, that cannot be corroborated by anyone else.'

'But the guy who saw me in the pub talking about the fruit machine can vouch for me.'

'He's changed his mind about that. Mistaken identity he said.'

'What?' Graham asked, alarmed.

'What happened to your hand?' Bill Fry asked, indicating the swelling and abrasion on his knuckles.

'I tripped and scraped it on a wall at home,' Graham replied, automatically putting his hand beneath the table out of view.

Ian continued. 'However, this new evidence does change things somewhat. When someone alters their story that many times, we just don't know what the truth is and what are lies. You appreciate the problem?'

'I'm telling you the truth now.'

'Why don't you just come clean and admit that you killed Tony?'

'I didn't. I wasn't diving that day. I was sick. I told you.'

'Yes. And now you've told us that you fought with Tony on the day he died and you've demonstrated the precise way that you created the marks on his wrists. You could have been so incensed by his continued denial of any involvement with Paula that you decided to go out to the sub before the others and kill him there, hoping to make it look like an accident. Isn't that right?'

'No, it's not right. It wasn't like that and I didn't do it.'

'I don't believe you. You've fed us one story after another. We're going to keep you here while we check things out.' Inspector Jamieson and Sergeant Fry got up and left the room.

'No. No. You've got it all wrong.' Graham was feeling confused. He hadn't really had time to consider the implications of what Ian Jamieson had said before they'd disappeared. This had not gone according to plan at all. He was just concentrating on getting the million for Paula and Jo. He was only doing what John had said was necessary to …

With a sick feeling in his stomach, he realised that John had just led him up the garden path and he had trotted along like some brainless poodle. 'It's not me,' he shouted in frustration, kicking the table. 'It's John.' The constable outside the door glanced in to check what he was doing but he was inured to suspects protesting their innocence and returned to his administrative tasks. Graham sat down, going over what he had just said, trying to work out how he could get out of the hole he had dug for himself.

★ ★ ★

Bill was completing the request for the search warrant for Graham's house as he and Ian sat in their office. Ian was sifting through messages that had been forwarded from their base in Plymouth. The investigative unit down there had been through the financial accounts of Kidcars and the personal finances of each of the main suspects.

'Listen to this, Bill. Over the last few months there have been several occasions when significant amounts have gone missing from the corporate account. By sheer coincidence large sums of money have also come in and out of Cleo's personal account about the same time.'

'She's been embezzling the company funds?'

'Well, yes and no. Overall, the end result is that the company is only down about twenty thousand, apparently. Maybe she was borrowing it for some reason, but so far she's managed to put it back within a reasonable time period.'

'Blackmail, do you think?' Bill suggested.

'If it were, she wouldn't be able to retrieve it, would she?

She'd be paying out and it would be gone for good.'

'What sort of system can they be using that hasn't shown up any irregularities before now?'

'She's the accountant for the company, isn't she?' Ian pointed out. 'She'd be able to manipulate the figures and ensure that they looked right in time for any audit.'

'Until now.'

'Yes.' Ian continued to study the papers, so it was Bill Fry who answered the phone on the desk when it rang. He sat up straighter and put his hand over the receiver as he offered it to his superior, saying, 'ACC for you, sir.'

The Assistant Chief Constable was not given to ringing his Inspectors for a friendly chat on a Sunday evening, so Ian dropped the papers and sat forward.

'Jamieson here, sir.'

'What the devil are you doing up there, man? That's what I want to know.' Jim Blane was a large man with a barrel chest and he could use his capacious lungs to create remarkable volume, which was not impaired by the medium of the telephone. He continued:

'I come back from my well-earned holiday to find that two of my detectives have been away for days,' he emphasised the word, 'on some fool errand involving other police forces and neglecting the stack of cases building up on their own desks, in their own area.'

'We are on a murder enquiry, sir, investigating an offence that was perpetrated in our area.'

'I might remind you that you are not part of some mobile task force that can investigate any event that takes your fancy in other parts of the country.'

Bill Fry wondered if it would be more discreet to leave

the room whilst Ian Jamieson endured this bollocking, but he was loathe to miss anything.

'I hope that fat oaf Fry hasn't been drinking the place dry whilst you've been away on your jollies.'

Bill now wished he had left and took another sip of water.

'Really sir, we've made good progress,' Ian Jamieson asserted.

'Have you arrested anyone?'

'Not exactly, sir.'

'For God's sake, Jamieson. Either you have or you haven't. Which is it?'

'We haven't, sir,' Ian was sinking lower in his chair, wishing that he could indeed report an arrest.

'Well, stop fannying about up there and get back here to deal with the cases on your desk. I don't suppose you've heard the news?'

'No sir.'

'There was an armed robbery down here. Brazen it was, but that wasn't the worst part. PC Cole was shot as he tried to intercept one of the offenders. He's in hospital and should be alright, but I don't need to tell you what the feeling in the station is like.'

'No sir.'

'You make sure you finish that case in double-quick time and get your asses back down here. Then you can try and find these morons who think they can shoot a police officer and get away with it. This is your priority. Do I make myself clear?'

'Yes sir.' Ian put the receiver down gently, as if it might still bark at him.

'ACC not happy then?' Bill asked unnecessarily.

'You could say that. Let's get out to Graham's house today and see if we can find any equipment that he could have used in the sub. Maybe we were wrong to rule him out before. Perhaps he was filled with a violent rage towards Tony and managed to pull it off. He certainly had the grip right and only the murderer would know that.'

CHAPTER 30

Ian led the way into the Bright's house with Bill following behind. Having to search someone's house always made him feel uncomfortable as it was an intrusion into the aspects of their lives they might prefer to keep secret. If it were after a death it was different, because they could not be personally affected in any way. In this case, with the family absent but very much alive still, they should take care to be as unobtrusive as possible.

'He's not going to keep his dive kit in the kitchen, is he? Come on.' Ian opened the door at the far end of the room which connected to the garage. There was so much stuff in there he doubted whether the car ever made it inside. Amongst the usual clutter of gardening items and decorating equipment, he spotted a diving cylinder in the back corner. 'In here, Bill,' he called. There were shelves above the cylinder which held Graham's fins, jacket, regulator and dry suit. His dive computer was nowhere to be seen. The two men looked reluctantly at the plethora of household equipment. It must represent years of accumulation as some items were broken, some covered in cobwebs and only those things which were easily accessible showed any hint of being used.

'We should have brought more pairs of hands with us,' Bill observed.

'No, it just means that we need to think, rather than plod through all this detritus mindlessly,' Ian responded. 'It's a computer after all. Isn't it likely to be with other computing stuff in the household, if they've got any? Or it could be hidden away somewhere in a bedroom, where Graham could check that it was still safe. We'll look at those first and then we'll come back here as a last resort.'

'Right,' Bill agreed, happy to leave the hunting ground in the garage.

They retraced their steps to the kitchen and passed through the living room, where Ian noticed an old fashioned sideboard along one wall. Climbing the stairs to the landing, they came to Paula's room first. Bill glanced in to confirm who the occupant was, but Ian paused in the doorway. He looked at the posters on the walls, the clothes strewn about on the floor and the pile of cuddly toys on the bed. 'Bill, if you didn't know any better, how old do you think the person that lives in this room would be?'

'I don't know, boss. It's a kid's room, isn't it?'

'Yes, my point entirely. I just wondered how old that kid is.'

'Sixteen, isn't she?' Bill asked.

'Now, yes, but how old was she when the baby was conceived?'

'Do you think John was consorting with a minor?'

'I don't know, but my feeling is it's worth investigating. Paula seems young to me. Some teenagers can pass for confident young women in their twenties, particularly when they're out clubbing and dressed to the nines, but Paula's not one of those.'

'But the baby came early, didn't it?'

'Yes, Elaine said that she was at thirty weeks when she collapsed at the bowling club yesterday. That means that the due date would be another ten weeks or so. Can you see a calendar anywhere?'

'There was one in the kitchen. I'll get it.' Bill disappeared downstairs as Ian went further into Paula's room, noting the baby development book on a heap of schoolbooks in a corner.

'Here,' Bill said, handing Ian the reverse side of the calendar which displayed a year planner. 'Thanks. So, what's the date now, 19th August,' Ian said, pointing at the month with his finger and moving it along as he counted up to ten. 'That takes us up to early November for the due date. Now if we go back forty we should get to the conception.'

'John must know it's an offence to have sex with underage girls,' Bill said as he watched Ian counting.

'Yes. That takes us back to the end of January/early Feb. I don't know how exact the timescale of forty weeks is, but I'd be very interested to know if Paula's birthday is in February or later.'

'So now we're looking for something that has her birth date on it,' Bill said thoughtfully. 'A birth certificate, obviously. That'll be hidden away somewhere with important documents or an ID card maybe, or a driver's licence.'

'She won't be driving yet, will she?'

'No, but I thought she might have applied for a provisional licence.'

'Doubt it. She'd have had more on her mind with the baby than with driving, I'd have thought. You go and see what you can find in that big sideboard downstairs and I'll go and look for the dive computer in Graham's room.'

As Ian went into Elaine and Graham's room, he felt sure that it was decorated to the woman's taste rather than the man's. There were frilly edges on all the soft furnishings, including the curtains, the tiebacks, the bedspread and the carefully arranged cushions on the bed. He suspected the pillowcases would be similarly adorned. He decided to start searching in the fitted wardrobes but found nothing of interest, apart from noting that Elaine's taste for lace extended to underwear as well. He hurried on, trying to dispel an image of the woman in her underwear. There was a dressing table with various feminine pots, lotions and jars arrayed on its surface and nearby there was a large basket of dirty laundry with a pair of underpants lying forlornly beside it. Suddenly the telephone on the bedside table started ringing, which made Ian jump. He felt like a burglar, or rather, as he imagined a burglar might feel. He left it to ring, and then heard the answerphone click into action downstairs. As he looked at the TV at the foot of the bed, he thought there was really very little storage space in this room. Then he lifted the bedspread and discovered the drawers beneath the mattress. In the last one, as he rummaged under sheets and pillowcases he came across a stack of pornographic magazines. Hurriedly sliding the drawer shut, he sat back on his heels, wondering where else there was to look. As he spotted the loft hatch in the ceiling, Bill came back into the room.

'Bingo,' he said. 'Found a baby book in the sideboard along with a nauseating envelope of baby teeth and locks of hair. Why do women keep that stuff? It's macabre.'

'Never mind that. What's the answer?'

'February 9th.'

'Hmm,' Ian replied thoughtfully, 'She'd have to get pregnant pretty much the first time they did it if they waited for her birthday in that case. Possible I suppose.'

'I hope not, actually. I'd like to get something on John. I

don't like the way he seems so superior, like he's just humouring us,' Bill commented.

'I know what you mean, but that's no rationale for charging a man. Who was on the phone?'

'It was Elaine ringing Graham. She sounds a mite pissed off about the length of time it's taking him to collect stuff and get back to the hospital. Says she hopes he hasn't decided to wet the baby's head.'

'Right,' Ian said, immediately losing interest. 'Can you see anything that'll open that trapdoor up there?' They both looked around the room and Bill opened a cupboard door, retrieving a long pole with a hook at the end. Once the door was opened and the ladder drawn down, Ian assessed the size of the opening and quickly checked it against Bill, concluding that it would be better to ascend the ladder himself. As he peered into the gloom, he said, 'Let's hope Graham is enough of a handyman to have installed light up here. Ah, he has.' As the attic lit up, Ian could see boxes of books and toys balanced on the rafters. What looked like a dismantled cot lay further away, but his eye was taken by a small package, partially hidden behind a large box of Duplo. 'There's something up here. I'll just have a look,' he called to Bill. Opening the bag carefully to preserve any fingerprints, Ian said, 'Aha. Two dive computers, no less.'

'Really?' Ian came down the ladder to show Bill his find.

'Well, that was certainly an inaccessible place to keep it, if it's just a spare for Graham,' he observed.

'Yes. I doubt there'll be any prints on it, but what's more important is the data inside. Do you think Sean Dixon will be able to send us the software up here so we can examine it back at the station?'

'I'll get on to it right away, sir.' Bill strode out of the room with the bag in his hand, leaving his senior officer to struggle with the extendable ladder and the trap door. When a breathless Ian rejoined Bill downstairs, he sat on the sofa, saying, 'Let's just think this through a minute.' As Bill sat down alongside him, his weight crushed the cushion, causing Ian to lean towards him. He pushed himself upright and asked,

'If this second computer shows evidence of a dive at a similar depth and duration to Tony's and Martyn's on that fateful Saturday, is that conclusive evidence that Graham did it?'

'Taken with the other elements that we know, I think so, yes,' Bill replied. He ticked things off on his fingers as he said, 'Graham's got the motive, he thought Tony had made Paula pregnant, he had the opportunity, he wasn't with the others that afternoon. He made violent threats about what he would do to Tony, he lied about what he was doing on the Saturday and I don't believe that story about the bruises being made during a scuffle in a back alley, do you?'

'No, I don't. Actually the duration of the dive must have been longer than Tony's and Martyn's. He had to be in the sub already, lying in wait. That's the bit I can't fathom, that Graham would be able to plan ahead and be patient enough to carry it out.'

'Maybe he could with sufficient incentive. I think he'd be the sort to carry grudges and let them fester in his head. If he thought he would have the last laugh perhaps he can control his temper in the short term. That reminds me, did you notice his bruised hand when we spoke to him just now?'

'The injury that looked like he'd recently hit someone

you mean? God, of course.' Ian leapt to his feet and ran towards the back door. 'Come on,' he yelled.

'Where are we going?' Bill cried as he tried to move his large body fast enough to catch up. Ian revved the engine impatiently as Bill toiled to get in beside him. 'Graham's only found out today who the real father is. Where do you think he'd go as soon as he left the hospital?'

'For a quiet little chat with John?'

'Precisely. Let's get over there and hope that nothing too bad has happened to him.'

'Can't we hope that something just a little bad has happened to him?' Bill suggested. Ian shot him a despairing glance as he turned the car towards John's house.

★ ★ ★

He lay back, his lust temporarily sated. The conquest of a new young body always gave him tremendous satisfaction. He reflected that his enjoyment was proportional to the amount of effort required in the seduction. If they capitulated too easily, there was little reward because he had not had to work for it. With this one he had used the full gamut of his charms, being at times funny, generous, flattering, persuasive and at others distant and uncommunicative. He compared it to fly-fishing; sometimes you needed the lightest of touches but when they were hooked, some perseverance was required and ultimately the strength to reel them in. God, he was good, he thought, sighing happily and falling asleep with the girl's head snuggled against his shoulder.

Some time later he awoke and glanced towards the champagne glasses on the bedside table. He moved his free arm to lift the bottle and found that it was empty, but the motion had disturbed his sleeping partner. 'This one's all gone. I'll go and get some more,' he said. The nap had revitalised him and he was already looking forward to round two.

'Hurry back,' she said languorously.

He smiled as he left the bedroom. She had already transformed from a naïve girl into a woman with an appetite. He was proud of himself and the service he provided to womanhood.

When he returned he knelt on the bed and unwound the wire top from the bottle, easing the cork out. It hit the ceiling and some of the liberated champagne spurted onto her chest. Rather than move to grab a glass, he put the bottle down and sucked at the pool of liquid lying between her breasts. As his tongue traced the rivulets up to a nipple, the girl writhed beneath him. She pulled his head up to hers, saying, 'I think we should drink a toast to your excellent planning.'

'We can, but I think it's only fair to toast yours as well. Credit where it's due.' He poured more champagne into the waiting glasses, handing one to her as she raised herself up on one elbow.

'To you, for having the foresight to keep the computer and plant it on that despicable Graham.' She caressed his face, gently skirting the area of bruising around the eye.

'And to you, for persuading Tony to change his will in our favour. That really was the masterstroke that underpinned everything.'

They clinked glasses and there was a corresponding chime from downstairs.

'Wonder who that is disturbing us on a delicious Sunday evening?' he said.

'Nobody important. I'm more important.'

'That you are.' He reached across her to put his champagne down. The doorbell sounded again and then again.

'Persistent, aren't they?' he continued, sliding down alongside her.

The ringing stopped as he took her glass and placed it next to his. 'I want your full attention.' He placed a proprietorial hand on the beautiful curve of her naked hip, but a hammering started on the back door. 'Who would do that?' he asked angrily, climbing out of bed and going into the bathroom. Wrapping a towel around his waist he went downstairs and opened the back door to find Inspector Jamieson and Sergeant Fry looking at him inquisitively.

'What?' he asked aggressively.

'Sorry to disturb you Mr O'Donnell. We'd like a word, if it's not too inconvenient.'

'Obviously it's bloody inconvenient. Couldn't be more so.'

'You seem to have been in the wars,' the Inspector commented as he slid past John into the house. 'Kitchen through here?' he continued. 'How did you get that black eye?' John and Bill Fry followed Ian as John answered, 'It was that maniac Graham. Came round here hurling abuse and then he just flipped and started attacking me.'

'You're much bigger than him. How did he manage to injure you like that?' Bill asked.

'He took me by surprise. One moment he's nice as pie. The next he's a dangerous madman with a violent temper. He should be locked up.'

'Possibly. You'll be able to discuss it with him when you come down to the station with us.'

'What for? I haven't done anything.'

'Maybe not recently, but you did about seven months ago.'

'Seven months?' John was thinking back. 'February? What did I do?'

'You had unlawful sex with a minor.'

'You mean Paula? No, she was sixteen.'

'You sure of that?'

'Course I'm sure. I'm not a paedophile.'

'Well, that might be the way other prisoners will see you when you're on remand. They tend to take a dim view of sex offenders you know.'

'I am not a sex offender,' John stated emphatically.

'What is it, John?' Rachel asked as she came into the kitchen, dressed only in a towel that matched her lover's.

Both policemen looked at her in disbelief. Bill's gaze quickly turned to appreciation, whilst Ian's switched to John. He asked, 'What is it with you and young girls?' but when John did not answer, he turned back to Rachel.

'How old are you?'

'Sixteen.'

'And when was your birthday?'

'May 8th. Not that it's any of your business.'

'It would be my business if you were under age. Did you know that John here is the father of Paula's baby?'

'Of course. He told me.'

'And it doesn't bother you?'

'No. He said that she was a mistake. It's me he cares about.' John was standing behind Rachel and smiled at the Inspector's continuing air of disbelief.

'I thought you and Paula were friends,' Ian said. Rachel

shrugged, looking guilty. As the movement caused the towel to loosen, she grabbed the top edge to secure it around her body.

'You do know it's a criminal offence for him to have slept with Paula before she was sixteen?'

'Surely it's not against the law to sleep?' John queried quickly, looking amused. Ian Jamieson looked uncomfortable as he floundered for a better phrase. 'Do you know when John and Paula first made love?'

'She won't know that,' John interrupted quickly. 'Only Paula and I know and it was definitely after her birthday, alright?'

'Well I wonder whether Paula will corroborate your story once she hears about the latest love of your life,' Ian said. 'Let's get you down to the station to make a statement.'

'We can get dressed first, I suppose?' John put an arm around Rachel to guide her back upstairs. The Inspector nodded briefly, watching the two of them in their matching white towels walk down the hallway. He saw John's hand move down to rest on her bottom and he was thankful that he did not have any daughters. As John was halfway up the stairs, he whispered, 'Shall we make them wait for a bit? I need a shower.'

CHAPTER 31

Elaine returned from the baby unit to find Paula asleep. The news was good about Jo as her condition had stabilised. She looked down on her daughter and decided not to disturb her because she needed the rest. Paula had some bruising around her lips where she had bitten them during contractions. Elaine had suffered simultaneously, feeling her pain through her virtual umbilical cord. She wondered how Paula would cope with the demands of parenthood; perhaps she would be a better mother than she had been. In some ways she thought that the baby stage was easy in spite of all the disturbed nights and the tiredness. It was these last teenage years that Elaine had found the hardest. When she had a moody individual on her hands and still wanted to do the best for her, yet seemed to have no key to communicating with her. She would do everything she could to be a good grandma and hopefully that would help her be a better mother as well. Whether Graham could undergo the same transformation was highly debatable of course. Her mobile started ringing and when she located it she saw it was Graham, as if summoned by her thoughts. She moved away from the bedside to take the call. 'Graham? Where are you? Did you get my message?'

'What? No. I'm in the police station. Listen, can you get hold of George Murmur and get him to come down here?'

'No, I'm in the hospital with Paula and Jo. Get him

yourself,' she answered irritably, thinking that he hadn't even asked about them.

'I can't, you stupid woman. I'm being held by the police for Tony's murder. I need a solicitor.'

'But you didn't do it.' Elaine was bewildered.

'For Christ's sake. I know that.'

'You haven't said anything foolish, have you?'

Graham hated the fact that she had an unerring way of focusing on his mistakes.

'I've got to go. You will get him for me, won't you?' he added plaintively.

'Yes, love.' Elaine closed her mobile feeling deeply confused. Why would the police be holding him for Tony's murder? She knew full well Graham had a violent temper, but whilst lots of people suffered verbal lashings, he did not attack them physically. Not since that terrible incident years back when he had injured someone badly in an amateur boxing match. He had sworn never to fight again. She wondered how she was going to get hold of George Murmur on a Sunday. She'd have to ring directory enquiries and find a number. Moving out of the ward to the visitor's room where she hoped to find a quiet corner, she fished in her bag for a pen and a scrap of paper.

* * *

Cleo put the phone down and turned to Martyn. 'That was Elaine. She sounds frantic. Paula's still in hospital with the baby but Graham's being held by the police. She says they think he did it.'

'But he didn't,' Martyn replied.

'I know. But it's a good thing if they think he did.'

'How can you say that?' he asked in astonishment. 'He's innocent. We know who committed the murder and how. We ought to tell the police and put them straight.' He moved towards the back door.

'Don't even think about it,' Cleo hissed angrily, pulling him back, 'Don't you realise you'd be sending me inside as well?'

Martyn was surprised by her strength as she gripped his arm. 'No. You're not a murderer. You said you told him not to do it but he went ahead anyway. It's not your fault.'

'I can't take the risk they'll see it that way.'

She released him and leant against the kitchen cabinet. One hand rested casually on the counter, within a short distance of the knife rack. Martyn thought he must be getting paranoid. Why would he notice something like that? It must be Graham's poisonous suggestion eating away at his faith in Cleo. His sense of unease was growing, seemingly increasing with every passing hour. He could not conceive how two apparently sane and normal people could conspire to kill another person, someone who was husband to one and partner to the other. He took her hands in his, reasoning that if he had hold of them, she could not pick up a weapon. What was he thinking? He loved this woman. He must trust her as well, otherwise how could they be together? But did he want to be with someone who had done what she had? He always had a strong sense of right and wrong, indoctrinated in him by strict parents. How could he stand by and remain silent if Graham was arrested for the murder of Tony? But if he spoke out he would lose Cleo.

'You can't let them think it's Graham when we know it's

John. He might spend years in prison for a crime he didn't commit. Surely you couldn't live with that?'

'It wasn't supposed to be like this. It was an accident. That was how it should have been.' Cleo put her face in her hands.

'But it was John, wasn't it? John who killed him in the submarine. John who got £1.4million in his will. What could they charge you with?'

'Are you forgetting John's promise that if we say anything, he'll tell them you killed Tony and it was us that cooked up the whole scheme?'

'I haven't forgotten. It's just sometimes you have to do what's right.'

'That's all very well for you to say. Maybe I haven't got your moral courage.' There was a long pause while they considered each other. Cleo continued, 'I don't want to go to prison.'

'It may not come to that. You'd be doing the right thing and telling the truth, rather than having that awful guilt playing on your conscience for years.' Cleo did not want to tell him the likelihood of her conscience being troubled over Graham was slim. People got wrongly convicted all the time. 'Maybe you need to think it over for a bit,' he suggested. She nodded, but knew her own self interest would take precedence over Graham any day. In an attempt to move on to a lighter topic of conversation he asked, 'Where's Rachel?'

Cleo looked around as if she had momentarily misplaced something. 'Oh, out with a friend, she said.'

'A boyfriend?' Martyn asked.

'I don't know actually,' Cleo answered thoughtfully. 'I had assumed she meant a girlfriend, but come to think of it she spent ages getting ready, cleaning and preening in the bathroom, agonising over what to wear. Maybe it's all for a boy.'

'You don't think there's someone special in her life then?'

'Now that you mention it, she's been secretive about talking and texting on her mobile recently. She used to chat away for hours, in the kitchen, on the sofa, in the bathroom, wherever, but now she tends to hide away in her bedroom to take calls or she goes outside.'

'That's a good idea,' Martyn said, glancing through the window. 'Shall we go for a walk in the woods?'

'No, we can't, sorry. That's why Elaine was ringing. She only got through to the office answerphone at the solicitors. We need to ask George if he'll go down to the police station to be there for Graham.'

'Oh.' Martyn couldn't help thinking it was bizarre for Cleo to get the solicitor for Graham, given that she wanted him to be wrongly convicted for a crime he did not commit. He should try to convince her of the right course of action. It was just a matter of working out how to do that. Cleo was ringing George's home number but gave up after a while. 'No answer. We'll have to go round.'

As they left the house, a police car turned into the track and made its way towards them. PC Tufthorn got out, saying, 'Evening, Mrs Fleming. Inspector Jamieson would like you to come down to the station, please.'

'Did he say why?' Cleo asked, uneasily.

'No. Just that I should come and collect you.'

'Well, actually we need to go and call on George Murmur on the way. Graham Bright needs him. Can we do that?'

The policeman looked unsure as this did not fit with his instructions.

'I'll come in the car with you and Martyn can follow us to George's. His house is almost on the way into town so it won't take us long.'

'Alright then,' PC Tufthorn replied, relieved that he had been offered a ready-made solution.

★ ★ ★

The police station had a problem with the plumbing in the basement which meant that anyone held in the cells had to be escorted up to the toilets in the offices above. Graham was being accompanied back from a visit when Inspector Jamieson and Sergeant Fry entered with John and Rachel. At the sight of John, Graham yelled, 'It was John. He killed Tony. It was him, not me.'

None of the policemen reacted to this outburst. John looked completely unruffled as he said, 'Really, he'll try and put the blame on anyone but himself.'

'What's he doing here then?' Graham shouted. 'What are you charging him with?'

Ian Jamieson answered, speaking more to the custody sergeant at the counter than to Graham. 'This is Mr John O'Donnell. I'm charging him with having unlawful sex with a minor, namely Paula Bright.'

'That's right,' Graham yelled, 'taking advantage of an innocent young girl.' John saw an opportunity to wind him up further. Rachel was looking about her with curiosity but no sense of alarm as she felt that there was no case against John. She noticed the posters on the walls advocating neighbourhood watch schemes, community policing initiatives and some planned visits to local schools. There was

333

also a plethora of notices about sources of advice which ranged from domestic abuse to substance abuse and on to credit control. With the plastic chairs lining the wall opposite the high counter, there was very little space for people, but then she supposed that there were never going to be crowds thronging the station at any one time. Graham's minder was distracted by a query from the custody sergeant so no one else was in earshot as John whispered, 'Not so innocent. And she'll be stretched now after the baby. No good to me now. I like them young and tight.' Graham flew at him in a rage, fists flailing. John tried to defend his already bruised head from more blows, but made no move to retaliate. PC Field, who was supposed to be minding his suspect, joined Ian and Bill as they wrestled to separate the two men. They pinned a panting Graham against the wall and John said, 'You see what he's like? He tried to kill me. He's a murdering psychopath and should be put away.'

'See to it, Field,' Sergeant Wood ordered brusquely.

'Are you alright, John?' Rachel asked, inspecting him carefully for any fresh injuries. As she caressed his bruised cheek, Cleo walked in, followed by PC Tufthorn, Martyn and George Murmur. The reception area was suddenly crowded with bodies as everyone was tightly packed into the 'public' side of the counter.

Ian Jamieson turned back to Sergeant Wood and continued smoothly, 'And this is Mrs Scarlett Fleming, known as Cleo, who is being charged with embezzling funds from the company account at Kidcars.'

A number of people reacted to his announcement simultaneously, but Cleo stood immobile, her gaze fixed on her daughter, whose hand still lingered on John's cheek. John and Rachel exclaimed, 'What?' together and stood frozen in position. Martyn looked shocked but said nothing, whilst George murmured, 'I would like to consult with my client.' As he tried to edge forward to assert his right to do so, Ian Jamieson asked, 'Which client do you mean? I believe Mr Bright asked for your services and I suspect Mrs Fleming might be requiring you very soon too.'

'Mum, what does he mean?' Rachel asked, glaring at her mother.

Cleo stared at Rachel and John white-faced. Finally she said, 'What...what are you doing with him?'

Rachel put her arm around John's waist and turned to face her mother, replying, 'We're together and we're going to run the company.'

'What do you mean?' Cleo was confused.

'John and I are a couple,' Rachel said slowly and clearly, as if speaking to someone retarded. 'We're going to use the inheritance to invest in the company and expand the business. What have you been doing embezzling our assets?'

'You and John are a couple,' Cleo repeated collapsing on to one of the plastic chairs. Her daughter was with a murderer. It must not be allowed to happen. She could not know the danger she was in.

'Have you been using company funds to feed your gambling habit?' John asked accusingly.

Martyn had remained silent but he was reeling from the revelations that assailed his senses. Rachel was with the man who had murdered her stepfather and had an affair with her mother. Should he tell her? Would anyone else tell her if he did not? John had referred to Cleo's gambling 'habit'. Did that mean that it was on the scale of an addiction? How bad was it and how much had she lost? Did he really know this woman at all? Apparently he did not even know her real name.

There was a temporary pause. Neither Ian nor Bill wanted to speak, in case there were further interesting secrets that might emerge from the mouths of those around them. The ensuing silence was broken by Inspector Macmillan who entered the station, took in the crowd and said, 'Inspector Jamieson, a word, please?' He lifted the leaf of the counter to go through to his office and gave a curt command to Sergeant Wood. 'Take Mr Murmur down to see Mr Bright. Put Mr O'Donnell and Miss Fleming in interview room one and Mrs Fleming and Mr Share in interview room two.' Bill Fry was quietly impressed that Ian's opposite number knew the names of all the individuals involved, as well as their apparent allegiances. Perhaps he had been keeping a closer eye on their enquiries than they had thought.

As Inspector Macmillan closed his office door behind Ian Jamieson, he lost no time in launching his attack. 'What the hell do you think you're doing, man? We have offered you every courtesy and facility while you've been working here. Then I find out that all of a sudden today you seem to have taken over my station. You've requested and obtained a search warrant and entered a suspect's home. You've sent one of my constables out to collect a suspect. You're expecting my sergeant to deal with suspects when you bring them in and all this without so much as a "by your leave" from me. It so happened that I was on a round of golf today with a local magistrate who mentioned the search warrant and expressed surprise that I had not personally authorised it. When I subsequently rang the station, Sergeant Wood told me that you're cracking on as if there's a pressing need to arrest half the population of the town within one day. I don't know how you run your operations down in Devon but I can tell you this is not the way we do things here in Gloucestershire. What have you got to say for yourself?'

Smarting as he was under this attack from an officer of the same rank, Ian Jamieson felt that the only way forward would be to apologise for his hasty actions. He needed this man's co-operation in future and the only thing to do was to plead pressure from above.

'I can only apologise,' he said disarmingly. 'I have let the pressure from my ACC drive my actions today and I am sorry for making free with your men and your station without consulting you first. I suppose we were made so welcome that it felt like we were all working together towards the same objectives. All your staff have been very helpful. I couldn't have asked for anything more. I realise that we should have kept you more closely involved with our investigations on an ongoing basis, but at the time I thought that would be more of an inconvenience to you. The thing is, we have to be back in our own station tomorrow morning and...'

'Not a moment too soon,' Inspector Macmillan said gruffly.

Ian Jamieson nodded, acknowledging the point. He continued, 'and that means that we will have to concentrate on our own case load down there. Whilst we will continue with the Tony Fleming murder case and will liaise with you in order to do that, there are the lesser charges of embezzlement for Mrs Fleming and unlawful sex for Mr O'Donnell. As these are subsidiary issues, but are essentially separate and on your patch, it would probably be better if you took them over.'

'You mean that now you've stirred the shit up over this one, you're handing some of it over to us?'

'That's about the size of it, yes.'

Inspector Macmillan sighed heavily as he saw the extra paperwork ahead of him. 'It's unavoidable, isn't it? I presume your squad will furnish us with the financial data to substantiate the case against Mrs Fleming? But it's up to us to investigate the case against John O'Donnell?'

Receiving a nod on both points, he continued, 'Well, what have you concluded about the murder?'

'We think Graham Bright did it. He had the motive and opportunity, witnesses heard him make threats and today we found a dive computer that we believe will link him to the murder scene.'

'I can't say I like the guy, but I didn't have him down as a murderer.'

'You can never tell though, can you? That's the one thing I've learnt from years of experience,' Inspector Jamieson concluded.

★ ★ ★

Cleo and Martyn sat opposite each other, across a battle-scarred table in a barren interview room.

'I can't believe it,' Cleo said.

'What?' Martyn asked, thinking there had been so many events that he could not believe over the last couple of weeks.

'Rachel and John.' Cleo spoke quietly, as if to herself. 'She mustn't be with him. He's a murderer. I'm afraid when I'm near him, knowing what he's done. If he can kill once and get away with it, he can do it again.'

'That's why we've got to tell the police.'

Cleo did not appear to have heard him. She looked up with calm resolution in her eyes. 'I've got to protect my daughter. Regardless of what it means for me, I'm going to tell the police everything.'